Elisabeth Carpenter lives in Preston with her family. She completed a BA in English Literature and Language with the Open University in 2011.

Elisabeth was awarded a Northern Writers' New Fiction Award, and was longlisted for Yeovil Literary Prize (2015 and 2016) and the MsLexia Women's Novel Award (2015). She loves living in the north of England and sets most of her stories in the area. She currently works as a bookkeeper.

Also by Elisabeth Carpenter

11 Missed Calls
99 Red Balloons
Only a Mother
The Woman Downstairs

The Vacancy

ELISABETH CARPENTER

ORION

An Orion paperback

First published in Great Britain in 2021
by Orion Fiction,
an imprint of The Orion Publishing Group Ltd.,
Carmelite House, 50 Victoria Embankment
London EC4Y 0DZ

An Hachette UK Company

3 5 7 9 10 8 6 4

A CIP catalogue record for this book
is available from the British Library.

ISBN (Paperback) 978 1 4091 8151 4
ISBN (eBook) 978 1 4091 8152 1

Typeset by Deltatype Ltd, Birkenhead, Merseyside

Printed in Great Britain by Clays Ltd, Elcograf S.p.A.

www.orionbooks.co.uk

The Vacancy

VACANCY

PERSONAL ASSISTANT to published author

Live-in position
Discretion essential. Experience preferred.
Duties to include taking dictation, research,
travel bookings, plus ad hoc tasks.
Contact: Dorothy Winters, Preston 229554

Chapter 1

The vacancy was advertised in one of the local newspapers. A live-in position was the perfect solution for someone practically homeless, like me. Dorothy Winters said she was a bestselling author (which made the prospect more attractive) and was looking for someone to type her handwritten manuscript along with other *ad hoc tasks*. I didn't admit that I'd never heard of her, and told Dorothy I could type a hundred words per minute after working at the City Council offices for three years.

It was a little unusual that the position was residential, but Dorothy said, 'I like to work in the evenings with a nice glass or two of something, but my eyesight isn't great in poor light. Sometimes I can't decipher my own writing the day after.'

I *deciphered* that to mean that Dorothy's pissed handwriting was so illegible, it was an evening's work (and a sozzled Dorothy) wasted. I hope I wasn't expected to take dictation while the woman drank herself into a coma. I didn't know shorthand, but I could record her on my mobile and pretend. And I actually was a fast typist. At least *that* part was true.

Dorothy had taken my CV at face value (though why wouldn't she?) and said she would write to request references *the old-fashioned way*, which was ideal because the Rachel Benson who'd been employed by Salford City Council between 2014 and 2017 didn't actually exist. I had listed my line manager as a Ms Eva Adams. She didn't work there either, so Dorothy's reference request would probably remain unopened. It was easy enough to find the council letterhead online to create my own.

I was surprised there were no other suitable candidates for the job. I thought I'd have been the last person she'd hire, especially after I turned up to the interview with a soup stain on my collar, flustered and tired after a sleepless night. But other, more sensible people, might've assumed Dorothy's advert was a bit ambiguous and that the whole set-up was dodgy. *Discretion essential* evoked all sorts of images (cannabis farm in the attic, sex slaves in the cellar) but after talking to her, I reasoned that the possibility of seedy intentions wasn't likely with Ms Winters. Though you never could tell with some people.

The weight of the suitcase was killing my shoulder. It was raining and the drains in the road were overflowing, making small ponds on the cracked road. I'd never been one for choosing weather-appropriate footwear and my soaking black canvas pumps sounded like flip-flops smacking soggy sand. It didn't help that tree roots were trying to escape the ground, creating little hills that dotted the concrete path. To an onlooker, I probably looked like a staggering drowned rat.

Another new phase of my life. I'd had too many fresh starts and they were never promising or exciting because most of the time I moved from one bad situation to another. I couldn't remember the first time because I was only two years old when my biological mother gave me away. I couldn't picture her face; I had no memories of her at all. I'm grateful to her for two things: bringing me into this world and giving me up. When I was a kid, I overheard various versions of my story: that she was an alcoholic or a drug addict or maybe both.

By the time I was eight, I'd been with thirteen foster families and in three different children's homes. This might not have been entirely accurate, but it didn't matter after I moved into Jenny and Phil's.

My last *fresh start* was when I married Matthew three years ago. He'd taken care of everything: sorted all the bills, the weekly shop, took my car for its MOT and always made sure it was filled with petrol. I made that sound like a practical arrangement, didn't I? It wasn't. Some relationships are complicated.

But he wasn't here now. And the bravado I felt walking here for the interview last week had vanished because the reality had hit that I was about to live with a stranger.

I stopped at number sixty-three. Opposite, was a large building with a wooden sign that read: *Whispering Oaks Residential Care Home*. In front of it was an elderly man, sitting on a wooden chair under the smoking shelter. It was as though he was looking in my direction, but his expression didn't change.

He shook his head and hollered, 'Strange shit goes on in there.'

'Are you talking to me?' I shouted back.

'I meant next door,' he said. 'That bloke and his mother.'

'Right.' I paused for a moment. 'Maybe the mother's not really there, like in *Psycho*.'

'I heard that,' he said. 'I'm not bloody deaf and I'm not a bloody psycho.'

'No, I said—'

'Ah sod it.' He stood and said, 'You're probably right,' before shuffling into the building.

I expected this suburban street to be quiet, but strange people weren't confined to city centres. They were everywhere.

I turned to Dorothy Winters' house: a red-brick four-storey end-of-terrace. The windows got gradually smaller the higher they were.

My new home.

There was no gate, and both of the sloping stone gate-posts were engraved with the house number. They were just above waist height and I gave them a firm shove to test their integrity: two Leaning Tower of Pisas which, thankfully, weren't going to fall down any day soon.

I walked towards the house. The path was made of uneven concrete slabs and loose bricks jammed into the gaps. I stopped halfway to swap the suitcase to my other hand and glanced at the house next door. A middle-aged man, late fifties perhaps, was standing at the upstairs window. He raised a hand to wave, so I held up my aching arm and waved back a bit too eagerly. He wrinkled his nose, turned, and walked out of sight.

What a nosy old git. Perhaps the smoking man was right. I'd have to keep my eye on him next door.

The knocker on the large red door was a small, dismembered hand made of brass. Why would anyone want such a thing on their door? I tapped it against the door three times and felt like I was shaking hands with a child.

It took Dorothy Winters (top twenty bestseller in 1999) only a few seconds to open up.

'Hello, Rachel,' she said, standing aside. 'You're early. I was going to change into something more presentable before you arrived, but never mind.'

She was dressed in a maroon knee-length leather pencil skirt and a cream silk blouse and was the first person I'd ever seen who could pull off wearing leather below the waist. Her platinum blonde hair was styled in a loose bun at the side of her neck. She held a half-empty martini glass in her left hand, and I could smell the gin fumes from the step.

Dorothy glanced at my rather pitiful suitcase. I felt bad for thinking of it like that because it was the one Jenny and Phil gave me when I first moved out. It hadn't aged well, but I couldn't part with it.

'Are the rest of your things arriving later?' said Dorothy.

'No,' I said, stepping inside. 'I travel light. We used to live on a boat.'

Why had I said that? I'd only ever been on a return ferry across the Channel on a booze run to Calais.

Dorothy raised her eyebrows.

'How very bohemian of you.'

'Not really,' I said. 'It was quite a nice one ... a canal boat. It had an Aga.'

It was as though some part of my mind believed what I was coming out with. I'd have to try to say as little as possible in future in case I tripped myself up.

Dorothy closed the front door. She downed what was left in her glass and placed it on the hall table. 'I'm so glad you accepted the position,' she said, turning on her heels. 'I've got a good feeling about you. The last couple of assistants haven't been ... hmm, what's the word ... *mature* enough for a position like this. One of them spent most of the time with her face in her mobile phone. Another one ... well, there's time enough for that story, isn't there?'

No, I need to know now. And just how many assistants had Dorothy been through?

She led me along the hallway, passing a closed door. The walls were clad in dark mahogany that matched the floor. A long red rug brightened it up a little, but it was still rather dark.

Dorothy stopped at the second door. She selected a key from a set held together with a large nineties smiley acid face keyring. I bet she had a lot of stories to tell (excuse the pun). I wanted to know where she got that keyring from and I tried to picture her thirty years younger in an outdoor rave, dancing with her eyes closed and arms in the air.

'A house is so much quieter without children, don't you think?' she said.

'I guess,' I said, wondering where that question came from.

'Though my children have never lived in this house. When they were quiet or asleep it was OK, but I just couldn't concentrate on my writing when they were pounding up and down the stairs, asking constantly when the next meal would be. As if *I'd* have known that.' She unlocked and opened the door. 'The husband was less tolerable, but I don't have to worry about him any more.'

'Do you have a lot of children?' I said.

Dorothy's mouth fell open slightly, but she'd made it seem as though she'd spawned a whole football team.

'That's a strange way of asking.' She smiled as she walked into the room, flicking on a switch that turned on three lamps and spotlights in the ceiling. 'I have three. Two girls and a boy. They don't visit much now, though. Not since I moved up north. You'd have thought I lived on the other side of the world, not the opposite end of the country. They say they can't understand what everyone says here. Ludicrous!'

The windowless room was about fourteen feet by ten and the floorboards were varnished in a rich dark teak. The rug in the middle was amber and russet with embroidered birds perched on branches. Against the walls left and right were units of white cupboards and shelves full of books.

'This is the library,' said Dorothy. 'I've always wanted a library.'

'Why do you keep it locked?' I asked.

Dorothy placed a hand on her hip and tilted her head to the side.

'Because there's a key for it,' she said. 'I've always wanted a house with keys, too. It's so gothic, don't you think?'

Locked doors were a given in some of the houses I'd lived in as a child. They were neither gothic nor intriguing, but I wasn't going to bring that up now. Tales of child abandonment tended to kill a jovial mood.

'Yes,' I said, catching my own reflection in the mirror hanging on a chain behind the door. I still wasn't used to having such dark hair. 'Very gothic.'

'Would you like a gin and tonic, Rachel?'

I looked at my watch as though it would give me the right answer. She could've been testing me, and I was sure to fail. What time was appropriate to start drinking alcohol with your new boss? Twenty past never, probably.

'I shouldn't, really,' I said, placing my suitcase on the floor. 'It's before five o'clock and you said in the interview that my normal working hours are eight until six.'

'Did I?'

I nodded, trying to smile and make it reach my eyes.

'Well, actually, this isn't your first day ...' Dorothy

sighed. 'Well, never mind. Drinking alone doesn't bother me.' She surveyed the rows of books, her eyes resting on several of her own. She glanced quickly at me and again at the books, but after a few moments' silence, she rolled her eyes. 'I suppose I'd better show you to your room.'

I should've shown more gratitude for being in the company of an author and gushed about the rows of books. Or maybe curtsied and bowed my head. I followed her obediently up the stairs.

The walls were covered with framed pictures of different sizes: a black-and-white photo of 'Women Factory Workers, Lancashire, circa 1908'; a recent wedding photo (the bride obviously wasn't Dorothy, far too young); and, near the top, a picture of a little boy, aged about three. I wanted to stop and look because there was something about the background that looked familiar.

On the first floor, Dorothy stopped at the door next to the bathroom.

'This is your room,' she said, pushing it open. 'Did I show you this during your interview?'

Had she been mentally present at the interview? She didn't seem to remember much about it.

'I don't think you did,' I said, as always, cushioning the negative with unnecessary words.

Dorothy leant against the door.

'Have you always spoken like that?' she said.

'Like what?'

'So well-to-do,' she said. 'I'm sure you had a stronger

accent when I interviewed you. A Yorkshire accent, wasn't it?'

So, she remembered *that*. I, on the other hand, had stupidly forgotten.

'It's when I get nervous,' I said. 'I've a Bolton accent.'

'They both sound the same, don't they? And there's no need to be nervous around me.'

Only confident people said that. *And no, the two accents don't sound the same, Dorothy*.

'You needn't pretend to be someone you're not, Rachel.' Dorothy knelt on the bed to open the pale pink curtains. 'I do like a Yorkshire accent. It reminds me of Heathcliff.'

I wished she'd stop saying the name Rachel so much. It was like she was talking to a different person.

'So, what do you think?' she said.

It was a small bedroom, about eleven feet by ten, dominated by two huge antique wardrobes. There was a bookcase on the left and a chest of drawers against the back wall that had a small television on top. The wallpaper was white with blue flowers and matched the print of the quilt cover on the single bed. It was hardly cutting-edge interior design, but it was warm and light.

Along the right side of the bed was a single-glazed window that overlooked a long, narrow garden.

'Sorry about the state of that.' She picked at the peeling white paint on the window frame, revealing rotten wood underneath. 'Oh, bloody hell, I've made it worse. I hardly ever come into this room. I'll have to get someone in to fix it.' She scooped up the flakes of paint

12

and put them in the pocket of her expensive-looking leather skirt. She wrinkled her nose as she stood and smoothed it down. 'Please just use that wardrobe.' She gestured to the smaller of the two that was next to the chest of drawers. 'The other one has my furs in. I can't wear them these days without some leftie accosting me. It's bad enough that I have to lie about this skirt.' She winked at me. 'I'll leave you to settle.' She glanced at my suitcase before walking to the door. 'Though I doubt it'll take you long to unpack.' She headed towards the stairs and shouted, 'Drinks in the library at five forty-five, prompt! We eat at six!'

'Thank you.'

I closed the door and yanked my case up onto the bed. I sank down next to it, putting my hands on the soft brown leather as I looked around the room.

How had it got to this? Sitting in a single bedroom, living with a woman I'd had met through a newspaper advert. Why couldn't I have been allowed to stay at home? I hadn't seen my family for over a month; the homesickness felt like pain in my chest.

I wiped the single tear that had run down my cheek.

There was no point thinking like this – no time to get sentimental. I hadn't received any hateful texts or poisonous emails in over three weeks. I hoped it was enough that I'd left. I hoped they thought I was hundreds of miles away.

No one knew me here. I could be anyone I wanted to be.

Finally.

Chapter 2

Kathryn had tried ringing him every hour on the hour six times. The contractions were now five minutes apart, and she should have known he wouldn't be here to drive her to the hospital.

'Has the mysterious Jack not shown up again?' Her mother was sitting at the dining-room table, smoking a cigarette, her eyes unwavering from *EastEnders* on the kitchen telly.

Kathryn stopped in the doorway as another contraction took over. Tears came to her eyes. Everyone had said there was no pain like it. They could've lied to spare her the dread, but they were right.

She didn't want to give her mother the satisfaction of seeing pain or anguish on her face. She wished she could cut this bloody thing out of her. What was the use of her going through this pain if Jack wasn't here to witness it?

'I'll order a taxi,' said Kathryn, walking to the hall telephone in short steps. Her hospital bag had been next to the front door for over a week now. It was one of the good things about having a sister – the only person in this shitshow of a family who actually gave a damn about her.

'Don't be daft,' her dad shouted from the living room. 'Your mum'll give you a lift, won't you, Marion?'

Kathryn knew without looking that her mother would be rolling her eyes and swearing under her breath.

'Let me finish *EastEnders* first,' she hollered from the kitchen. 'Babies don't actually shoot out of you, especially the first one. They take bloody hours … days, if you're unlucky.'

Kathryn wished she could sit on the bottom step – or any step – of the staircase to sulk and wait, but she wouldn't be able to get back up again without a hoisting hand. It was all so undignified, pregnancy. You had to give your body away to this thing growing inside you. Doctors and midwives prodding you, poking you. It was disgusting. Kathryn always took her mind somewhere else when she had check-ups.

'Thanks, Mum,' she said. 'I'd appreciate a lift.' If Kathryn told her what she was really thinking (*Fuck you and your lift, you uncaring bitch*), her mum wouldn't bother. And as much as Kathryn made a show of attempting to call a taxi, she'd rather walk it alone than show up in a hired car with a stranger.

Even though the driver's window was open, her mum's cigarette smoke wafted towards her in the back. Kathryn inhaled it deeply, quietly, through her nose. She hadn't had one for at least four months now. She didn't want to be seen as someone who didn't give a shit. There was a pack of ten Regal in her hospital bag and she couldn't stop thinking about them.

'Sorry, I can't stay,' her mum said when she pulled up in front of the entrance. She didn't even attempt to get out of the car. 'You know what your dad's like about being on his own in the house.'

Kathryn heaved herself out and slammed the car door shut before bending slightly. The strength of the latest contraction made her want to pass out. If she did, her mother would have no choice but to get her fat arse out of the car, wouldn't she?

Marion leant across the passenger seat and wound the window down.

'Have you packed enough pads?' she shouted. 'You don't want to be bleeding everywhere when it's all over. You might be in there for days.'

Kathryn picked up the holdall, shook her head and walked towards the doors of Bolton Royal Infirmary.

Tears mingled with the rain on her face. She shouldn't have expected anything from her mother – she was lucky to have been given a lift. She wouldn't usually have cried about it, but all the bloody hormones made her feel needy and vulnerable and she hated it.

By the time she got to the delivery suite, she was begging the midwives to put her out of her misery. 'Just kill me,' she screamed. 'I am not having this baby any more. I didn't want it in the first place.'

'Now, what sort of talk is that?'

Kathryn turned to the familiar voice and a wave of relief washed over her.

'Chrissy,' she whispered between breaths.

Her sister reached for her hand.

'Squeeze as hard as you like,' she said.

'But ... what ...'

'I couldn't let you do this on your own, could I?' She clung to Kathryn's hand and perched on the end of a plastic chair. 'Had to get the bus, mind. They'd already started on the lager by the time I came home from work.'

'I wish they'd put me under a general anaesthetic.'

'You don't want to miss out on seeing your baby for the first time, Kathy.'

'I don't care.'

She really didn't. She wanted to be put to sleep and wake up when everything was back to normal. And she'd find a way to get back to normal.

Six hours later it was over, and Kathryn was on a ward with three other mothers – one of whom snored like a tractor. At least she was in a bed next to the window.

She had arrived in hell; it was so baking bloody hot. Didn't germs breed in heat?

'Ten little fingers and ten little toes,' said Chrissy. 'You've made something so perfect, Kathy. I can't wait till it's my turn.'

'You can have it if you like,' she said.

Chrissy laughed. 'I'm just popping to the canteen. I haven't eaten since yesterday. I've been too excited.'

Kathryn wished *she* was excited. The thought of being alone with it made her want to run away yet feeling it in her arms was more enjoyable than she thought it'd be. Like a moving hot water bottle. There was an angry red rash across its forehead, though. Was there such a thing as concealer for babies?

It began to stuff its little fingers into its mouth. Shit, it was hungry. Kathryn couldn't bear the idea of putting its mouth to her breast. What man would want her after knowing a baby had been there, too? It was disgusting to think about. She grabbed one of the three bottles of ready-made formula.

Chrissy came back in and laid a plated sausage roll on the bed.

'I can't eat that,' said Kathryn. 'I'm fat enough as it is.'

'Don't be silly. You've just had a baby. It's not fat, it's your muscles. It'll take a while for them to go back to normal. I read it hurts when they're contracting, too.'

'Great. Something else to look forward to.' Kathryn pushed the pastry away. 'It stinks.'

Chrissy grabbed it from the bed and put it on the cabinet.

'Ah,' she said, stroking the baby's cheek. 'Feeding time, is it? Do you want me to do it?'

Kathryn cradled the baby tighter. 'No. It's mine.'

'It?' Chrissy stood and went to the window. 'You're going to have to think of a name.' She sighed. 'I'll have to be getting home in a bit. I'm meant to be starting work in an hour.'

'Don't leave me on my own,' said Kathryn. 'I didn't mean to snap.'

Chrissy turned and smiled. 'OK.' She sat on one of the plastic chairs. 'I'll ring in sick. I could stay with you all day if you need me to.'

After downing over half of the small bottle, the baby wouldn't stop crying.

'It's wind,' said Chrissy. 'If you support the chin and rub the back, it'll come up and out. Yes, that's right.'

White vomit landed on the covers.

'God, that's disgusting. Chrissy, can you wipe it off for me, I'm not good with sick.'

Her sister rolled her eyes and plucked out a wet wipe.

'It's not like proper sick, is it? And you're going to have to deal with the nappies yourself soon.'

'Why won't it stop crying? The wind must've gone by now.' Screaming and screaming and screaming. The baby looked so ugly when it was red and shrieking. 'There, there,' said Kathryn, bringing the baby close to her chest, stroking its head. 'You're mine, little one. Be good for Mummy.' That was what babies liked to hear, wasn't it? She didn't like the sound of *Mummy*, though. Perhaps she'd make it call her by her name.

Chrissy stood and almost lunged towards her.

'Here, I'll walk around with—'

'No, you won't.'

Kathryn slid off the bed and paced the room, rocking the baby up and down. Her head was going to explode if it carried on like this.

Outside, she saw a couple. The man was carrying the

car seat with their precious little bundle. Pair of smug bastards. Kathryn pictured the man as Jack and the woman as his wife. How dare they be happy when she was left to go through this alone? How fucking dare they?

She went to the plastic cot and placed the baby inside; its face was almost purple from crying and fretting.

Kathryn slid on her shoes and took her coat and cigarettes from the small bedside cupboard.

'I'm going for a walk,' she said.

She knew her sister was shouting after her as she walked along the corridor towards the lift, but she didn't care.

What an ungrateful little shit. After she'd carried it for nine months, living inside her like a parasite. And then having to go through all that pain.

If it couldn't behave then she'd bloody well teach it a lesson.

Chapter 3

There were only a few items in my make-up bag: concealer, eyeliner, mascara, and tinted lip balm. I learned from the age of five – when they finally let me choose a few precious items to pack – to always travel light. It was pointless having too many nice or expensive things because they always got pinched. Everything was a little bit tainted by the ugly sticky labels with my initials written on them in thick black marker. That didn't stop other kids peeling them off and replacing them with their own. I still haven't forgiven Adele Marsden for stealing my Rainbow Brite doll. I tried to get revenge by sticking my label on her new toy, but everyone knew she'd been given the Girl's World because she'd bragged about it for weeks. I suppose that was the start of my downfall.

I didn't use to think about my childhood all the time. The last time I saw Gina, my counsellor, she said that people who experienced trauma tended to constantly look back on their lives to see which events had led them to that point. I told her that I didn't *want* to think

21

about these things and I'd obliterate every memory if I could. She did that thing with her lips where they almost disappeared and said, 'But you *are* your memories. You *will* get over this.'

What the hell did she know anyway, with her yoga pants and cream sofas? She probably stood in front of her mirror every night and asked herself what she could have done better today. I didn't think people like Gina actually existed, but they do.

I dabbed on the tinted lip balm and stood before the full-length mirror on the back of the door. It'd do. It was subtle, but at least I'd made some effort. And my hair had dried from the rain with a wave that looked intentional.

I went out onto the landing. I like to familiarise myself with my surroundings, so I noted that there were two other doors on this floor. One, slightly ajar, was the bathroom; the other one was shut. I tried the handle, but it was locked, which was just as well. It wouldn't make a great impression if I were to be caught snooping on my first day.

I headed downstairs. It was after five thirty and almost dark outside; the lamp on the hall table had been switched on. I tiptoed towards the library, even though I'd taken off my shoes. Was it bad form to be wearing only socks to dinner in a house like this? I put an ear against the door. Dorothy was humming along to a jarring piano concerto and I envisioned her floating around the room in a floaty dress. My imagination kept turning her into Bette Davis in *Whatever Happened to Baby Jane?*

The music stopped and the clock struck the quarter hour. Dorothy opened the door; she raised an eyebrow. 'Right on time, Rachel.' She opened the door a little wider. 'Though that's not surprising, considering you were lingering outside. How long have you been waiting there?'

I felt heat gather in my right ear. *Left for love and right for revenge.*

'Not long,' I said, walking inside.

The room was lit by ten or so candles dotted around the room. The flickering light illuminated the dust on the mirror on the back of the door. I was surprised Dorothy had placed naked flames so close to this many books, but the glow made the room look even more beautiful.

'You should've just come in. We're not at all formal here.'

Dorothy held a champagne saucer in her left hand as though she was cradling a delicate dandelion clock. The glass was half-empty, though that wasn't saying much; at full capacity it only held a large gulp.

She had changed outfits, even though her previous ensemble was perfectly fine. She probably didn't have many guests, preferring the solitude needed for writing. Maybe she didn't like people that much – I had a low threshold myself, so I totally understood.

Dorothy left the door open, walked over to one of the bookcases and rested an elbow on one of the deep shelves. It was a pose she must've learnt in the *What Writers Must Do* handbook. I expected her to place a

23

hand on her forehead and lament. She took a longer than passing glance at my socks, which were red with white polka dots. She raised her eyebrows again.

'Hmm,' she said lightly, before taking a delicate sip from the glass. 'Don't worry, you won't have to dine with me every night. I thought it'd be nice for us to eat together on your first night – a welcoming party of sorts. I expect you'll meet people your own age soon enough ... Wouldn't want you to feel you had to keep company with an old lass like me.'

I didn't think anyone could describe Dorothy as an *old lass*. She was about the same age as Jenny, early seventies, but Jenny dressed for practicality rather than vanity. I don't think I've seen her in anything but jeans, except for my wedding day three years ago.

Dorothy handed me a glass of fizz.

'We'll eat in five minutes or so,' she said. 'I hope you're not a vegetarian or anything.'

She didn't wait for a reply. She looked around the room, surveying the hundreds of books she must've collected over decades. There was a faint smudge of mascara under her eyes. It was either that or she'd had a late one last night.

'Have a sip,' she said, pointing a finger at the glass in my hand. 'I haven't poisoned it.'

There was a pause a moment too long before Dorothy laughed.

'You must forgive my dark humour.' She flicked a hand in the air. 'You'll get used to me.'

I put the glass to my lips and let the wine coat them.

I knew it would taste horrible; it was warm after sitting on the shelf for God knows how long.

'Hmm,' I said. 'Very nice.'

The clock struck the hour and Dorothy downed what little was left in her glass and turned on her heels. 'I am bloody starving.' She walked into the hall. 'I was so caught up in a chapter today I totally forgot to eat.'

I couldn't imagine that; I've never been so absorbed in something that I couldn't hear my stomach growl. And, during the past few weeks, breakfast, lunch and dinner was all I'd had to look forward to.

I followed Dorothy through the next door. The brightness in the dining room hurt my eyes after the gentle glow of candlelight. It was no ordinary big light; it was a two-tiered distressed brass chandelier with imitation candles. The somewhat unusual wallpaper was white with bright green leaves and it covered every wall. A large mahogany dining table dominated the space; it was set for two and had a small white candle burning in the centre. I spotted several antiques around the room: a walnut bureau with intricately carved legs, and suitcases in different shades of brown leather piled in a corner near the window. Just one of those would be worth a hundred quid at least.

Phil used to take me to car boots sales on Sundays in the summer holidays. He'd get me up at 6 a.m., always optimistic he'd find hidden treasure. Of course, he never did. 'Bloody dealers,' he'd say. 'They always get here first. Everyone's onto it these days. Damn that *Bargain Hunt*. We'll get up at five next week.'

We didn't, though.

Heavy cream curtains surrounded a window that looked out onto the garden and the wall between this house and the next. The drapes were open, and our reflection was of a strange couple no one would put together.

Dorothy sat at the table with her back to the fireplace and gestured for me to sit opposite.

Humming came from behind the door next to the fire before the clatter of metal landing on a hard floor. Dorothy didn't flinch.

'Who's in there?' I hissed.

She leant forward, frowning.

'You don't have to whisper, Rachel,' she said. 'It's only Louise, my housekeeper.'

'Oh.'

'Haven't I introduced you to her yet?'

I shook my head.

'Lou!' shouted Dorothy. 'Come in here a sec.'

I watched the doorway, expecting a large lady, dressed in a long black skirt and a flour-coated apron, clutching a dead pheasant.

Louise was, in fact, tall and slim. She looked younger than Dorothy by at least ten years. Her (obviously dyed) black hair was in a bob just above her shoulders. It wasn't as sleek as it could've been – she was at least two months late for a trim. She *did* have an apron on, though. Over black trousers and a shirt with tiny birds printed on it.

She stared back, probably scrutinising me in the

same way, and smoothed down her hair that had gained a halo of frizz from the heat of the kitchen.

'Hi, Rachel,' she said. 'It's nice to have you here. Dorothy's told me so much about you.'

Dorothy's head jolted and her mouth twitched.

'Have I?'

'Bits here and there,' said Louise, her cheeks flushing under pale make-up.

'I'm absolutely ravenous,' said Dorothy.

She unfolded the napkin from the table and laid it on her lap.

'I'll take that as my cue,' said Louise, smiling warmly. She went into the kitchen and came back carrying a huge tray with two silver cloches on. 'Thanks for letting me leave early today, Dorothy,' said Louise after setting them down in front of us. 'I've left the main course in the warming oven – be sure to use the mitt.'

'Thank you,' said Dorothy. 'I can't wait to see what delights you've conjured up for us.'

Louise bowed slightly. 'I'll see you tomorrow, Rachel,' she said. 'Bon appetit!'

She returned to the kitchen.

Dorothy waited until a door – presumably, the back door – slammed shut before lifting her cloche.

'Soup,' said Dorothy. 'And it's pea green to match the dracaena leaves on the wallpaper. Jesus.'

I lifted the lid, slightly annoyed that Dorothy had ruined the surprise.

'I don't mind pea soup,' I said.

Dorothy sighed, got up and returned from the kitchen with a bottle of gin.

'Let's have a little bit of fun, shall we?' she said. 'This ought to loosen things up.'

Chapter 4

'And that was the year I was nominated for an RNA award. Even though that wasn't my genre at all!'

I had no idea what RNA stood for and wasn't about to ask. It was nearly midnight and I'd listened to Dorothy go on and on all evening about books I'd not read and people I'd never heard of. I drank the three gin and tonics (quadruples at least) that she'd placed in front of me and the urge to talk about Matthew was getting stronger. About how much I missed him, but at the same time was afraid that—

'You're a quiet one, aren't you, Rachel?' said Dorothy, leaning back in her chair with a cigarette in her hand (she was pretty much a chain-smoker). She frowned in my direction, but her eyes wandered from side to side. She must've had a lot more alcohol before sitting down for dinner. Mascara dregs still lined her eyes, and her red lipstick was now a pink stain that bled into the wrinkles around her mouth.

'I don't mean to be quiet,' I said (I couldn't get a bloody word in). 'But your stories are so interesting.'

I cringed at the sound of my own words. Sycophant.

'Oh, stop,' said Dorothy, standing. 'I tell the same boring crap all the time – it's just that you've never heard it before.' She took a final drag of the cigarette before grinding it into the glass ashtray. She blew out the final lungful with a hiss. 'I bore myself constantly. Need the lav.'

When I heard her footsteps on the stairs, I got up and wandered over to the sideboard, running my fingers over the highly polished carved wood. If it was Jacobean, it'd be worth a fortune. What had Phil said about the tell signs?

The top drawers slid open easily; the weight and smoothness of the wood was so satisfying. The first drawer contained placemats and coasters; the second held folded napkins and rolls of lace. There were two small cardboard boxes in the final drawer labelled *Angel* and *Tarot*. Next to them was a red velvet tote bag. When I poked it, it sounded like there were marbles inside. I reached into it, feeling the coldness of the stones and pulled one out. The symbol on it was an X with a long straight line running through the middle. It was a rune stone. Gemma had a set years ago that she used to try to predict her future or reflect her feelings or whatever rune stones were supposed to do.

The sound of water came running down the pipes in the wall. I crouched down to chance a quick look inside the cupboard doors. Board games were stacked neatly. On top of them was a large black box with a brass hook and clasp at the front. I pulled it out slightly, but the top gave no clue as to what was inside.

'It's a Ouija board.'

I jolted back.

Shit.

How had Dorothy managed to be right behind me? The woman was stealth personified.

I slid the board back and shut the door quickly, trapping the tip of my thumb in the top corner of the left cupboard. My eyes watered as I tried to stand, but my hand was still stuck.

Dorothy grabbed the wooden handle and yanked the door open.

'Good grief,' she said, reaching for my hand as I began to sway.

Instinctively, I brought it towards my chest and cradled it in my other hand.

Dorothy tentatively took hold of my hand and drew it towards her for a closer look.

'It's a bit dented,' she said, squinting. 'But the skin's still intact.'

She opened the middle drawer, took out one of the rolls of lace, and wrapped it around my thumb, tucking the end inside.

'It's not very secure,' she said, 'but it'll make you feel better. And I bet that's the most elaborate bandage you've ever had.'

'Yes,' I said, my voice a whisper.

It did make me feel better and it was nice to be taken care of.

She rubbed the top of my arm.

'Oh, bless you, love,' she said, guiding me back to my chair. 'I'll get you a shot of whiskey. That'll calm your nerves.'

After she'd been in the kitchen for about a minute, there was a screech, followed by the shatter of glass. 'Don't worry,' shouted Dorothy. 'I forgot about the step.' She staggered back in and, luckily, landed in her chair after falling backwards. She slid towards me a shot glass of amber liquid, which had remarkably survived the flight and landing in the kitchen.

I grabbed it with my right hand and downed it. The buzz went straight to my head. It dulled the pain slightly, but my thumb throbbed so much it felt as though it might burst open.

'I'm sorry about snooping about in your cupboard.' I held up my hand. 'I've never gotten away with misbehaving without someone finding out.'

God, I needed to shut the hell up. What on earth was I on about?

'Well, that doesn't sound like much fun,' said Dorothy. 'Not all mischief is bad.' She lit another cigarette. 'So, tell me about you.' She poured more gin into her tall glass. Two thirds gin, one third tonic. 'You didn't mention children or a husband during the interview. Have you ever been married?'

No, would have been the easiest answer.

'Yes,' I said quietly, my gaze focused on the empty shot glass in front of me.

'You don't have to talk about it,' she said. 'Was it a very long time ago?'

I looked up at her. I'd put a false date of birth on my CV, but I hadn't changed the year.

'I don't mean to suggest you're old,' said Dorothy, wafting smoke from her face. 'It's just that some people marry quite young, before they're ready.'

'Is anyone ever ready for marriage?' I said. 'People never stay the same.'

'That's a good point. I'm a bit of a chameleon myself.'

'That's not what I—'

'Yes, I know,' she said. 'I know you meant over time. I was just trying to bring the conversation back to me.' She flashed a mischievous smile. 'I could tell you were feeling uncomfortable ... I sensed you didn't end your marriage on good terms. But you'll meet someone else soon enough. Anyone can start their lives again. Even me.'

'I'm not looking for another relationship right now.'

Dorothy's shoulders relaxed and she scooped up her glass.

'Cheers to that,' she said. 'Men are so overrated.' She leant forward again and looked to the candle on the table. It had nearly burnt out. 'I wish I could edit my speech like I can my words. It would make me so much more thoughtful.'

'It's OK,' I said. 'It's just something I don't like talking about.'

Dorothy's lips parted for a moment.

'Have you always lived in this area?' she asked.

33

'Around Bolton, mainly. My childhood wasn't conventional.'

'Is anyone's?'

I doubted that Dorothy had ever known despair – she'd probably always had money. The way she drank, the way she ate, the way she dressed.

'My biological mother was too young when she had me,' I said, not mentioning the various versions I'd heard over the years. 'By the time I was eight, I'd lived in three care homes and with thirteen different sets of foster parents.'

I waited for a reaction – there was always a reaction. No one I'd met had ever just said nothing. Not that I often gave this information away. But I'd drunk too much, and my words were progressively unfiltered. Hopefully, Dorothy wouldn't remember in the morning when I officially started. She must've drunk at least a bottle of gin on her own. How the hell was she still sitting upright? Perhaps she *had* known despair and used alcohol to bury it.

She took a deep breath.

'Have you tried to find your biological mother?'

'No,' I said quietly. 'I'm not interested in finding her.'

'Well, you've done very well,' she said. 'And your references were amazing.'

Dorothy stood and left the room without saying anything. It was ten minutes before she reappeared at the kitchen door.

'Darling,' she said, 'I'll have to cut the evening short.

My friend has just texted to say she needs an ear. Hope you don't mind.'

I didn't mind.

I got out of there as fast as I could without running.

Chapter 5

The cold pavement felt delicious under Kathryn's feet, as did the breeze on her bare legs. Twenty-six hours ago she'd been somewhere else. She'd wanted to go to Paris, but accommodation was too expensive. Now she was in York after following Jack across the country.

Last night he told her not to stand outside their house any more.

'Eleni's afraid you might break in,' he said.

Eleni. She didn't suit the name at all. Far too tall and thin and pointed. She should've been worried about far more harmful things than Kathryn breaking in.

Flashing lights flooded the ground, the railings.

'You all right, love?'

Someone from behind wrapped a foil blanket around her like she was a turkey being primed for the oven.

'Of course, I'm all right,' said Kathryn. 'Why are you asking me that?'

She was sure she'd left a child somewhere. Had she left it behind? She couldn't remember now. Everything important was becoming blurred. Had she had a drink tonight? Had someone spiked it? That must be the only sensible explanation. She hadn't meant to come here, but she had nowhere else to go. She supposed getting into the ambulance wouldn't be a terrible thing. At least it wasn't a police car. She was sure she had done something bad but couldn't remember who she'd done it to.

She supposed she'd find out eventually.

Chapter 6

In my bedroom, I grabbed my mobile phone out of the bedside drawer. There were three unread text messages on the lock screen, all from Gemma, the friend I'd known the longest. It took me longer than it should have to read them because the letters danced in front of my eyes. **Why aren't you replying?** and **Everyone's really worried about you** and **Come on, Bee. Just a few words to let me know you're OK**.

I didn't mind when Gemma used it, but I hated the nickname Bee. It wasn't as though I were called Beatrice or Bianca (a name I yearned to have after watching *EastEnders* when I was twelve). I put the phone under my pillow.

The rain tapped on the window. It was single-glazed – only a thin barrier between me and the weather. The curtains were still open, and a blob of rain collected smaller drops until the weight of them all dribbled down the glass like a giant tear.

I loved it when it was pouring down outside, especially in the summer. It was a good excuse to stay inside.

It was harder to be miserable when the sun was shining, with people going on about what a great day it was.

It had been raining the day I met Matthew, although we actually met on a flight to sunny Malaga. He was sitting with one of his friends in the row in front of Gemma and me. She had gotten so pissed that she shouted at him after he reclined his chair – it almost rested on her lap. She flicked vodka and orange onto his head.

I watched between the seats as he ran his fingers through his hair. He stood and turned round. He was so tall, he had to bow his head to avoid the luggage compartment. His hair was a reddish brown and his fringe a little too long. His arms were tanned and dotted with tiny freckles.

'What are you doing?' he said, with a slight smile. He licked his lips. 'A slight hint of orange juice in that vodka.'

'You,' said Gemma, resting her arms on his headrest, her head clearly wobbling, 'put your seat back and nearly spilled my drink.'

'So, I *nearly* did you a favour, then,' he said. 'You look like you've drunk *everyone's* drink.'

I covered my mouth in case Gemma spotted me laughing (though when she was that drunk, she wasn't her most observant).

'Actually,' I said. 'You *did* spill a bit of her drink. Everyone knows you're not meant to put your seat right back on planes.'

He rested a knee on the seat and his hand on the

39

headrest. 'I must've missed that part when reading the instructions,' he said, grabbing the laminated safety leaflet from the pocket in front of him. 'Oh, right! That's because it doesn't say anything about it.'

I wrinkled my nose. 'Who reads the safety instructions? If this plane were to crash into the sea,' I glanced out of the window, 'a bit of oxygen's not going to save us.'

Gemma sat upright. 'We're about to crash?'

'No, Gem,' I said. 'Try to sleep for a bit.'

I took off my cardigan and draped it over her after she'd arranged her handbag into a pillow.

'Matt,' said his friend sitting next to him, 'stop being a dick and say sorry. Everyone knows you shouldn't recline your seat that much.'

Matt raised his palms and said, 'Yeah, I know, Richie. I was just messing. I can't concentrate on my magazine and I've run out of peanuts.' He looked at a sleeping Gemma. 'She could've just said *excuse me*. There was no need to flick her drink all over me.'

Matt sat down and looked through the gap between the seats.

'Sorry about that,' I said. 'She's scared of flying and tends to drink a lot at the airport. Even though it was a 10 a.m. flight.'

'And you'd been at the airport since ...?'

'Half seven,' I said, laughing.

'So, you've tasked yourself with looking after her?'

'We've known each other since we were kids,' I said. 'Everyone needs looking after sometimes.'

Matt rested his head against the seat.

'That's a nice thing to say,' he said. 'Who looks after you?'

'I don't need looking after.'

At that point, his friend Richie elbowed him and said, 'For fuck's sake, Matt. Grow a pair.'

Matt and Richie, it transpired, were staying at the same hotel and by the final night we had spent most of the two weeks together as a foursome, mostly talking rubbish, drinking lots of alcohol and realising what friends from home we had in common – even the most tenuous of acquaintances.

On the final night, Gemma had sneaked off with Richie, and Matthew and I were on Malagueta Beach behind a cluster of palm trees that shielded us a little from the sea breeze. We lay on his blue and white Bolton Wanderers beach towel that smelt like it hadn't been washed in a fortnight. But that didn't matter because I liked him, and we'd spent too many hours drinking *cervesas* and margaritas on a beach bar terrace.

He propped himself on his elbows and looked down at me.

'Do you think we'll see each other when we get home?' he asked.

I'd never heard a man be so direct. Usually, it would be a guessing game of *did he like me*? or wondering if they'd call. 'When you meet the right person,' Jenny said when I cried into my pillow as a teenager, 'there'll be no time for games because they'll want to spend as much time as they can with you.'

Yeah. I'd thought that was bullshit, too.

'I don't see why not,' I said.

Matthew flopped back down into the sand.

'Good,' he said, taking hold of my hand. 'I can't believe we live just five minutes' drive apart.'

'Yeah, it's weird,' I said, because I was the same sparkling raconteur I am now.

I was glad Gemma had taken Richie for a walk as I was sure Matthew would never have been so open with him around.

'What was it like,' he said, 'living in a children's home?'

'As you'd expect, really. No privacy, no special treatment. They tried to make sure we were treated the same.'

'How old were you when you were adopted?'

'Eight,' I said. 'And Jenny and Phil gave me the news on my actual birthday ... and they filmed it on his camcorder, which was a bit embarrassing.' I grabbed a handful of sand. 'It kinda made up for the fact that no one came to my birthday party.'

'Shit,' he said. 'That's awful.'

'Yeah. It was Sam Grisdale's party on the same day and apparently his parents hired a bouncy castle.'

'God, that's harsh,' he said. 'Why didn't Gemma come?'

'I hadn't met her yet.' I turned my body towards him. 'And I'm sure she would've come if I had. Even if it'd meant missing out on a bouncy castle.'

'I don't know about that,' he said, twisting to face me. 'Unless you had ice cream and Turkey Twizzlers.'

'Ha!' I said. 'I know for a fact we'd never have had Twizzlers. I always wanted to try them. Ice cream on the other hand ... What was it like for you, growing up?'

'Really, really average,' he said, laughing. 'Two-up two-down ... played out until we were called in for tea.'

'I yearned for average.'

He kissed the end of my nose.

'I'm your man if that's what you're after.'

My phone vibrated under my pillow and brought me back into the small bedroom in Dorothy Winters' house. I wiped the tears that had dripped from my face into the collar of my nightshirt. By the end of that two weeks, I thought I knew everything about Matthew.

I was so wrong.

I wished I could stop thinking about him. I could be anyone I wanted now – an assistant to a famous author who travelled around the world if this new book was successful.

I closed my eyes. I could dream of a better life.

Anything was possible.

Chapter 7

Camera_3>bedroom>time_00:24

She puts her phone under her pillow then lies back on the bed. Her hands are clasped together.

She turns onto her right side and opens the bedside cabinet drawer.

She takes out what appears to be a blister packet of tablets (product name unclear. Suggested: Diphenhydramine).

She reaches for the switch on the lamp and turns it off.

Camera_3>bedroom>04:32>

She is asleep but moving.

'Please no ... No ... No ... Stop it ... Please ... I won't do it again.'

Chapter 8

'A young lady arrived at Dorothy's with a suitcase, yesterday, Mother.' Gordon stood at the kitchen window. 'I wonder what she's doing there.'

The lights were still on in the dining room next door even though it was eight in the morning and there was plenty of light outside. He couldn't help but notice; the end of her house (before the extravagant kitchen extension) was near enough in front of him. Especially if he stepped on the small plastic step kept in the cupboard under the sink. His mother had ordered it online because she couldn't reach the biscuit cupboard any more. She seemed to be shrinking an inch every year.

'Did you hear me?' he said. 'A young lady with a suitcase. Don't you think it's a bit strange?'

She didn't reply. Too busy watching *Good Morning Britain* from her chair next to the fire in the living room. Last month, her area was the tiny sunroom (or *solarium*, as she called it) that had been added onto the kitchen in the eighties. But she was permanently cold now and it was too draughty in there.

45

At least Gordon had the rest of the house. Mother only frequented the living room, the bathroom, her bedroom, and the kitchen (on very rare occasions). The heating bill after the first month of her relocation was astronomical. He decided, then, to only put the heating on between 7 a.m. and 10 a.m. (sometimes she had a lie-in) and to let her have the fire on all day. His world was a quieter place when Mother was warm and fed. Like a newborn baby.

It hadn't always been like this. Two months ago, his wife Audrey lived here, too. They'd only been two years into their marriage. First time for Gordon, fourth time for Audrey.

She was apprehensive about leaving their rented apartment overlooking the river but once she realised they'd have most of Mother's house to themselves, she soon became accustomed to the idea.

Gordon's father made him promise to look after Mother. How could he have gone against the wishes of a dying man?

'You know what she's like, son,' he said. (Dad hated Gordon's name as much as he did.) 'Your mother won't like to admit she hates being alone ... even after mithering me just for being in the same room as her. She's only like that because that's how her mum and dad were.' He paused for a moment to take a few breaths. 'Keep on top of the servicing for the car, too, won't you. You know how much your mother likes to be driven around.'

'I know, Dad,' said Gordon. 'But let's not think about that. You've plenty life in you.'

Dad gave a wheezing, choking laugh. At least, Gordon *thought* it was a laugh.

'You've always been an optimist, son,' he said, once his airways had cleared. 'And I know you'll do good by your mother. Plus, the house'll go to you eventually. Might as well make yourself at home.'

Dad died only a few days later.

That was nearly three months ago, but it felt like last week.

When Gordon told Audrey the plan, he was sure, now, that the only words she heard were that Gordon was going to inherit the house. They'd been together for three years, but it was like she'd been waiting for an excuse to end things. She kept saying things like, 'Sometimes I miss the days when I could wake up alone and have the whole day to myself.' He had spent most of his thirties and forties wishing the opposite.

'And you say your mum's not in very good health?' she said.

As if Gordon couldn't see the meaning behind that question. He wasn't an idiot. And it was only a week after his dad's funeral when she asked. She should've kept that to herself for at least a few weeks.

That should have told Gordon all there was to know about Audrey. He wouldn't make that mistake again.

She only lasted six weeks in this house. She'd probably expected living quarters the size of a Kensington Palace apartment – fancied herself as an older Princess Diana.

He dried the two cups, saucers and his cereal bowl

and put them away. He wiped the few crumbs that he'd missed near the kettle. He sighed as he looked out of the window again. More jobs that needed doing. The Creeping Jenny had spread almost overnight towards the ornamental grass section. A bit of anarchy in the garden. Gordon smiled at the thought.

He stood on the plastic step from under the sink with a view to seeing the bottom of the garden. The top of the garage was just visible above the back wall, but he didn't want to think any more about his dad's car. He still hadn't brought himself to drive around in it – even though he'd let the engine run a few times to make sure it still ticked over.

He chanced a glance over the wall into next door's garden.

For goodness' sake, it was getting worse. Ms Winters wasn't green-fingered like he was. Her garden stretched out a good six feet longer than theirs, but she didn't do anything with it. If it were his, he'd put an extra shed down there – maybe kit it out with a sofa and a television so he'd get a bit of peace away from the house. Mother was always within shouting distance – even over three floors, she'd mastered the art of being heard.

He couldn't see anyone in next door's dining room. The woman who arrived yesterday looked to be in her early thirties. He didn't get a clear look at her yesterday; there's only a certain amount you can tell from a bedroom window.

'Gordon!' Mother shouted from the living room.

God, he really did hate his name. No one else was called Gordon at school. He'd tried out a few nicknames (Gordy, G-man, Donny) but none of them caught on. He'd hoped that when *Flash Gordon* came out when he was fifteen, it'd give the name a bit more street cred, but it didn't.

He stepped down from the step and flung the tea towel across the kitchen.

In the living room, the remote control was lying not far from the television.

'Is Piers Morgan annoying you again this morning, Mother?'

He picked up the remote and placed it on the arm of her chair. He tucked in the sides of her blanket.

'Stop mithering me, Gordon,' she said. 'I could've got the flicker myself. And the reason I called you in is nothing to do with the telly. Piers Morgan isn't on *GMB* anymore. You really should keep up with current affairs.'

'What did you call me in for, then?'

'I saw an ambulance outside, but it's gone now.'

'There's always an ambulance across the road,' he said, leaning on the windowsill. 'I wonder if they're killing them off, one a day.'

'You should take me over the road,' she said. 'I'd be gone a lot quicker than in this waiting room. They'll be expecting me soon, you know ... You'd better make the most of me while I'm still here. There's my sister Rita ... and your father ...'

Gordon tuned out from his mother reeling off all the

interesting dead people she'd known. The undertone was always that she'd been left with the most boring of the lot.

If she really understood him, she wouldn't think like that.

'Oh,' she said, finally. 'Another reason I called you in is because your phone beeped.'

He suddenly felt quite queasy. He thought he'd put it on silent. Why did people need to feel connected all the time? If it weren't for his mother, he'd rid himself of that bloody phone.

'It's on the mantelpiece,' she said, pointing at it with the walking stick she didn't really need.

'Yes, thank you.' *I know where it bloody is*. 'I'll take it through to the kitchen.'

'It's probably from Audrey.'

'Rightio.'

He walked back into the kitchen. Mother had probably peeked at the message preview on his home screen. And not for the first time.

It probably *was* from Audrey. He had a vague recollection of emailing her in the early hours after three whiskies too many. He hadn't worked up the courage to check the sent folder on his PC.

Right.

Nothing to be scared of.

Only Audrey.

Still, he opened her text message with only one eye open.

God, another essay. Who on earth felt compelled to write so much in a text message?

Audrey, that's who.

Gordon,
I'd appreciate it if you could stop sending me
passive aggressive emails under the guise
of memes. If you need to speak to me about
something important, please go through my
solicitor.
   In the meantime, I've blocked your email address.
Audrey.
PS. Sending 'funnies' by email is so 2003.

It was typical Audrey. Such a superiority complex. And as if she'd have blocked him. She was far too nosy to do that. She wanted to keep in contact with him, otherwise she would've just deleted his email. She was probably waiting for his mother to die. Then she would come slithering back like the snake she was. Such a cold heart. He'd just have to stop his fingers contacting her again.

Chapter 9

Luckily, my super-strength painkillers had kicked in to get rid of the cracking headache I woke up with. They gave me a nice buzz that made all of this seem like a dream.

I leant back in my chair and swivelled around in a circle. The office I was to work in was surprisingly small compared to other rooms in the house. The walls were painted deep red, which clashed with the mustard-coloured velvet curtains that framed the window. The eighties-style office blinds completed the look of English eccentricity (and that was being generous).

My battered wooden desk was placed in the bay window, so I was on display to everyone walking past the front of the house. Fabulous.

To the right of the desk was a small fireplace. The ash in the grate was covered in cobwebs and a pile of scrunched-up newspaper. A painting hung above the mantelpiece and, at first glance, it looked like a normal family portrait. The mother was dressed in a shin-length flapper dress, the father in a boxy suit. One of the three children was dressed to match his father, the other two boys in sailors' outfits.

I stood and rested my hands on the mantelpiece for a closer inspection. Their eyes were black and their expressions blank as though all five of them had been posed post-mortem. It felt as though their eyes bored into mine.

I shot back, my hand grazing against a metal box. It crashed onto the wooden floor.

Damn.

I hoped Dorothy hadn't heard me messing with her stuff. She was probably still sleeping. Like I wished I were when my alarm sounded at eight o'clock this morning. The only sign that she'd been in here recently was a list and a notebook decorated with fairies.

I sat at the desk and flicked through the notebook as the laptop booted up. Inside the front cover was the title *Vindicta*. Dorothy's looped slanting handwriting filled most of the pages.

I placed it back on the desk and picked up the list.

Research undetectable contemporary (also historical but still available) poisons; legalities of death in absentia; buy The People's Friend, *send the package on the hall table and get a book of first-class stamps.*

Andrea, one of the care workers at my last children's home, used to read *The People's Friend*. After she'd finished reading it, she'd leave the copy on my bedside cabinet – even though some of the stories were a bit grown up for a six-year-old. I loved looking at the illustrations. I kept all the copies she gave me under my bed until Jade my roommate – the little shit – decided to create a mini bonfire in a metal wastepaper basket at 2 a.m. one morning in the first-floor bathroom. The fire alarms went off and everyone had to stand in the car park for two hours, freezing cold in crappy pyjamas, until the fire brigade declared it safe to re-enter. Even though I'd already put the fire out with one of the little red extinguishers that were everywhere.

That, unfortunately, had put me at the scene of the crime. *The People's Friend* magazines were still recognisable when the firefighters presented the manager Mrs Renner with the evidence. She was convinced I was *poisonous* and *a bare-faced liar* and the mean cow decided that my being in an environment with other children was dangerous to everyone. So that was the beginning of my many foster homes.

The phone on my desk rang.

I grabbed it quickly as the bloody thing was so loud; I'd have heard it from my room upstairs.

'Dorothy Winters' residence,' I said. I felt posh just saying those words.

'Oh,' said the caller. It sounded as though he was in his eighties. 'I must have the wrong number.'

'Who are you after?' I said, now sounding more *Coronation Street* than *Downton Abbey*.

'Estelle Williams,' he said. 'But I haven't talked to her in a long time. I probably typed the number in wrong. I'm always doing that. My granddaughter said I should get a mobile phone so the numbers are already typed in, but my eyesight's shocking and the bloody things are too small to read from.'

'I'm afraid it's only Dorothy and me here,' I said.

'Dorothy who?'

'Winters. The author.' *Don't you know.*

I grimaced at myself for sounding so pretentious.

'Oh,' he said. 'I've heard of her. My wife used to read her books.'

'Really?'

I shouldn't have been surprised – they even stocked Dorothy's books in the library in town.

'Yes. But I thought Dorothy was ...' The man's voice trailed off.

Dead? Eccentric? Crap?

'I'm so sorry to have bothered you,' he said, instead. 'I'll try to press the numbers in the right order this time. If it rings again in a minute, don't answer it.' He chuckled. 'Bye-bye now. I hope you have a wonderful day.'

I replaced the handset and the silence in the room wrapped itself around me. I'd been alone for weeks now. First at the hotel room, where I hid away through fear. But after nothing happened, I realised that maybe nobody was chasing me after all.

What had I expected here, though? Glamour? Parties? I knew this job might've been merely a glorified typist but the temptation of somewhere to live had made me accept it too hastily.

Movement out of the window caught my eye. A woman was walking slowly along the pavement towards either the church or the lone detached house at the end of the street. She was wearing an electric blue coat that tied at the waist. Her near-black hair was in a bob that rested on her shoulders, but the peaked beret she wore cast shadows on her face.

A memory flashed in my mind. A woman with shiny dark hair in a navy-blue coat bending down to stroke my cheek. Whenever she came to visit at the children's home, they used to say, 'Your grandmother is here to see you,' but I never believed them. Grandmas weren't meant to look like that – glamorous and young. Nearly every kid at the home had had visitors – sometimes their parents. That was worse, I thought. Even then. I couldn't imagine how it felt to say goodbye to their mum or dad time and time again.

The last time the woman in the blue coat visited, I'd been placed with Jenny and Phil. It was about a year after the fire, so I would've been about seven. 'I'm going away for a bit,' she said, as though that would mean something to me. 'And I won't be able to visit for a long time.'

'Oh,' I said. 'It doesn't matter.' Though I remember thinking at the time that she'd probably heard I'd been branded an arsonist and a liar.

Jenny murmured something about, 'What was best for everyone,' when I asked her about it. It didn't matter anyway because Jenny and Phil were my family now.

The woman outside the window had gone and it began to rain again.

I brought Facebook up on the laptop and typed

Matthew's name in; the phone began to ring again. The man obviously had the right number, but the wrong person.

I scrolled through Matt's pictures until I reached September 2017. I clicked on one of the photographs of us together. It was the night I'd first met all his friends and I was sitting on his knee, our heads close together. He rested his hand on the top of my leg. I was pretty drunk that night and I looked it: eyes glazed and focused on the ceiling.

'I can tell,' he whispered in my ear that night, 'that we're going to be together for a very long time.'

'That's if you don't get fed up with me,' I said. 'I can be a nightmare.'

He laughed as he linked our hands together with his fingers.

'You keep trying to put me off you, don't you?' he said.

I shrugged. 'I'm just saying these things before you do.'

The phone finally stopped ringing – the echo of it lingered in my ears.

I was right, in the end. It was my fault Matthew and I weren't still together.

Mrs Renner was probably right.

I was poisonous.

By two in the afternoon I'd crossed off most of the tasks on the list. Considering it was my first day, I hadn't seen Dorothy at all since last night. Perhaps she checked up on what I'd done when I went to the Post Office at lunchtime. I did prefer not to be monitored all the time while working but being totally ignored was a first for me.

Rain began tapping on the window. The clouds were heavy, and it looked like the streetlights should be on already. I flicked on the desk lamp. I couldn't concentrate on any of the research Dorothy had tasked me with. Looking up ways to kill people by poisoning was a little macabre – even for me. Dorothy must be used to it. In most of her books, there were at least two murders, all committed in gruesome ways. It was hard to believe those ideas were invented in her mind. She seemed so well-to-do. But then, so was Jeremy Bamber and he murdered his own family.

My gaze focused on the horizontal blinds in a rare moment where my mind went completely blank for a few delicious seconds. A gust of wind forced a shower of rain to batter the window and my eyes drifted to the street outside where a man was standing at the end of Dorothy's path. He was tall – almost double the height of the gateposts he stood between. He had jet-black hair, dark-rimmed glasses and a bright red scarf. His grey overcoat ended just below his knees and in his right hand was a black doctor's bag. He had a look of Mole from *Wind in the Willows*. With the reflection of the lamp, it was hard to tell if he was looking back at me.

I got up and stood close to the window, resting my bottom on the desk.

Still, he stood there. What the hell was he doing?

I raised a hand and waved slowly.

The man raised his in return.

We mirrored each other for a few seconds longer than a normal polite greeting until I grabbed the long handle of the blinds and twisted them shut.

Shit. Why had I done that? I couldn't see where he was going to go next. He might come up the path. He might be some sort of investigator hired to find me. I'd been gone from home for over a month now. Was that enough time to hunt me down? I should've travelled further.

No, no. An investigator would have been more discreet – not stood at the window and waved at me. I smiled at the thought, but it wasn't funny. If someone knew where I was, I wasn't going to know about it.

I peeped through the narrow slats and saw him opening the gate to the house next door. He walked briskly up the path; his yellow socks flashed with each step because his trousers were a few centimetres too short. Yellow socks and a red scarf. Perhaps everyone who lived on this street was eccentric.

He slotted a key into the front door.

I stepped away from the window and tiptoed towards the party wall, leaning against it and cupping my hands around my right ear.

'Hello, Poppy.' His voice was quiet, but his words were clear. 'Did Mother feed you your lunch?'

God, the walls were thin. He could probably hear everything in *this* house if he tried.

'I'm back, Mother,' he said, louder. There was a light thud against the wall – maybe he'd hung up his coat. 'They had those egg custards you like. And I managed to get four more of those Myada 108ops from the photography shop ... super high quality.' A cat's meow. 'At least I'm not talking to myself with you around, eh, Poppy?'

I flattened my ear against the wall. I couldn't hear a reply from Mother (who called their mum *Mother* these days?). Maybe she wasn't even there, like the smoking shelter man suggested yesterday – like Norman Bates and his *mother*.

Or maybe it was quiet because he had his ear to the wall, too.

I went back to my desk. The room was now lit mostly by the lamp because I'd shut out the daylight.

It was too quiet in here. Why hadn't Dorothy given me a radio or something? Perhaps because *she* needed silence to write she didn't think about anyone else. Maybe that was too harsh. She probably hired me because I emphasised how competent I said I was at prioritising my workload and working independently. God, I'd written a load of meaningless crap in my personal statement. Didn't most people?

I got the earphones from my handbag and plugged them into my mobile phone (three new text messages from Gemma that I'd read later) and selected a classical music radio station. I wasn't really into that type of music, but I couldn't listen to Radio 2 in case I typed the lyrics instead of Dorothy's handwritten words.

I turned to the first page in the notebook, eager to be the first to read Ms Winters' new bestseller and scanned the first couple of pages. The main character was called Kathryn. She was in labour and from looking at the first few pages, she didn't seem thrilled at the prospect of giving birth. Alone and resentful of the baby. I turned the handwritten pages to find that she was no longer taking care of her child.

It was a story that sounded almost too familiar.

Chapter 10

Kathryn had been on the psychiatric ward for almost a week and there had been no chance of getting a proper night's sleep. All the moaning, shrieking, screaming, murmuring. People were so selfish. Didn't they realise she wasn't like them?

The doctors didn't understand that either. For the past five days they hadn't let her be alone. Even when she showered, there had to be someone present. What did they think she was going to do? There was nothing in there to hang herself with, and no plug to collect enough water to drown in. And it was usually that ugly nurse Marjorie or Maggie or whatever she was called who chaperoned her. Bloody pervert. She wasn't meant to be looking at her that intently, was she? Kathryn should've put on a little show for her. That would've got them talking in the staff room, though they had enough fodder from the real patients in here. One of them – let's call him Peter – took off his trousers and underpants and wandered around, shaking his dick for everyone to see. Kathryn knew full well he was aware of what he was doing.

Technically, though, she had nowhere to live, so at least she had meals and a bed. Jesus, since when had that become her bare minimum? Jack. That was when. Empty promises and shit sex. Of course, he thought it had been amazing because she was always so enthusiastic.

Kathryn put down the book she was pretending to read. She could use this time out to gather her thoughts, plan what she was going to do next. Something always came along – she was lucky like that. Though luck seldom came into it. She wished she were allowed a phone call. If Jack knew she was in here, he would come to her rescue. Wouldn't he?

No. Kathryn should be cleverer than that. She didn't want to be seen as someone in dire need. What man would be attracted to that? She'd rather not have to explain why she was sectioned. She'd gloss over that when she saw him again. And she would. She'd make sure that it happened.

'Have you got your menu, Kath?' asked Jim, addressing her in that artificially friendly way. His blue nurses' outfit would look a lot better on him if it matched his eyes, but they were an insipid hazel. Neither green, blue or brown.

'It's right there,' she said, pointing to the end of her bed. He picked it up and her gaze was drawn again to the new man in the corner. 'What's happened to him? He hasn't spoken a word since he arrived yesterday morning.'

'Gone vegetarian today, then?' said Jim.

How bloody rude. Did he look in her dirty laundry as well?

'No,' she said. 'The shepherd's pie could be made from God-knows-what meat and the corned beef hash probably has cow eyes in it.'

He attached the piece of paper to his clipboard. 'Fair enough.' He wasn't bothered. It wasn't as if *he* was cooking it.

Kathryn watched as he took orders from the rest of the *clients*. The man in the corner said nothing; he just handed over his menu.

'Jim!' Kathryn shouted. 'Can you help me a second?' She beckoned him closer with her index finger. 'So? The man in the corner?'

He sighed. 'You know I can't say anything.'

'Oh, come on, Jimmy.' She stuck out her bottom lip slightly. 'Who am I going to tell? Everyone else in here is crazy.'

He pursed his lips and leant in closer.

'His name's Andrew. Some sort of breakdown.'

Oh. A high-stress job maybe? A company director? An overworked doctor? They put anyone in here, at first. It didn't matter what you did for a living.

'Did he have a high-powered position?' she said. 'Maybe someone famous I don't know about?'

'That's all I'm saying. I'll be in trouble if I say any more ... not that I *know* any more. He's barely spoken.' He rolled his eyes at his own indiscretion. 'See you later.' He reached the doors. 'And stay out of trouble.'

Now, where would the fun be in that?

She slid down in her bed and brought the book up towards her face. Andrew was looking out of the window. He was probably quite sensitive. He had *The Notebook* paperback on his cabinet. She could ask him if she could borrow it.

She closed her eyes and imagined a day, perhaps a year from now. She'd get into her BMW, with the recovered millionaire Andrew at her side. Jack would knock on the window and say, 'Kathryn. You look amazing. How have you been?' And Kathryn would say, 'I'm sorry. I can't stop now. Nice to see you. Take care of yourself.'

That would be all it would take for him to come running back to her. But for now, she would have to forget about Jack.

For now, it was going to be all about Andrew.

The group was sitting in a circle in a conference room. Wood-panelled walls and a suspension ceiling. One of the counsellors, Georgina, had suggested Kathryn take part in group therapy. 'It might help,' she said, 'if you realise other people have been through similar experiences in their lives.'

'You mean I should realise there are people worse off than me?' said Kathryn. 'I know there are people who have been through horrific things, but aren't problems relative?'

Georgina sat cross-legged on her plush cream sofa. So unprofessional.

She wanted to ask if Andrew would take part, but her asking would reveal a motive. She needed to appear open, honest.

'OK,' said Kathryn, exasperated, as though giving in after hours of convincing. 'I'll do it.'

It was her third time now and the first time that Andrew was in the same group.

On the table (that took up most of the room) was a large oval plate piled with biscuits. Six Jammy Dodgers were dotted around the edges. Perhaps they were a test: if you chose one, it meant you were cured. No one had picked up a Jammy Dodger so far.

'So, Kathryn,' said Dave the group leader, councillor, whatever. 'Do you want to say anything today?'

She felt Andrew's gaze on her – along with everyone else's. Kathryn looked at him and immediately his eyes went to the floor.

'Not really.'

Dave sighed. They weren't meant to do that, were they?

Kathryn thought about grabbing the plate of biscuits and jumping out of the window with it. Why did they put a bunch of suicidal patients in a room on the fourth floor?

'OK,' he said. 'Let's hear from Jean.'

God, not Jean. Always going on and on about her mother (who didn't sound too bad considering she had to put up with a daughter like Jean).

'Hang on,' said Kathryn, aware that Dave had manipulated her into silencing Jean. Jean was probably a plant, ensuring each one of them would say anything for her not to speak again. 'I'll do it. I'll say something. Where do you want me to start?'

He gave a sickly smile and opened her file. 'Hmm,' he said, sounding like Kaa the snake from *The Jungle Book*. 'Perhaps how the feelings you have about abandoning your child have affected your present?'

A buzzing sounded in her ears. Even the bloke who usually stared at the ceiling was staring at her. Were they supposed to reveal personal information like that in front of everyone? She looked at Andrew again. His eyes were focused on the floor again. She could tell he was on her side. An unspoken respect between them.

'That's a loaded statement,' said Kathryn, leaning back and folding her arms. 'It's the nineties.' She noted the raised eyebrows because it wasn't the nineties any more. 'You wouldn't ask a bloke that kind of question.'

The whole thing would've been pointless had Andrew not been waiting for her outside the group after the hour and a half was up.

'Kathryn is it?' he said. His voice was louder than she thought it'd be.

'That's right.' She leant against the wall.

'I think we have a few things in common,' he said. 'You seem the most,' he glanced around, 'down-to-earth person here.'

'That's one way of putting it,' she said, smiling.

'Is it OK if we have a chat sometime?'

'Of course it is.'

She walked away, back to her new room and closed her door.

It was always so very easy to get them. Keeping them was another matter. She might actually put some effort in this time. It was all about compartmentalisation.

Chapter 11

The room was in semi-darkness after I closed the lid of
the laptop and flicked off the lamp. Outside, a streetlight
was flickering into life and the rain still poured, beating
against the window. Dorothy – well, I assumed it was
her – came downstairs at around three but didn't come
into my office. Now it was six o'clock and I still hadn't
heard from her. I might buy a magazine for tomorrow
– might as well make the most of being left to manage
my own time.

I printed off the pages, stapled the corner and headed
out of the office door. On the hall table near the front
door was a candle in a glass dome, casting giant shadows of the vase of fresh flowers. Neither had been there
when I left the house earlier.

'Dorothy?'

There was no reply.

Where was she? There were doors everywhere. The
one under the stairs rattled slightly as though a breeze
had blown through the gaps. Was it a downstairs loo or
did it go down to a cellar?

It was locked, but the door to the library was open.

There were several lamps in the room, but it felt presumptuous to turn one on. I took my mobile from my pocket and switched on the torch.

Every wall was covered with bookcases. I started from the left, nearest the door, illuminating the spines of the books with my phone light.

Dorothy's novels took up three rows of the bookcase next to the door. There were a few I didn't recognise that hadn't been stocked in the library. I picked out one of the older-looking ones – *The Visitor in the Picture* – and flipped it over where there was a large black-and-white photograph of the author. Her blonde hair was hidden mostly by a scarf wrapped around her head and she wore huge gold loop earrings. Her chin rested on her hand in a typical author pose of its day. Her symmetrical features were covered in make-up – heavy black eyeliner, painted lips, and blusher sculpted on her cheeks. She looked about forty but could've been a little younger. Inside the front page was the publication date: 1986. That meant Dorothy must be around seventy years old now. She'd definitely had some work done to her face – there was no way her skin could look as good as it did without some surgical intervention.

Why had she bothered, though? She was cooped up in here all day. It wasn't as if she mingled regularly with the rich and famous. There was nothing on Google about her attending book launches or celebrity red carpets. Still, there were at least twenty different titles to her name; she must have earned a fortune. Enough to pay for this house, at least. And to hire an assistant she wasn't really bothered about.

On the other side of the room were about fifty red leather-bound editions – mostly the classics: *Treasure Island*, *Middlemarch*, *Dracula*. The spines were free of creases; those books were probably just for show.

I tucked Dorothy's pages under my arm and took *The Count of Monte Cristo* from the shelf. I loved the smell of old books: musty and slightly sweet. The pages inside were yellow around the edges. It was a 1983 book club edition, like the ones that used to be advertised on the back of Sunday newspaper magazines. It probably wasn't worth much. Inside, on the title page, was faded black handwriting: *To Mother, on your birthday, with lots of love from your favourite son, David xx*.

I replaced it and moved my mobile's torch along the shelf until I came to a gap between the books. There was a porcelain shape of a human head labelled *Phrenology by L.N. Fowler*. It wasn't an original; some of the lettering was wonky. Different characteristics were inscribed on the head: *Selfish Propensities* just above the right ear; *Sympathy, Liberality, Philanthropy*, at the top of the head. It had a very plain-looking face that would benefit from some drawn-on eyelashes ... maybe a bit of lipstick.

Alongside the head was a row of non-fiction books: *Spiritualism in Late Victorian England* and *Contacting the Other Side*. I took another one from the shelf. *Practical Spiritualism: An Intermediate Guide*. The front cover had a photograph of two men and two women sitting

around a table with their hands resting on the planchette of a Ouija board.

I flicked through the first couple of pages in the hope
of finding another personal message for the recipient.
Instead, my eyes landed on the epigraph.

*Les morts savent tout ce qu'il y a. Demandez et ils
répondront.*

The dead know all there is. Ask and they will answer.

I stared at the words. I'd never believed in ghosts
or anything like that. I'd been to a medium in the local
pub, but she hadn't revealed any details relevant to my
life. I'd primed myself to resist offering confirmations
of her guesswork, but in the end, I couldn't bear the
awkwardness of it all. 'Yes, Cassandra,' I said. 'My dog
was called Misty and now she lives in the eternal gar-
dens of heaven.' She wasn't convinced of my sincerity
and obviously I wasn't by hers so that made two of us,
which was ridiculous. Such a waste of money.

Dorothy was probably a believer. There were too
many titles on the subject for it to be a passing interest
and none of her novels had touched upon the subject of
spiritualism so it couldn't have been for research.

After placing the book back on the shelf, I froze.

Tapping came from behind the bookcase. What room
was behind that? It couldn't have been the dining room.
I side stepped to the right until I reached white wood
panelling shaped like a door, but there wasn't a handle.
A small round metal disc was where a lock would be. It
slid to the side when I brushed a finger across it. A keyhole. Surely this end-terrace house wasn't big enough

72

to have a secret room. There was the sound of a closing filing cabinet. A sigh. Footsteps coming from—

'Rachel!'

Dorothy had opened the door; my phone torch shone into her face, making her scrunch up her eyes. She *did* look seventy years old up close.

I handed over the typed pages.

'I'm sorry,' I said. 'I was coming to find you. I finished the jobs on the list.'

'Why are you using a torch?' said Dorothy. 'There's a light switch by the door and at least three lamps in here.'

'I didn't want ... I didn't mean to seem ...'

'Seem like what? A murderer in the dark? Miss Scarlett in the library with the mobile phone?'

'Well ... no.'

'Treat this house as your home.' She flicked on a lamp, turned her back on me, and locked her study door. 'What were your thoughts? Did you find it authentic?'

I frowned.

'The manuscript, dear.'

Dorothy rolled her eyes and pouted slightly.

'Authentic in what way?' I said. Dorothy's gaze was fixed on me. 'I only did English at GCSE ... and I don't remember the technical terms for anything.'

'You don't have to be an expert. You read books, don't you? And I'm sure you've watched dramas or comedies on the television and thought, *This is a load of crap – as if that character would say that.*'

73

'I believed what your characters said. Absolutely. Nothing stood out as—'

'Good, good.'

Had I put that I studied English on my CV? I knew I'd highlighted I was an avid reader.

'I noticed that the main character comes from Bolton,' I said. 'What a coincidence.'

Dorothy frowned and wrinkled her nose slightly.

'Did I write Bolton?' she said. 'Oh gosh. It must've been subliminal when I finished the chapter last night.'

That made sense: the handwriting on a few of the sheets was large with only one paragraph per page.

'If you need any help with the area,' I said, 'just let me know.'

'That's kind of you,' she said. 'You can't beat a bit of local knowledge. Google Street View only offers so much.' She turned to the mirror on the back of the door and smoothed down flyaway strands of hair with the palm of her hand. 'What are your plans for tonight? I'm having guests this evening. You don't mind, do you?' She pondered a moment. 'Did I show you the other room upstairs?' She placed a finger on her chin. 'I don't think I did, did I? I'll have it sorted for you. It's like a living area, but I don't think it's been cleaned. All my previous assistants have used it with no bother.'

'It's OK,' I said. 'I've still got some of my lunch and I'm quite tired. I was thinking of an early night anyway.'

The sound of canned laughter came from another room.

Matthew used to love *Only Fools and Horses*. He'd watch it on a Sunday morning, nursing a hangover from the night before with his friends. Episode after episode. His favourite scene was Del Boy falling through the bar. I still couldn't watch it now.

'Are you all right?' said Dorothy, folding her arms. 'You've gone a bit pale.'

'Yes, yes,' I said. 'I'm fine.'

'I hope you have a lovely evening,' she said. 'My friends are quite a noisy bunch, but you should be OK up on the first floor, high ceilings and all that.'

She turned and walked out of the library.

The first-floor landing was in near darkness, lit only by a light in the garden shining through the bathroom window. My bedroom looked smaller than I remembered it this morning.

A night surrounded by the same four walls. The only difference between this and the hotel room was that I was getting paid to be here. If I'd been at the hotel, though, I'd have run a bath and watched some television. But tonight, I felt as though I was intruding in someone else's home.

I plugged my mobile phone in to charge. There were no missed calls or unopened text messages. I'd been annoyed at the constant texts from Gemma, but now there were none, I yearned for contact from home. I knew, though, if I spoke to anyone, my homesickness would overwhelm me. I had to stay away from there, stay hidden. I couldn't risk my life again.

I got under the quilt, still fully dressed, and closed my eyes.

Chapter 12

During brief moments of sleep, I dreamed of Kathryn. Dorothy hadn't described her appearance, yet my subconscious pictured her to be the same height, build and colouring as me but slightly older. She was standing outside the house I shared with Matthew and our eyes met as I watched her from our bedroom window. The room behind me was filled with people I didn't know, drinking and laughing. It must've been my mind processing the noise from downstairs.

The doorbell had rung four times and Dorothy opened the door to whoever it was with loud, over-enthusiastic greetings. The more people that came, the louder they were. With no bathroom on the ground floor, they used the one next to my room. At first, I listened at the wall, trying to gather clues as to who they were, but they weren't the most pleasant of noises. The younger woman liked to sing as she peed, flushed, and then talked to herself in the mirror. One of the men had obviously eaten something disagreeable at some point, which was when I took my leave of that line of investigation.

What outfit had Dorothy picked for the evening? She was glamorous in the day – what might she look like when she was seeing her friends, people she wanted to impress? I thought, by her lack of presence online, that she might have been a recluse, but this obviously wasn't the case. Were there celebrities downstairs? Did famous people automatically befriend each other simply with that in common?

There was an old television in the corner of my room, on the chest of drawers. The aerial on top would be useless now everything was digital, but there was a video player integrated into the base. There were three videos to choose from: *Season 1 episodes 7–12 of The Golden Girls*, *Beaches*, and *ET*. *The Golden Girls* was the least depressing.

The fast-forward button didn't work so I had to sit through adverts for films I'd long forgotten. The antiquated nature of it all reminded me of the ancient television in the bedroom I shared with Gemma at Jenny and Phil's.

Gemma had come from Manchester. Her mum had just died, and she stayed with us for six months. Her dad had withdrawn into his grief and didn't give her the attention she needed. Those were Gemma's words; she didn't want to talk about it much.

We had to have the telly on all night, every night, with the sound on low. She was afraid her mum would appear as a ghost at the end of her bed if the room was in total darkness. She cried every night the whole time she stayed when she thought I was asleep.

'Are you OK?' I asked, the first time, but she didn't reply. 'If you ever want to talk about it, I'm here. Just wake me up if I'm asleep – I won't mind.'

I got used to the television being on all night – it was kind of soothing. It had a sheet of glass in front of the screen and we pretended it was flatscreen when we bragged about it at school.

The volume on this one at Dorothy's didn't go above twelve, but it was nice to have some company in the room, even if it didn't totally drown out the sounds from downstairs.

I peeked out of my bedroom window. A man – tall, fair-haired and dressed in jeans and a white shirt – stood a few feet from the house, staring into the darkness of the garden. He had a cigarette in one hand and a glass tumbler in the other. He kicked the small stones in the flower bed. Had Dorothy pissed him off?

Someone inside must have said something because he replied, 'As if you care about a few stones. It's not as if she'd notice.'

He spoke loudly, in the way drunk people do. I chanced a better look, resting my hands on the window-sill to see who he was talking to. All I could see was a sparkly turquoise skirt. A cloud of cigarette smoke was exhaled into the cold air. Why were they outside when Dorothy was smoking inside yesterday?

'I'll be in in a sec,' he said, his cigarette only two thirds smoked.

A few minutes later, he downed what was left in his

glass and took a last drag before tossing the cigarette onto the pavement slabs.

He paused before retrieving the still-glowing butt from the ground. He doused it in the bird bath before flinging it into the black wheelie bin. As he stepped towards the back door, his phone must've beeped. He paused to take it out of his pocket and frowned as he squinted to read it.

He looked straight up at my window.

I wished I'd ducked out of view; my hair was a state, and I was, by this time, in my nightshirt. I was the mad woman near the attic and held his gaze as though I were shameless. My cheeks were burning, and my nose was itching.

Shit, shit, shit.

Slowly, a smile spread across his face as the canned laughter sounded from the television at the end of my bed. There was no way he could've heard it. What had made him look up?

'Brett!' a woman shouted from the house – a voice that didn't sound like Dorothy's.

'Coming, darling,' he shouted, still looking up at me.

He shook his head, still smirking, his eyebrows raised.

I flopped down onto the bed and covered my face with a pillow. How bloody embarrassing.

More laughter from the television; they found it funny too.

I flung the pillow away, sat up and tried to concentrate on the programme.

There was a gentle tap on my bedroom door.

It couldn't be the man from the garden, could it? Had he mistaken me looking at him as some sort of come on?

I lowered the already-quiet television to zero and waited a few moments.

There was no second knock. A step creaked on the staircase.

I got off the bed and opened the door to an empty landing. On the floor was a silver tray with a plate, a tall glass of milk and a package wrapped in tin foil. I picked it up and kicked the door shut.

I'd lied to Dorothy earlier about having leftover lunch and my stomach had been rumbling for over an hour. I placed the tray on the bed and sat cross-legged. A note was placed on the side: *A little snack in case you get hungry x*

It wasn't in Dorothy's handwriting. It must've been from Louise.

I put the glass of milk on the bedside cabinet and unwrapped the foil. It was a sandwich: brown bread, turkey, lettuce and mayonnaise. My absolute favourite. It wasn't such an unusual combination after all. The lettuce was crisp and fresh, and the turkey was that proper carved deli stuff – not those pre-packed slices I used to buy.

By the time I finished, and just as the VHS tape began to auto-rewind, music began playing even louder from downstairs. The back door was open again; I could hear nearly every word of Jarvis Cocker singing 'Disco 2000'.

I got up, placed the tray outside and closed the door.

I lay in bed with the lights off, wishing I were

somewhere quiet. My mind always went to places I didn't want to visit when I couldn't sleep. To home, to Matthew.

I'd introduced Matthew to Jenny and Phil when we'd been seeing each other for nearly three months. Jenny didn't lay out the posh china or anything, but they'd set the table rather than unfolding the TV dinner tables in front of the telly like they usually did when all the children had been fed and watered. Matthew had brought a bottle of red wine.

'Well, look at that,' Phil said as he accepted it. 'That's very generous of you, Matthew.'

Matthew shrugged and said it was no bother, which was just as well because I knew the wine would never be opened. Phil didn't touch red because it gave him a hangover as he was drinking it.

Matthew was dressed in a black leather jacket I'd never seen before because I'd told him that Phil was mad keen on motorbikes. I knew Phil forgave him for the red wine after Matthew asked to see his Triumph Bonneville. They were out in the garage for ages.

In the kitchen, Jenny poured me a glass of white wine.

'You sit down,' she said. 'You can talk to me as I finish up. Fish pie – I hope that's all right. I've got some fresh peas from the allotment, too.'

'Sounds perfect.'

Jenny glanced at me.

'Look at you,' she said. 'I've never seen you grinning so much.'

'I know. I didn't think I'd ever meet someone funny *and* good-looking.'

Jenny threw a tea towel over her shoulder and took a sip of wine.

'You know that men can have looks *and* a personality, don't you? I mean, we have a shining example with our Phil.'

She winked at me as Phil and Matthew walked back in through the patio doors.

'I think we have a convert,' said Phil. 'He said he's never ridden a motorbike before. And I thought he'd know a bit about bikes with that jacket on.'

Phil patted him on the back; Matt smiled and rolled his eyes.

'I wanted to make a good impression,' he said. 'I'll have to get some lessons in.'

'See,' said Phil. 'A convert. You'll be coming with me and the gang to Devil's Bridge before you know it.'

Almost two months later, Matthew finally introduced me to his parents. Their house was a two-up two-down just outside Bolton. His mum Tina had organised a barbecue and invited most of the street. When I arrived, all the other guests were already there.

'Sorry,' I said. 'Am I late?'

'Don't worry, don't worry,' she said.

I sat on the plastic chair next to Matthew. It was a small yard laid with concrete slabs, but pots of pretty flowers brought colour to the grey.

'I thought it started at two o'clock,' I said to him. 'I feel awful.'

'Not to worry.' He kissed my cheek. 'It doesn't matter. Mum has threatened to get my school photos out later. Hopefully, she'll forget. I told her parents don't show baby pictures these days.' He glanced at me as he took a swig from a bottle of lager. 'Just warning you.'

'I quite like old photos.'

Matthew's dad Shane walked over and handed me a glass.

'There's a nice cocktail for you, love.'

'Oh, what's in it?'

Matthew turned to look at me. 'He's not trying to poison you,' he said, laughing. 'Though I wouldn't put it past him to try to get you pissed.'

'Language, son,' said Shane.

The cocktails were lethal because after my third I could barely stand without Matthew's help.

'They really liked you,' he said a few hours later when we were back at his house and I'd almost sobered up. 'Especially Dad. He likes someone who can have a drink and a laugh.'

'Are you sure?' Anxiety after drinking had dialled up to ten.

'Definitely,' he said, kissing the end of my nose.

He always kissed the end of my nose.

I blinked away the tears and wiped the sides of my face. It was futile trying to block out memories. I needed to feel the pain that came with remembering good times. It made the awful times so much darker.

Chapter 13

It was half past seven in the morning and my body ached. I'd only walked for an hour yesterday lunchtime, so it must've been from sitting in the same position at the desk for hours.

I'd had a terrible night's sleep. Several times I sensed Matthew in the room — that somehow he'd followed me here, but when I opened my eyes, I was alone. At around three, I heard what I assumed was Dorothy tripping up the stairs and banging around the floor above. From the sniffs and the sobs, it sounded as though she was crying.

I got up, washed and dressed. The only clean clothes I had left were my sage green jeans, pale pink blouse, and a mustard-coloured cardigan. I looked like a children's TV presenter from the nineties.

The clock chimed once for a quarter past eight as I walked downstairs. I hadn't heard the other guests leave and dreaded the idea of them still awake and partying. Those creative types might've been into all sorts.

I pictured opening the door to a pile of middle-aged naked bodies after a night of depravity.

I listened at the dining-room door.

No sound.

I needed to walk through there to get to the kitchen. That would be my excuse if there was still an orgy going on (on the off-chance they'd actually notice me tip toeing past).

I turned the handle and pushed open the door.

Thank God. Empty.

The room was immaculate. There were no empty glasses, no smashed bottles, no overflowing ashtrays, no naked heap. Dorothy had almost certainly left the tidying up to Louise.

I headed to the galley kitchen, which was longer than it was wide, and the glossy white units and white laminate floor were at odds with the traditional décor in rest of the house.

Inside the fridge, three bottles of half-drunk wine (red, pink and white) were in the door compartment. Three unopened bottles of champagne lay in a row on the bottle rack. The rest of the shelves were crammed with food in neatly stacked Tupperware containers.

I made myself a coffee – avoiding the fancy coffee machine and going for the instant – and gazed out of the back-door window. The kitchen extended beyond the house next door by about twelve feet and the garden was almost the length of the house. The grass was neatly manicured with small ornamental walls that separated the lawn from the flower beds, which were bare save for a few ferns that had survived the cold.

Frost coated the grass, and the water in the birdbath was topped with a thin layer of ice that sparkled in the sunlight. A shed at the bottom of the garden stood against the party wall and was painted a dark muddy brown; some of the timber lengths were warped. A hearty shove could probably raze it to the ground.

Movement caught my eye. It was the strange man from next door. His head was bobbing above the wall.

I leant forward, putting my face too close to the window.

He yanked a blanket across his washing line, making the cord sag in the middle. Surely, a wet cover would freeze solid in this weather.

He turned his head quickly.

Shit.

I ducked down below the glass of the door, hot coffee splattering onto my jeans. I dabbed it with my cardigan sleeve, hoping it wouldn't leave too noticeable a stain.

This was silly. I'd never lived in such a street with all this sneaking about. Or perhaps it was just me.

I was still crouching when I heard the music.

'Creep' by Radiohead.

I thought I'd imagined it at first; it wasn't loud. Had it been playing all along?

I stilled my breath. It was coming from another door, next to the entrance to the kitchen. I hadn't noticed it before because it was covered with aprons that hung from a coat rack.

I stood straight, placed the cup on the drainer and

ran my fingers along the top of the surfaces as I walked towards the music.

Matthew loved that song.

I didn't mind it, but I'd told him I wasn't a particular fan.

Whenever it played on the car radio, he'd turn up the volume and sing loudly, badly. 'How can anyone not like Radiohead?' he said. 'This guy's a genius.' He'd light up a cigarette, maximising the pleasure of it all, only opening the window a tiny bit.

Close to the door in the kitchen, I smelt tobacco.

I pulled it open to find a windowless pantry. The wallpaper was buttercup yellow with a brown wheat pattern, peeling in places. The radio was on a shelf to the right alongside tins of food and packets of sauce mix.

A lit cigarette, half smoked, rested on a thick glass ashtray on a small square table. 'Dorothy?'

I don't know why I shouted – there was nowhere in here for her to hide.

I stubbed out the cigarette, rushed to the back door and stepped outside. It was bloody freezing. My breath clouded in front of me and damp frost soaked through my socks.

There was no one in Dorothy's back garden, no footsteps imprinted on the grass.

I needed to stop being so paranoid. No one knew I was here – I wasn't in danger any more. But, on the other hand, it wouldn't be sensible to relax too quickly. He'd found me once before.

'Hello there.'

I almost fell against the wall. It was the man from next door, standing on something to raise himself to about eight feet tall.

'Hello,' I said.

'You're up and out early,' he said, looking to the end of Dorothy's garden.

'Oh,' I said. 'It's not that early.'

He glanced up at Dorothy's house. The man had no shame.

'It is for *that* house. It was gone four thirty by the time the last of your guests left.'

'I wasn't invited to the party,' I said, feeling a little disloyal.

'Oh, you wouldn't want to be invited to one of *those* get-togethers,' he said. 'I've got my security cameras fixed on my back garden in case they sneak over the wall. I imagine they get up to all sorts.'

'Do you?'

His neck coloured slightly.

'Just a turn of phrase,' he said quickly. 'How are you settling in?' He reached an arm over to shake my hand. 'I'm Gordon.'

'I'm Rachel, Dorothy's new assistant.'

'Oh, I see,' he said. 'I did wonder.' He flicked a leaf off the wall on to Dorothy's side of the garden. 'How are you finding it so far?'

'OK,' I said. 'I'm still waiting for the all-night partying and debauchery.'

He wrinkled his nose slightly.

'Do you work from home, then?' I said. 'I've noticed you don't leave the house till later in the morning.'

Oh God, I sounded like a stalker.

'Have you? Nice to know someone's looking out for me. And technically, I do, yes. I'm a private investigator ... well, I'm training to be. Today's library day, though. They have someone in to talk on Tuesdays. It's "Foraging Wild Food in the British Countryside" today. You never know when something like that might come in handy.'

'I suppose you don't,' I said. I took a few steps back and rubbed my hands; the cold was seeping up through my now-soaking wet socks. 'I'd better get back inside.'

'Yes,' he said. 'You don't want to get on the wrong side of *her*.'

'Really?' I said. 'She seems pretty relaxed ... a bit eccentric.'

'Well, before she started having these parties, I used to hear her crying and ranting.' He pointed to the house. 'My bedroom must be right next to hers.'

'Oh,' I said, frowning. Did he really have nothing better to do than spy on number sixty-three?

'The shared wall ... they're so thin because they didn't build them with sound protection or insulation.' He must've noticed he was losing me and leant forward, resting his arms on the wall. 'I think she's having man trouble.'

'Really?' I folded my arms. 'Has she told you that?'

'No. It's what I've gathered. It was always when that man was here. I can't remember his name. Tall, younger than she is by at least a decade. Blond hair, a bit smarmy.'

'I take it you're not a fan of his.' I tried to stop myself smirking. 'I think he was here last night.'

Gordon's eyes widened; he raised his index finger.

'Brett!' he said, like an excited child. 'That's his name ... Fancies himself as an author as well, but I've only read the first chapter of one of his books – free on Amazon – and I didn't rate it much. I could've done a much better job of it.'

My whole body was shivering, and I knew I should walk away, but I did love a gossip. 'So, Dorothy's in a relationship with Brett?'

'I don't think so,' he said. 'But relationships can be complicated, can't they?'

A window slammed shut from upstairs.

'Oh no,' I whispered. 'I'd better go.'

Shit. What if Dorothy had heard us? I'd only been here a few days and had already breached her rule of discretion.

'Don't worry,' he said, whispering too. 'There's no way she could've heard us talking from upstairs. It's your room up there, isn't it? It was probably Louise making your bed.'

'How ...?'

He jumped down from whatever he'd been standing on.

'Nice talking to you, Rachel,' he shouted from behind the wall.

I dashed towards the back door in case someone was

still watching. Inside, I peeled off my socks and stood next to the narrow radiator in the kitchen. My toes were bright pink and prickled with the sudden change of temperature.

I hoped Dorothy or Louise hadn't heard me gossiping; the shame of it. I was no different from the people who talked about me in my hometown.

I walked towards the dining-room door, hoping there'd be no one there.

The pantry door was closed again. I was sure I hadn't shut it.

I pushed it open to find that the radio and the ashtray were gone.

Chapter 14

Footsteps were heavy behind, running towards her. The sound of breathing, too, although that would have been impossible as her hearing wasn't *that* good. Kathryn had only been in this city three months (two of them against her will), and she still had the feeling that someone was following her.

There were umbrellas everywhere, making it hard for her to see who might have been behind her when she chanced a look over her shoulder. She ducked into a shop doorway as a man came out. He held the door open for her and instead of thanking him, she held his gaze.

He shook his head, tutted at her, and muttered, 'Entitled bitch,' in a broad Yorkshire accent.

At the retreat (she preferred to call it that), hardly anyone talked with a broad accent. It was as though they'd all congregated in this northern city with no roots or accent to place them – dropped from nowhere into a hellish nightmare together.

Kathryn couldn't remember much about the day she was brought in, but the date was 31 December 1999. In her notes, it was recorded that she'd been wandering barefoot near the A64, wearing shorts and a T-shirt when it was minus three degrees.

She couldn't imagine herself doing that, but the doctor had no reason to make it up. She *could* imagine herself so desperate on the eve of the new millennium that she wouldn't have cared what happened to her. *New starts*. Everyone went on about them in 1999, but her life was at a dead end. *That* she could remember. It was odd because she couldn't recall ever wanting to go to York.

She sighed aloud when she realised it was a home-wares shop she'd stumbled into. If she ever got to the stage in her life when she browsed cups and plates for pleasure, then she knew her life would be totally with-out joy. And here she was.

She never wanted to be sensible. Where would the fun be in that? Perhaps those thoughts were why she ended up staying in York for longer than she intended.

She was holding a ceramic York Minster saltshaker when the door slammed open, causing the floor to vibrate.

'Kathy!' the woman said, bending over briefly, strug-gling to breathe. It wasn't a good look. And with what she was wearing (black hair extensions, black skirt to the floor), she looked like a screaming banshee who had been dragged through a hedge. She'd probably been going for the Kate Bush look, but it really hadn't worked. 'Why didn't you stop? I've been calling your name since Blake Street!'

'Sorry. I must've been in a daydream.'

She couldn't remember this woman's name. She was from one of the classes they made them take. *French for Beginners* or *Cooking for the Five Thousand* or *Sit in a circle and tell us why you wanted to kill yourself*. Something like that. Kathryn thought she might be called Jean or Jenny. Those women all blended into one – they all seemed to say the same sort of banal things they thought the counsellors wanted to hear.

'Are you coming to the meet-up tonight?' said Jean, snapping Kathryn's attention back into the homewares shop. Of *course*. Her name was Jean. 'There are a few guys from *Art for Life* coming. They're meant to be a right laugh.'

'No.' Kathryn couldn't think of anything worse. 'I've something I need to do ... it's an appointment I can't get out of.'

She left Jean standing in the middle of the shop, walked slowly to the door, and slipped the saltshaker into her pocket.

Andrew was waiting for her outside York Register Office. It was a beautiful Georgian building, three storeys high with huge white pillars either side of the doors. It was impressive, considering it was a council building.

He hugged her (he must've had a sneaky cigarette while he waited) and handed her a small bunch of flowers: a couple of bright pink roses, a smattering of daisies, all surrounded by sprigs of lavender. She didn't like to say that pinks and purples weren't exactly her favourite colours because he looked so pleased with himself.

That was one of the many things she hated about relationships with people like him: she had to keep these judgements to herself. He was so easily upset or offended. But, anyway, it was much easier to be pleasant when she had a long game ahead.

Andrew was wearing a suit she'd never seen him in. It was dark grey with tiny white pinstripes. His shirt was navy, and he wore a purple tie to match the flowers. He'd slicked back his auburn hair; the curls tickled the back of his neck and the top of his collar.

She really could picture looking at his face for the next few years. At least.

'I thought you weren't going to turn up,' he said. He gestured to the man and woman sitting on a bench. They were passing a can of Tennent's super-strength lager between them. 'I've found us a pair of witnesses.'

'A pair of pissheads more like,' she hissed in his ear.

'They're not as drunk as they look,' he said, shrugging his shoulders.

Kathryn thought Andrew might have chosen more appropriate adults after his past relationship with booze. But who was she to monitor his behaviour? She wasn't going to be *that* kind of wife.

'Do you know their names at least?' she said, wrinkling her nose.

She wasn't sure if the tatty suits they wore were by choice for the occasion or if they'd stolen them from a bin bag of clothes outside one of the charity shops.

'You can be such a bloody snob sometimes, Kathy.'

She detested the shortening of her name without her permission – it had been bad enough when the counsellors called her Kathy. If Kathryn had the chance to start her life again, she'd choose a name that couldn't be abbreviated.

Hopefully, it wouldn't come to that.

'This is Kathryn,' Andrew said as the seated man displayed an enviable talent of pouring beer into his mouth from the can three inches above his face. 'Kathryn, this is Clarence, and this is his wife, Esther.'

Clarence tipped an invisible cap.

'You're married?' said Kathryn.

'Common law,' said Esther.

'Oh, right.'

'There were slim pickings around here,' Andrew said quietly, guiding Kathryn towards the steps by her elbow. 'It's pouring down – everyone else was in a rush. It's lunchtime, you know ... for people with proper jobs.'

Jesus. Nothing like the wedding of your childhood dreams.

They'd said at the retreat that she shouldn't make any important life decisions so soon after being discharged, but Andrew was in the same boat. They couldn't arrest them for getting married.

He'd only sat in on one of the same group sessions as her, so she'd only told him what she wanted him to know. She'd said that her child was adopted, and she wasn't permitted to see her any more. She'd embellished her relationship with her parents, too. It would ensure he'd never want to meet them.

Andrew bent his arm at the elbow, and she threaded hers inside.

'Where did you get that suit?' she said as he tugged at the cuffs. 'It doesn't even fit.'

She couldn't help saying it. It was like her soul wouldn't rest until her observation was voiced. A handful of things *had* to be released. It wasn't good for one's mental health keeping everything inside. She'd heard that enough times.

Andrew rolled his eyes and smiled.

'Are you sure you don't want to call your sister?' he said. 'She doesn't live that far away.'

'No.'

If she were to marry again, she would invite her sister. It would be better than this.

She'd make sure of it.

Chapter 15

I sat down at my desk a few minutes before nine.
My adrenaline surged with every sound made in the
house and I prayed Dorothy hadn't heard me talking to
Gordon earlier.

It had taken me over half an hour to find the details
about two poisons for Dorothy's new book.

*Succinylcholine: a drug often used in anaesthesia to
cause the muscles to relax/stop working. It is untraceable
soon after death as it is metabolised by the body.*

*Potassium chloride: an overdose can mimic a heart
attack but is also metabolised easily. A naturally occurring chemical in the body.*

Good to know. You could actually buy them online,
but you'd probably need to set up a lab before they
supplied you.

Which character was going to poison the other? Will
Kathryn get bored with Andrew or will Dorothy introduce another character? God, I hoped no one would
search this laptop's internet history. Perhaps she was
going to set me up; that there wasn't a book she was

working on at all and she wanted to kill Gordon from next door. A bit elaborate, but you never know.

I brought up one of the photos of Matthew. His hair was cut short, and the freckles around his nose and cheeks had gone darker in the sun. It was a photograph that Jenny had taken in their back garden about a month before our wedding. Phil had donned an apron with *Dude with the food* printed on it. He stood at the barbecue and kept beckoning Matthew to join him, which he was keen to do to escape the constant talk of weddings: the cake, the flowers, the car, the favours. Jenny was as obsessed as I was.

Maybe that was why I hadn't seen the signs, though they were obvious now when I looked at this picture. He was smiling but I could tell from his eyes how he felt. I glanced at the family in the portrait above the fireplace. Matthew's eyes looked like theirs: dead inside. It was though he'd only revealed it to the camera.

My office door opened, and I closed the lid of the laptop.

'Good morning!' said Dorothy, popping her head around the door. If it had been her at the window earlier, she mustn't have heard my conversation with Gordon. She was actually smiling. 'I hope we didn't disturb your sleep last night. They can be a bit of a loud bunch.'

'No, no,' I said. 'I slept fine.'

I was hardly going to tell the truth, was I?

She opened the door wider and handed me her notebook.

'I've got another chapter for you here, but would

you mind taking a dress to the dry cleaners for me first? I've hung it near the front door.'

I almost stood straight away. An escape from these four walls.

'Of course.'

'Good, good,' she said. 'I'll see you later.'

She closed the door, which meant I had to wait until I could no longer hear her footsteps before opening it again. Why was she in such a good mood? If *I'd* had only a few hours' sleep, I'd be on my hands and knees.

I grabbed the dress from the coat rack and headed outside.

The chill of the morning had lifted, and cloud now covered the sky. I should've picked somewhere warmer and brighter than Preston. I'd only ever seen signs for it on the motorway, and even from a distance it looked unexciting. But that was what I needed.

After dropping off the dress and scanning the street for any faces I recognised from home, I saw a familiar figure about a hundred metres in the distance. It was Gordon, heading towards the library. Without thinking, I crossed the road and followed him.

There was a vestibule before the inner doors, its walls plastered with posters of various events (*Christmas Wreath-Making in the Park – weather permitting*) and items for sale (*Exercise Bike £50 ONO*).

I peered through the glass doors. A man, dressed in a khaki shirt and matching combat shorts, was standing in front of twenty plastic chairs. Only three seats were filled, and Gordon was sitting at the front with a note-pad already on his lap.

I nearly fell into the room when a man opened the door.

'I thought there was someone in the foyer,' he said. 'It's so dark outside for this time of day. The lights in here reflect on the glass doors.'

'Oh, right.'

He was younger than all the people I'd met so far in this town. He was a few inches taller than me and his hair was almost jet black, as were his eyebrows. His lips were pink, but not so much that they looked painted; his eyes were brown with flecks of amber. He didn't look like the type of person to work in a library, but I hadn't frequented many.

'I work here,' he said. He gestured to the people on seats. 'Are you here for the talk?'

My nose wrinkled. It was a reaction I wished I'd grown out of.

'Erm.'

His cheeks flushed. I hadn't seen a man blush since secondary school.

One of the audience members turned around and frowned at him.

He winced. 'Libraries aren't usually quiet these days, but they don't like disruptions while a discussion is going on. Which is fair enough.' He smiled. 'It's not exactly a sell-out – you've caught us on a bad day.'

He didn't seem to notice I hadn't spoken much yet. He walked towards the counter in the centre of the room, away from the tiny gathering.

I followed without thinking.

'I haven't seen you in here before,' he said. 'Have you just moved to the area?'

I stopped at the counter and waited as he flipped up the shelf. The name on his badge was Adam but it seemed too familiar to address him before he introduced himself.

'Sort of,' I said.

'What do you mean sort of?'

He frowned slightly but the corners of his mouth turned up.

'I've just got a new job,' I said. 'It's a live-in position.'

'That doesn't sound temporary.'

'I haven't decided if I'll stay yet.'

Why was I telling a stranger this?

'Sorry for being nosy,' he said. 'I'm used to people telling me everything about themselves here. Sometimes we're the only people some of the older folk speak to all week.'

'I'm like your *older folk*,' I said. 'I haven't spoken to a normal person for nearly a month ... well, apart from this old guy who rang by mistake the other day.'

'An old guy, eh?'

He pursed his lips and his eyes flashed. Was he trying not to laugh? A voice boomed from the other side of the room.

'And now I'm going to elaborate on my ten rules. Number one: never eat anything you haven't 100 per cent identified. Failing that, there are ways to make sure your find won't kill you if you ingest it. Firstly, you rub the item on the underside of your forearm ...'

The foraging action-man stood in front of his audience, clutching a collection of leaves and wild mushrooms.

'Take a seat if you want,' said Adam. 'It's meant to be four pounds, but I'll let you in for free seeing as it's already started.'

'It's OK,' I said.

'Not your thing?'

'Um.' I paused, thinking of how to word it so as not to offend him. I glanced at Gordon, who seemed to be enthralled by the Ray Mears wannabe. 'My neighbour's in the audience. I'm not sure what to make of him. He seems a bit too familiar.'

Adam glanced behind me.

'Oh, you mean Gordon,' he said quietly. 'He's not so bad. He gets caught up in different projects. One month it's photography, the next it's conversational Japanese. He's researching spy novels. I think he wants to become a private detective.'

'I heard that.'

'He got to you pretty quickly, didn't he?'

'He seems the lonely type.'

His smile faded when he looked at me. 'Do you think so?'

I broke from his gaze and scanned the room. Why did I always say the wrong thing?

'Shall I register you then?' he said. 'Even if you're not staying around here for long, you might as well have access to free books.'

'OK.'

He bent down to open a drawer and pulled out a form that seemed to be the result of photocopy after photocopy.

I filled it out and slid it towards him. I didn't mention the issue of identification – he was busy dealing with someone else anyway.

I wandered into the crime-fiction section to see if Dorothy's books were there. I expected a whole display of them, seeing as she only lived around the corner. Perhaps she'd never set foot in this place.

There were two of her novels, *The Elements of Insanity* and *Burning Perfect*, which I hadn't yet read. The author photo on the back was tiny and the same as the large picture on the rest of her books.

There was a bank of computers at the other side; only one seat was empty. A woman sitting at the end terminal caught my eye. She raised her eyebrows and wiggled her fingers in a tinkly wave. She stood and walked towards me – exaggerating her shoulders as though she was trying to tiptoe.

'Hello there,' she said.

The woman stood three inches shorter than me and had white hair, cut in an elfin crop. Her green parrot earrings almost touched her shoulders. Blue eyeliner framed her blue eyes. Someone had probably told her in the seventies it brought out the colour.

'Are you Dorothy's daughter?' she said.

'No.' I stood back slightly; she was standing far too close. 'What makes you ask that?'

'I saw you going into her house the other day. You had a suitcase with you.'

'I . . .' What the hell did it have to do with her? 'I'm her new assistant.'

'Ah, I see.' She folded her arms. 'She's a very private person, is Dorothy.'

Clearly not doing a good enough job of it.

'She is.'

I reminded myself that I shouldn't gossip, especially after this morning.

'I was just checking you weren't related to her,' the woman said, 'before I said anything too indiscreet.'

My ears tingled. Why were people doing this to me? I must've had *Tell me everything* written on my forehead.

'I've only been working there for a few days,' I said.

The woman stepped forward and rested her hand on my arm.

'You might not have heard what some people have been saying about her, then.' She glanced across the room at Gordon. 'Apparently they get up to all sorts at that house. I've heard she hosts parties where they contact the dead.'

I frowned.

'That's hardly *all sorts*, is it?'

She put her palm on her chest.

'Well, no, but it's very odd. And Dorothy herself is a bit of a recluse. I didn't know she lived in this town until last week. I thought she lived in London.' She leant even closer and took a sharp breath in. 'There are two types of people who live in this town: ones that have lived here most of their lives and the others who just pass through. Has she ever left the house while you've been there?'

What was she asking? If Dorothy Winters was a figment of my imagination?

'To be honest,' I said. 'I don't think she *has* left the house since I arrived, but I expect that's quite common with writers, isn't it?' I folded my arms and widened my eyes. 'But saying that, there *have* been some strange noises coming from the cellar.'

'Has there? Do you think it's haunted?'

'It's probably just a draught,' I said. 'Common with old houses.'

'I suppose.' She seemed a little disappointed. 'It's just that Gordon—'

'I wouldn't listen to him,' I said. 'He barely knows Dorothy.'

The woman's eyes travelled to Gordon and glazed over. She was obviously seeing something in him that evaded me.

'He's such a lovely man,' she said. 'He's so sincere, so reliable. We've become really good friends over the past couple of months. So helpful. He showed me how to set up my blog.'

'That's very nice of him,' I said, but the woman caught my tone.

'Well, I'll leave you to your browsing,' she said. 'Can't stand around chatting. I'm doing a new blog post. Do have a look. It's called *Gillian's Not-So-Secret Diary*. I try out different activities each month and write about them, obviously. I have over a hundred subscribers, you know. Anyway, it was nice to meet you, Rachel.'

She wiggled her fingers in a wave again and went back to the computer.

I watched as she put on her glasses and leant forward to look at her screen. Every so often she glanced at Gordon. He must have told Gillian my name. Could no one keep a secret in this town? Obviously not Gillian, given her blog title.

It was possibly the worst place I could have picked to be invisible.

Chapter 16

'Do you think we should invite my mother for Christmas?' said Andrew, placing his book on his lap. 'It's her first one alone since my dad died.'

Why wasn't Andrew psychic? If he were, he'd have known not to ask Kathryn absurd questions like that.

Three months married and it wasn't how she thought it would be. She'd had too much time to think at the retreat, imagined a life so different. She thought Andrew would get back to his banking job, work long hours so they wouldn't have to spend too much time together and when they did, she'd watch him cook while sipping cold white wine.

But marriage was so terribly dull, especially with his constant musings. *What shall we have for lunch today?* Even when they'd just finished breakfast, and even when lunch was always tinned soup or ravioli on toast. It was as though he'd run out of interesting things to say because most of the time they were in each other's company. Sharing a bed meant she barely slept with his snoring and shifting about all night. And it wasn't as though Andrew was all that bad, really. She knew there were worst men out there.

'I'm not sure,' said Kathryn, staring into the three bars of the electric fire. Only one was glowing red. 'It's our first Christmas as a married couple. I hadn't imagined sharing it with anyone else. Can't your sister have her? She has children – I'm sure they'd love to see dear old granny at Christmas.'

'You know they call her Nan,' said Andrew, 'and she's not exactly a dear old granny, is she? She's only fifty-seven.'

'I forget these things, what with my mother and father never being around.'

Kathryn got up from the chair and walked towards the back window of their first-floor flat. Jesus, it was so depressing around here. All they could afford to rent was a one-bedroomed flat that had been converted from a semi-detached house with views of a garden they couldn't use. An older man lived below them, and he'd let the back get into a right state. What a waste. Kathryn could've been sitting out there, enjoying the sunshine with a nice glass of wine.

The doctors were right when they said she shouldn't make drastic life decisions so soon. What kept her going was the money in her Post Office account – the one Andrew didn't know about. She had saved three hundred and twenty-five pounds so far. It would only get her a week or two at a bed and breakfast. She'd have to make sure a job was already lined up, but she hadn't even been looking. She had sales experience, but that was taking a step back. Plus, she wasn't sure if she wanted to leave yet; she changed her mind daily.

She took out the black-and-white photograph from her dress pocket. It was a little battered after she'd kept it in her purse for years. She should have found a frame for it, really, but Andrew would've asked too many questions.

She'd often thought of putting a letter with the gifts she sent. But she couldn't find the right words. *Love, your mummy*, was all she'd written. There was never an acknowledgement in return, but she was never going to stop sending them. She was a mother. She would make sure she was never forgotten.

She stroked the face in the picture. Just like her as a baby. Beautiful curly hair and chubby little legs sticking out from the christening gown that Kathryn had bought second-hand from an advert in a newsagent's window. She hadn't asked why they were selling it – people were terrible about droning on and on about themselves.

'What's that you're looking at?'

She'd almost forgotten Andrew was in the same room.

'Oh, it's just an old photograph,' she said, walking back to her chair.

He leant forward and took it out of her hands.

'Is it you?'

Now could've been the time to tell him more – describe how they took her child from her. She couldn't remember the details, but when had that stopped her? Her version of the truth was surely true somewhere, wasn't it?

'No,' she said, instead. She couldn't be bothered

111

making up something elaborate. She wasn't in the mood. 'It's my sister.'

'Oh.'

He tilted his head to the side and wrinkled his nose for a moment.

Indeed, why would she be carrying a photo of her sister when they weren't at all close? They could've been close, but Chrissy was too headstrong. A little sister shouldn't be headstrong and disrespectful.

'She's very cute,' he said.

'I ...'

Kathryn couldn't finish the sentence.

'It must've been hard looking after her when you were so young,' he said. 'To think your parents swanned off to the pub every night and left you to it.'

'It wasn't as bad as that,' she said.

'But you said your sister complained constantly about being hungry, then moaned about the meals you made her for tea. You made sure she was washed, and her uniform was clean for school. And you couldn't wash as often as you wanted to ... because your dad complained about the cost of heating the immersion and he rationed the fifty-pence pieces for the meter.'

'I don't want to talk about it.'

'I can't believe your parents came back drunk nearly every night. And that you had to get into your sister's bed to comfort her when you heard them shouting downstairs.'

'Oh,' said Kathryn. 'Did I say that?'

'Wasn't it true?'

'I wouldn't have made it up. I forgot you were in the same group session as I was. I'm surprised I was so ... *open.*'

'It was only one session, Kathryn, but it was talking treatment – we were meant to be honest. Otherwise, what was the point?'

'We were there for different reasons,' said Kathryn. 'I had nowhere else to go.'

'Technically,' he said, staring at the photo in her hands without actually looking at it, 'we were all there because we were sectioned. If you're saying you tried to get in because you were homeless, then ...'

'I didn't mean it like that.' Kathryn stood and went to the window again. 'I thought we said we weren't going to talk about being in there any more.'

Andrew put his head in his hands.

'There's not a lot we *do* talk about these days.' He got up from the chair and walked the few feet towards the kitchen area. He opened the fridge and fetched out a green wine bottle. 'Now it's past six, I thought we could open this.' It was the sparkling perry that had been in the fridge since they won it at a tombola in the community centre down the road. 'It's nearly a year since we met,' he said, trying to find two matching glasses from the cupboard. 'Hasn't it flown?'

Kathryn walked towards him. He looked at her with such trusting eyes – thinking he knew everything about her. He was so open with her, but there was so much she hadn't told him.

113

Andrew handed her a glass; the sickly sweet drink hissed inside.

'To us,' she said, clinking his glass.

She should've said, *You shouldn't be drinking that, Andrew*.

Instead, she took a sip and pursed her lips so she wouldn't spit it back out. It tasted like cider and she had awful memories of cider – even just the smell of it. Being sick in the park after drinking in the afternoons. But cider had been cheap; it still was.

'We should take a holiday,' he said, reaching over to touch her arm. 'We didn't have a honeymoon.'

'With what money?' she said. She placed the glass on the counter between them. 'Sorry, I didn't mean to snap. This is harder than I thought.'

He put his glass on the counter next to hers.

'By *this* do you mean us?' he said.

'No, no. I mean having no money. Being cooped up in this place all the time.'

'We could move,' he said. 'I can get bar work anywhere.'

She sighed loudly.

'Do you think that's enough? To work behind a bar for the rest of your life?'

'I thought that's what you wanted. You said you hated being alone during the day. I thought I was doing it for you.'

She looked out of the window, just as the man from next door flung a bulging carrier bag of rubbish into his silver dustbin.

'And I appreciate it, Andrew,' she said. 'Really I do. But I think things are going to have to change.'

Chapter 17

I waited until ten in the morning to check my phone. Three text messages: Jenny, Phil and Gemma each wishing me a happy birthday. No one here knew because I'd put a different date on my CV.

My phone beeped before I could reply. Another message from Gemma.

And sending hugs for tomorrow. Try to keep busy.

It was my wedding anniversary tomorrow. I was glad I wasn't among people who, however well meaning, would be constantly reminding me. It felt wrong to remember happy days when it ended so badly.

The night before the wedding, on my birthday, Gemma had organised a girls' night in the flat we used to share. I was glad to be able to finally relax, knowing that Jenny was looking after any last-minute arrangements – collecting the flowers, decorating the hall. She loved doing those things, and I was often in the way when she wanted me to leave her to it.

It turned out the girls' night was just Gemma and me. She had run me a bath and said to take as long as I liked, but after fifteen minutes I kept hearing the floorboards creak outside the bathroom.

'I can hear you, Gem,' I shouted, peeling off one of the chilled cucumbers she'd placed over my eyes.

'Sorry, sorry,' she said, centimetres from the door. 'Relax, relax.'

'I can't with you hovering outside, can I?' I laughed. 'Shall I get out now?'

'Only if you really want to,' she said, which meant yes. 'I've got the next bit of your surprise ready. I can't wait for you to see it.'

'Obviously,' I said, getting out of the bath and patting myself dry.

I put on the pink velour tracksuit she'd hung on the back of the door for me. I opened the door to find her wearing the same outfit, grinning. She handed me a pink cocktail with a cherry on a stick, took me by the hand and led me the short distance to the living room.

She'd covered the small coffee table in the middle of the room with a gold-coloured tablecloth and laid out a bottle of champagne in an ice bucket, along with a selection of my favourite snacks.

Gemma sat cross-legged on one side and patted the table.

'Sit, sit,' she said, her face beaming.

My eyes filled with tears.

'Oh God. You hate it, don't you?' she said. 'Everyone

117

said you didn't mean it when you said you didn't want a big party.'

I sat on the floor opposite her. 'I'm crying because I'm happy, Gem. This is perfect. I wouldn't want to spend tonight any other way.'

Gemma frowned. 'Not even with Aidan Turner?'

I looked around the room. 'Have you tied him up somewhere? Hidden him behind the curtains?'

'He was otherwise engaged tonight ... said he's thinking of you, though.'

I sipped my pink cocktail as Gemma poured the whole lot into her mouth.

'God, that's too delicious,' she said and licked her lips. 'Triple sec, vodka and grenadine.'

'Shit, Gem,' I said. 'I can't be hungover on my wedding day.'

She picked at the foil around the top of the champagne bottle.

'It's not till three,' she said, resting the bottle on her legs and twisting the cork. 'You'll be fine.' It popped out and hit the wall, and she sucked the fizz that leaked from the top of the bottle. She filled two glasses. 'Are you nervous?'

'A little,' I said. 'You know how much I hate people looking at me – it's embarrassing.'

'But you'll look amazing,' she said. 'And I've another bottle of this in the fridge for us to drink while you're getting ready tomorrow.'

'I might trip up. I'll—'

'Stop!' She put a hand up. 'You won't trip up. Phil

will be there to steady you and Matt will make sure you don't fall at the altar. He'll probably be pissed, too. You know what that Richie's like.'

'So do you,' I said, raising my eyebrows up and down.

'Ha! Very funny. That was just a holiday fling, nothing like you and Matt.' She rested her elbow on the table and rested her chin on the heel of her hand. 'I can't believe that was nearly two years ago.'

'I know.'

'He's great for you, Bee,' she said. 'I know he'll look after you.' She held up a hand again. 'And before you say you don't need looking after – I know you don't. But sometimes it's nice.'

'I know.' I opened my mouth to speak. I knew I shouldn't say it. Everyone thought our relationship was perfect. 'He treats me *too* well, sometimes.'

'What do you mean?'

'It's like he's doing it ... things ... because he thinks he's supposed to, especially when other people are around.'

'You don't have to go through with tomorrow if you're having doubts.'

'I couldn't not go through with it. I wouldn't want to hurt anyone.'

'He loves you, Bee. Everyone can see that.'

'I know.' I stared at the champagne bubbles rising to the top of the glass. 'I've always wanted to be someone's favourite.'

She stood up, wobbling on her feet.

'Right! We are going to have fun because that's next on the list!' She switched on the stereo. 'I've made a playlist for tonight, starting with Steps.'

At a little over midnight, we lay side by side on her double bed, still dressed in our pink tracksuits.

'I'm so looking forward to tomorrow, Bee,' she said, staring at the ceiling. 'Do you think you'll start trying for kids straight away?'

'We've talked about this, Gem. I'm still not sure I want to get pregnant. There are enough children out there who need parents. And me and Matt need to be completely ready for responsibility like that.'

'I guess.' She rolled onto her side and I turned my head to face her. 'You know what you said before, about wanting to be someone's favourite?'

'Yeah.'

'You're already *my* favourite.'

I took hold of her hand.

'And you're mine,' I said. 'But don't tell Matt.'

She giggled. 'Deal.'

I wished I could press rewind and go back to that night with Gemma. Instead, I was on my own in a tiny office in a strange house. I could go out at lunchtime and buy myself a cream cake – maybe even a present, but I didn't have much cash left after spending a small fortune staying at the hotel.

I wouldn't think about it. It was just any other day. I was too old to get excited about birthdays anyway.

I scrolled down the pages of Dorothy's manuscript.

I didn't know how I felt about the main character,

Kathryn. She was unlike anyone I had met before, and not at all like the characters Dorothy had created in her other novels. I felt sympathy for her when she was dropped off and left by her own mother at the hospital. I'd never given birth but imagined it to be one of the most frightening and vulnerable of experiences. I understood too well what it felt like to be abandoned; there were so many variations of it. It left a mark and I've never felt good enough. Was that how Kathryn felt?

Dorothy hadn't mentioned in her manuscript where Kathryn's child was – was she ever going to? The character seemed to feel no emotion towards her, or anyone for that matter.

The postman whistled as he strode up the path. Before I had a chance to hide, he saw me sliding off my chair.

Oh, bloody hell. I hated answering the door. Matthew used to say that I'd stay indoors with the curtains shut all day if I could.

'Parcel for Ms Winters,' the postman said when I opened the door.

I reached out a hand.

'New here, then?' he said.

'Yeah.'

There was no need for us to chat – it was a simple exchange. Why did people want to talk to other people so much? And about such boring, mundane things.

'I bet you haven't heard the history about this house, then, have you?'

'No.'

I went to close the door.

'Hang on.' He reached into his pocket and took out a handheld machine. 'I need a signature.' He didn't seem to be in a rush to hand it over. He prodded it with a stylus gripped in his fat fingers. 'They say it's haunted, this place.'

'Who says that?' I said.

He glanced up, his eyebrows raised. 'I get about a bit, you know.' He smirked and I wanted to swipe the machine out of his hands. 'Apparently there was a body buried at the bottom of the garden. And the spirit never left. Some have even seen his face in the window up there.' He stood back and pointed his plastic pointy stick to the third floor.

'I don't believe in ghosts,' I said.

I reached out a hand to sign the device.

He shrugged and passed it over and without thinking, I scribbled the wrong initials. My old initials.

He barely glanced at it, but the parcel wasn't for me anyway.

'Have you read any of her books?' he said. 'I've read three of them, but that was years ago.'

'I've read a few.'

'So? What did you think of them?'

'I liked them,' I said. 'Although you couldn't get away with a group of strangers locked in a house with no way of contacting the outside world. Not these days.'

Why had I blurted that out? It was bordering on a proper conversation, now.

'You're talking about *Made of Broken Things*, aren't

you?' he said, folding his arms. 'I love the idea of being secluded somewhere with a murderer in the house.'

'As long as you're the murderer, you'd be fine.'

His eyes widened.

'I'd not thought of it like that. I'd assumed I'd play the role of the detective.'

'But if there was a murderer in the house then you'd be a potential victim, don't you think? There's nothing fun about that. And what was to stop the criminal leaving the house, just because some weird old man told them they couldn't leave? Totally unbelievable.'

He frowned. 'Sometimes you just have to not think about things like that. Suspend your disbelief.' He leant forward. 'Did you hear about what happened between her and—?'

'No. I haven't heard anything about her. There's nothing much online – not recently, anyway. Should you be gossiping about your customers?'

His mouth dropped open and he took a step back.

'It's not gossip! I'm just making conversation.'

The church bells began to ring. Slowly, he turned to face the cemetery.

'It always seems cloudy over that church, doesn't it?' he said. 'You shouldn't go alone into those grounds, you know. There have been a few people gone missing from there.'

'I doubt that's true,' I said.

Why did people always make connections where there were none? Something that made their boring lives more interesting.

123

'Are you sure about that?'

He glanced up again at the top window before walking back down the path.

I leant on the front door after closing it.

God. I understood people liked to talk about fellow residents, but this was three times in just two days. The postman, Gordon, Gillian.

It was just like it was at home. I couldn't go anywhere for months without having the feeling people were talking about me. Once, I walked into the local shop and caught the tail end of, '... and he was such a lovely man ... someone should've seen it coming—'

They stopped when they saw me. Gemma had grabbed me by the elbow because I couldn't move, frozen to the spot.

She walked me out of the shop before shouting loudly, 'They don't know what they're talking about.'

The landline in the office rang, bringing me out of the daydream.

'Hello?' The sound of traffic sounded down the line. 'You'll have to speak up – I can't hear you.'

There were no breathing sounds or the movement of strides, which sometimes happened when someone's phone called from a pocket.

Abruptly, the sound of traffic stopped. Silence before a deep intake of breath.

'*I know who you really are.*'

I dropped the handset onto the desk and quickly replaced it on the cradle. Could I have imagined the words – my mind trying to make sense of jumbled noise?

No one from before knew where I lived now; well, except for Jenny. She wouldn't have told anyone else, would she? Gemma could be very persuasive. Her heart was in the right place, but she didn't half love a gossip.

I reached for the telephone again, but before I had the chance to pick up the handset and dial 1471, it rang again.

'Rachel.' It was Dorothy. 'The postman knocked on the door nearly half an hour ago – were you planning on bringing me my parcel?'

'Yes, of course.'

I picked up the package from the desk and my hands were still shaking when I reached Dorothy's study. I knocked on the door.

'Come in!'

Her voice was sharp. I hesitated. I'd not seen her in a bad mood yet. Perhaps I'd soon find out why all her other assistants had left.

Well, I was a big girl now. What could she do – tell me off for chatting with the postman?

I pushed the door open with more force than was necessary.

It was the first time Dorothy had allowed me into her study. It was lighter and warmer than mine, but it was her house, and she should have the best office. The walls were cream, and a mirror hung above the log burner on the right. The fire crackled with two freshly placed logs. The flames curled from the outer edges, trying to meet in the middle.

'Do you see your demons in the flames?' said Dorothy.

I looked up quickly.

Dorothy held a fountain pen mid-air in her left hand. Round silver-rimmed glasses rested on the end of her nose.

'What?' I said.

'You were daydreaming for a good full minute.'

What had demons got to do with anything? I stepped towards her and held out the parcel.

Dorothy put her pen down and folded her arms on the desk.

'He doesn't half go on a bit,' she said. 'In future, just take the parcel and go. I don't pay you so you can stand nattering on the doorstep.'

She *was* telling me off for chatting. She stood and took the parcel from my hand.

'And I bet he had a few words to say about me, didn't he?' She didn't wait for a reply. 'It's because I didn't sign a few books for his wife a couple of weeks ago. Why should I do that for her when she couldn't be bothered to come and see me herself?'

'Perhaps she was too afraid to bother you.' Shit. I hadn't meant to say that. 'I mean – she was probably a bit intimidated with you being such a famous author.'

I held my breath. Slowly, Dorothy smiled.

She stood and went to the window, placing both hands on her hips. There wasn't much of a view, but there were pots of purple heather and lavender and little glass lanterns that were draped along the white wall.

'I'm working on another story,' she said, still looking

out. 'In addition to the one you're typing for me. But I just wanted to get a feel for the idea – see if I like it before I show it to someone.'

'That sounds exciting.'

Maybe I should've knelt down and kissed the woman's feet, too.

'Hmm.' She turned round and swiped a packet of cigarettes from her desk. 'Do you think the dead stay dead?' She took one out and lit it.

'Yes,' I said. 'What else could there be? I don't believe in ghosts.'

'Quite a few people do, you know.'

She flung the packet and lighter back onto the desk.

'Do you?' I asked.

Dorothy sat in her chair, leant back, and crossed her legs. Her feet were bare, and her toenails were painted shocking pink.

'I believe the dead follow the living, but not in the way you think ... not like unearthly spirits. They're inside us.'

Her eyes twinkled; I couldn't tell if she was winding me up.

'Like parasites?' I said.

Dorothy swatted the smoke away from her face and pounded the almost-whole cigarette into the ashtray.

'No, no. You're thinking too literally.' She sighed. 'Oh, I don't know. At the interview, I thought you'd be someone I could bounce ideas off.'

I hesitated for a moment.

'If you're writing about a character who senses a

127

dead person – perhaps you could create a point of view from that dead person?'

She pursed her lips and furrowed her brow.

Had I sparked an idea? Was I handing her the key to a masterpiece?

'Yes, I suppose I could,' she said, picking up a pencil and tapping each end on the desk. 'Although that would be stretching the realms of probability.'

I tried not to let the flash of disappointment reach my face.

'I'd better get back to the typing,' I said.

I walked out of the door and went to pull it shut.

'One more thing,' said Dorothy. 'I'd appreciate it if you didn't gossip about me.'

Back at my desk, I selected Gemma's number on my mobile. The call before still bothered me. *I know who you really are.* Chances are it was a wrong number, especially after that man telephoned yesterday asking for a stranger.

Gemma answered after two rings.

'Hey, Gem,' I said. 'It's me.'

'Bloody hell, Bee,' she said. 'I thought you were dead or worse. Why haven't you answered my texts?'

'What's worse than being dead?'

'A lot of things,' she said. 'But I'm not going to reel them off to cheer you up.'

I smiled. Gemma was always inappropriate in a way that bordered on offensive.

'People are asking where you are,' she continued. 'What should I tell them?'

'Tell who?' I said. 'It's not as though I went out much before I left. I pretty much hid away at Jenny and Phil's.'

'Whoever sent you those letters knew you'd be there, though,' she said. 'You should've gone to the police about it instead of going into hiding.'

'It might have made things worse if I reported it. Especially after the—'

'—dead bird on the doorstep.' Gemma exhaled down the line. 'You know, it was probably killed by a cat.'

'But after those letters, Gem,' I said. 'Whoever it was, wished me dead – threatened to make my life a living hell. And then the silent phone calls ... the unwanted take-aways. I couldn't risk staying there in case it escalated.'

'I miss you, Bee,' she said.

I could tell she was crying because her words trembled to match her bottom lip.

'I know,' I said. 'I miss you too. When I'm settled and I'm sure that no one has followed me here, we can meet up.'

'You don't think someone will follow you, do you? I thought what they did was meant to make you leave town. They got what they wanted.'

'I don't know.' I picked up a pen and began to dig lines into a notepad. 'I had a phone call about half an hour ago. Someone – I think it was a man – whispered down the line. *I know who you really are.*' I hissed the last words.

129

There was a few seconds' silence.

'Shit,' she said. 'That's really creepy.'

I paused. 'It sounded like Matthew.'

'Oh, Bee. It can't have been Matthew.'

'I know.'

'Try to do something nice for yourself today, won't you?'

'No. I'm just going to forget about it.'

'OK.' She sniffed. 'God, Bee. Won't you come home? You'd be much safer around family.'

'I'm not so sure about that,' I said. 'Anyway. I'd better go. I'm not paid to chat, apparently.'

'You've got a job? But—'

'I'll ring you soon, Gem. Love you.'

I waited until she said it back before ending the call.

I ached for home, to be sitting with her and chatting about everything and nothing; watching *The Notebook* and crying before the sad parts because we'd watched it so many times.

A piece of paper slid under my office door.

Oh God. Had Dorothy heard me talking to Gemma? I hadn't spoken loudly, but I knew from the way she talked about the assistant before me that she didn't like people talking incessantly. I'd have to rein it in and act professional. I had nowhere else to go and my money had almost run out.

I picked up the note from the floor and opened it.

I'm sorry for snapping earlier. Please join me and
Louise for a late lunch/early dinner in the garden. I
feel like finishing early today.
  3 p.m. prompt.
  D

My shoulders relaxed. She mustn't have heard me.

I looked out of the window to see the sun escaping from the clouds. Lunch outside would be perfect. It was as though she knew it was my birthday.

Chapter 18

At three o'clock on the dot I stepped outside. I've always loved finishing work early when it was unexpected. A rectangular wooden table had been placed on the small patio and was laid with white plates and glasses that sparkled in the winter sunshine. At either end were thick white candles inside large glass domes.

Dorothy was at the head of the table, smoking a cigarette and reading the newspaper. I was glad I hadn't changed as Dorothy was wearing jeans and a polo neck jumper and had sunglasses on the top of her head. She was sitting cross-legged; her painted toes peeked out from under both legs. She couldn't possibly have been comfortable like that (unless she practised yoga on the quiet). Jenny always used to complain about her knees, but it seemed Dorothy didn't have the same problem. Maybe the volume of alcohol numbed the pain.

'Hello there,' she said, tossing the newspaper onto the grass. 'What a lovely afternoon it's turned into.'

'Yes,' I said. 'Though I hope the wasps keep away.'

Dorothy barked a laugh.

'I think we'll be all right at this time of year.' She patted the seat next to her. 'Though I'm always surprised by those little bastards.'

Louise stepped out of the back door carrying a large jug of water, ice and lemon slices, and placed it on the table.

'Don't worry,' she said, winking at me. 'I'll just be a sec with the wine.'

'I haven't drunk wine in the afternoon for years,' I said.

'One of life's decadent pleasures,' said Dorothy. 'Though sometimes daytime drinking can have me asleep by 7 p.m.'

I seriously doubted that.

'And it's pink fizz today,' she continued. 'I think the day calls for it, don't you?'

'Are you celebrating something?'

'Just the sunshine.' She pulled the sunglasses over her eyes and put her face up to meet the sun's gentle rays. 'And I finished another chapter today. I'll leave it on your desk later when I've tweaked it a bit. How are you finding it so far?'

'I'm really enjoying it,' I said. 'Does it take you long to write each chapter?'

'Oh, you know. How long's a piece of string?'

'Right.'

I was glad Louise arrived back with the wine. She poured it into three glasses.

'Thank you, darling,' said Dorothy, picking up her glass with delicate fingers. 'Cheers, ladies.'

We took tiny sips, as one must do after raising one's glass.

'Right,' said Louise, getting up again. 'You two relax while I prepare the last bits of lunch.'

She said it so nicely, too. If it were me, I'd have probably stomped off and clattered a few dishes about in the kitchen.

'What would I do without Louise?' said Dorothy.

She leant back in her chair surveying her beautiful house.

'I don't know,' I said. *Maybe get up off your arse and do something yourself?*

I shouldn't have been thinking like that, should I? It wasn't as though Louise was kept here against her will. Even if I had money, I don't think I'd ever employ staff unless I was physically incapable. Which was why I'd never become rich in the first place.

Louise brought out a large oval platter and put it in the middle of the table. Mini scotch eggs, samosas, tiny quiches, and slices of mozzarella and tomato.

'Wow,' I said. 'This looks amazing.'

She brought out a basket of different breads and a plate of tiny crustless sandwiches. I wanted to eat all of it, but I knew I'd eat too little out of politeness and be starving two hours later.

'Do tuck in, ladies,' said Dorothy, refilling her own glass.

I took a scotch egg and a cucumber sandwich and placed it on my little side plate.

'Drink, drink,' said Dorothy, leaning over with the bottle.

I downed what remained in my glass, trying not to retch after the bubbles caught the back of my throat.

After refilling my glass, she lit a cigarette, taking drags between tiny bites of food.

They talked about the previous evening and I didn't have any words to offer so I made the most of the opportunity to eat and daydream. Wine always went quickly to my head in the afternoons. I felt a warm fuzzy blanket around me already. Actually, it was starting to get a bit cold. I rubbed my arms.

'Here you go, love,' said Louise, handing me a beautiful chunky-knit blanket.

'Where did that come from?' I said, wide-eyed as though she'd magicked it from her sleeve.

'The wicker basket under the table,' she said, pointing to it with her foot.

'Oh yeah.'

They must've though they had a right idiot here. I stuffed another mini scotch egg into my mouth to soak up some of the drink. It must've been the bubbles.

'And,' continued Louise, 'Sophia was all over Brett – and her boyfriend didn't bat an eyelid.'

'That's because he was busy making eyes at Brett as well,' said Dorothy through almost closed lips as though she was trying to be subtle.

The solar lanterns hanging along the wall began to glow, and the candles cast shadows on the table. It was nearly five o'clock already. A lovely breeze ran through my hair as I picked up my glass by its stem. This was what it was like to have no worries. To eat lunch, and drink outside in the winter sunshine wrapped in a blanket. I was borrowing this life for one delicious afternoon.

'How did you two meet?' I asked.

Dorothy glanced at Louise.

'We met a long time ago,' she said. 'Didn't we, Lou? Introduced by mutual friends.'

'That's right.'

'Where was that?'

'Liverpool,' said Dorothy. 'We both left the area around the same time.'

'Oh right,' I said. I was sure she had mentioned living down south. 'That's a coincidence.'

'Not really,' said Dorothy, lighting another cigarette mid-meal. She placed it in the ashtray and grabbed the second bottle from the cooler, tipping what little was left into her glass. 'So, what are your plans for the rest of the evening? Have you met anyone outside the house yet?'

'Gordon, the man from next door,' I said. 'And Adam, who works at the library.'

'I wish I made friends so easily.'

Dorothy hadn't put as much make-up on as the other night and the redness effect of alcohol was crawling from her neck to her cheeks.

'I wouldn't call them friends,' I said. 'We only chatted for a few minutes.'

'I know what you mean,' she said pointedly, looking

136

over to the house next door. She leant forward and raised her chin. 'I'm surprised he's not crouching behind that wall, listening to everything we're saying.'

'Dorothy!' said Louise, but I knew she was trying not to laugh.

'Is he that bad?'

'He's probably harmless enough,' said Louise.

Dorothy cackled. 'Yeah, but someone probably said that about Ted Bundy once.'

My eyes widened and the breeze caught them, making them water.

'Don't worry,' she said. 'We'll protect you from the bad man.'

The telephone in the hall sounded through an open window. I half expected Dorothy to instruct me to answer it, but slowly she got up. She walked back into the house still laughing and muttering, 'He's a very, very naughty boy.'

Louise smiled as she rested her chin on her hand, obviously not used to so much alcohol.

'So, you grew up in Bolton,' she said. 'What are your parents like?'

'They're lovely,' I said. 'I wish I'd gone to live with them sooner. I was eight when they adopted me.'

'I'm glad you found them. Dorothy told me. I hope you don't mind. It must've been hard being in foster care.'

'It was all I'd known. I was only about six when I realised not everyone moved around all the time.'

'Well, well, well,' said Dorothy, almost tripping over

137

the threshold and back into the garden. 'That was an interesting phone conversation.' Her lips were pursed, and her eyebrows raised as she sat sideways on the chair and crossed her legs. She flung a blanket around her shoulders and reached, again, for her cigarettes. 'That was my dear friend Brett,' she said. 'He was round here the other night. It seems he saw you looking at him from the window, Rachel.'

Oh God. I should've realised he'd tell Dorothy.

'I thought I heard something in the back garden,' I said. 'I wanted to check no one was breaking in.'

Dorothy wafted a hand in response, causing smoke to float across the table.

'Well, whatever,' she said. 'He said that he'd love to meet you ... said you looked far more interesting than any of my other assistants.'

'Really?' I said. 'I'm hardly remarkable.'

'Now, don't fish for compliments, darling, it doesn't suit you.' She leant backwards. 'I suggested tomorrow night, Lou, as we've nothing planned. Would that be OK? Just a few nibbles, nothing too heavy. Eating's cheating, after all.'

'Of course.'

Louise collected the dishes and Dorothy let her. She must be used to people working around her.

I stood, picking up my plate and followed Louise into the kitchen.

'Now you're both making me feel bad,' said Dorothy. She got up, walked towards the house, and leant against the back door. 'Though not so bad that I'm actually going to join in.' She stood aside as we brought in the remaining dishes. 'I think we should dress up tomorrow night, don't you, Rachel?'

Louise placed leftovers into Tupperware containers.

'I don't have anything dressy to wear,' I said. 'I could go into town tomorrow and buy—'

'No, no,' said Dorothy, stepping inside and closing the door. 'I've got plenty of things that would fit you. I'll dig something out tomorrow.' She walked towards me. 'How exciting.' She downed the rest of her drink. 'And now, I must rest for a while.' She placed the glass on the side, not far from the open half-empty dish-washer. 'See you later, all.'

I watched as she walked away.

'I suppose I'll get used to her,' I said, before I had a chance to think. I turned round quickly. 'Sorry. I was thinking out loud. I didn't mean to sound ...'

'Don't worry about it,' said Louise. 'There are plenty who've said worse. And to her face.'

'Was she like this when she was younger?'

'Like what?'

Louise folded her arms.

'So confident ... so unusual.'

'For as long as I've known her, at least. She's had some very tough times, though. From what I've heard.' She folded the tea towel and hung it on the oven handle. 'But we shouldn't talk about that.' She flicked the kettle on. 'I know it's only early, but would you like me to do you a hot water bottle?'

'Really?'

She laughed.

'Yes, of course.' She got one out from one of the bottom cupboards.

'I haven't had one of those since I was a child. Jenny would do them for us. I used to love the smell of hot rubber. I used to cuddle it when my feet got too hot.'

I was more than a little bit pissed.

The kettle clicked and Louise poured boiling water into the hot water bottle and screwed on the lid. She passed it me and I pressed it against my chest, relishing the way the material softened with the heat.

'Now you get yourself off to bed,' she said. 'I'll lock up and I'll see you tomorrow.'

I went towards the door before Louise stopped me. She handed me a Tupperware box of goodies.

'Take these up with you,' she said. 'You might get peckish later.'

I could've hugged her.

'Thanks, Louise.'

I walked up the stairs.

It was the best day I'd had since I arrived.

And then I caught sight of the photograph on the wall again and a weight seemed to crush my chest. It was the picture of the little boy sitting on a wall. It reminded me of Matthew in the photos his mum showed me. It was another reminder that I shouldn't be laughing and drinking fizzy pink wine in the garden.

I sat on my bed and placed the plastic box of food on the bedside cabinet.

This small single room made everything more apparent. Our house had been lovely, filled with things we'd bought together. Before everything started to go wrong. After the wedding, nothing was ever the same again.

Chapter 19

Camera_1>bedroom>time_04:22

She sits up in bed and opens the quilt.

She swings her legs to the floor and walks to the door.

Camera_3>livingroom>time_04:24

She walks to the bookcase and takes out every book on the shelf.

She flicks through each one before replacing them.

Camera_3>livingroom>time_04:35

She leaves the room.

Camera_1>bedroom>time_04:42

She enters the room and tiptoes to the bed.

She pulls the quilt over herself.

Chapter 20

Gordon poured Mother's leftover cream of tomato soup down the sink, rinsed the bowls and placed them on the drainer.

They'd been making a racket outside for nearly three hours now, and it was freezing. All that wine they were drinking must've made them oblivious to it. Dorothy often entertained outside. The other day they'd gone on till the early hours of the morning and after midnight he'd heard (only because he thought Poppy was trapped in the cupboard under the stairs) them playing with what sounded like a Ouija board, like a bunch of overgrown school children. So much squealing and shrieking and after another hour, crying.

He didn't tell his mother what they'd been up to because she was rather superstitious, and she'd only start worrying about wandering spirits. It wasn't that Gordon *didn't* believe in otherworldly things – he had an open mind until science could prove it one way or another – but why were they inviting bad luck into their lives?

Gordon grabbed the handle of the window over the

sink and pulled it shut. Their cackling began immediately, and he tried to push away the suspicion that they were laughing at him.

Mother appeared at the doorway.

'Were they annoying you, too?' he said.

She scrunched up her face. 'Was who annoying who?'

'Never mind.'

'I came in to see if you had any of those nice egg custard tarts left from yesterday.'

Gordon folded his arms. 'I don't know,' he said, knowing full well there were two left in the packet. 'It's *your* house, you should know where things are.' He grabbed the tea towel and picked up a bowl from the drainer. 'You didn't eat all your soup.' He buffed the bowl with a little too much force.

'I didn't eat all my soup?' she said. 'Who are you – my mother?'

She walked to the fridge, making a show of slowly reaching for the box of cakes.

Gordon sighed and glanced at the ceiling.

'I'm sorry, Mum,' he said, taking the box from her. He fetched out one of her favourite china plates from the cupboard. 'I was going to do a bit of tidying up in the garden this afternoon, but next door have been out there shrieking and laughing.'

'Why didn't you put your headphones on?' she said. 'I thought you had a new talking book on your mobile phone.'

He plated up the egg custard and put the box in the fridge.

144

'Does it annoy you that she's an authoress?' she said. 'I know you've always wanted to write a book. Perhaps you could go round and ask her for tips.'

Gordon walked to the living room with his mother following.

'Ask her for tips?' he said. 'I'd rather ...' He waited for her to sit before placing the plate on her lap. 'I'll leave you to enjoy your tart.'

'Any chance of a cake fork, Gordon?' she called after him. 'And maybe a nice cup of tea.'

It was far too late in the day for caffeine, but he shouted, 'Of course, Mother.'

He was essentially his mother's maid now. *What's for tea, Gordon? Can I have another biscuit, Gordon?* Life had gone full circle. She was getting her own back for all the times she was *chained to the kitchen*. He shouldn't begrudge her, really. This was *her* house and he lived here rent-free.

'I'm going upstairs now,' he said, putting her cup on the side table. 'Give me a shout if you need anything.'

She paused the programme.

'You're a good boy, Gordon,' she said. 'You know that, don't you?'

'Thanks, Mum.'

He left the living-room door ajar before walking up the first flight of stairs. It worried him when she said things like that – as though she had a premonition she was about to die and wanted to make sure he knew she loved him. That was how she'd always told him. *You're a good boy, Gordon.*

145

He couldn't imagine living in this big house alone.

He closed his study door and sat at his desk. He didn't know why he disliked Dorothy so much. Perhaps his mother was right, and it was jealousy, though it wasn't as though Dorothy Winters was relevant any more. He brought up the Goodreads website and tapped in Dorothy's name. There wasn't anything about her in the biography section, nor was there a photograph. She probably didn't have a publisher at the moment. Her most recent book was published in 2002: *The Dance of the Fireflies*, and its average review was 3.97 out of a possible five. Not bad. He had given it three stars, which he thought was fair, and his comprehensive review had received nine likes so far.

Winters was obviously influenced by her contemporaries, but The Dance of the Fireflies *lacked the pace of Lee Child and the flourish of Sarah Waters.*

He was particularly delighted with that line. It had taken him days to get it right.

He closed the page. He shouldn't be so scathing. It was probably quite difficult to write a book. It took him at least a week to compose and edit a blog post of five hundred words.

There was banging on the front door of Dorothy's again. Where did the woman find the energy to entertain so much? Gordon wouldn't be able to relax if he had to be listening out for people knocking on his door at all hours.

He couldn't hear who it was and forced himself to remain seated. He brought up his camera feed, but the night-vision wasn't working on one of them. Damn. He couldn't do anything about that now.

A back door slammed shut.

He went to the window. Dorothy and that slimeball Brett were standing in the middle of the garden. She must be pissed again. Their heads were close together before Dorothy tried to walk away. Brett caught her hand and yanked her back towards him. She pressed her hands on his chest and shoved him away. She was stronger than she looked.

As Dorothy walked back to the house, Brett stared after her. His eyes were dark, and his lips were parted. He looked as though he hated her, but it was hard to tell given the distance and the darkness.

Gordon sat down and drummed his fingers on the desk.

No, he shouldn't.

He should try to concentrate. Lord knows he had enough of his own work to do.

Perhaps he'd just check.

No, no. He mustn't.

He was already opening his study door; the television was blaring from downstairs. Mother had probably fallen asleep in front of it, so he went down from the second floor two stairs at a time towards the first room at the top of the stairs. It was Dad's music room. The piano used to stand against the back wall, but Gordon had moved it to another. Much better for the acoustics.

He pressed an ear to the cold wall.

Rachel was crying softly. Not noisily, in the way Dorothy did, but with gentle sniffs.

He wished he could whisper something to make her feel better – or tap Morse code onto the wall so she wouldn't feel so alone. As lonely as *he* felt.

Why was she so upset? Was she homesick or had Dorothy or Brett said something to upset her? Gordon would have to keep a closer eye on number sixty-three.

Something very odd was going on.

Chapter 21

I didn't feel too bad after yesterday's afternoon drinking, which wasn't surprising after almost twelve hours' sleep and a pint of water before bed. That didn't stop me feeling embarrassed when I recalled being pissed in front of my boss. Had I said something inappropriate – had I let slip something about Matthew? I wasn't sure. I couldn't picture myself saying the words. I hardly spoke at all.

I tried to concentrate on work, and it was almost two o'clock when Dorothy came into my office.

'Good morning, Rachel!' she said. She waved a leather-gloved hand. 'Afternoon, whatever ... I've got a meeting in town.' She was wearing a turquoise beret, big yellow hooped earrings, and a white woollen coat tied around the waist. 'Brett's due here at seven and I thought it would be fun if you could answer the door to him. You can finish early again today – when Louise arrives at four to prepare the food. I've left a dress on your bed – I hope it's OK. See you later!'

'Bye.'

It was apparent that my fear of saying too much last night was unfounded.

Three hours to get ready. I could shower, dress and put my make-up on five times over in that time and still have time to watch an episode of *Come Dine with Me*.

I waited until Dorothy had been gone thirty minutes before I left the office. Finally, I had the whole house to myself. It was unsettling living in a house I'd only seen some of. Apart from my room, the bathroom and the office, I'd been in the library, the dining room, Dorothy's study and the kitchen. There was one door downstairs left.

It was panelled to match the side of the mahogany staircase. I grabbed the small round handle, turned and it clicked open with a satisfying clunk. I pulled the white cord that dangled from the low ceiling, the bare bulb cast light down the narrow stone stairs. Either side, white paint peeled from damp, freezing cold bricks.

I dabbed the top step with my foot. I pictured myself toppling down them, cracking my head and collapsing in a bloody heap at the bottom, lying undiscovered for days.

But I went down anyway, gripping the cold metal rail with both hands.

When I reached the bottom, I flicked on the second light switch. A bare amber bulb hung from the centre of the low ceiling. The bottom of the bare brick wall was coated with patches of black mould. A window to the left at the front of the house was barred; leaves and debris were plastered to it from the outside. Chairs were

150

stacked to the right – dark mahogany with dirty pink satin seats. Against the back wall were two wooden cupboards as tall as me.

I opened one of the doors. There were stacks of papers, buff folders and opened envelopes held together with a rubber band. I couldn't resist the lure of someone else's correspondence and reached for the letters, peeling off the elastic. They were to a Mr Jack Lawrence, but the address was crossed out. *Return to sender* was scribbled across the top. The postmark was dated 24 January 2001. I took out the note.

Dear Jack,
I was so very sorry to hear about the death of your
wife, and in such a gruesome manner. It must have
been devastating to have to identify her when she was
barely recognisable to even you.
I sincerely hope they find her attacker.
If you ever need a loving ear to listen, I am here for
you.
As always, you are in my heart.
x

I slid the letter back into its envelope and took out the next one.

It was addressed to the same person, postmarked 13 April 2001, and written in the same handwriting. I opened the yellowing note, and the exact words were transcribed again.

Dear Jack, I am so very sorry to hear about ...

I laid the letters out on top of a blue plastic folder. Again, identical writing, and the same shape and colour of envelope. I picked another at random.

Dear Jack, I am so very sorry ...

This woman didn't give up. Assuming it *was* a woman.

I replaced the letter and picked up a blue envelope from underneath. The writing was in capital letters to a Ms Holden at an address in Tuebrook, Liverpool, and postmarked January 2002. The writing inside was bold and in a biro so heavily pressed it embossed the paper.

Dear Ms Holden,
If you continue sending these letters, I will have no
choice but to involve the police. They're causing great
upset to my wife (who you know is very much alive),
and to our children.
I deeply regret ever meeting you.
My wife knows everything. You cannot blackmail
me any more.
Sincerely,
Mr J Lawrence

Lawrence. Wasn't that Louise's surname? It was the oddest thing. Why did Dorothy have these? Was this the same Jack she had written about in her story; had she collected these letters for research? Phil used to collect old photographs. Most of them were from the last century – weddings, portraits. He said he hated that they were for sale and no one wanted them. Was this the case with these letters? Dorothy didn't strike me as the sentimental type, though Louise said she had had some difficult experiences. Had these toughened her up over time? Dorothy probably wasn't always the way she was now.

I bundled the letters back together, replaced the elastic band and closed the cupboard doors. It was intrusive of me to have read them. Nothing good ever came from snooping.

A large, gilded frame caught my eye from the back of one of the cupboards. I reached down the side and yanked the picture out. Unlike everything else down here, it wasn't covered in dust and dirt. It was a painting of a woman in a lemon yellow dress sitting on a chair. She held a book on her lap and gazed to her left. Her blonde hair was set in large curls and swept to the side of her head.

She looked so much like Dorothy, with the blonde hair, red lipstick and slim figure, but her outfit looked as though it was from the last century. Unless it was created to look like that. If it *was* of Dorothy, why was it down here? I was surprised it wasn't centre stage in the dining room where everyone could admire it.

I turned the painting around. There was a message in the bottom-right corner.

To Estelle,
She reminded me so much of you, I had to buy her.
With all my love, Henry x

I froze when a sound came from the front of the house. Footsteps on the path, followed by a metallic bang. I held my breath. Dorothy hadn't been gone long; she couldn't have got back so quickly from town. Louise wasn't due to get here for at least another hour.

I laid the painting across the top of the cabinets.

Whistling came from outside.

At first, it sounded like wind blowing through the tiny cracks in the glass. I went to the window and stood on a pile of boxes, but they were damp and gave way slightly. Someone was standing on the front step above. I grabbed the bars on the window and tried to hoist myself up. Men's shoes: green and white Vans. The same ones Matthew wore.

Whoever it was, was only a few feet away. He loitered at the front door.

The box gave way from underneath.

'Shit!'

I covered my mouth, but the sound was already out there.

His hands wiped the cellar window. 'Is anyone there?' he said. 'Do you need help?'

I was shaking. Had someone from home found me?

The man stood up and posted something through the letterbox. I couldn't see who it was from behind as he walked away. He was wearing a navy blue jacket with the hood up and dark blue jeans. He was about six inches shorter than Matthew.

I ran back up the cellar stairs. That would teach me to go sneaking about.

But it didn't, of course. Once in the warmth and light of the downstairs hallway, I opened the door to the library. I had only been in Dorothy's study once. She needed privacy and quiet for her writing and I shouldn't have expected to be in the same office space. It wasn't like the film I'd seen where an assistant was hired by a once-famous-now-forgotten writer to be some sort of beloved muse.

The key was hidden in a little wooden box on one of the bookshelves. Dorothy probably thought I hadn't noticed her putting it in there the other day.

I unlocked the door and went inside. The room was the lightest in the house; the sun shone through the large window. Dorothy's notebook lay on the large leather-topped desk. The computer was switched on but when I touched the mouse, a prompt for a password appeared on the screen. I wasn't even going to try to guess it. Instead, I casually flicked through the pages of the notebook. There weren't any new chapters. She said yesterday that she'd finished a new one, but it wasn't in this book.

I straightened the notebook, lining it up the way I found it, and put the fountain pen back at the same angle.

The clock on the mantelpiece chimed three times. Dorothy had only been gone an hour.

The small metal filing cabinet stood next to the fire-place. It was a matt grey colour and rusty at the corners. I pulled at the handle of the top drawer and it opened smoothly.

All the tabs were labelled in handwritten script. There were only six or seven hanging in the large drawer. I picked out the one labelled 'personnel' and laid it on Dorothy's desk. I opened it, expecting to read about the previous assistants – to see what they'd put on their CVs to land this job. But inside was a cutting of the newspaper advertisement, my covering letter and CV, a photograph – of what appeared to be a screen-capture of me standing at Dorothy's front door on the day of my interview. Behind these papers was a photograph of a baby, lying in the carrycot of a pram. I turned it over; there was no description, but the year 1985 was scribbled in the bottom-right corner.

The year of my birth.

No, no. It couldn't have been me. It was just a co-incidence: one of Dorothy's research photographs that dropped into my file by mistake.

I closed the file and replaced it. I flicked my fingers through the other tabs, looking for a collection of photographs the picture might have escaped from. Utility bills, letters from solicitors and—

The door to the study opened. It was Louise.

'What are you doing?'

I slammed the filing cabinet shut.

'Dorothy asked me to do a bit of research,' I said quickly. 'I thought I might find it in here.'

Louise folded her arms. 'She wouldn't ask you to research something she had in her own cabinet, would she?'

I couldn't interpret her tone. She was either bemused or seething. She stood aside as I made my way towards the door. She grabbed me by the top of my arm.

'You shouldn't snoop, Rachel,' she whispered. 'She won't like it.'

'I won't come in here again.'

She let me go.

It was only when I sat back at my desk that I realised my heart was pounding. Adrenaline made my hands shake. Why was that photograph with my CV? I had no pictures of me as a baby; for all I know there were none. The earliest one I have is from Christmas 1990 when I was standing next to a man dressed as Father Christmas. I was always told that my biological mother was too young, that she couldn't cope. What if that had been a lie?

Chapter 22

They'd been in Liverpool for just over two months now and the novelty of living somewhere new had faded. They were renting a whole house now, but the backyard was tiny. A bright blue shed took up most of the outside space and the neighbourhood cats used the small square of gravel as a giant litter tray. Pretty much useless. Kathryn wished Andrew were more into DIY. Did he expect her to do *everything*?

He was asleep on the sofa again. Kathryn couldn't understand how he could sleep so early in the evening. All the signs were there that he was having a relapse of sorts. It didn't help that his working schedule was so sporadic. She wanted to shake him sometimes.

It didn't matter anyway because she was going out tonight. She'd told Andrew she was meeting a few of the girls from work in the pub in the next town. His apathy towards life had extended to her whereabouts.

She'd be bothered about that if she cared about him, but their arrangement suited her for now.

Her dress was laid out on the bed – the emerald green

one with the sequins around the hem. A little dressy for mid-week perhaps but it felt like a special occasion. The earrings Andrew bought her for their first wedding anniversary went perfectly.

She sprayed more Dolce & Gabbana *Red* behind her ears. Maybe it would trigger Jack's memory of when they were good together.

She smoothed down her dark hair – freshly cut into a sharp bob that rested on her shoulders – and put an extra coat of mascara on. Kathryn had sold eight of these at work today. She'd told the last woman – who appeared to be about ninety – that it made her eyes look magnificent when in fact it looked like she had spiders' legs for lashes. Still, Kathryn had the second-highest sales this season and she'd only been working at Lewis's department store for six weeks.

Jack always said he liked her eyes; he said they intrigued him.

She put on her heels, went downstairs and into the living room.

She stood over Andrew with her hands on her hips. He hadn't moved in the hour it took her to get ready, still with his hands behind his head, legs crossed at the ankles and a serene look on his face. He didn't have much to worry about, did he? He only worked three days – he didn't know what it was like working six days a week.

His eyes opened, as though he sensed her standing over him.

'What are we celebrating?' he said, stretching out

his long legs and arms. 'You look gorgeous.' He pushed himself up. 'I can be ready in ten.' He swung his legs to the floor.

'There's no good news,' said Kathryn flatly. 'What do you think could possibly be worth celebrating?'

His mouth opened and his eyes watered.

For God's sake. How would he have reacted had she told him what she really felt? *You're not who I thought you were; I thought you had ambition; I thought you'd help me get to where I want to be.* Sometimes she was tempted to let it all out, but she hadn't found anywhere else to live yet.

'Sorry, Drew,' she said quickly. It was the name she called him to make him think she loved him. She hated the nickname Andy – it reminded her of that ridiculous puppet that used to be on television. She bent down and kissed him on the forehead. 'It's Trisha's leaving do tonight. Thought I'd make an effort. I hardly ever go out.'

He rubbed the sleep from his eyes.

'You're out nearly every day.' He raised a palm. 'I know, I know. You're out because you're working.'

What went on in that head of his? She took a deep breath, and walked towards the kitchen, wobbling on the ridiculously high heels she wasn't used to yet.

She exhaled slowly, trying to expel the hot rage inside.

She took a four-pack of Carling from the fridge and put them on the coffee table.

'I got you these,' she said, planting a smile and

turning round. 'And I've left a tenner in the biscuit tin for you to get yourself a takeaway.'

He stood and walked towards her, slipping his arms around her waist.

She shook her shoulders and stepped aside, patting him gently on the arm before going to grab her winter coat from the tiny hallway.

'You don't have to wait up for me,' she said, popping her head around the door. 'Although the amount of sleep you've had this afternoon you probably won't be tired later.'

He flicked open a can.

'I doubt that.'

She rolled her eyes at the front door, stepped outside, and slammed it shut.

The walk to the pub should've only taken ten minutes but it took double the time in the stupid heels.

Jack was standing at the end of the bar when Kathryn walked in. He didn't look up from his mobile telephone. It was typical that he was the first person she knew to get one. Always wanting something others didn't have. She mounted the bar stool next to him as gracefully as she could. He downed his whiskey and placed it on the bar before turning and kissing her on the cheek.

'Kathryn,' he said.

She nodded in a greeting, trying to be cool, but when her eyes met his, she felt it again.

'So that's what you're calling yourself these days?'

He looked up to the barman and ordered her a gin and tonic. It wasn't her favourite drink any more.

'I've always been called Kathryn,' she said. 'But you chose to call me something else.'

Katie. She hated the name Katie. It was a completely different name to Kathryn.

'So, how's the girl?' he said, sliding the drink towards her.

Kathryn stared at her reflection in the mirror behind the bar.

'She's not a girl any more,' she said.

She turned to face him again, the eyes so familiar sometimes it was hard to look into them – the same eyes as their child.

'Bet it makes you feel old, doesn't it?' he said. 'I know I do.'

'You haven't seen her for decades, and even then, it was every few weeks, whenever you felt like it,' she said. 'So don't get all sentimental.'

He leant an elbow on the bar.

'Ouch.'

He wouldn't have accepted her spite with such grace if he knew Kathryn hadn't seen their daughter for years either.

His eyes glistened, but it wasn't out of sadness; it was mischief. He lit a cigarette.

'We have a lot to catch up on, Kathryn,' he said, exhaling.

She downed the drink in one.

*

She waited until he was five drinks in before she asked, and even then, he didn't appear drunk.

They'd found a table behind a pillar that shielded them from most of the pub.

'What did you really want to see me for, Kathryn?' he said. 'I've not heard from you in years.'

She knew she couldn't use the excuse that she wanted to see him about their child. The last time they saw each other, they'd rowed in the street. He'd called her a stalker for following him to York.

He was back in Bolton now, but she didn't tell him she knew. It was easier to keep track of him now he had a website for his business – she'd seen it when she used the computer in the city centre library. Kathryn wondered where Jack had told his wife he was tonight. Eight o'clock on a weeknight, an hour away from home. Perhaps she could convince him to book a hotel room, spend the night together reminiscing.

'I wondered if you could lend me some money,' she said. It had taken three double gins to garner the courage. 'It's Andrew. He barely lets me leave the house. He wants to know where I am all the time.' She reached across and put a hand over Jack's. 'I need to escape.'

He swiped his hand away and folded his arms.

'I was waiting for that,' he said. 'I'm surprised you endured my company so long before asking. It must be really hard for you this time.'

'We have history, Jack,' she said. 'We have a child together.'

'It's not as if you need money for the kid, is it?'

'Don't you care that I'm slowly losing my mind? Would you rather I was stuck, living with someone I don't love? It needn't be much, just a couple of hundred. Enough for a deposit on a new rental.'

He shook his head slowly. 'It's of your own making, Kathryn. Everything always is.' He grabbed his jacket from the back of the chair and stood. He bent down and kissed her cheek. 'Don't contact me again, Kathryn,' he said, before walking off.

Her eyes were fixed on him as he walked out the door. Not once did he look back. It was as though the whole pub had gone silent, but the people standing at the bar looked deep in conversation, throwing their heads back with laughter. Why couldn't she hear them?

Fucking bastard. How dare he humiliate her like that? Never before had she been left alone in a pub, let alone at a table by herself.

She got up, but the pattern on the carpet danced, like gymnasts swirling ribbons.

She felt tingling in her hands, on her forehead. She sat back down, lowered her hand into her hands and cried for the first time since she was a child.

Kathryn hesitated at their front door. She reached into her handbag and placed the wedding ring back on her finger. The television was blaring through the walls and was twice as loud when she got inside. If Andrew was sleeping on the sofa again, she could tiptoe past him and have the bed to herself for one glorious night.

But he was sitting in the armchair just a few feet from

the telly. He'd also moved the small occasional table and the wastepaper basket, so they were next to him.

'I thought the pub shut at eleven,' he said, not looking at her.

'It did,' she said. 'But they had a lock-in for Trish. It isn't that late, anyway. It's not even midnight. I left them all still drinking. I was worried about you.'

He turned in his chair to face her.

'Ha! As if,' he said. 'Who was out? Anyone special?'

She took off her shoes and the relief was delicious.

'No one special,' she said, taking off her coat and draping it on the sofa.

'Why aren't you looking at me?' he said.

She met his gaze. 'What? You expect me to stand here and stare at you?'

'I expect you to meet my eye when you're lying to me.'

'Why would I lie about a leaving do?'

She looked at the ink stain on the arm of the chair. She'd been attempting a crossword last night and had absentmindedly rested her pen.

Kathryn wished she could tell him who she'd met tonight. In some ways, Andrew was the closest she'd had to a best friend, the person she told most of her thoughts to. But not all of them.

'I'm going to bed,' she said. 'Night.'

He didn't reply. Instead, he turned the volume up on the TV – even louder than it had been.

She placed the eye mask over her face.

Why was she being so weak? It wasn't as though she

165

needed Andrew. She was the one bringing in the money. If he spoke to her like that again then she'd leave.

The bedroom door opened and the cheer of a football crowd on the television roared from downstairs.

She heard Andrew breathing and smelt the beer on his breath with ... what else was it ... whiskey? He must have used the money for more drink instead of food. He was so bloody ungrateful.

'What do you want, Andrew?' she said. 'It's obvious I'm trying to sleep.'

'I saw you with him, Kathryn.'

She felt his weight as he sat on the edge of the bed.

'You're imagining things,' she said. He didn't even know who Jack was. 'You're pissed. You should've got a takeaway instead of more booze.'

'I popped into the pub,' he said, 'so I could say good-bye to Trish, and I saw you sitting there with him. Your friends weren't even there.'

'That was my boss,' she said. 'You can't even remember that, can you? He stopped me for a chat before we headed somewhere else.'

'Was it really your boss?'

'Yes!' She was glad of the eye mask. She turned over to face the other wall. 'And Trish isn't *going* anywhere – she's only leaving Lewis's. You can talk to her next week when she comes round for tea. She'll tell you all about the leaving do.'

'She will?'

'Yes.'

Andrew would never remember this in the morning.

He never did when he drank whiskey. He rubbed her shoulder.

'Night, love,' he said. He lingered at the door. 'Sorry if I've been a bit of a dick tonight. I worry I'm going to lose you.'

'You won't lose me.'

'Promise?'

'Yes,' she said. 'I'm knackered. Bugger off.'

He laughed, probably thinking she was joking, and closed the door.

Images from the evening kept flashing through her mind.

Jack taking his hand away from hers. His amusement at being asked for money, knowing it was coming, waiting for it. She wanted to erase the whole thing. It was so embarrassing. She would never put herself in that situation again. Never. She would have to think of another way to escape this house and this marriage.

Jack would wish he'd never met her.

Chapter 23

'Dream a Little Dream of Me' was playing when I walked into the dining room. It was The Mamas and the Papas' version – the song Jenny and Phil chose for the first dance at their wedding.

I was nearly at the kitchen door and could see Louise taking a tray out of the oven, when I noticed Dorothy sitting on the window seat in the dining room. She was turned to the side, gazing out.

She swivelled to face me when the music ended.

'Put it on again for me, would you, Rachel?'

I lifted the lid of the record player and brought the stylus to the beginning, savouring the exquisite crackle of old vinyl.

Dorothy patted the seat.

'Come and sit next to me.'

I walked over and perched on the green velvet cushion. It felt odd sitting so close to her. She was still wearing the denim jumpsuit she had on earlier.

'Did I ever tell you about my first husband?' she said.

'I don't think so. Is this the man you had your children with?'

An inappropriate question, probably, but she didn't react.

'No,' she said. 'It was before all of that. I met him in York.'

'Like Kathryn in your story?'

She tilted her head to the side.

'Perhaps,' she said. 'Sometimes writers use places they've been to, but it was nothing like that.' She swung her legs to the floor and clasped her hands on her lap. She wrinkled her nose slightly. 'Poor Kathryn.'

The song had almost finished again.

'No,' she said. 'This was my soulmate. The love of my life.'

'Oh,' I said. 'What happened?'

She put a hand over her eyes and sniffed, but when she brought her hand down again there were no tears. 'He died, Rachel.' She stood, folded her arms around herself. Her brows furrowed, and she blinked quickly as though trying to stop herself from crying.

'That's awful, Dorothy.'

I got up and raised a hand close to her back. Was I meant to comfort her? It was like being in school when a teacher said something about her personal life.

She turned quickly to face me.

'It is, isn't it?' She walked over to the record player and switched it off. 'Anyway.' She wiped a finger under her eyes. 'You look amazing tonight, Rachel.' She beckoned me with her hand. 'Let's have a look at you.'

I shuffled towards her like a reluctant bridesmaid in the turquoise dress she'd left for me on my bed. It was sleeveless and beaded on the bodice; the skirt had a chiffon overlay that skimmed my knees.

Up close, I could see the broken capillaries on Dorothy's nose and cheeks that were usually masked by make-up.

'That dress looks great on you,' she said. 'Do a twirl for me.'

'What?'

'Oh, go on. Don't be a spoilsport.'

I turned around slowly.

Oh God. Was Dorothy planning to pimp me out to Brett? Was this what the *discretion essential* part of the job entailed?

The doorbell rang.

'Shit,' said Dorothy. 'It can't be that time already. Though I should've guessed from your impeccable timekeeping.' She walked quickly towards the dining-room door. 'Give me a second to sneak upstairs before answering it, won't you?'

'Of course.'

I counted to ten after hearing Dorothy start up the stairs.

The doorbell rang again, followed by three knocks.

My mouth felt dry, but, for once, there were no alcoholic drinks on the dining table for courage.

I felt my heart pounding across my chest as I approached the front door. This man thought I was spying on him the other night. I'd made a bad impression before I'd even met him (though that probably wasn't a bad thing if there was anything seedy on the agenda).

His silhouette was visible in the small window. He stood close to the door and must've seen me getting nearer because he stood back as my hand reached the handle.

'Face to face at last!' he said, lifting his arms slightly at the sides.

Brett looked younger than he had from a distance. He had an air about him as though he might have been a famous actor in the nineties but now treaded the boards in local theatre. His complexion was smooth and tanned and I wondered what foundation he used. I'd probably end up asking him later, given my big gob yesterday after too much fizzy wine. I cringed at the thought. There should be an app that stopped the mouth opening after five drinks.

'I'm Brett. I've been looking forward to this all day.' I stood aside as he stepped in. 'Though from your expression, I'm assuming that's not mutual.'

'I ... erm.'

'Just kidding,' he said. 'Everyone tends to scowl when I walk into a room.'

'I wasn't ... I mean I didn't—'

'Bloody hell, it's freezing out there,' he said. He rubbed his hands and took off his coat. 'Lou-Lou Lawrence not around to answer the door, then?' He hung his coat on the end of the banister, ignoring the three empty coat hooks on the wall. He stood staring at me and leant closer. 'Are you all right?' he said, frowning. 'Have I said something wrong already?'

I smiled, hoping it looked genuine.

'No,' I said. 'Not yet.'

'Don't worry. There's no need to look so petrified. I won't bite.' He linked his arm through mine, kicked the door shut, and escorted me down the hall. 'It's a lovely house, isn't it? I couldn't believe it when she first showed me around.'

'Have you known Dorothy long?' I said as we walked into the dining room.

'Feels like forever.'

He released my arm and walked straight to the drinks cabinet.

'Ah, I think I'll have a whiskey,' he said, pouring a large measure into a crystal tumbler. 'And whiskey is always the first of many bad decisions I make of an evening.' He took a sip of his drink. 'Now that's what I call a good one. I can't afford this one on my paltry royalties.'

'I thought it paid well, being an author.'

He pulled out a chair at the dining table.

'Only if you're lucky,' he said, sitting down. 'And if you write well.' He waved an arm in the air. 'Sit, sit. I'm sure Louise will be in soon if you're too polite to get yourself a drink.'

I sat in the chair opposite him.

'Don't you write well?'

He threw his head back and laughed.

'A lot of writers will tell you what they write is shit, but they don't believe it when they say it. They hope someone will interject and say, *No, you're wonderful, darling*.' He drank the rest of the whiskey and reached over for the rest of the bottle. 'And we all think we're undiscovered geniuses, though I suppose that's true no matter what you do. Perhaps most people think that, someday, someone will think we're special.'

'I don't.' I picked at the hem of the dress. 'I'd rather be invisible and just get on with things.'

He reached inside his jacket pocket for a packet of cigarettes. Another evening of spraying dry shampoo into my hair before bed. I thought people who thought themselves enlightened would care about their health, but apparently not. He tapped his cigarette on the table before lighting it. He inhaled, and slouched back on the chair, exhaling.

'Don't you think that's rather sad?' he said. There was a hint of Scottish in his accent that I'd only just noticed. 'I couldn't imagine wanting to be invisible. What did Oscar Wilde say?'

'Probably a lot of things—'

'*There is only one thing in the world worse than being talked about, and that is not being talked about.*'

He leant forwards and placed an elbow on the table, resting his chin in his hand. He tilted his head to the side, slightly wobbling (it probably wasn't his first whiskey of the night).

Was he expecting a round of applause for remembering a quote? People like this probably expected praise for sentences they hadn't put together themselves – that merely saying them at the right moment demonstrated the connections they made between life and art.

173

Educated rather too much and wanted to show it off. Or something like that. Maybe I should start writing myself. There was a book inside everyone, wasn't there?

'Are you working on anything at the moment?' I said.

He probably expected that question and I didn't know enough about him to ask anything else.

He flapped a hand.

'Just working on a character piece, which no one seems to want these days. It's all plot, plot, plot now.' He took a drag of his cigarette. 'And rightly so.' He still had smoke inside him when he said the words and he almost choked. He blew out what remained. 'Anyway, I'm awful when I talk about myself. More about you. What made you want to work for Dorothy?'

'The live-in position was ideal for me,' I said.

'How old are you?' He picked up the drink, tilting it mid-air, looking at the bottom of the glass. He held it higher and tipped the whiskey into his mouth. He fixed his gaze on me. 'Are you offended by that question, Rachel?'

I felt as though a camera had just zoomed in on me.

'Thirty-five,' I said. 'How old are you? Fifty-five, fifty-six?'

'Ouch!' he said, almost slamming the glass on the table. 'Actually, I'm fifty-two.'

'So why the *ouch*? I wasn't that far out.'

'Ah,' he said, smiling. The creases around his eyes deepened. 'She bites back.' He leant back in the chair; the cigarette poised near his face. 'I don't know. I've always been told I look younger than my age.' He got up and stood five inches from the mirror. He smoothed back his hair with the palm of his hand. 'It must be the new shade,' he said quietly. 'It drains all the colour from my face. Grey is ageing but it's better than this.' He shrugged and sat back down. 'So, you're not married?'

'What makes you ask that?'

He looked around the room in an exaggerated manner.

'Hello? You're living here – alone.' He pointed to my hand. 'And you're not wearing a ring.'

My left thumb automatically rubbed the back of my ring finger. There was still a slight smoothness at the bottom.

He got up again and replaced the whiskey bottle onto the drinks tray. He poured two gin and tonics, passed one to me, and stood in front of the record player.

I took three long gulps and winced slightly with the mostly-gin concoction I wasn't used to.

'Oh,' said Brett. 'She's been playing that bloody song again.'

He lifted the lid, set aside the stylus, and removed the record by its edge. He picked up the sleeve and delicately placed it inside. I'd half expected him to throw it across the room like a frisbee. He flipped through the line-up of vinyl before placing one on the turntable and sat back down at the table.

'Have *you* ever been married?' I asked.

The voice of a crackling Bob Dylan came through the speakers as Brett's eyes fixed on the hanging lights outside.

'Yes,' he said.

175

The only ring he wore was a gold signet on the little finger of his left hand.

'So, you—' I began.

'I'm so sorry I'm a bit late with the drinks.' Louise appeared at the door carrying a tray with three champagne flutes. 'I had to help Dorothy with something.'

'There must be a secret tunnel here,' said Brett. 'I didn't see you go through. Unless you scuttled past and we were too deep in conversation to notice.'

I felt my cheeks flush.

Louise offered the tray to me and my hands trembled slightly as I took one of the glasses.

She placed the tray on the table.

'I'll just help myself then, shall I?' Brett winked at me as he grabbed a glass. 'And when do we expect the lady of the house to grace us with her presence?'

'I'm so sorry,' Louise replied, but her eyes were on mine. 'Dorothy's had a wardrobe malfunction. She'll only be a few more minutes.'

Brett sniggered.

'Bloody hell. Who does she think she is? Britney Spears?'

Louise wrinkled her nose.

'She's invited you for dinner.' She rolled her eyes. 'You should show a little appreciation.'

'Oh, I should, should I?'

He downed the champagne in one and took the other glass from the tray.

Louise cleared her throat loudly and looked directly

at him. They held each other's gaze until Brett raised his glass.

'I am very sorry for my behaviour,' he said. 'And I apologise to you, dear Lou-Lou Lawrence. You are the most wonderful of housekeepers and I am a little bit pissed.'

'Right, well,' she said. 'I'll get a move on with the starters.' She turned and walked towards the kitchen. 'Otherwise everyone will be shitfaced in no time.'

I leant across the table.

'Did she just say shitfaced?'

Brett brushed flakes of ash from his sleeve.

'Probably,' he said. 'Don't let her fool you with this *Downton Abbey* act. Her previous job was in a pub.'

'There's nothing wrong with that,' I said, chancing a sip of champagne.

It was as acidic as I thought it would be. I wondered if there was any orange juice to improve the taste.

'I know there's nothing wrong with that,' he said, slurring slightly. 'But you'd think she'd come straight from Windsor Castle, the way she's acting.'

'Have you known her for the same amount of time you have Dorothy?'

He inhaled and exhaled slowly.

'Enough about me.' He took another cigarette from the packet. I wished for the confidence to open a window; I was suffocating in here. He patted his jacket pocket and fished out a Zippo lighter almost the size of his palm. 'Oh, I wondered where that was.' He flicked it open, lit the cigarette, and clanked it shut. 'So, what did you do before you came here?'

'Temping, mostly,' I said. 'I wanted to see different parts of England.'

He wrinkled his nose. 'And you ended up here?'

I shrugged. 'It's as good a place as any. And there are so many cities within driving distance.'

'Ah, so you drive.'

'No.'

The dining-room door slammed open.

'I'm so sorry I'm late.' Dorothy walked over to Brett. He kissed her twice on the cheek; she kissed the air. 'I hope you've managed to get better acquainted.'

She had taken only twenty minutes to get ready but looked as though she'd been up there for hours. Her make-up was plastered on, but the colours suited her. She wore a white silk jumpsuit with a wide gold belt. She flopped onto the chair next to Brett.

'God, I barely leave this house.' She leant to the side and rested her head on Brett's shoulder. 'One day, you're going have to rescue me from this torture.'

'Again, ma chérie?' he said, slightly stiffening.

Dorothy straightened when Louise came in to set the rattling plates on the table. On top of them were little pots with mashed potato. They smelt like mini fish pies.

'I'm absolutely starving,' said Brett, tucking the linen napkin into the collar of his shirt. 'I haven't eaten all day.'

'I can believe that,' said Dorothy. 'The booze has gone right to your head.'

'Unlike you, my darling,' he said, 'who has the constitution of a heavyweight boxer.'

'You've got your metaphors mixed, *darling*,' she said, glancing at the food on the table. 'I don't recall requesting a sit-down dinner.'

Dorothy took a fork to her mashed potato and lifted a minuscule amount to her mouth.

'So, Brett,' she said. 'What interesting things have you done today?'

He grabbed the hot ceramic pot, scraped whatever was left with a spoon and jammed it into his mouth. He ate it quickly and licked his lips.

'That was bloody lovely.'

He wiped his mouth with the napkin before letting it drop back onto his chest.

Dorothy's nostrils flared and her mouth dropped open.

'God, you're a pig.'

Brett rested his elbows on the table.

'Thanks, love,' he said. 'And to answer your question, I got up at noon, watched an episode of *Frasier* then had a bath. Best day I've had all week.'

'Good grief,' said Dorothy, spearing a piece of salmon. 'You should do something useful with your life.'

'You hardly lead by example, Dorothy.'

She took a small bite of the fish and placed her knife and fork together on her plate.

'I'll ignore that.'

I silently ate my starter while I listened to the pair of them. I tried to eat slowly so I didn't have to look at them properly when I finished, but it was so delicious I couldn't help but rush it.

I was glad when Louise came in to clear the dishes. She didn't react to Dorothy having barely touched hers.

I stared at my hands until Louise brought the main course in.

It was roast beef, accompanied by dauphinois potatoes, glazed carrots, and the tiniest Yorkshire pudding I'd ever seen. I could've cried it looked so beautiful. I was constantly hungry in this house.

'Thank you, Lou,' said Dorothy. 'Eat, Rachel, eat. Don't wait for me.'

I picked up my knife and fork. It was obvious these two thought *eating was cheating*. Louise had obviously gone rogue with her instruction of *just a few nibbles*.

Brett picked up his lighter and pointed it towards my plate.

'You're not going to eat that and ruin my cigarette, are you?'

'I . . .'

'Leave her alone, Brett,' said Dorothy. 'Let her eat in peace.'

'I was only messing,' he said. 'Hey, do you remember that time Victor Bartholomew slated you?'

For a moment, Dorothy stared at him with unblinking eyes.

'I don't know what you're talking about.'

'Oh, *I* remember it vividly,' he said. 'He said you copied his life in your last book – said that every detail he told you, you used, and that—'

180

'That's enough, Brett!' She stood and grabbed the whiskey from the drinks trolley. 'Remember whose house you're a guest in.'

She poured the liquid into a tumbler and downed it.

'Lighten up, Dorothy,' he said. 'After that critic tore it to shreds, didn't you say you'd never take yourself seriously again? What did he say ... "Winters was obviously influenced by her contemporaries"?'

Dorothy returned to her seat and placed the decanter in front of her. She took a cigarette out of the packet and reached behind her for a cigarette holder.

He raised his eyebrows as she lit it, a slight upturn to his lips.

She exhaled the smoke in a perfect O.

'It wasn't a critic,' she said quietly. 'It was a reader on *Goodreads*. Comparing my work with that of Sarah Waters and Lee Child, which was hardly fair. We write in completely different genres. It showed the reviewer's ignorance if you ask me. And anyway, Brett, don't you have anything more productive to do with your time than read my reviews?'

'But they're so entertaining,' he said. 'In fact, there was this woman who said that—'

'You're boring me now,' Dorothy said. 'Isn't your wife giving you enough attention at home?'

'Don't be sexist,' he said and laughed. 'I don't need attention from my wife. We are separate people who happen to like each other. We don't live in each other's pockets.'

'Or the same house, most of the time.'

'It works for us,' he said. 'At least I didn't end up alone, having to pay people to live with me.'

'Oh, fuck off, Brett.'

Dorothy stood, walked over to the solid mahogany sideboard, and opened one of the heavy doors. She took out a large flat cardboard box and placed it on the table.

'Let's play a little game. Louise!' she shouted. 'Grab yourself a drink and come and join us.'

Dorothy lifted the lid; I already knew what was inside.

The Ouija board.

Oh, bloody hell.

Chapter 24

'I don't think this is a good idea,' said Louise, cradling a cup of tea with her hands. 'I had a bad experience with a Ouija board once. The spirit followed me home, I'm sure it did. The next day my son ended up in hospital. Attacked on the street.'

Dorothy flapped the objection away with her hand.

'Don't be a spoilsport, Lou-Lou,' she said. 'That was obviously a coincidence.'

Louise shrugged slightly, looking towards me, and bit her lip.

I tried to smile in return, but my face seemed to have frozen.

There are no such things as ghosts. There are no such things as ghosts.

'Well, I'm up for a bit of spooky shit,' said Brett, a cigarette hanging from the corner of his mouth, 'as per usual.'

Dorothy took the lid off the box and a spider the size of a two-pence piece crawled out.

'Bloody hell,' she said, sweeping the creature off the

table with a hand. 'This hasn't been open in years. It smells so musty.'

'We played it the other week,' said Brett. He lifted his bottom off his seat, took the cigarette from his mouth and rested his hands on the table. He looked at each of us in turn as he said, 'It was the ghost of Dorothy's past ... one of the husbands who mysteriously disappeared.' He sat back down with a thud.

'You make it sound as though I've had dozens of husbands,' she said. 'And you can't remember yesterday, let alone last week.'

Brett glanced at me. 'She adores me really.' He rubbed his hands together. 'I'll be on my best behaviour.' He patted the seat next to him. 'I think we'd all better sit a little closer. Rachel, come and sit next to me.'

Dorothy switched off the two lamps and lit candles around the room. The light danced on the walls; Louise's silhouette was double her size.

'I'm not comfortable with this,' I said, remaining in my seat. 'We shouldn't mess with things we don't understand.'

Dorothy blew out the match.

'Don't take things so seriously, Rachel,' she said. 'Relax for a bit, will you? And I thought you said you don't believe in ghosts?' She unfolded the board at the end of the table. 'Come and sit next to me if you don't want to sit near Brett.'

'I'm not some drunken lech, Dorothy,' he said. 'I can keep my hands to myself.'

'Well, you're one out of two,' she said. 'Come on, Rachel. You're holding up the fun.'

I stood, grabbing my drink from the table, and walked slowly to the seat next to Dorothy.

'There we go,' said Dorothy. 'That wasn't too difficult, was it?'

I pulled my chair closer to the table.

'Don't look so worried,' said Brett. 'We've done loads of these and nothing interesting's ever happened.'

Dorothy placed the planchette in the centre of the board.

'Fingers on, everyone.'

Considering Louise had been hesitant to play, I was surprised her finger was the first on.

I reached a hand over; my finger tingled with the proximity of the others.

Dorothy cleared her throat.

'If there are any spirits with us,' she said. 'Please go to *yes*.'

The silence was almost crackling with electricity until a gust of wind made the curtain billow. Two candles near the window blew out, casting darkness on half the table.

'Fuck,' said Brett. 'I nearly shit myself then.'

'Shh,' hissed Dorothy.

She took a deep breath. Wasn't she going to reignite the candles? I felt the darkness on my right side like fingers creeping up my right arm.

'If there's anybody here,' said Dorothy, 'please go to *yes*.'

It was so quiet I could hear her breathing and the candle nearest me hissing.

The planchette vibrated.

'Oh God,' said Louise, pulling her hand away. She turned to Brett. 'Was that you?'

He took away his hand and reached for his glass, downing several gulps of whiskey.

'No!'

'It was probably just someone's finger twitching,' snapped Dorothy. 'Let's try one more time.'

I pressed my finger harder on the planchette. If someone were manipulating it, I wanted to know who.

'If there is anyone here,' said Dorothy, sounding impatient, 'please make yourself known.'

A thick silence descended; even the wind seemed to have disappeared.

The counter slowly travelled to *yes*. It was almost slipping away from under my fingers.

'Who's moving that?' I whispered.

'Not me,' said Dorothy.

Louise's eyes were fixed on the board.

'My God,' mouthed Louise.

'Please identify yourself,' Dorothy commanded.

The counter glided over the board. I couldn't tell where the force came from. Brett read out the letters it stopped over.

'K ... A ... T ... H ... R ... Y ... N.'

The planchette stopped in the middle of the board.

'Who's Kathryn?' I said. 'Was she a real person?'

Dorothy's eyes were fixed on Brett. 'Was that you?'

Brett shook his head. 'I swear it wasn't.'

'It wasn't me either,' said Louise.

'Nor me,' I said. 'The only Kathryn I know is from your—'

'Maybe Kathryn's a ghost in this house,' whispered Brett. 'You didn't murder her, did you, Dorothy?'

'Shh.'

The counter moved more quickly this time.

M . . . A . . . T . . . T . . . H . . . E . . . W

'Matthew,' whispered Dorothy.

My face went cold. It was as though my blood had turned to ice. This couldn't be right. I should've whipped away my hand at the start.

I pictured Matthew's face in between Brett and Louise, and he was laughing at me. It must've been my subconscious controlling the counter. I should've closed my eyes.

I scrunched them shut and the planchette began to move again. Brett read out the letters.

'M . . . Y . . . L . . . I . . . T . . . T . . . L . . . E . . . B . . . E . . . E.'

'My little bee,' said Louise. 'That's a strange combination of words.'

I opened my eyes.

I knew what these words meant, but this couldn't be happening – no one around this table knew about that. I felt as though I was sitting just outside of my body, looking over my own shoulder.

'It's three different names,' said Dorothy. 'Kathryn, Matthew, and Little Bee.'

'Which one are you speaking to?' said Louise.

187

The counter began moving, round and round, faster and faster. Brett's eyes were wide. My finger was only lightly touching when it stopped.

The tip of the counter pointed towards me.

'Rachel?' said Louise. 'That can't be right.'

'You're not dead, are you, Rachel?' said Brett. 'Or perhaps we're all dead and we don't realise.'

'Does it mean the spirit is talking to her?' said Dorothy.

The planchette moved to *yes*.

I withdrew my hand, my fingers still tingling as though hundreds of tiny spiders were crawling under the skin.

'This is stupid,' I said, rubbing my hands. 'I don't know a Kathryn or a Matthew.'

'They might be distant relatives,' said Dorothy. 'You should ask your mum about them.'

'Jenny won't know about my distant relatives,' I said, grabbing a napkin and wiping my hands. I stood, blew through the hole of the planchette and folded the board before placing it back in the box. 'I don't even know my biological mother's name.'

Louise stood and put an arm across my shoulders.

'It's just nonsense,' she said, rubbing the top of my arm. 'That's all. It's just a game.'

I picked up the box and put it back in the cupboard.

'I didn't know you felt that strongly about it,' snapped Dorothy. 'We could've had another go ... see if someone else came through.'

'There's no one coming through,' I said, flicking on one of the lamps. 'It's all bullshit.'

Brett cleared his throat; a smile lingered on his lips.

'If you don't mind,' I said. 'I'm going to go to bed. The darkness makes me tired.'

Dorothy sat back and crossed her legs.

'By all means, dear,' she said.

I walked out of the room, closed the door gently and leant against it.

My knees, arms, and hands were shaking.

'I've never seen anyone react like that before,' I heard Brett say.

'Do you know,' said Dorothy, 'that's the most personality she's displayed in the whole week she's been here.'

I lay in bed and tried to erase Matthew's face from my mind. I snapped the elastic band around my wrist. It was the one useful tool I'd picked up from my counsellor Gina; a short, sharp shock of pain to take me out of my thoughts. Most of the time it worked. This time, it didn't.

Our wedding day was three years ago today.

I *was* a bit tipsy walking down the aisle after sharing the bottle of champagne Gemma had bought us to drink while getting ready. I had to grip Phil's arm to steady myself, but the day was perfect.

At half past midnight, we left the few remaining partying guests downstairs. Gemma was slow-dancing with Richie, even though the music had long since finished and the date she brought was actually another man I can't recall the name of.

Matt opened our hotel room and held it open with his leg.

'Stand back a bit,' he said, bending slightly and holding out his arm.

'What the hell are you doing?'

He wrapped his arms around my legs and hoisted me over his shoulder.

'You're not meant to give me a fireman's lift.' I giggled as he released the door. 'It's meant to be face-to-face, romantic.'

He patted my bottom. 'I quite like this view, thanks.' He turned and laid me on the bed.

Our suite was decorated with the usual: rose petals and a bottle of champagne, which was floating in melting ice. I grabbed a handful of petals and scattered them on my dress.

'I want to wear this for at least a week,' I said. 'It's the nicest dress I've ever had.'

He flopped down next to me.

'My God,' he said, 'I haven't talked that much crap to so many people before.'

'You did a pretty good job of it.' I laughed and turned over. 'It was a great day, wasn't it?'

'I suppose.'

He got up, walked to the bathroom and closed the door. He was in there for at least ten minutes before I fell asleep.

When I woke, he was sitting in the corner in an armchair. He'd taken off his tie, his shirt was unbuttoned, and a glass of whiskey dangled from his hand. He was looking straight at me.

'What time is it?' I said, sitting up, the rose petals still scattered on my dress. 'I'm sorry, I was so tired.' I glanced at my phone. Twenty past six in the morning. 'Have you been awake all this time?'

'Hmm,' he said. 'It was nice to have some peace at last.'

I shuffled to the end of the bed. 'Aren't you going to join me?'

'I'm not sure I can do this.'

'Do what?' I said. 'We can just sleep. First night ... well, morning, as husband and wife.'

'There are things you don't know about me. About my past.'

I knew there'd been something. I'd often catch him staring at me. He used to dismiss it as *daydreaming without realising*. It was as though he was trying to work me out.

'Sometimes,' he said, 'I worry that you're going to get bored with me. It's happened to me before.'

'What do you mean?'

He circled the glass, the whiskey millimetres from the rim.

'Rejection,' he said. 'It's the worst thing that can happen to someone.'

'I know that.' I slid down from the bed and crawled towards him, sitting at his feet. 'You know I'd never reject you. Whatever it is, you can talk to me about it.'

He rested the glass on the arm of the chair, leant forwards and stroked my hair.

191

'I know,' he said. 'You're my little Bee.' He stood and stepped over me. 'That reminds me. I have something for you.'

He flung his holdall onto the bed, unzipped it and fished out a little black bag.

He sat next to me on the floor and handed it to me.

'Oh,' I said. 'I didn't get you anything.'

'It doesn't matter.'

I reached into the bag and pulled out a small box. Inside was a delicate little bee on a sterling silver chain; its wings were encrusted with tiny crystals. I took it out and held it gently in my hands.

'I love it,' I said. 'Will you put it on for me?'

He took it from me. 'Turn round.'

He must've been a bit drunk and tired after drinking so much and staying up late.

'Shit,' he said. 'I'll have to do it later.'

He threw the necklace into its bag, took off his jacket and flopped on the bed.

Within minutes he was asleep.

There were so many awful memories tangled with the good. It was difficult remembering any of it.

My Little Bee. The words that were spelt on the Ouija board tonight. If I believed in ghosts and spirits, I might've been convinced it was him trying to contact me. But I didn't. The dead remained dead; their spirits didn't magically float to a heavenly place.

Matthew was gone and he was never coming back.

Chapter 25

Camera_3>bedroom>05:34

He stands over the bed, bending down, close to her face.

He opens the bedside drawer and takes out her mobile phone. He scrolls through it before putting it back.

She turns in her sleep and faces away from him.

He sits on the floor and crosses his legs. He watches her for one hour and twenty-three minutes.

Chapter 26

The next morning, still in bed, with a clearer head, I thought about the Ouija board. Dorothy, Brett, Louise, couldn't have known about what happened to Matthew. My bank cards with my real name were inside my mobile phone case and I kept that with me all the time. There were no recent pictures of me in connection with Matthew's case online. The only explanation was that my subconscious spelled out the words.

I hadn't thought about our wedding for ages. There was something about being here in this house that made the memories come tumbling back into my mind.

The first two days of our honeymoon had been perfect. Matthew had visited Budapest before and took me to the thermal springs in the River Danube and on a boat ride where we saw the beautiful buildings that were a world away from our hometown. On the third and final night we went to the restaurant we'd eaten at every evening.

'I think I'll try something different from pizza

tonight,' I said, holding the menu with two hands. 'The chicken paprikash sounds delicious.'

'I recommend the steak hortobagyi,' said Matt. 'Best thing I've tasted in years.'

'I'm sorry,' said the waiter, who appeared next to our table. 'If I may interrupt. If you are choosing between the two, I recommend the paprikash. Seeing as it's your last night here in Budapest.'

'Thank you, Laszlo,' I said, handing him the menu. 'That would be perfect.'

Both the waiter and I looked to Matthew. He wasn't reading his menu; his eyes were focused on mine. He raised his eyebrows and his nostrils flared.

He passed the menu to Laszlo without looking at him.

'I'll just have the same.' He waited a few moments until the waiter had left. 'Why did you call him by his name?'

'Because we've seen him every night,' I hissed. 'And we had a drink with him last night. It seemed rude not to.'

'We didn't have a drink with him!' he said. 'Did you come back here when I was asleep?'

'Of course not,' I said, a little too loudly, causing the people on the next table to glance at us. 'Although you probably had a bit too much to drink and can't remember.'

'That's typical of you, isn't it?' he said. 'Making me believe something that's not true to get yourself out of shit.' He drank his remaining wine and grabbed the

195

bottle from the ice bucket. 'I've lost count of the times you've flirted with the men here.'

I laughed. 'Very funny. Everyone knows how bad at flirting I am. Gemma says that—'

He shoved the bottle back into the bucket; drops of water landed on my face and shards of ice fell to the floor.

'You know how I was treated in the past, and then you go and flirt with all these tall, dark, handsome clichés ...' He shook his head as he fixed his gaze on the table. 'There was the man sitting opposite us on the boat cruise ... even the woman in the red bikini at the springs.'

'What?' I dabbed the water from my face with a napkin. 'Now I know you're not being serious.'

I grabbed my wine glass and took three gulps of the rosé.

The rest of the meal was endured in silence and the next morning he was already in the shower when I woke.

'Morning, beautiful,' he said when he opened the door. He bent down to kiss my forehead. He laughed. 'You slept well. Must've been all those shots after dinner.'

'We had shots?'

'About seven,' he said. 'I'm not surprised you can't remember.' He held up his mobile phone and showed me a photo. 'And you did this, too.'

It was our initials carved into a tree.

'I can't remember doing that,' I said. 'We came straight back after the meal.'

He picked up his watch from the bedside cabinet.

'You'd better get ready. Breakfast finishes in half an hour.'

I sat up. 'You don't think we should talk about what happened last night?'

'What are you talking about?'

He sat on the bottom of the bed.

'We argued, remember?'

'I can't remember an argument,' he said. 'I think I mentioned you being overfamiliar with the waiter, though. How would you feel if I were like that with a waitress? Calling her by her name, taking her recommendations and ganging up against me?'

'I'm sorry, Matthew.'

'There you go,' he said, smiling and stroking my cheek. 'All better now.' He stood and walked to the bathroom. 'I'll run you a nice bubble bath. How's that?'

'Good.'

I undressed in the bathroom, staring at myself in the mirror.

Had I expected it to be like this? No relationship was perfect.

We always had different versions of events. He said, she said. How did the saying go? There are three versions of the truth: mine, his, and what actually happened. We'd both had a few stressful weeks. Things would settle down soon.

I stood back a little from the mirror as the steam obscured my face and words appeared on the glass.

Remember I will always love you.

197

I blinked the words away. I've spent too much time wallowing in bed recalling events I couldn't change when I should have just got up straight away after waking. It was just gone eight and I needed to get ready for work.

I sat up and reached for my phone but stopped when I caught sight of my hand.

Tiny white lines of scratched skin covered the tops of my fingers; small bits of dirt were wedged into my fingernails. I flicked some of it out onto the bedside cabinet; they were little splinters of wood. I turned to open the curtains; the windowsill had no marks. I got off the bed and knelt on the floor to look for signs that I'd scraped my nails on the floorboards.

Nothing.

My heart began to race. No, not again.

A fear crawled around my mind, the fear of having done something I couldn't remember. People had never believed me when I told them I didn't remember carving our initials into the tree. 'You can tell you did it,' Gemma had said, when she looked at the photograph. 'You put his initials first. Matthew would never have done that.'

I looked to the large wardrobe in the corner. It seemed to suck the colour from the rest of the room and was almost bulbous in shape. Dorothy had said it wasn't to be opened, which was like telling a small child she was forbidden from taking a sweet from a bowl right in front of her.

One of the wardrobe doors wasn't shut properly. I

got up from the floor and walked slowly towards it.

The handles were a wide oval shape in a distressed gunmetal grey. I grabbed both of them, cold as pebbles in my hands. I turned them in opposite directions.

The smell of mothballs hit the inside of my nose and the back of my throat. It was so strong they obviously hadn't seen daylight for years. It was as though the skins were decomposing.

Inside, were five or six fur coats of different shades. I touched one with my finger but couldn't shake the image of the animal who wore it first. A fox? Rabbit? Mink? How could someone wear fur and not think about a creature being skinned?

Without thinking, I stroked an arm. A velvety softness that artificial fur could not replicate. I looked down at the base of the wardrobe. There were scratch marks in the wood as though a toddler had taken the point of a pair of compasses and gouged scribbles in erratic circles. Ten, twenty times. Jesus. It was like someone had been locked inside.

I sliced through the middle of the coats and pulled them apart, shedding light from the window onto the back of the dark wardrobe.

A name was scratched into the wood. Twenty, thirty times.

I stumbled back, slamming both doors shut.

The name was Matthew.

Oh God. What had I done?

Chapter 27

Brett was in the kitchen when I went to get a coffee. Both of his hands gripped the sink as he gazed at the brick wall outside. There was a deep vertical line between his eyebrows, and his bottom lip stuck out slightly. The dressing gown he had on was obviously Dorothy's; it was blue silk with tiny feathers printed on it.

Had he heard what happened in my bedroom last night? The scraping of wood, carving out Matthew's name over and over again. What had I used? I'd searched my bedroom for any sharp objects but found none.

It was anxiety, that was all. I needed to keep on top of my medication. I could see if there was any sandpaper in the shed at the bottom of the garden. The wood inside the wardrobe wasn't perfect – I could easily get rid of the scratches.

Brett turned when I cleared my throat. His frown disappeared, and a smile transformed his face.

'Morning, sunshine!' he said.

Sarcastic bastard.

'Morning, Brett,' I said, flicking on the kettle.

'Great night last night,' he said. 'Though I can't remember much past midnight.'

He laughed as he took two mugs from the cupboard. I used the noise of the kettle to feign deafness, but he side stepped to stand next to me. He placed the two mugs down and folded his arms. The hair on my arms tingled, the way it did when people I hardly knew stood close to me.

'Did you stay up late?' I said, rubbing my arm.

'I'm guessing about three or four judging by the way I'm feeling this morning.'

'How's Dorothy?'

I couldn't imagine those two kissing, let alone sleeping together.

The kettle clicked off and Brett heaped instant coffee into each cup.

'Do you take sugar?' he said.

'No thanks,' I said, reaching for the milk.

'And as for Dorothy,' he said, 'I imagine she's still out for the count. I've never known her to wake before ten.' He nudged me with his elbow, causing the milk to land in my cup with a giant splash. 'Are you wondering if we slept together?'

I tried to hide my burning cheeks.

'No.'

He winced as I stirred in the milk.

'Jesus,' he said. 'That's like a bell ringing inside my skull.'

'Sorry.'

He grabbed his mug. I could see from the corner of my eye that he was looking at me.

Don't mention it. Don't mention it. Say something quickly.

'I've got to start work—'

'Weird about that Ouija board,' he said, 'wasn't it?'

God.

'Yeah,' I said. 'Really weird.'

'*My Little Bee*. Are bees significant in your life? Perhaps you used to be a beekeeper?'

I faked a laugh. Trust it to be the bloody Ouija board incident that featured in his limited memory of last night.

'No,' I said. 'I've never worked as a beekeeper. I've never met a beekeeper, either.' *Bee, bee. Busy little bee.* 'Which shows it was all a load of rubbish.'

'Do you think? Dorothy's really into all that stuff ... Has been since someone close to her died.'

'One of her ex-husbands?'

'She told you then?' He glanced at the ceiling. 'It was a long time ago, though. She's convinced she can feel his presence around her.'

The people in this house were batshit crazy.

'Did you meet him?'

'No,' he said. 'That was all before I came onto the scene.' He drank the rest of his coffee. The now-empty mug dangled from his index finger as he clasped his hands and rested them on the top of his legs. 'What about you, Rachel? You're quite mysterious. All the other of Dorothy's assistants never stopped talking about themselves.'

I wanted to ask why Dorothy hadn't kept their details – had they offended her so much she got rid of their files? – but that would've revealed my snooping.

'That was probably why they were fired.'

He went to the sink and rinsed his cup. 'Probably.' He put it upside down on the drainer. 'So, you've never known someone called Matthew?'

I picked up my coffee – untouched and getting cold – and walked towards the door.

'No,' I said, my back towards him. 'I don't know anyone called Matthew.' I glanced over my shoulder. 'I'd better get to work.'

'See you later, then,' he said. '*Rachel*.'

Chapter 28

Gordon was on his third cup of filter coffee, and at last the caffeine was kicking in. Perhaps a bit too much. His heart was hammering, and he felt agitated as he paced the kitchen.

He'd just had a conversation with Audrey. The first time in their two months of separation that she'd actually called *him*.

'Gordon, it's me,' she'd said, needlessly. 'This is the last time I'm going to contact you.' She took a deep breath. 'Please, please stop whatever you're doing to me. I know you've had someone watching me.'

'What the heck are you t—'

'Don't try to deny it. I know what you're like. Stop sending flowers, stop ringing my office and stop sending me creepy emails from other addresses.'

'I haven't sent you any—'

She hung up.

He stared at the phone as he paced. The woman was clearly insane. Why the hell would he waste money buying her flowers? And the insinuation of hiring someone to follow her? She knew full well he was perfectly capable of doing that job himself and wouldn't be sloppy enough for her to notice.

Gordon poured the rest of his coffee down the sink. What counteracted caffeine? He wasn't sure. He ran up two flights of stairs, but it only made his heart pound harder. An appointment with the doctors was needed – he could keel over at any moment with all this stress. Who knew what it was doing to his heart?

He switched on Classic FM and rested his hands on the windowsill. He took several deep breaths. He'd read about a certain technique that mimicked the act of sleep. Inhale for the count of four and exhale for the count of seven.

He glanced at his Fitbit. His heart rate was now seventy-five.

Why had he taken early retirement? It had seemed like a good idea at the time and Audrey had gone on and on about all the holidays they could take. 'Canal boating in the Norfolk Broads would be amazing, wouldn't it, Gordon? Or what about renting a lodge in the Highlands?'

He tried not to get sentimental, even though he thought, sometimes, that being with the wrong person was preferable to a life alone.

He should've steered clear of internet dating. Their late-night conversations over *Messenger* had convinced him that they knew each other so well. He'd kept their chat transcripts and went through them a couple of days after she left. He highlighted the red flags he should've noticed at the time had he not been blinded by the three photographs she'd sent him (that were obviously taken at least two decades ago).

He powered up his PC and took out his logbook.

Relationships were too problematic. He should concentrate on his new business. Yes, that was it. He could register with The Association of British Investigators, do a couple of courses; perhaps he'd get himself a slick new website.

He typed in his password (changed every two weeks) and clicked onto the camera feed recordings from last night.

His mobile sounded the Morse code tone with a text message.

It was from Mother.

There is someone at the door.

He closed his logbook, put it back in the drawer and turned the key.

'Who is it?' he shouted when he'd nearly reached the hallway.

'How the devil should I know?' Mother hollered back. 'You've not opened the living-room curtains yet.'

Great. Whoever it was would think they're a pair of lazy reprobates. He smoothed down his hair and widened his eyes to look as awake as he could.

'You all right, mate?' the young lad said when Gordon opened the door.

'Yes. Why wouldn't I be?'

'You look surprised.' He shrugged. 'Parcel for you.'

The lad was dressed in black. Not the usual Royal Mail get-up. Was he chewing gum on the job?

He handed Gordon the package.

'Do you need a signature?'

'Not this time, mate,' he said.

Gordon watched the lad get into his van and drive away.

'Good morning.' It was a voice to Gordon's left.

That smug git Brett. He had a cigarette hanging from his mouth and looked as though he hadn't shaved yet. Gordon wouldn't have been surprised if he'd caught him zipping up his flies as he strutted down Dorothy's front path.

Gordon shut the front door without replying and glanced at the parcel. It wasn't for him at all — it was addressed to someone next door. The postal service wasn't like it used to be — far too many companies doing the same job. Never mind. He liked receiving mail intended for someone else. It often indicated their interests (*Digital Photography*: number fifty-one) or problems they might be having (brown envelope, *This is not a circular*, red font inside: number fifty-nine).

This one for number sixty-three, however, had no sender details and was postmarked *Greater Manchester*. He took out his phone and took a quick snap. It was someone new to investigate: Bethany Arnold.

As Mother would say, who the devil was that?

Chapter 29

Matthew, Matthew, Matthew. How could I have scratched his name into wood so many times without waking? But who else could it have been?

His eyes met mine from the laptop screen. It was a picture they'd used over and over again online.

'Who's that?'

Dorothy's voice made me jump in my chair.

My face went cold. Her head was just inches from mine as she stooped to look at Matthew's face.

I watched as she read the headline. I'd rehearsed what to say if I were ever asked about it – however remote the chance – but the words had vanished from my mind.

'Is this part of the research I asked you to do last week?'

She frowned slightly and the foundation on her forehead creased. Eyeliner was smudged under her eyes, but it might have been by design rather than by accident.

'Not quite,' I said. 'I went down a bit of a rabbit hole.'

'Oh,' she said. 'Was he poisoned?'

'No. At least I don't think he was. I didn't get a chance to read the whole article.'

I knew every word of it.

'I see,' said Dorothy. 'Well, I can't blame you for keeping his picture up. He was a good-looking man, wasn't he? So heartbreaking for someone to die so young.'

'He wasn't that young,' I said. 'He was thirty-four.'

'Well, you certainly remembered *that* part,' she said as she scanned the rest of the article. 'It's awful what happened to him, isn't it? So tragic when a man dies when they have so much more life to live.'

I closed the news page.

'Yes,' I said. 'It was.'

'I'll let you get on with your work,' said Dorothy. 'Here are another couple of chapters for you to type. I've had a very productive afternoon so far.'

'Very good.'

Dorothy stood straight, rested her bottom on the edge of my desk and folded her arms. Chanel N°5 wafted towards me.

'And to celebrate me reaching the halfway point of the book,' she said, 'I thought it'd be fun to have a murder mystery party. What do you think?'

'Erm ...' *That writers celebrate bloody everything.* 'It sounds lovely. I'm sure you'll have a great time.'

Please don't say it. Please don't say it.

'You're coming, too, Rachel,' she said, patting me on the shoulder.

Shit.

'Wouldn't want you to miss out.' She walked around my desk and slid her fingers between the slats of the blinds. 'I've invited a couple of others you haven't met yet.' She whipped her hand away from the window. 'Bloody hell. Gordon's walking up the path.' She darted towards the hall. 'You deal with him for me, will you? I'm going to hide.'

'Yeah, sure,' I said, to myself.

I waited until Gordon knocked before heading to the door.

'Morning, Gordon.'

He was carrying a brown parcel the size of a Next catalogue.

'This was delivered to mine by mistake,' he said, making no attempt to hand it over. He held up the parcel. 'Funny thing is, though, it's addressed to someone who doesn't live here.'

'Perhaps it's for one of Dorothy's friends,' I said, folding my arms to shield from the cold. 'She has a lot of friends.'

'OK,' he said, presenting me the parcel with two hands. 'Here you go, Rachel.'

I took it from him. 'Thanks, Gordon. I've got to get back. I've so much to do.'

'I bet you have,' he said.

I closed the door and put the package on the hall table, glancing at the name on the package. My knees buckled; I grabbed hold of the end of the banister and crawled to the bottom step.

No, no.

My hands were shaking as I reached for the parcel. I stood, ran up the stairs, and slammed my bedroom door shut. I lifted the mattress and slid the parcel out of sight.

I knelt on the floor and buried my face into the quilt.

Whoever sent the poison letters to me at home had found me again.

Chapter 30

Gordon settled himself at the dining table. He fancied a change of scenery; it was detrimental to mental health being cooped up in one room for most of the day. He'd head down to Homebase this weekend (or B&Q – less pricey) to get himself some paint. His office needed freshening up, especially if he were to invite clients over. Yes, it was his office now. A study was for amateurs.

Mother had been snoozing away in her bedroom for over an hour now, but he knew better than to keep checking on her. She'd wake up at just the creak of a floorboard.

He pressed send on his mobile phone and it took only a few minutes for the email to arrive on his laptop. Two photographs filled the screen. The first was a close-up of the handwriting on the address label and postmark, and another of the package as a whole. When he'd shaken it earlier, there had been a gentle thud as the contents went from side to side. Nothing heavy or noisy. A small item of clothing perhaps, or a soft toy? Or something small and precious, effectively wrapped.

He typed *Bethany Arnold* into the people search on Facebook. He disliked using the site, but it was an effective way of getting an idea how common a name was.

He recognised no one in the results displayed.

Gordon tried a generic search engine of the name plus *Preston*, focusing on the images results. Pages and pages of strangers' faces. It could have been any of them. Could the sender have sent it to the wrong number?

This was pointless. He stood and went to the window.

Poppy was chewing grass again. He'd have to make sure she wasn't allowed in for the next half an hour or so in case she was sick again. He banged on the window, and she ran in the opposite direction.

Was Bethany one of Dorothy's friends? Rachel was right – she did have a lot of them, and he was good at remembering faces. Perhaps she wasn't from Preston. He had to be patient. Nothing worth doing was easy and he had a feeling there was something he was supposed to discover. Some things happened for a reason; that was why he'd received the parcel when they were in all along.

Gordon sat back at the dining table and typed in *Bethany Arnold* and *northwest*.

He scrolled through the first, second, third, fourth pages. All the faces started to blend into each other. Brown hair, blonde hair, young women, older women. A few men thrown in. Staircases, people receiving awards, shaking hands. Groups of ten or more, which made it more time-consuming.

And then he saw her. After sixteen pages of scrutinising photographs of strangers.

It was as though his subconscious knew all along.

He clicked onto the website linked under the image
and leant back in his chair as he absorbed the words of
the news article.

He put his hands behind his head.

WOMAN STABS HUSBAND TO DEATH.

'Well, well, well, Rachel,' he said aloud. 'I knew you
were hiding something.'

Chapter 31

I had to get out of the house at lunchtime. I walked through the gateposts and along the street, with the feeling that the whole street was watching me.

I glanced at the house next door; there was no shake of the net curtain, though that didn't mean he wasn't looking. Gordon knew my real name. Would he connect it to Rachel? I needed to get rid of that package. I should've ripped off the label and destroyed it. What if Louise were to find it if she changed the sheets?

The first anonymous parcel was sent to me when I was staying at Jenny and Phil's. It was after Matthew died and, before I opened it, I thought it was a gift from Gemma because she used to do things like that. But it wasn't. It was a knife that looked like it was covered in blood. It turned out to be red nail varnish, but Jenny made me report it to the police. They couldn't trace who sent it.

I found myself outside the library and pushed open the door; the warmth inside was comforting. Adam was standing behind the counter and he looked up as the door opened. Would Gordon tell him about the package or was I being paranoid? Perhaps he already knew.

'You got the card, then?' said Adam.

'The card?'

'Your library card,' he said. 'I dropped it off on my break the other day.'

'Oh, it was *you* who came to the door.'

'Were you in?' he said. 'I did knock. I wasn't sneaking around.'

'Oh, yes. I was in, sorry. I was on a phone call.' I glanced over to the bank of six PCs; only one space was occupied. 'I've left the card at home. I was wondering if I could borrow one of those computers?'

'Is the internet down at your place?' he said. 'Sorry, I'm being nosy. Course you can.' He stepped out from behind the counter. 'I'll even throw in a coffee if you like, or I might even stretch to a hot chocolate.'

'Thanks.'

What if Gordon were to come in? He was the curious type who'd search for the name online. There was only one, blurry picture of me, but it would take determination to scroll through all the search results.

'It's as easy as that,' said Adam.

'Sorry. What?'

'Just log in with these details, though I've done it for you this time.' He frowned. 'Are you OK? Aren't you enjoying your new job?'

My eyes darted to the glass doors as they opened.

It was a woman lugging a bag for life, which she dumped on the counter.

216

'Bloody hell,' she shouted over to Adam. 'I'll kill the little scrote who stole my shopper. Nearly had a heart attack walking up the hill carrying this lot.'

'Sorry to hear that, Pauline.' He headed back to the counter. 'Will I put a sign on the noticeboard to ask if anyone has a spare shopping trolley?'

'God, no,' she hissed. 'Can you imagine them all at Tuesday's book club? They'd think I was begging. Even if it was anonymous, they'd know it was me.' She leant towards him, resting her elbows. 'Though between you and me, I wouldn't be surprised if one of them had swiped it. John Crenshaw was always eyeing it up and stroking it. The tight git, they're only fifteen pounds down the market.'

'I could put up a Missing Shopper poster,' he said.

There was a smile in his voice.

I turned away quickly when Pauline caught me watching.

Please don't let her shout at me. It would only take that for me to break down in tears.

Pauline chuckled.

'Eh, wouldn't that be funny?' she said. 'Especially if we could put up mugshots of John or Gillian and her not-so-secret online diary, eh?' She was still laughing as she wandered over to the True Crime section. 'Eh, I don't know.'

I wondered if Matthew's case would ever feature in True Crime books. There were at least two or three magazines dedicated to the topic.

A hand waved in front my face.

'You all right, love?' It was stealth Pauline.

'Yes, thank you,' I said, glancing around. Three other people were sitting behind computers, their heads up after Pauline's hollering. 'I was miles away, then.'

'A million miles, more like.' Pauline sat at the station next to me. Oh God, was she going to keep talking to me? She flicked on the switch. 'Don't worry, I'll not bother you,' she said. 'I've got some researching to do myself.'

She nodded towards my screen.

VICTIM'S MOTHER SLAMS THE JURY: 'SHE SHOULDN'T HAVE GOTTEN AWAY WITH MURDER'

'That's some serious stuff you're looking at,' she said.

'It's for an assignment,' I said quickly. 'I'm studying with the Open University.'

She placed a hand on the arm of my chair.

'What a coincidence! Me too. I'm studying for a Geography degree. It was my husband that convinced me, but I told him, *It'll take me six years. I'll be seventy-eight when I finish*. He said, *You'll be seventy-eight anyway*.' She sighed. 'But he's dead now, bless him. What about you. What are you studying?'

'Criminal Psychology,' I said.

'How depressing,' she said, typing in her login details. 'Though I'm sure you're bright enough to switch off when you sit down of an evening.'

'I don't really sit ...' I started, but Pauline wasn't listening any more.

She stared at her screen with narrowed eyes and placed giant headphones over her ears.

Jenny and Phil used to *sit down of an evening*, each in their own chairs. Phil by the telly and Jenny next to the fire with easy access to the door for snacks they munched throughout the night. I wanted to be transported back to that place and time.

I looked at my screen and comforting thoughts slipped from my mind. I was here to search for my photograph – to see how persistent Gordon would need to be to find my picture. Because he would – he was the determined type.

I felt a dab of pain as my fingers touched the keyboard.

The scratches from the wardrobe last night.

Something like that happened about a year after we married. I'd been pretty drunk after Matthew and I had shared three bottles of wine. He'd cooked a meal of chicken fajitas, which he knew was one of my absolute favourites.

We ate at the small table in the kitchen that his parents had given us while we saved up for a new one. He'd lit candles and put Radio 2 on in the background.

'When did I get so old,' he said, 'that I'm offended by the dance music on Radio 1 on a Friday night?'

I laughed. 'I don't know. These young people getting ready for a night out, eh? Think they're the only important people in the world.'

'And as if they listen to the radio while getting wasted before going *out* to get wasted.' He got up to bring over dessert. 'Chocolate cheesecake,' he said. 'One of your seven favourites. Don't worry, I bought this one so you're safe.'

'I could get used to this,' I said.

'Ha! Well one of us has to make an effort. The last time you cooked, you burnt a frozen pizza.'

We ate in silence until he'd finished.

'Did I mention I've got a work thing next weekend?'

I placed my cake fork on the plate.

'No,' I said. 'The whole weekend?'

'Yeah.' He stood and took both plates to the sink. 'It's a team-building thing or something ... going to be a nightmare.'

'OK.'

He turned round, leant against the sink, and folded his arms.

'You don't sound thrilled.'

'I only said *OK*. I thought we were going to the pictures to see *The Girl on the Train*.'

'That can wait,' he said. 'It'll still be on the weekend after.'

'I suppose.' I stared at my hands. 'But I didn't turn up to my own leaving do because you wanted to go and see *Star Wars* on the night it was released.'

'I wish you'd gone to it now. You mention it every time we make plans.' He sat down and topped up our wine. 'You didn't even want to go ... said you were glad of the excuse. You said you never wanted to see any of them again. Why do you always put a different spin on things?'

220

'I'm sorry,' I said. 'I wasn't aware I did that.'

'Oh,' he said. 'That reminds me. I've bought you a present.'

I laughed. 'Me being wrong made you remember that?'

He went out of the kitchen and opened the cupboard under the stairs.

He was grinning as he walked towards me and placed a silver hologram box with a big red bow in front of me.

'I got one of those present boxes you keep mentioning,' he said, 'when we watch American Christmas films.'

'It's lovely.'

He laughed. 'The present isn't just the box, silly,' he said. 'Open it.'

I lifted the top off the box.

'A mobile phone.'

'You're always saying you can't do much on yours,' he said. 'You can watch films on this one.'

'It must've cost hundreds.'

'You're worth it.' He stood and took another bottle of wine out of the fridge. 'You don't seem happy with it.'

'It's just that I'm used to the phone I've got.'

He pulled the box towards him.

'It's OK,' he said. 'I can take it back ... get you something you really want.'

'No, no,' I said. 'I'm sorry. I love it. Really, I do.'

He took out the phone.

'I've set it up for you already,' he said. 'All you have to do is put your contacts in.'

'It's great.' I got up, sat on his knee, and wrapped my arms around his neck. 'Thank you.'

We spent the rest of the night lounging on the sofa watching *Gogglebox* and *The Graham Norton Show,* drinking glass after glass of wine. The last thing I remember was glancing at the clock at ten to midnight.

'Bee,' Matt whispered my name, 'Bee,' shaking my shoulders.

I opened my eyes.

I was sitting on the cold kitchen floor, leaning against the cupboards, dressed in my nightie.

'What happened, Bee?' he said. He was wearing only boxer shorts; his hair was messy from sleeping. 'What have you done to your hair?' He knelt in front of me. 'You could've hurt yourself with these.'

I followed his gaze.

My index finger and thumb were wedged in the rings of some nail scissors. Small clumps of hair were scattered around me.

I screamed, shaking my hand frantically to rid them of the scissors.

'Matthew!' I shrieked. 'Help me.'

'Calm down,' he said. 'Calm down. Don't hurt yourself.'

He clamped hold of my wrist and gently prised the scissors from my hand.

I reached to my hair, expecting there to be none left.

'Don't worry,' he said, getting up and putting the scissors on top of the freezer. 'I think you only gave yourself a trim.'

'It's not funny,' I said, tears falling from my face onto my nightdress. 'I could've killed myself. I could've hurt you.'

'I know it's not funny,' he said. 'I was trying to make you feel better. You didn't hurt anyone.'

He crouched next to me.

'God, you're shaking,' he said. 'Come on. Let's get you back to bed.'

He pulled me up from the floor, guided me up the stairs to the bedroom and into bed.

'Have you ever sleepwalked before?' he asked, draping the quilt over me.

'When I was younger,' I said. 'But they were night terrors. I didn't remember them. Jenny used to tell me about them in the morning. I'd wake up screaming and crying, talking nonsense.'

He wiped the fresh tears from my face.

'It's probably from the stress of your new job and meeting all those new people. Try to get some sleep. We can talk about it in the morning.'

'I don't want to fall asleep,' I said. 'What if it happens again?'

'Hold my hand,' he said. 'I'll wake up if you leave the bed.'

'But you might let go.'

'I won't.' His eyes were already closing slowly. 'Don't worry.'

'Hey, Rachel.'

I lay awake for hours, keeping hold of Matthew's hand until I woke up alone...

'Rachel!'

Adam was standing next to me.

'Sorry,' I said. 'I didn't realise you were talking to me.'

'Oh, OK.' He looked around. 'You're the only Rachel in front of me.' He put on a black winter coat that went to his knees. 'I'm just going for lunch. I don't suppose you'd like to join me?'

'Um ...'

He raised a palm.

'Don't worry. It was just an idea. I thought you might be hungry, seeing as you've been sitting there for nearly three hours.'

'Have I?'

The clock read almost one o'clock.

Pauline took off her headphones.

'Is it that time already?' she shouted. 'Oops, sorry. The voices in my ears were so loud.'

'I'm just off for lunch, Pauline,' said Adam. 'But Mary's covering if you need anything.'

'Not to worry, love,' she said. 'I'm meant to be meeting Gillian at the pub for lunch. I probably won't see daylight again. She's having man trouble. Are you two off out together?' She smiled and raised her eyebrows as she wrapped the scarf around her neck. 'He's all right is Adam,' she said. Her theatrical whisper wasn't at all discreet with him standing right next to her. 'I don't know why he's single.'

'Oh,' I said. 'I'm not look—'

'Stop touting me out, Pauline.' He rolled his eyes.

'Last week she was trying to set me up with Emily,' he said, 'who's seventy-three years old.'

Pauline's eyes widened. 'You shouldn't reveal a lady's age,' she said. 'And Emily is very flexible. She still practises yoga.'

The café Adam said he went to nearly every day was only a few minutes' walk away. The place was small with only eight tables and we managed to get one by the window.

Adam was oblivious to the two women who tutted at us.

'I knew we should've reserved our view, Maggie.'

'I should try somewhere else,' he said as he read the menu. 'But I know I like the food here. I look forward to lunch all morning and I'd be gutted if I ended up with a crap one.'

The waiter took our orders and brought over the drinks.

'This town gets so busy at lunch,' he said, looking out of the window. 'I don't know where everyone comes from.'

'They must all work from home.'

'Maybe.'

I told you I wasn't blessed with sparkling conversation.

'It's always bigger than I thought it'd be,' Adam said after the waiter placed the all-day breakfast in front of him.

My toasted teacake was smaller than I thought it'd be.

'Are you sure that's all you want?' he said.

'Yes, it's fine.'

Nothing's ever *fine* when someone says it's *fine*, is it? And my coffee was almost cold. It was the Universe's way of saying I shouldn't be here, sitting with another man. Well, it would've been if I believed in all of that.

'I'm sorry I'm terrible company,' I said. 'I've a lot on my mind, what with the new job and everything.'

'That's OK.' He slopped a squidge of egg yolk onto a slice of toast with his knife. 'So where do you come from? You've a bit of a Manc accent unless I'm very much mistaken.'

I laughed. 'It's not Manc. I'm from just outside Bolton.'

'I didn't want to say you sounded like Sara Cox,' he said. 'What made you come here? Preston's not the first place I'd think of as an ideal destination.'

'The job was in the paper,' I said, tearing the teacake into pieces. 'My finding it was serendipitous. I needed somewhere to stay, too.'

'A happy accident, then. I suppose Preston's had worse descriptions.'

I smiled.

'You're not on the run, are you?' he said, a glint in his eye. 'Perhaps Blackpool would've been better for that. The number of tourists who pass through there, a person can easily become invisible.'

'I'll make a note of that,' I said, not altogether joking. 'Have you always lived around here?'

He put down his knife and fork and closed them together on his plate. He'd left an egg, a slice of toast, half a sausage and the fat from the bacon. He wiped his mouth with the napkin.

'My nan always said I had eyes bigger than my belly.' He took a sip of his coffee. 'Yeah. Here or hereabouts. I went to uni in Liverpool, but I couldn't find work there relating to my degree.'

'Which is?'

'Drama and English Literature.'

'I expect finding work anywhere with that might be difficult – unless you want to go into acting or teaching.'

'I'd be useless at both,' he said. The café was beginning to empty. We'd been here for nearly forty minutes. 'Hey, you don't fancy coming for a drink with me tomorrow night?'

'Don't I?'

His cheeks flushed. 'You know what I mean.' He raised a palm. 'And before you say it, I know you're not looking for a relationship or anything, but I thought it'd get you out of that house. Can't be fun staying in all the time.'

'OK.'

He took out his mobile and I read out my number.

'Great,' he said. 'Shall we say seven?'

Outside, walking past the estate agents, was a man in his early forties. He was wearing a black woollen jacket and dark suit trousers. His chestnut hair was scraped back – something Matthew never did. But his skin colour was so much like his.

I stood and grabbed my coat from the back of the chair and placed a ten-pound note on the table.

'I'm really sorry, Adam,' I said, putting on my coat. 'I have to go – I've seen someone I know.'

I rushed towards the door.

'A tenner's too much,' he said after me. 'You only had a teacake, and it was ...'

His words faded as I ran outside and across the road, searching for the figure in black.

I scoured inside shop windows as I passed.

He was in the sandwich shop.

I hesitated for a few minutes as he stood in line. He grabbed a newspaper from the display on the wall and took a bottle of water from the refrigerator.

I couldn't go inside. It was far too small – the sort of place that people turned around when someone came in. He ordered from the counter, and a few moments later was handed his sandwich. I stood a little back from the door as he headed towards it, hiding behind a huge potted plant.

The same tanned face, the auburn hair.

He walked towards the pelican crossing. I followed, pretending I wasn't trying to run. When he stopped at the kerb, I almost ran into the back of him.

He turned around.

'Are you all right?' he said.

'Yes, yes,' I said. 'I thought you were someone else. I'm sorry.'

How could I have thought it was Matthew?

The man grinned and narrowed his eyes slightly. 'No need to be sorry. You haven't done anything wrong.' He pulled his scarf tighter around his neck. 'Good afternoon,' he said, before walking across the road.

I was shaking, feeling as though everyone was whispering about me.

And she killed her husband. She shouldn't be allowed to walk free on these streets.

I broke into a run and dashed down an alley, leaning against the wall next to a wheelie bin. Slowly, I slid down. What was I thinking, wandering the streets alone when someone from back home knew where I lived now?

Chapter 32

I waited for Adam, leaning on the edge of the desk at the office window. I had convinced myself to go out again after chasing that stranger yesterday. If I didn't go back out now, I'd become a hermit again. I barely went out in the months before Matthew died.

Brett had been staying at the house since Ouija board night. I didn't know what room he slept in and I tried not to listen out for any intimate murmurs coming from upstairs. It would've been like listening to parents having sex.

He appeared every morning in Dorothy's dressing gown.

This lunchtime I saw him and her talking in the kitchen, their faces inches apart and not in a romantic way. I stopped halfway towards the door when she took his face in her hands, squeezing his jaw with her fingers. I must've gasped because they turned to look at me and she dropped her hand.

'Louise made you a sandwich,' Dorothy said, striding towards me. 'It's in the fridge.'

'I'm just stepping out for a smoke,' Brett said when I walked into the kitchen.

I'd expected him to say it wasn't what it looked like, but he didn't. Perhaps Dorothy was annoyed with him again, but I knew first-hand that whatever a person said was no reason to put your hands on them in anger.

It was five to seven when Adam came into view. I smiled when he blew into his hands to check his breath. I was glad to see he hadn't brought flowers. I always felt awkward when presented with traditionally romantic gifts, as though I were expected to swoon and be grateful. Not that this was a date. Not at all.

'I was thinking we could go bowling,' he said, trailing behind me down the garden path.

'Really?' I stopped at the gatepost. 'I'm not really dressed for bowling.'

'No, not really,' he said. 'I'm crap at bowling. Don't want to show you my worst points straight away. There's a nice pub nearby – it overlooks the river.'

I glanced at Gordon's house. There were no silhouettes lurking at the window.

'What was that look?' said Adam. 'You looked angry for a second there.'

'No, I'm not angry. It's just that Gordon seems to be always watching every time I go outside.'

'He's not that bad, really.' We came to the main road and he guided me to the right. 'I think he's lonely. He took early retirement and moved here to take care of his mum. His dad only died a couple of months ago.'

'Oh. I assumed he'd lived with his mother his whole life.'

'No. He was married until a few months ago.'

'Really? What happened?'

'I don't know,' he said. 'Blokes don't usually ask those types of questions unless they've known each other a while.'

'That's a bit of a generalisation.'

He laughed. 'No, it's a bit of experience.'

We walked along the main road until we reached a bridge over the river. The moment was spoiled slightly by the sound of cars and buses on the road next to us.

'Where are we going?' I said. 'We've been walking for ages.'

'It's only been about fifteen minutes. Are you not much of a walker?'

'I don't mind, if I know I'm going for a walk.'

'Fair enough,' he said. He pointed to a row of terraced houses that overlooked the river. 'I live in the second one from the end.'

'It looks nice,' I said, ever the conversationalist. 'Do you have it all to yourself?'

'Yeah,' he said. 'But it looks bigger from the outside. It only has two bedrooms.'

'Like a reverse TARDIS.' I touched his arm. 'Oh. Did you walk all the way to Dorothy's and now we're walking back?'

He shrugged.

'Yep. But I didn't mind. It's a lovely evening and I like to listen to music as I walk.'

'What kind of music do you like?'

Please don't say Radiohead.

He got out his mobile phone, clicked onto Spotify and passed it to me.

'This was my playlist walking up.'

I scrolled through it: 'Hollandia' by Ethan & The Reformation; 'Every You Every Me' by Placebo, 'I Bet You Look Good on the Dancefloor' by Arctic Monkeys. There were at least fifty songs. I handed the phone back.

'Does it meet your approval?' he said.

'I've heard of about three,' I said. 'I'm not really into music.'

He stopped and took hold of my hand.

'What? You're kidding me, right?'

'No.' I laughed at the horror on his face. 'Some songs evoke memories so it's easier not to listen. Though I do put Radio 2 on sometimes. That I can cope with.'

'So, in a way,' he started to walk again, still holding my hand, 'it's that you feel music a little too much.'

'Yes, I suppose that's true. How do you do that?'

'Do what?'

'Get people to open up to you? You know all about Gordon, and you got me talking about my feelings about music.'

'Just asking the right questions, I guess. And being interested in other people.'

'Sorry,' I said. 'I've not asked you much.'

We came to a pub just off the riverside footpath.

'Don't worry.' He opened the door and held it open.

'There's plenty of time for me to talk about myself. I'm good at that, too.'

I followed him to the bar. It wasn't busy as it was still early.

For nearly twenty minutes I had forgotten about the parcel, about Bethany.

I hoped it would last all night.

We stood at the bar and I was paranoid people would think Adam and I were on a first date. I wished I'd brought a handbag or something to fidget with, but I only used pockets when going out. Money, phone. That was all you needed, wasn't it? And a spare tenner in my shoe in case of emergencies.

'Shall we sit over there?'

He nodded to a conservatory with late sunshine landing on the tables. God, we were going to sweat in there.

'Yes, that's fine.'

I reached for my drink on the bar.

'I'll carry it,' he said, heading over to the table.

Why was I pretending to be such a sap?

It was probably a good thing he took it for me because my hands were shaking, and I mightn't have any drink left by the time I reached a seat.

I was on my third large glass of wine; Adam had tired of pints – 'I'm far too full' – and was drinking a JD and coke.

'Is this the first time you've been here?' he said.

'Erm.'

'Of course it is.' He reached for his drink. 'You didn't

234

know where we were walking to.' He took a quick sip. 'Sorry, I'm a bit nervous.'

'You don't strike me as the nervous type.'

'It's all an act.' He held out a steady hand. 'Look at that. I'm shaking.'

'Oh, right.'

No, he wasn't.

He laughed. 'Sorry. Nothing's coming out in the right way. You probably think I'm a weirdo.'

'Not at all.' I was pleased we weren't talking about me again.

'So.' He took another small sip. 'Has anyone famous popped round to Dorothy's yet?'

'I don't think she knows anyone famous. I'm sure she'd have let me know. There'd be photographs on the walls, no doubt.'

'Ha! That reminds me of my brother. He brought home a signed photo when he was eleven or twelve ... said that Warren Beatty came into his friend's parents' restaurant.'

'No way! Was your brother in Hollywood?'

'Nah, Southport. When he handed me the photo, I realised it was actually Derek Beattie from *Mr and Mrs*.'

I laughed. 'Easy mistake to make.'

'Quite.'

The couple on the table next to us were trying to row quietly.

'*You could've told me your ex would be here*,' he said.

'*I didn't know, did I?*' she said.

'*He posts his whereabouts online every five seconds.*'

'Well, why don't you just go and talk to him instead of stalking him?'

Adam cleared his throat and leant towards me. 'I think they've cottoned on to us eavesdropping.'

I looked around the room. 'I really want to know who her ex is.'

'Me too. And where does he go every five seconds?' He took his mobile from his pocket and took off his jacket. 'Anyway ,.. more about you living with an author. Has anyone been round to Dorothy's? I can't imagine she's a total hermit.'

'It's not as interesting as you might imagine. There's the housekeeper Louise and another writer Brett, who's staying at the moment. I don't know how long for, though.'

'Brett Daniels?' Adam picked up his phone. 'I think I've seen him around. I might have seen one of his books in the library, though wasn't his last one published in the late nineties?'

'I don't know. I've only read Dorothy's because I was going for this job.'

'His stuff is a bit purple prose. Three pages to describe a landscape in Derbyshire, from what I remember. I doubt his books would be your thing.'

'How would you know that?'

'A librarian's intuition.'

'Is that your superpower?'

'Yes, ma'am.' He saluted. 'The world's most boring and inconsequential of all superpowers. At your service.'

Adam's phone pinged with a notification.

Motion detected Camera 3.

'Sorry,' I said quickly. 'I didn't mean to be nosy.'

'That's OK. Though I'm the nosy one with cameras everywhere.' He tapped something into his phone and switched it off. 'I like to keep an eye on my house. There's been a few break-ins round my area in the past couple of weeks.'

'Aren't you going to check it?'

He put it in his jeans pocket. 'It'll just be next door's cat.' He stood up. 'I'll just nip to the gents.'

The rowing couple were now sitting in silence. Him on his phone and her with her arms folded, staring at the carpet. I never knew where to look when I was on my own in a pub.

I swiped my phone from the table as a text silently appeared on the screen from an unknown number.

The floor seemed to move beneath me. I gripped the table with my other hand.

Hello, Bethany.
I hope you're having a nice evening with your new friend.
Nice jacket.

'I have to go,' I said to Adam. 'There's something wrong and I have to go back to the house.'

'I'll walk you back,' he said, getting up.

'It's OK. There were some black cabs outside. I'll be fine.'

I hopped into the nearest one and gave the driver Dorothy's address.

I stared at my phone screen.

Whoever had written that text had been watching me. Had Gordon been in that pub? He was the only one so far around here to know that Bethany Arnold was connected to Dorothy's house.

I ran down the path after the taxi dropped me off and ran straight up to my room, opened my drawer, and took out two of my tablets so I could sleep without dreaming.

Chapter 33

Brett was in the kitchen again. The smell of bacon had infiltrated the hallway and nearly made me vomit.

'You excited for tonight, Rachel?' he said, standing at the back door smoking.

'What's tonight?'

I found a packet of Berocca in the cupboard and dropped one into a glass of water. I downed it, trying not to retch as the fizzy liquid went down my throat. I hoped the vitamins would help remedy the slight hangover and the constant intrusive thoughts.

Brett hurled his cigarette and closed the door.

'The murder mystery party, of course,' he said, tying the floral dressing gown tighter around his waist. 'Don't tell Dorothy you forgot – she's really looking forward to it. She's planned it out meticulously.'

'She's the murderer, then?' I rinsed out the glass and filled it with fresh water.

'No one knows yet.' He took out the grill pan and laid the sizzling bacon onto one of two slices of bread on a plate. 'That's the point. It's a mystery.' He tore off a piece of kitchen roll and wafted the sandwich past me as he walked. I tried to not visibly gag. 'But who knows, eh? Best be on your guard, Rachel. See you later!'

God, another party. Why had I gone out last night? Hopefully the mystery party wouldn't last all night. I did one at college when someone's parents had gone away for the weekend and we played at being grown-ups in their house. Gemma's boyfriend at the time (can't remember his name) was a hardcore heavy metal fan and surprised us all by really getting into it – he even wore a white lab coat and insisted on listening to everyone's heartbeat with his stethoscope.

'Good morning, Rachel!' Dorothy came up behind me as I stared into space. 'What a beautiful morning it is today.'

'It is?'

It was still raining, and the cloud was heavy, but I supposed she didn't see many mornings.

'I hope you haven't forgotten what tonight is?' she said, flicking on the posh coffee maker.

'The murder mystery party,' I said (thank you, Brett). 'I can't wait.'

She came up behind me and put her warm hands on my shoulders, close to my neck.

My whole body tensed. It was the first time she had touched me, and I wanted to wrangle myself from under her.

'I am so excited!' she said. *You don't say*. 'We haven't had one of these for months!' She smelt of stale perfume and cigarette smoke. 'You're going to be Nina Beckett, personal assistant to the murdered mogul.'

She finally removed her hands and my shoulders felt lighter.

'I don't have to act, do I?' I said. 'I haven't the confidence to do that sort of thing in front of strangers.'

She stared at me for a few seconds, narrowing her eyes. 'I'm sure after a few cocktails you'll get into the spirit of things. We'll have a little reception in the library to oil the wheels.' She grabbed an espresso cup from the cupboard next to my head and placed it under the coffee machine. She pressed a button to fire a shot of coffee into the cup. She downed the hot liquid in one. 'And you'll meet some new people. What could be better than that? I've left some new pages on your desk.'

She waltzed out of the kitchen, through the dining room, and the door to her study slammed shut.

I couldn't concentrate on work, even though Dorothy had left three new chapters for typing. Until yesterday I had looked forward to reading what happened to Kathryn, but now it seemed frivolous to be distracted by the life of a fictional character when my life was going to shit again.

It was three o'clock already and I hadn't left the room.

It was just like being at home again. Too afraid to go outside.

Louise had been cleaning and tidying for nearly four

hours now and must've finished hoovering upstairs. She galloped down the stairs and opened my office door.

'This was under your mattress,' she said. She placed the parcel on my desk. 'What a strange place to put it. Do you remember putting it there?'

'I was in a rush the other day and just put it there without thinking.' I glanced at the address label again, the words like a flashing beacon. 'I ordered it for a friend on Amazon. I put this address in by mistake.'

Louise picked up Dorothy's handwritten pages.

'Is it any good?' She scanned the first page; her eyes widened for the briefest moment. 'Kathryn,' she whispered. She snapped the notebook shut, placed it on my desk and walked to the fireplace. She gazed at the family portrait of the living dead, and her shoulders shuddered. She spun on her heels. 'Have you sorted your outfit for tonight?'

'No,' I said, swiping the parcel and sliding it to the floor. 'I don't think I've anything suitable. What are you wearing?'

'I can sort you something out. I'm going to be Adeline Carmichael, wife of the deceased. I have a white trouser suit with massive shoulder pads.' She leant on the mantelpiece. 'The last time we did one of these I was the murderer, and it was so stressful. I kept thinking people could see right through me.'

'Did anyone guess?'

'No,' she shrugged. 'Hardly anyone suspects the quiet ones – especially when we pretend to have our heads in the clouds.'

242

'Is that what you pretend to be?'

'Is that how you see me?' she laughed. 'No, it was written on my list. *Your character is scatty*, that sort of thing.' She walked towards the door. 'Are you nervous about it? You needn't be. I know Dorothy's invited some younger ones tonight, so you'll have some interesting people to talk to.'

'More interesting than Dorothy?'

She looked around the room and her shiny hair swished like a hair dye advert. She must've had it done today. 'Do you think she's filming us?' She laughed again. 'But you're right. She is one of a kind ... unpredictable.' She wiped along the windowsill and then across one of the slats. The cloth was coated in dust. 'Oh God. I haven't done these in a while, have I? Let's pretend we didn't see that. I'll do it next week. See you later.'

I waited a few minutes before I placed my foot on top of the package. When I pushed down, the cardboard collapsed easily. I knew it wouldn't have been a birthday present from Jenny – I hadn't given her this address yet and it wasn't her handwriting.

I pushed the chair away from the desk and slid to the floor. I picked at the brown tape on the box to get purchase and ripped it off.

A musty, decayed smell escaped – like the smell of a decomposing rat under floorboards.

I opened both sides.

Blood-coated white cotton; buttons; a collar.

I reached for a pen from the desk and prised out the fabric.

A white shirt. But millions of people had white shirts. The label was purple: Ralph Lauren.

I ran my fingers along the buttons and stopped at the last, turning it over.

It was sewn on with cream thread because I had no white.

It was Matthew's shirt. Blood-soaked and torn open. The shirt he died in.

Chapter 34

Kathryn was sitting cross-legged on the windowsill. It wasn't technically a window seat, but she'd lined it with a folded bedspread and laid cushions along it.

Wales wasn't what she'd been expecting – rolling hills, sheep, people singing in the streets – but she hadn't been able to afford anywhere in the countryside. Her one-bedroomed flat had the most perfect view, even in bad weather. The Irish Sea was pounding the promenade, soaking careless pedestrians: a woman with a buggy and a bloke dressed in shorts and a T-shirt who walked with his hands by his side.

She put her book aside; it wasn't capturing her. Nothing she read recently held her attention for longer than five minutes because her mind always drifted.

How dare Andrew leave *her*?

'You're not the person I thought you were, Kathryn,' he said, eleven months ago. 'Or maybe *I'm* not the same person any more.' Bloody cliches. He'd probably practised saying them for days before. 'You're so heartless,

Kathryn. You have no empathy for anyone.' Blah, blah blah.

How *dare* he?

She'd heard from one of their mutual friends – well acquaintances – that Andrew had moved in with a woman who had four children. Four! Kathryn would put her money on him not lasting a year with that amount of noise in the house.

Four children. Jesus.

Kathryn had begged him to stay. She had impressed herself with the performance. She'd had ugly cried, too. She could always cry on demand.

'You don't need me,' he said. 'You even abandoned your own child. You don't need anyone.'

That might've been the case, but it should've been *her* who ended their relationship. That had been her plan. And technically they were still married. He wanted her to demonstrate that she had *feelings*. She had an idea of how she could make him see that.

Nestled in her lap was a tiny cardigan and a fluffy bonnet with the ribbon she was always afraid would be a choking hazard, so she never used it. See, she had been responsible at some point.

After she had given birth, Jack had given her the deposit for an even smaller flat than this. Paid her to keep her mouth shut, no doubt, because he only met his baby twice. He hadn't even lied to her that he was going to leave his wife. They had two children. Kathryn couldn't remember their names or ages. She just had to get on with it herself.

When the baby had cried at night, the man living upstairs used to bang on the ceiling and shout, 'Tell that little brat to shut the fuck up.'

It must've been colic or something. Going out with the pram did nothing to quiet the screams. The only thing Kathryn had found that worked was sitting in the launderette listening to the washers and the dryers. Sometimes she would fall asleep on the bench with the pram tied to her wrist, glad of a few hours' peace.

When it was a few months' old, it finally started sleeping through the night. She chanced a drink down the pub and when she got home the flat was in silence and the baby sound asleep. Easy, really.

She'd been going for the odd night out, and it was only by chance that she was discovered. They said Kathryn was neglectful and there was no second chance. She argued that no harm had come to the baby. It wasn't as though she were starving or beating the thing.

Her final day as a mother was a day like today. It was two in the afternoon and Kathryn was still sleeping after the night before. Her sister had come in and snatched the baby from the cot.

'For God's sake, Kathy,' she shouted, shaking her awake with one hand. 'You can't keep doing this.'

'I'm fine.'

'No, you're bloody not.'

Her sister packed a bin liner full of the baby's things and Kathryn just watched from the sofa. She couldn't find the words to protest. She felt like shit from too many brandies.

Having the flat to herself was bliss, but she had to think of what was next. She wasn't going to stay around and watch her sister bring up her child. How humiliating. Even when her mind suggested she be the glamorous aunt, swanning in and out with expensive gifts, she countered that it would only hold her back.

And now, over thirty years later, she was in Wales with a shitty part-time job.

A bird landed on the windowsill; she was glad of the distraction.

She could change the future, though. Get back into their lives. Convince Andrew that she could be a caring person. She was far too old to be on her own. She could arrange an emotional family reunion, invite him along to watch it. He still loved her. There was no doubt about that.

There was a letter from him still on the telephone table. He probably thought she was asking for money when he saw her handwriting last week, but bless him, he was always prompt with his reply (unlike Jack).

She got down from the window and went over to it. He always did have messy handwriting; it was surprising it arrived at the right address. It was postmarked a few days ago. He had, more than likely, written to her on the same day he received her letter.

She tore it open and scanned the niceties.

Hope you're well, Kathy. I've managed to start a car cleaning business and so far, it's doing really well ... Angela and the kids are well (as if Kathryn would give a shit about that). *There's always some drama, but I love being busy. She's the perfect mother.*

He hadn't written that last sentence, but of course it was implied.

Kathryn had spent a decade of her life with him and he only chose now to start to love *being busy*. A new business? It wasn't as if she'd held him back. She was always telling him to get off his arse and do something with his life, supported him when he took up all sorts of hobbies to try to *find himself*, and this was the thanks she got. He was doing it all now with someone else and *Angela* would have all the benefits.

There was a knock at the door. She glanced at the clock; the rest of the letter would have to wait. Her colleague, Barbara, called on her to walk to work with her nearly every day now and Kathryn was getting sick of it. It wasn't that she was bad company, but sometimes Kathryn liked to walk alone, especially when she knew she'd have to speak to people all night at work.

She was tempted to ignore her.

But she didn't. She hadn't spoken to anyone all day.

She grabbed her coat.

The strong wind kept blowing her skirt up and now she didn't feel so smug about her inner criticism of the pedestrians earlier on.

She would move closer to home. Get her child back and get Andrew back.

They belonged to her.

Chapter 35

I was surprised Dorothy hadn't left me a waitress's outfit for the evening, as I was supposed to be the one opening the door to guests. Instead, Louise had brought some of her clothes from a *previous life* as an admin assistant at an accountant's. Black high-waisted trousers and a pale blue blouse with a giant bow at the collar. The look was completed with my hair in a messy side bun and black-framed glasses.

'You do look the part, Rachel,' said Dorothy, flouncing into the dining room. 'I love it when people make an effort. Makes everything a bit more special.' The large dining table had been moved near the window so the guests could *mingle*. Dorothy twirled in the centre of the room, her fifties-style turquoise dress billowing. 'What do you think, ladies? Do I look the part, too?'

Louise gasped and clasped her hands together like the ever-faithful housekeeper she was (although tonight she was actually Adeline Carmichael).

'Yes,' she said. She turned and went into the kitchen. 'Come here a sec, Rachel,' she shouted over her shoulder.

She opened a bottle of champagne and poured it into seven glasses.

'If you're a bit wary about answering the door to everyone, I can take over. I doubt Dorothy'll notice after the first guest arrives.'

'I'll be OK.'

She took a bottle of vodka from the freezer and poured some into two little shot glasses. 'I think we're going to need this to get us started. Dorothy has been on the gin since four.' She picked up a glass and knocked it back.

I shrugged and did the same.

'Now, ladies,' said Dorothy, 'look sharp.' She leant on the door frame. 'Rachel, are you still all right to open the door to the guests?'

'Are you sure you don't want *me* to do it?' said Louise. 'I'm wearing an apron.'

Dorothy wrinkled her nose. 'What does wearing an apron have to do with answering the door?' She clasped her hands. 'Go stand near the door. I don't want anyone waiting more than a couple of seconds. And take the tray of champagne. Give each guest a glass after hanging their coats.' She rubbed her hands together. 'I've been looking forward to this evening all week.'

At dead on seven, I leant on the banister looking through the glass like a kid waiting for friends to arrive at a birthday party.

I hadn't met Dorothy's other friends yet and a wave of stomach cramp hit.

One of them was walking up the path: a woman with long hair and a coat that flowed behind her like a wedding train. I opened the door before she had a chance to knock.

'Get that for service,' she said.

Sophia is the one with the long mousey-coloured hair. Hopefully, she won't be pissed before she gets here.

'You must be—'

'Ooh, is that champagne?' Sophia stepped inside. Her hair wasn't mousey at all, but a dark golden blonde that has been tonged into ringlets. Her skin was glowing, iridescent, and her lipstick was the perfect shade of natural pink. 'She told me I wasn't to drink before I came, but I'm here now.' She picked up one of the glasses before I had chance to take her coat. 'Is it down here?'

She walked down the hallway and I slipped past her to open the dining-room door. Dorothy and Louise stood in the middle of the room, their eyes on the first guest.

'Sophia has arrived,' I said, as grandly as one shot of vodka afforded.

Dorothy's shoulders dropped. 'Oh, it's only you.'

'Charming,' said Sophia. She tipped the glass to her lips and downed it in one. 'Any more?'

Dorothy tutted and swiped the glass from her hand. 'For God's sake, Sophia. I'm getting the Prosecco out for you — that champagne's far too expensive for you to be glugging it down like water.'

Sophia turned to me and whispered in my ear. 'I never drink water.'

I wasn't at all surprised.

There was a knock at the door and it took me a few seconds to remember I was supposed to be answering it. I wanted to stay and watch Sophia get pissed and make a show of herself. I recognised the silhouette in the frosted glass.

'I thought you were already in the house,' I said.

Brett stepped inside. 'I didn't want to just come down the stairs,' he said in a dubious Boston accent. He grabbed a glass and flashed his invitation. 'And tonight, my darling, I am Jasper McKendrick. *Hugely* successful actor in the nineties, but now I do voiceovers for insurance commercials.' He placed a hand on his middle and bowed slightly. 'May you do me the honour of letting me escort you?'

'Why, yes, sir,' I said in a terrible cockney accent. 'But don't tell the missus or I'll get into terrible trouble.'

He stared at me for a few moments then raised his eyebrows. 'We couldn't have that, could we?' He took hold of my hand and pulled me towards the dining room. 'Are you playing a chambermaid?'

'Er, no.'

'Good evening, ladies. And nice to see you, Sophie,' he bowed in front of her, 'how wonderful it is to see you again.'

'Get us a refill, will you?' she said, resting against the wall. 'I'm absolutely parched.'

'I doubt that for one moment,' said Dorothy, glancing at the clock. 'It's five past. Where is everyone else?'

'Who else have you invited?' said Brett, pouring champagne into Sophia's glass. 'Here you go, Sophie.' She didn't seem to mind (or notice) that he kept getting her name wrong. 'Dorothy, can you get her a bigger glass?'

253

'Just drink it slower, Sophia ... I mean Daisy Travis, actress,' said Dorothy. 'Have a little self-control.'

'I'll try.' Sophia wiped her mouth with the back of her hand.

How on earth did Dorothy and Brett know this woman? She looked to be in her late thirties but behaved like a teenager.

'A surprise for Louise,' said Dorothy, 'and a woman from the library.'

'Really?' said Brett. 'You invited randoms to make up numbers? Wouldn't Christopher and Oliver have wanted to come?'

'They're far too busy for something like this,' she said.

There was another knock on the door; Dorothy and Brett turned to me.

'I'm going.' I walked down the hall, muttering, 'Can't have the lady of the house answering her own fucking door,' like the ungrateful homeless person I was.

I took the tray from the hall table and balanced it on my upturned palm before opening the front door.

The man was dressed in jeans, a white T-shirt, leather jacket and Ray-Ban sunglasses.

For a moment, I thought it was Adam. The same height, same dark hair.

'Hello,' I said, almost dropping the tray.

'Hello there, ' he said, removing his sunglasses. 'I'm Louise's son, Jamie. Though I've been told to be Gabe Maddox, actor, tonight. Apparently, he's currently starring in the sci-fi trilogy *Galaxy Wars, One, Two* and *Three*. Who might you be?'

'Nina Beckett, personal assistant to producer Marcus Carmichael.' He shook my hand firmly. 'Please come in. Daphne de Florier is waiting for you.'

It was hard to say that name out loud with a straight face, but his expression remained unchanged. He didn't seem the booky type.

He swiped a glass from the tray.

'What's your real name?' he said. 'I'm sure I've seen you before.'

Oh God. He had a Bolton accent. I thought Louise had said she was from Liverpool.

I swallowed the nausea that was rising in my throat. If he knew who I really was, he'd have just come out and said it, wouldn't he?

'It's Rachel,' I said, putting on a posh accent. 'But I have to be Nina tonight.'

He stared at me as he folded his sunglasses and slid them into his top pocket.

'Oh, right.' He walked towards the open dining-room door. 'Come along, *Nina*,' he said. 'I never make an entrance alone.'

Chapter 36

The final guest was Gillian from the *Not-So-Secret Diary* blog fame. Dorothy was scraping the barrel when it came to local celebrities. Gillian had previously hinted at them being more than passing acquaintances, so her presence didn't altogether surprise me. Unlike Louise, who had paled when she saw her son walk through the door. It took her longer than it should have done to register it was actually him.

Dorothy dinged a glass with a fork.

'Now, everyone.' Dorothy took a little bow. 'Welcome to Lethal Fame. I am Daphne, your host for this evening.'

'Why have I got such a rubbish name?' said Gillian to no one in particular. 'Everyone else has such exotic names.'

'There's nothing wrong with the name Elaine Pettigrew,' said Dorothy, glancing at the ceiling. 'In fact, it rather becomes you. And I'd appreciate everyone staying in character. Otherwise, what's the bloody point?'

'OK,' said Gillian. 'I'm so sorry, *Daphne*.'

'Jesus,' said Brett. 'I wish I'd thought better of

putting on an accent. There's no way I'm going to be able to keep this up all night.'

'I'm sure you'll manage, darling,' said Dorothy, smoothing down her hair.

'Are those two shagging again?' Sophia had said it quietly enough for only me to hear. 'Sexual tension or what?'

'I don't think so. I haven't seen or heard anything like that,' I said. 'What do you mean *again*?'

'They used to have a thing. Well, that's what Daphne de Dorothy told me once.' She was swaying a little now.

'How did you meet Dorothy?'

'In a pub. Miles away. And I was miles away most of the time. She felt sorry for me, I suppose. Was really kind to me when the bloke I lived with treated me like shit. God knows why. No one else noticed.' She looked down at the sticker (*Daisy Travis*) on her top and patted it. 'But it doesn't matter because I'm someone else to-night. Dave Lee Travis.' She snorted a laugh. 'I need another drink ... need to stop blabbing to everyone.' She headed towards the kitchen in a remarkably straight line. 'Have you got another of those nice cocktails, Lou— I mean, *Adeline*?'

'Sophia!' Dorothy shouted so loudly that all conversations in the room ceased. 'Turn around and come back into this room. I am about to read out the murderous turn of events.'

Sophia leant on the doorway and pivoted on her heels.

'Very well, Daphne,' she said, saluting her.

Dorothy cleared her throat in an exaggerated manner.

'Now, dear friends. We were gathered here today to dine with the legend that is – was – Marcus Carmichael. I am very sad to announce that he has, this evening, been found dead in his hotel room.'

She paused, raising her eyebrows and circling a raised wrist.

'Oooh,' said Brett.

The rest of us echoed him.

'I've never heard of him,' said Gillian.

Typical Gillian.

'Will she ever shut the fuck up?' said Sophia into my ear, without a hint of irony.

'I express my deepest condolences to his dear wife, Adeline,' said Dorothy, 'who I am sure is devastated.'

Louise took this as her cue and, after reading from her card, sobbed loudly into a handkerchief (an inspired accessory).

'Sadly,' continued Dorothy, 'we must assume that one of the persons here tonight is responsible for the death of our dear friend.'

I was the only one who didn't gasp. Everyone else seemed to have read their booklet, but I still hadn't opened mine.

'We will shortly be sitting down for dinner,' said Dorothy. 'But first, I hope you will join me in the library for a pre-dinner drink.'

Nothing like a pre-dinner drink after the murder of one's dear friend.

'I'm just popping to the ladies,' I said, in my best Nina Beckett voice. 'I will be as fast as I possibly can.'

No one replied because no one was listening to me.

I bolted the bathroom door, sat on the closed toilet, and ripped down the perforated edge of my game booklet. It looked professional enough; at least Dorothy hadn't created it herself.

<u>Nina Beckett</u>: Since childhood you have always wanted to become a director of independent films. After completing your degree, you gained work experience in television studios where you met Daisy Travis who yearned to be a Hollywood star. After she earned a small part in one of Marcus Carmichael's films, she became his mistress and introduced you to him. In time, you worked your way up over two years to become his main personal assistant. You found out, however, that he had started another affair behind your friend's back, and then you discovered Daisy was pregnant. You decided to confront him, and he threatened to end your career.

What a load of sexist nonsense.

I peeled off the section at the bottom.

YOU ARE THE MURDERER.

Of course I bloody was.

'I knew all along,' said Dorothy. 'It was the hard-faced ambition that gave it away.'

I didn't know why I was taking her words so

personally; it wasn't as though she was actually talking about me.

'It wasn't hard-faced, was it?' said Brett. 'She was sticking up for her friend.'

We were sitting around the dining table that had been reinstated in its rightful place. I was sitting next to my new best friend for the evening.

'I do appreciate that,' said Sophia, resting her head on my shoulders. 'Not many people would kill someone for their best friend.'

'My best friend would kill for me,' I said, running my hand along the edges of a silver coaster.

I hadn't expected anyone to have heard, but the room went silent.

'Really?' said Dorothy. 'Would she really?'

'It's just an expression,' I said.

'It's not though, is it? Not when you think about it.' Dorothy looked to Brett on her left and Louise on her right. 'I mean, I love my friends, but I wouldn't go to prison for them.'

'You probably wouldn't get caught, Daphne,' said Sophia. She tapped both hands on the table. 'Can anyone lend me a cig? I quit last week, but I can't be arsed giving up any more.' She nudged my shoulder. 'I might die tomorrow. Might as well make the most of tonight.'

Slowly, everyone congregated into huddles of conversation and at some point in the evening, time seemed to have fast-forwarded. Dorothy announced that she'd had enough and the stress of organising the whole thing

260

had left her totally drained. It didn't take long for the rest of them to leave.

'Seems it's just you and me left now, kid,' said Brett, sitting next to me at the dining table. 'Do you want to go out for another cigarette?'

'Nah,' I said. 'My throat's hurting. I don't usually smoke. I'm far too drunk tonight. I don't think I can even lift my hands.'

'No worries,' he said, getting up. 'I won't be a sec.'

I slid down in the chair. I really wanted to go to sleep and I must've closed my eyes for a few minutes because Brett was standing in front of me. I was exhausted.

'You'd better go to bed, love,' he said. He held out a hand. 'Come on, I'll walk you to your door.'

Chapter 37

Camera_4>kitchen>02:44

He reaches into the cupboard above the microwave and takes out a small bottle (brown). He removes the lid and takes out what appears to be a capsule. He pulls it in half and pours the contents into a glass (wine glass containing approximately 200 ml of liquid).

He opens the drawer next to the sink and takes out a teaspoon and stirs the liquid in the wine glass.

He washes and dries the teaspoon and replaces it in the drawer.

He picks up the glass and leaves the kitchen.

Camera_4>room3>02:47

She is seated.
He hands her the drink and she places it on the table.
She sips the wine and finishes drinking it at 03:24.
They both leave the room.

Camera_1>bedroom>04:31

He enters the room and then removes her bed covers.
He picks her up and carries her out of the bedroom.

Chapter 38

I woke to the sound of banging from next door. The sound of a wooden spoon hitting a pan. Or maybe it was the ringing of church bells from the end of the road. It seemed to surround my ears.

Jesus, my head was killing me. I was lying on top of the covers, still wearing the outfit Louise had lent me. I hoped Dorothy didn't expect me to do much work today because I felt like shit. I remember the first shot of vodka with Louise in the kitchen, the four proper champagnes that I asked her to mix with orange juice. There were cocktails, too. That'd do it.

It felt as though my pulse was beating in my temples.

I closed my eyes and the image of Matthew's face flashed before me.

'Go away, Matthew. Not now.'

I was probably still a bit drunk.

I closed my eyes again and another scene flashed in my mind.

It was a Thursday night, almost six weeks before he died. Matthew had come back from the pub at just

263

gone midnight. He woke me by banging things about downstairs: slamming the front door, flinging his shoes against the hall wall. What was the point of being angry if no one noticed?

The fridge slammed shut and ice tumbled to the floor.

'Shit,' he said. 'Fucking stupid bastard ice.'

I had tried doing two things when he was like this: to ignore it and pretend I was asleep (he always shook me awake to tell me what had pissed him off), or secondly, go downstairs and ask what was wrong.

It was usually something trivial, like his phone wasn't working properly or he'd lost a bet on the football, made worse by one of his mates winning. The weekend before, on a rare night when we had gone out together, Richie had ribbed him mercilessly about Bolton Wanderers losing in a friendly against Halifax.

'Aren't they as bad as Accrington Stanley?' said Richie, nudging Matt, causing his lager to spill over the glass. 'Oh, hang on.'

My body was shaking. I wanted to tell Richie to shut the hell up, but then I'd have looked like the crazy one again, wouldn't I?

'Yes, very fucking funny, Rich,' Matt said, smiling.

But I knew what he'd be like when we got home. It was why I didn't like going out with him any more. It was prolonging the anticipation of trying to guess his mood. It was easier to just deal with the aftermath. At least I couldn't be blamed when I wasn't even there.

I grabbed my dressing gown and stepped loudly

down the stairs. I didn't want to be accused of sneaking up on him again.

Simple. That was how I wanted my life to be. And it was if I abided by the rules.

The unwritten, silent rules.

He was sitting at the kitchen table, staring at a can of lager.

'Are you all right?' I said.

'Do I fucking look all right?'

I flicked the kettle on. 'What happened?'

'Nothing, really.' He got up and stood next to me. The smell of whiskey made me want to cough and retch. 'Well, not nothing.'

For fuck's sake, spit it out and let's get it over with.

'Oh?'

'Come on, Bee,' he said. 'You know what this is about.'

'I really don't, Matt.'

I flicked the kettle off, pulled out a dining chair and sat down.

'It's been bugging me since yesterday,' he said. 'One of many things, really. Last week when you said you were going for lunch with Gemma ...'

Shit. He couldn't possibly know, could he? There was no way Gemma would have let it slip to him that she hadn't met me.

'... I'd thought to myself that maybe it wasn't a bad idea – you hadn't seen her in months. I'd even worried about coming home to you passed out on the sofa ... worried because I know how alcohol makes your

265

anxiety ten times worse. You know I do these things because I want to protect you, don't you?'

'Yes.'

'But here's a funny thing. You didn't go to the pub you said you went to, did you?'

What did he know? Did he know where I really was, and this was a test? Do I tell the truth but not the reason? My heart pounded and he wouldn't take his eyes from my face. He said I always touched it when I lied.

'There was a change of plan,' I said. I was already sitting on my hands.

'Ah, there it is. I knew it!' He stood and paced the length of the kitchen. 'And there was you, telling me what Gemma had been up to, describing what you had for lunch. *Oh, the spaghetti was lovely, Matt. We should go there some time.*'

My mind went through all the reasons I could have been at the solicitors. I had thought of loads last week but they'd vanished from my memory. I'd been caught out before, when I went to see Jenny and Phil. I didn't understand how he could have possibly found out.

'I went to the solicitors,' I said. 'I was making my will.'

He stopped pacing. 'Go on.'

He *did* know where I'd been.

'I didn't want to worry you,' I said.

'I wouldn't have worried about that, would I? We could have got them done together.'

'I found a lump,' I said.

He sat in the chair next to me. 'What?'

266

'I saw the doctor last week, when I said I was going to the shop next door. She's going to arrange a hospital appointment for a biopsy.'

He reached for my hand and I slid it from under my legs.

'Oh, Bee.' He put my hand to his face. 'Oh, Bee. Why didn't you tell me? I could've helped.'

'You've been so stressed with work and—'

'Please don't keep something like this from me again,' he said. 'We're a team.' A tear ran down his face, onto my hand and down my wrist. 'I don't think I could live without you.'

'I'm sure it'll be fine.'

'I'll come with you to the hospital, OK?'

'OK.' I got up and picked up his coat from where he'd dumped it on the floor. 'Is it OK if I go back to sleep – I'm drained.'

'Of course,' he said. 'My poor little Bee. You must be exhausted from all the worry.'

I waited as he got up and staggered to the living room. I didn't want him looking in the cupboard under the stairs where my suitcase had been for the past four weeks. I just had to work out where he'd hidden my birth certificate and passport. The solicitor said to get my marriage certificate, too, if I could find it.

But I'd have gone without them.

There was another sound now, coming from upstairs. Dorothy couldn't be awake already.

I sat up too quickly and scanned the room. I had

vague recollections of talking with Brett all night. Or *someone* all night. God, I hoped it wasn't Louise's son, Jamie. I could've let something slip.

There was no sign of anyone or any—

Blood on the floorboards.

Shit. Had I hurt myself again? I always did that years ago when drunk, though never enough to leave a trail of blood. Just bruises on my arms, shins, the tops of my legs.

I swung them to the side and slid to the floor.

There were three circular drops in a line: the largest was the size of a two-pence piece. Dark red, almost maroon on the outside, and bright red at the centre.

Maybe it wasn't blood.

I looked around for an empty wine glass; there were two on my bedside cabinet, but I could see from here that neither had the remnants of red wine.

Did someone have a drink with me in here last night?

I reached over for my phone to look at the time but stopped when I saw my hands.

Brown and red coated my fingers. It was almost black under my fingernails.

I stood and scanned my clothes.

Tiny splatters were scattered on the pale blue blouse, and smears – five lines each side where my hands must have wiped.

I unzipped the trousers and unbuttoned the blouse, rolling them into a ball.

Fuck. They weren't mine to dispose of. I couldn't burn them in the fireplace like I had Matthew's shirt. I'd have to wash them with my other clothes and hope

Louise didn't ask for them back straight away. I stuffed them into a carrier bag next to the bed. I must have put it there in case I was sick in the night.

I sat on the edge of my bed in my underwear and thought back to some of the events I remembered last night: me revealed as the murderer; Dorothy saying she thought that all along; me thinking everyone knew what I had done to my husband. Did I tell everyone? Or had I just gone to bed? What time would it have been? Midnight? What time was it now?

I picked up my phone. Six minutes past six; it was too early to deal with these questions. I checked for any outgoing messages that I might have sent, but there were none. One less thing to worry about.

Nearly a month ago at the hotel, in a drunken mess at three in the afternoon, I had messaged Matthew's mum saying how sorry I was and that I hoped she would still think of me kindly. My face still burns with shame just thinking about it. She hadn't replied. I hoped she'd got a new number and hadn't read it at all.

I reached for the door.

Silence.

It was still early and hopefully it would be quiet for at least another few hours. Right now, I wanted Gemma here. I wanted her to tell me exactly what I did last night and not to worry because everyone makes mistakes, or for her to say that I wasn't bad at all, that I had been funny and everyone else was as drunk as I was.

But she wasn't there on the night Matthew died and she wasn't here now.

I was alone with blood on my hands.

Again.

I grabbed the dressing gown from the back of the door and dashed towards the bathroom. The door was open slightly and I pushed it open, my feet still on the landing carpet.

I smelt it before I saw it: blood. Lots of blood. On the floor, splattered on the walls; a trail of five lines across the mirror; splashes on the shower curtain. Toilet lid closed, sprays of red on white.

My knees gave way and I collapsed at the threshold.

What the hell had I done?

Chapter 39

Ever since he moved here, there hadn't been a quiet night. Gordon wasn't surprised his mother hadn't warned him; she didn't hear any of the noisy antics next door because she took out her hearing aid at night.

Gordon supposed, briefly, that a bestselling author added a little more fascination to his life, but without external stimuli, he had always been good at occupying himself. His mother often used to point it out to relatives when they judged him to be a painfully quiet child. She wasn't enamoured with his makeshift bug sanctuary with empty jars on his windowsill, though. 'Why have you pinned their wings to leaves?' she asked before throwing the lot in the bin. 'I hope they were already dead, Gordon,' she carried on, muttering something about serial killers practising on small creatures before turning their attention to human beings.

Gordon had only had three hours' sleep last night. It couldn't go on. Perhaps he could convince his mother to sell up and get somewhere smaller, perhaps near the countryside. But he knew what she'd say. She's never been one for living in the middle of nowhere. 'I like to hear people going about their business around me, so I know I'm not dead yet.'

Dorothy Winters had people around again last night. It was a wonder she got any writing done at all. It was probably the reason she hadn't had anything published in decades – just living on the minimal success of her past seven novels. They weren't up to much, but they might be generating a steady income. Perhaps there was something else going on in that house, but he didn't want to speculate about that.

Probably some kind of orgy, and she was the madame. He'd read about that scenario in one of the Sunday papers a few years ago, and apparently it was pretty lucrative. But then, so was drug dealing and there weren't enough comings and goings for *that*.

That said, he didn't see much evidence of anything illegal last night. He should have realised it was going to be a loud evening because there was a string of oddly dressed individuals making their way to number sixty-three. One of them looked strikingly like Adam from the library, but Gordon must be mistaken. He had never seen Dorothy in the library.

Even Mother had heard the shrieking. It started at nine o'clock in the evening as they were both watching the film *The Talented Mr Ripley*. It was a rare evening together; Gordon didn't fancy a night alone in front of his computer when he couldn't concentrate.

There's a murderer next door.

If someone could kill the person closest to them, what

else were they capable of? Had Bethany and Matthew been close – or did they have a relationship similar to that of him and Audrey? Ultimately, they had been strangers with only a sketch of what the other person was like.

'Good grief,' his mother had said, 'is someone being attacked next door?'

'I wouldn't be surprised if there was,' said Gordon.

'What do you mean?' she said. 'I was only joking.' She picked up the remote on the arm of her chair and turned the volume up to twenty-one. 'If they go on for much longer then you'll have to go round and have a word, Gordon.'

He glared at her, but she stared at the television, playing ignorant. Never in his life had he been the type of person to *go round and have a word*, and she knew that very well.

At 2 a.m., that Brett fella was sprawled on the grass. What surprised Gordon was that Bethany was lying next to him in very close proximity. As he watched her take a drag of Brett's cigarette, pass it back and lie down, Gordon found it difficult to imagine her stabbing her husband to death. Why the hell wasn't she in prison? There was talk online of him being abusive, but the victim's mother said that wasn't the case. He'd have to do a bit more digging on the subject. No one knew what went on in private. The shrieking from number sixty-three had turned into screaming at four o'clock this morning. It sounded like someone *was* being murdered.

He sat at his desk and switched the monitor back on.
The screen still showed the article about Bethany:

VICTIM'S MOTHER BLASTS THE CPS.

God knows what happened in that house last night,
but enough was enough.

He picked up his mobile and dialled the local police
station.

Chapter 40

I dressed quickly and rushed downstairs to the kitchen to wash my hands. It was still early and there was nothing downstairs to suggest that anything bad had happened last night.

I turned on the hot tap and waited until the steam came. I pumped the soap dispenser five times, coated my hands and lower arms with the gloopy liquid and placed them under the scalding water. I grabbed a scourer and scrubbed until my hands seemed to glow red.

I opened the cupboard under the sink, reached for the bleach and smothered the sponge with it. I couldn't leave any traces of blood on that – it would be mixed my skin cells. I doused the sink with the thick bleach and rubbed it clean with my hands, then gouged out the remaining blood from beneath my fingernails. I rinsed the sink, my hands, the cloth, with freezing cold water before drying my hands on three sheets of kitchen roll.

What should I do with them? There was a smoke alarm in the kitchen, so I couldn't burn them. The toilet. Scrunch them up and flush them away.

There was a scream from upstairs.

I stuffed the ball of kitchen roll into my jeans pocket and slowly walked down the hall and up the stairs, climbing two at a time as I neared the landing of the second floor.

Dorothy was standing at the doorway of the bathroom next to my room.

'What's happened?' I asked, standing next to her.

She pushed open the door; it slammed against the bath.

'Haven't you seen the blood?' Her skin was pale, and the spider veins across her cheeks were a map of tiny red rivers. She turned to face me. 'What happened here, Rachel? Has someone been hurt?'

'I ... I didn't see it,' I said. 'And I've no idea what happened.'

'But you *must've* seen it. It's *your* bathroom. Why didn't you come straight to me? What were you doing downstairs? Is anyone down there?'

'There's no one downstairs,' I said, even though I hadn't checked my office or Dorothy's study. I turned and gripped the banister. 'I'll double-check.'

'Double-check? How can you possibly miss an injured person lying in a room?'

My heart hammered as she followed me down the stairs. I opened my office door; pages of Dorothy's handwriting littered the floor. I rushed to the floor to gather them.

'Now's not the time for that,' she snapped. She walked along the hall and stopped at the cellar door, turning the handle. It was locked. 'I don't have a key to this door. No one could possibly have got themselves down there.'

'But it was open the other day,' I said, grabbing the handle and turning it, shaking it.

'Don't you believe me?' she said. 'It's never been opened. Not while I've been here.'

That couldn't be right. Why was she lying to me? I definitely went down there.

Didn't I?

I stayed in the hallway as she checked the library, the dining room and the kitchen. I prayed that I'd left no blood splatters in the sink, on the cupboard, on the floor.

She opened the back door and went outside.

I waited, shivering, even though I wasn't close to the cold air of the morning.

Dorothy slammed it shut as she came back inside.

'There's nothing outside,' she said. 'I need to check the second floor.'

'What should I do?'

She stopped and took hold of my left arm, holding it up. She pushed down the cuff of my jumper and ran her hand along it. She dropped it and did the same with my right.

'What are you doing?' I said.

'I'm making sure you haven't harmed yourself.'

'I would've told you.'

'I don't know you well enough to know that for sure, do I? I barely know you at all.'

I followed her upstairs again, like a puppy, as everyone else who knew her did.

I stayed near the first-floor window that overlooked the front garden as she checked the other bedroom. I heard her footsteps above me, the opening and shutting of doors. Outside, the early morning drizzle made everything look cloaked in mist. No one was outside – no one was looking out of the care home opposite, even though the lights were always on on the ground floor.

Dorothy walked slowly downstairs.

'What's wrong?' I gripped the edge of the window-sill. 'Is there someone hurt upstairs?'

'No,' she said. 'It's not that. But Brett's not in his room.'

'Perhaps he went home with someone. He was talking to Sophia all night, wasn't he?'

'He was talking to everyone last night, including you. Are you sure he's not in your room?' She strode towards my room and pushed open the door. 'Brett? Are you in here? Come on, darling. I'm as open-minded as they come.'

'He's not in there.'

She came out of the room and wiped the sweat from her forehead with the back of her hand. 'You're right, he's not.' She tried the door next to mine, reaching into her pocket for the keys after realising it was locked. I stayed on the landing and hoped that he had fallen asleep inside another room. 'Nothing.' She didn't lock the door behind her. She walked to the top of the staircase. 'Come on. Let's see if we can contact him.'

'It's only early,' I said, still clinging to the window-sill. 'Anything could've happened. Someone might've had a nosebleed or cut themselves on glass.'

'Yes, yes,' she said. 'It must be my overactive imagination ... it's what writers do, you see. Imagine every possible scenario when the truth is the simplest of explanations: Occam's Razor. Brett used to always go on about that ... so annoying.' She started down the stairs. 'But there was so much blood.'

'My sister Gemma used to have nosebleeds,' I said. 'It seemed like there were pints of it, but she was fine.'

'Yes, it's probably something like that, you're right. But Brett said he was staying for a few weeks. His clothes and his wallet are still in the room. It's not like him.'

Banging came from the front door. I looked out of the window.

My stomach contracted; a flash of pain across my chest. My knuckles were white.

A police car was parked outside the house.

Chapter 41

I ducked below the windowsill, even though from this angle they couldn't see me from the front door. The sound of blood pumping raced in my ears; dots of light flashed in front of my eyes. I couldn't be found at another scene like this. There was no way they would believe I had nothing to do with this after what happened to Matthew.

'Well?' Dorothy's feet were now behind me; the woman loomed over me.

'It's the police,' I said in little more than a whisper. 'What if they've found a body?' I leant against the wall under the window. 'Have they got their hats on or off?'

She stood on tiptoes and leant over me, trying to see the officers at the door. 'Their hats are on,' she said.

The police banged on the door again. They weren't going to go away. '*We* don't know what happened in the bathroom last night — how can the police possibly know?' She breathed in deeply. 'Shit. I need to pull myself together. It's far too early. What do you think they want?'

'I don't know,' I said.

The letterbox flapped open – it echoed in the hallway.

'Dorothy Winters?' It was a male police officer. 'Can you open the door, please.'

'Right,' said Dorothy, a faraway look in her eyes. 'We can't just ignore them. You wait here and I'll see what they want.'

She dashed down the stairs.

'Good morning, officers,' she said, opening the front door. 'You're up nice and early.' There was a smile in her voice – she was so calm; it was as though there wasn't a blood-coated bathroom just a few metres above her. 'Is everything OK?'

'Can we come in?' said the officer. 'It's freezing out here.'

'Of course, of course,' said Dorothy. 'Would you like a hot drink?'

What the hell was she doing? Was she going to invite them to breakfast as well?

'No, thank you.'

I couldn't determine the tone of his voice. There was no way the police could know about the blood in the bathroom. Unless Louise had witnessed something and phoned them. She might have been the only one who knew what happened last night – she wasn't a big drinker.

'Come into the study,' said Dorothy.

The door to my office slammed shut. They would be seeing the pages all over the floor. Dorothy should've let me tidy them. Would she tell them it's my office? Might they check the search history on the computer – the articles I'd searched about Matthew? I lowered my head to the floor and pressed an ear into the carpet.

All I could hear was muffled voices. I stayed with my head resting on the floor and watched the seconds ticking on my watch. My stomach flipped with nausea. I must have drunk more than I thought last night. My mouth was dry and tasted bitter; my brain felt as though it had turned to stone.

It was me who called the police after Matthew died.

I was sitting in our bedroom, against the radiator under the window, for ten minutes after it happened. He was lying on the bed, his arm flopped over my side of the bed, his eyes fixed on the ceiling.

His blood had started to seep through to the bed covers underneath, slowly spreading like an ink stain on blotting paper.

I still had the knife in my hand when I got up. I clung to it as I walked down the stairs to the telephone in the hallway.

'Police, please,' I said when I was connected. I should've asked for an ambulance as well. 'I think I've killed my husband.'

The study door opened downstairs, thirteen minutes after they went in.

'Of course, officer,' said Dorothy.

It was the friendliest tone she'd spoken in since I'd known her.

'Bye now, Mrs Winters.'

Dorothy closed the door, bolted it quietly, and pushed across the chain and latch.

I got up from the floor and went to the top of the stairs as Dorothy walked back up, slowly, as if to prolong my agony.

'What did they want?' I said. 'Did you mention I was upstairs?'

Dorothy sat on the top step.

'No, I didn't,' she said. 'Why would I? They don't know about what happened in my bathroom. Do you think they'd have gone off with a cheerio if they thought something sinister had happened in this house?' Dorothy rubbed her face with both hands. 'I'm sorry. I didn't mean to snap. It was so stressful. That weirdo Gordon from next door complained about the noise last night.'

'Oh, thank God,' I whispered.

'He said there was banging and shouting last night. What were you and Brett up to ... before you went to sleep, that is?'

'I didn't hear any shouts or bangs,' I said. 'Something must've happened after I'd gone to bed.'

I put my head in my hands. I felt like crying, but the tears never came.

Dorothy sighed and leant on the banister.

I glanced at the bathroom door. I could almost taste the blood, though I must've been imagining it.

'You're shivering,' said Dorothy, rubbing my back.

'Can you ring Brett?' I said. 'Or some of the other guests. One of them will know what happened.'

She frowned. 'I was going to do that anyway.' She glanced at her watch. 'It's only just gone half seven. I don't know if they'll be up yet. It was a late night.'

'But this is worth waking them for, isn't it?'

She grabbed the banister and pulled herself up.

'Yes, it is.'

'What are we going to do about the blood? Should we clean it?'

'I think we should leave it until we know what happened,' she said. 'If you need to use the bathroom, use mine.' She began walking down the stairs. 'Try not to worry yourself. I'm sure there's a benign explanation for it all ... that it's not as bad as we think.'

I waited until she'd walked down the stairs, along the hall and closed the dining-room door before rushing up the second flight of stairs. I pushed open Dorothy's bathroom door and vomited into the toilet.

Chapter 42

Before I went back downstairs, I checked inside the room Brett had been staying in. Dorothy was right when she said that his wallet was still there – it was lying on the vanity table near the window, but the single mattress was bare and covered with an immaculate mattress protector. There was a chest in the corner; its top two drawers were filled with men's clothes. On a long table against the back wall were several taxidermy animals: a mouse sitting on top of a model spitfire, dressed in a leather jacket, helmet and flying goggles. Next to that, a fox with an angry snarl, wearing a yellow checked waistcoat, propped against a pile of books.

I wasn't surprised Dorothy kept these hidden away. Even by her standards, it was bizarre. How had Brett not had nightmares with these objects in view from the bed?

I closed the door and went down to the first floor. The curtains were closed in the room at the front of the house. The single bed was made, with a blue cornflower bedspread. Under the pillows was a folded silk nightdress. The room was so old-fashioned – one I imagined a grandmother's room might be like. The width of the dresser under the window was almost the size of the wall – nearly six foot long. On top, in the centre, was a large three-part mirror that looked straight out of an Argos catalogue in the eighti—

There was a thump against the window.

A rush of adrenaline flashed across my chest; my right arm raised itself, protecting my face.

What the hell? It was nearly twenty feet above the ground.

I leant over the dressing table and pulled aside the curtain. On the glass was an imprint – a grey and brown smudge the size of a football.

I rushed out of the room; the front door was open by the time I reached it.

Dorothy was standing near the small cellar window, tapping a bird with her foot.

'I'd say that was dead,' she said, kicking it again. 'Wouldn't you?'

The poor thing still had its eyes open.

'Perhaps it's just stunned,' I said, bending down. 'Look. It's staring at the sky, wishing it was up there.'

Dorothy grabbed a stick. 'Don't be sentimental, Rachel.'

She poked it and flipped it over.

'Wait,' I said, picking up a smaller twig to spin it back over.

I picked up a brown leaf and placed it over its chest.

'You're not going to try to resuscitate a pigeon, are you?' said Dorothy.

'No. I'm feeling to see if it's still breathing. I didn't want to touch it – pigeons carry disease.'

'I imagine they do.' She crouched down to look closely. 'So, is it alive, Dr Rachel?'

I closed my eyes, but no amount of wishful thinking would make the bird start breathing again.

'No.'

Dorothy got up and walked into the house, coming out a few moments later with a carrier bag. She picked up the pigeon and placed it in the bag. She flipped open the lid of the wheelie bin and dropped the dead bird inside.

'I don't think we're meant to put dead animals in the bin,' I said. 'We should bury it.'

'Ugh,' she said, ignoring me. 'I need to disinfect my hands now.'

She went back inside, and I looked up at the house. The mark of the bird on the window looked like the shadow of an angel. My eyes wandered across to the house next door. There he was – standing by his living-room window, holding his mobile phone up.

I walked towards Gordon. Bloody shameless, that man. Filming me after trying to tend to a dead bird had to be the strangest thing I'd seen.

I stopped at the small boundary wall that divided us.

Slowly, he lowered his phone and had the grace to slightly wince and bite his bottom lip. He mouthed the words, 'I'm sorry.'

'We couldn't save it,' I said, not knowing if he was sorry for filming me or for the poor bird.

I went inside, still shaking. Anxious was my new normal; it seemed to follow me wherever I went. I supposed that happened when you took another person's life.

In the kitchen, Dorothy was scrubbing her hands with a nail brush at the sink. I stood behind her, looking out at the brick wall.

'Are you OK?' she asked, turning the tap off. 'This has been such a peculiar morning.'

'Have you managed to contact anyone from last night?'

Dorothy grabbed a tea towel and briskly dried her hands. 'No one's answering yet, but I'm not surprised given the hour. The only reason I woke so early was because I heard—'

'Good morning, ladies.' Louise stood at the kitchen door. 'Are we having a crack-of-dawn meeting?'

She smiled and placed a bag for life on the kitchen counter. It looked as though it had exhausted three lifetimes already.

'They didn't have Wensleydale,' she said, unpacking the groceries, 'so I got Cheshire. They taste almost the same, don't they?'

'For God's sake, Lou,' said Dorothy, walking towards the door. 'I don't care what bloody cheese you bought.'

She walked out and her study door slammed shut.

'Oh dear,' said Louise. 'Someone woke up a little too early. Perhaps she's near the end of the book and wants to crack on.'

'I don't think so,' I said. 'She gave me about fifty new

pages yesterday. And from what I've read, it's nowhere near the end.'

Louise frowned.

'Are you sure?' She put tins of soup, peas and coconut milk into the cupboard. 'She told me everything was coming together.'

'Perhaps she's getting to it in the pages she gave me last night,' I said. 'I haven't gone into my office yet. Have you heard about what happened?'

'No.'

She turned her back on me as she opened the fridge door. Was it meant to be a secret? Dorothy hadn't told me to keep it from Louise.

'The bathroom on the first floor,' I said. 'There's blood all over it. On the walls, floor, in the bath.'

Her arms stopped in mid-air and the weight of the two-litre milk carton made her hands shake. She shoved it into the door compartment and slowly closed the fridge.

'What do you mean *blood all over it*? Where has it come from?'

'I don't know.' I leant against the kitchen counter. 'And the police came around at seven this morning complaining about the noise. Gordon had rung them.'

'Oh.' She rubbed her face. 'I'd better take a look. Come and show me.'

I didn't want to – Louise knew where the bathroom was – but I went with her up the stairs, both of us in silence. She took a breath before pushing the bathroom door.

'Jesus.' She put a hand to her mouth. 'What the hell happened here?'

'I don't know.'

'What time did you go to bed?'

'I think it was about one-ish, but I can't really remember. There was so much champagne, so many cocktails. Did you stay last night?'

'No,' she said. 'I didn't have anything to drink after that shot of vodka, so I drove home about midnight.' She leant further into the bathroom. 'Has Dorothy talked to everyone from last night?'

'I don't know. She's in her study.'

'Right.' She closed the bathroom door. 'No one is to go in there. I'll go and have a word with her. We can't just leave it like that.' I raced down the stairs behind her. 'Why didn't she tell the police when they were here?' she asked.

'I think it was in case someone had a nosebleed or something. She didn't want to waste their time, I guess.'

'Or maybe she doesn't want the police snooping around.'

'Why wouldn't she want them here?'

'I don't know.'

She reached the bottom of the stairs and walked into the library without saying anything more.

Was Dorothy hiding something?

It seemed I wasn't the only one keeping secrets.

Chapter 43

Gordon couldn't believe the police weren't more interested. Even after he told them that Ms Winters' soirees went on until the early hours almost every night. If he'd had the correct equipment to measure sound levels, he was confident they'd have exceeded the permitted levels. The police officer with the ridiculous moustache (it wasn't the eighties any more, fella) said that if the noise was above twenty-four decibels between 11 p.m. and 7 a.m. then it was a council matter anyway. Gordon would have to get one of those digital sound-level meters from Amazon. They sold everything on there. He couldn't buy anything in town these days because nearly everything had closed down. He boycotted Amazon for nearly ten years until he realised no one noticed and he really needed some haemorrhoid medication and was too embarrassed to go to Boots. When he'd tried to get it at Morrisons, the damn scales on the self-checkout didn't register the packet's weight. Cue a mortifying intervention from Sandra manning the masses of flashing red lights.

Gordon preferred to be anonymous. One who could disappear from a person's mind moments after they passed him on the street. It had happened to him a lot over the years, people not remembering his name.

Bethany from next door always remembered his name (though *he* needed to remember to use her alias in public – he didn't want to be the one to give her game away). From their conversation a few days ago, it was apparent she wasn't included in Dorothy's extracurricular activities, so hopefully the police presence next door wouldn't have been a worry for her.

It was as though they had a connection – or perhaps it was his morbid fascination with her. He'd watched plenty of true crime documentaries on Netflix and always wondered if he'd recognise a murderer if he met one. He didn't, as it happened. Then again, if a murderer looked like a murderer, there would be no need for a judge and jury.

He'd used Bethany's computer after she'd finished with it at the library the other day and he'd been thinking about it ever since. She was so distracted when she left, she didn't notice him, and didn't think to log out and clear her search history.

'Did you hear that, Gordon?' shouted Mother.

She was sitting near the living-room window. Obviously *Good Morning Britain* wasn't holding her attention.

Mother was always hearing something. Probably the sounds in her own mind.

'Gordon!' she hollered again. 'There was a bang from next door!'

She hammered her stick three times on the floor.

'You're not upstairs, Mum,' he said, walking into the room. 'There's no point doing that.'

'So, you *did* hear me,' she said. 'There's some commotion outside. Come and be my eyes and tell me what's going on.'

'You're not blind, Mum,' he said.

Just blinking lazy. He swept the net curtains aside and stood at the bay window.

'What's happening?' she said. 'Has someone died?'

He leant closer to the window, resting his hand on the sill. Dorothy and Bethany were only a few feet away, kneeling on the grass.

'They're poking at a dead body,' he said.

Bethany had a husband; now he's dead.

Gordon's wife was still alive. Mother never liked her. He wasn't sure *he* liked her either. The feeling was probably mutual. People who stuck together through habit rather than love. Would he feel more affection towards her if she were dead?

'They never are!' said Mother. 'A dead body!'

He glanced behind; she had a hand to her mouth.

'With a stick!' he said. 'The new woman is putting her fingers on its chest.'

'Her fingers? How very odd. Who is it?' she said. 'Whose is the body?'

How long could he keep this up for before she actually got up from her chair to have a nose for herself?

'I can't see from here,' he said.

'Film it on your phone, Gordon,' she said. 'Don't let me miss this.'

'It's a bit macabre,' he said, getting out his phone anyway.

Dorothy Winters went inside and left Bethany kneeling before the fat dead pigeon. Horrible things. Carry all sorts of disease. What was that expression on her face? She looked at the dead bird with such pity. Had she looked at her husband like that after she'd stabbed him in the heart? Did she love him more after she killed him? There were reports that said she had acted in self-defence. Matthew's mother said otherwise. 'Everyone loved Matthew,' she was reported as saying. 'He would do anything for his family, for his wife. She wanted him out of the way because she was seeing someone else.'

Had that been true? Bethany hadn't given any interviews. She didn't have to of course – she'd had her life exposed in a courtroom. Why should she have fed the appetites of a hungry public to satisfy their need for entertainment?

Bethany stood and looked up to the sky. Was she a spiritual person?

Dorothy came out of the house with a Waitrose carrier bag. Typical Dorothy, flashing her cash. She was just like her books: style over substance. What was one of her opening lines? *Constance lay, incessantly, messily, weeping on the doorstep of Mr Powers' house; she happened to notice a crack at the bottom of the wood that had initiated a tiny, almost imperceptible, split to almost halfway up*. The *crack* certainly hadn't been a metaphor for anything in the rest of the melodramatic thriller. What a load of verbose rubbish.

Bethany looked as though she was about to cry when Dorothy put the bird in the carrier bag and flung it in the bin. When Ms Winters went back into the house, Bethany looked straight towards Gordon. What was she trying to convey to him? That her heart was breaking – could it be that she was projecting feelings about her dead husband onto the bird? He wanted to comfort her, tell her everything would be all right.

No. Bethany wasn't looking at him; she was staring at the phone in his hands. Oh Lord. How was he going to recover from this pickle? Slowly, he lowered the phone.

'I'm sorry,' he whispered.

She said something back, but he couldn't make out the words.

What was wrong with him? He was turning into one of those bizarre individuals who found killers so in-triguing, beguiling. He never understood it when he'd read about it.

'Why have you stopped filming, Gordon?' said Mother. 'Have the police arrived?'

'No,' he said through an almost-closed mouth.

'What did you say?' she said.

He watched as Bethany turned and went back inside number sixty-three.

'For goodness' sake, Gordon,' said Mother. 'Don't leave me hanging.'

'It was a bird, Mum,' he said. 'Just a bird.'

He drew the net curtain across.

'Oh, you're such a card, Gordon. You had me going then,' she said, giggling. 'There was me thinking we had a dead body on our hands.'

'Not yet, Mother,' he said, walking across to tuck her blanket in at the sides. 'Would you like a tea?'

'You're a good boy, love. Let's have a biscuit as well, shall we?'

He wandered into the kitchen. He'd read the articles about how she'd plunged the knife into his chest. He wondered if Dorothy knew she was sharing her house with a killer. Gordon smiled.

'Yes, Mum,' he shouted. 'Good idea. I'll open a packet of fig rolls.'

Chapter 44

Kathryn stood outside the terraced house. It hadn't changed from the outside: the same red front door with a gold knocker. She couldn't hear a sound from inside, but that didn't mean there was no one inside.

Kathryn brought a hand up to knock on the door.

In some way, she hoped it wouldn't be answered. She'd been in Bolton for nearly three weeks and it had taken her three trips to this street to come to the door and think about what she was going to say.

No, she wasn't ready for this yet. She wanted to get her life in better order, to appear settled with a job and a place of her own. But she'd turned up again like a vagabond, a wandering soul. A bad penny.

Yet, she couldn't wait another month, another year, another decade. She might be dead in ten years. She'd been away too long. The longer it had been, the harder it was to come home. Why should she feel guilty? It had been in everyone's best interests for her sister to look after the child.

Her hand still lingered in the air as the door flew open.

Kathryn hadn't seen her for nearly fifteen years. She used to love her long blonde hair, but now it was cut short and was blonde with white highlights.

Chrissie's eyes narrowed.

'Jesus fucking Christ,' she said. 'What the hell are you doing back?'

'I . . .' said Kathryn. 'I got your letter.'

'But that was nearly a year ago.' She reached out and touched Kathryn's hair. 'It's like bloody straw. Since when have you been blonde?'

There were tears in her sister's eyes. Kathryn had half expected her to slam the door in her face or to be chased down the street, and she had been prepared for that. She'd saved her heels for a proper reunion when she could look the part for Andrew.

Chrissie peered out of the door, no doubt looking for neighbours having a nose.

'I think you'd better come in.'

Kathryn followed her into the living room. The narrow hallway was nothing like it used to be. The tatty carpet had been taken up and the floorboards sanded; the radiator was hidden under an intricate wooden cover. The cream living-room carpet was spotless, and in the fireplace was a log burner instead of the old gas fire with the plastic light-up coal. There were family photographs on the mantelpiece. On the living-room table was a half-completed jigsaw puzzle.

This was the life Kathryn could've had. Thank God she'd escaped.

Chrissie stood in the middle of the room and held

Kathryn by the tops of her arms. She was slightly anxious that her sister might slap her across the face.

'I can't believe you're standing in front of me,' she said, more tears forming in her eyes. 'I haven't heard from you in so long. I thought you might be dead.'

Kathryn wiped the tear that fell down her sister's cheek. Her hands were shaking. It didn't help that she'd had too much to drink last night. She should have had a quick shot of vodka before she left the B&B this morning. Chrissie probably thought she was nervous.

'Is she around?'

Her sister frowned.

'No,' she said. 'You're shaking, love. I'll go and put the kettle on, make you a nice cup of sweet tea.'

Kathryn's stomach churned at the thought of putting anything sweet in her mouth.

'Have you ...'

Her sister stopped at the living-room door and Kathryn nodded to where the drinks cabinet used to be.

'Have I what?' she said. 'Anything stronger?'

'It doesn't matter.'

'We don't tend to have drink in the house these days,' she said, walking out the room and into the kitchen.

It hit Kathryn that she didn't know her sister any more and nothing had stayed the same since she'd left. She had pictured everyone and everything on pause while she'd been away. Andrew had said to her before he left, 'You think the world revolves around you [he always talked in cliches] and that everything stops when you leave the room.' She wasn't like that at all,

299

she told him. He didn't believe her, and neither did she.

She perched on the settee. It was a mistake coming back. She did the whole *leaving her hometown* wrong. She should've changed her name and embarked on a profitable career. But she'd wasted her life yearning for a man she loathed, working crappy jobs and drinking in pubs with wasters. She deserved more than this – the nothing she'd ended up with.

Kathryn should've got up to look at the many family photos, been curious to see how they'd all got on, but she couldn't be bothered. She could try to sneak out of the front door and never return, but Chrissie came back into the room, carrying two mugs of tea.

She placed one on the carpet at Kathryn's feet.

'It's lovely in here,' said Kathryn.

'Not what you were expecting?' she said, one eyebrow raised. Kathryn always wanted to be able to do that, but never could. 'We had a lot of help from friends and family.'

Kathryn was dying to ask – she thought her sister might have mentioned something by now. She always loved having the high ground over Kathryn.

'I sent you another letter a couple of weeks ago,' said Chrissie, blowing onto her drink. 'But it was returned. It was lucky I put my address on the back, else I wouldn't have known you'd moved. Aren't you on the same mobile number?'

'I'm always changing mobiles,' said Kathryn. 'I usually get given other people's hand-me-downs.'

Kathryn felt her sister's eyes travel down her jeans

to her boots. She had deliberately dressed down for the visit.

'You know,' said Chrissie, 'I always thought I'd see you pop up on the television or in a magazine ... or maybe you'd marry a millionaire.'

'Or made a million pounds myself ...'

'Yes, I suppose that, too.'

Chrissie slurped her hot tea.

'What did it say?' said Kathryn. 'The letter?'

'She's getting married.'

Kathryn's hand had been reaching for the mug of tea, but she stopped. The nausea travelled from her stomach to her throat. Getting drunk last night had been a very bad idea.

'When?'

Kathryn should've been the first to know.

'Next month. She met him last year. She didn't want to waste time.'

'Do you think she'd meet with me? Has she talked about me at all?'

Chrissie placed her mug on the mantelpiece, rested her arms on the chair and crossed her legs.

'You look so different,' she said. 'Your hair. How do you get the blonde to look so natural?'

Kathryn put a hand through her hair.

'What makes you think it's not natural?'

'Come on, Kathy,' she said. 'I'm only blonde so my roots aren't as obvious. I went grey when I was twenty-one.'

'She hasn't talked about me, then?'

'Mum's been asking after you recently. Her health's not so good, you know. She wants to say goodbye before ...' Chrissie must've noticed Kathryn's blank expression. She pursed her lips before reaching into her bag and took out a small card. 'Her mobile number's on here.' She took out a pen and wrote on the back. 'She's on Manchester Road. They own the house, you know. She's done very well for herself.'

Kathryn took the card and ran her finger along the embossed lettering.

'Thank you,' she said. 'For everything. You know ...'

'She's still a bit troubled, you know.'

'What do you mean?'

'She hides it well, but as her ... as her guardian ... I know her better than anyone.'

'Do you think she'll talk to me?'

Her sister rolled her eyes.

'Why aren't you listening to me?' said Chrissie. 'Why is everything always about you?'

Kathryn stood and placed the card in her handbag.

'Thanks, Chrissie,' she said, walking down the hall towards the front door. 'I'll be in touch.'

She was fed up with those words: *everything is always about you*. People said it in such a negative way. Chrissie wouldn't have had the chance to be a mother if it wasn't for Kathryn.

From the corner of her eye, she saw a pathetic figure walking on the opposite side of the road.

'Kathryn,' the old woman said. 'Is that you, love? Have you finally come home?'

302

'Oh, fuck off,' Kathryn hollered.

She was 99 per cent sure it was her mother.

Chapter 45

I listened at Dorothy's study door as she paced the length of the room, with a strange soft sound of marbles clanging. Worry beads perhaps. It must be unusual for Brett to go AWOL.

'I can hear you lingering outside, Rachel.' She opened the door. 'Just come in.'

There were shadows under Dorothy's eyes; they reached the top of her cheekbones. She was still wearing her dressing gown – the one Brett had been wearing. Did it smell of him? Technically, he wasn't missing. He just hadn't slept here. Dorothy wasn't his keeper.

She shuffled through the chapters I had printed. I couldn't remember the words; they hadn't registered.

Dorothy placed the pages on her desk and smoothed them with her palms.

'What do you think of the story so far?' she said. 'Does it make sense? Do the characters seem authentic?'

'I think so,' I said. 'Sometimes people marry people they don't love.' But those were the words I typed last week. Wales was today and Kathryn and Andrew had separated. Good on him. 'It's sad she couldn't get close to anyone. Did you purposefully create her to be a bit of a narcissist?'

'You think she didn't love him?' she said, ignoring my unqualified observation.

'Would she have been that mean to him if she did?'

Dorothy stood, walked to the front of the desk and perched on it. She crossed her legs and let her foot swing to and fro. 'You don't think love is more complicated than that?'

'Probably. But I said she didn't love him in the first place. I don't think she is capable of love or getting close to anyone. Why else abandon her child like that?'

Dorothy brought up a hand and examined her nails. She got up and went back to her seat. 'I suppose that's an issue close to your heart. Abandonment. I haven't experience of it myself.' She kicked the leg of her desk to make her chair swivel. She stared outside. 'Don't you think she's justified in her actions, though? I've tried to make it obvious that she'd been hurt in the past.'

'I ... I don't know.' I caught a glance of myself in the mirror. I hadn't even brushed my hair; a halo of frizz made me look wild, unkempt. My eyes, like Dorothy's, had dark circles and my skin was pale – even my lips. It was as though it were *my* blood that had been drained onto the bathroom floor. 'Did you manage to contact everyone from the party?'

She swivelled back to face me. 'Most of them. Gillian said she and Jamie left together at about one – though I can't remember that. What an odd pairing. They must've left without saying goodbye, which is a bit ungrateful if you ask me, considering the effort I put into the night.' She rubbed her right temple. 'I can't get hold of Brett or Sophia. I asked Gillian if anyone had had an accident or a nosebleed, but she couldn't recall.' She bit her bottom lip. 'Of course, Gillian wouldn't notice anything apart from what *she* was doing. So self-involved, that woman. Perhaps Sophia and Brett spent the night together.' She frowned. 'But I just can't imagine that.'

The landline on her desk began to ring. Dorothy grabbed the handset. 'Brett, is that you?' Her shoulders dropped as she listened to the voice down the line. 'Oh. I see ... yes .... OK ... Well, let me know if you hear anything.' She replaced it in the cradle without saying goodbye. 'That was Sophia returning my call.' Her gaze lingered on the telephone. 'She said Louise gave her a lift home at around two. It seems you were the only one left with Brett. Are you sure you can't remember anything?'

'I'm sure.'

But I wasn't. Fragments of conversation, snapshots, were coming back to me.

Brett had been in my bedroom.

I switched on the television in my room to take the edge off the constant feeling of doom and the butterflies in my stomach. I put one of the unnamed videos into the player and recognised the music as soon as it started: *Anne of Green Gables*. Jenny had taped it on big cassettes and one summer holiday I watched the whole series at least three times.

I plugged my phone into the charger, got into bed, propping the pillow higher, and typed Brett's name into Safari. There were no new articles, no missing person reports, but then he'd only been out of contact for a few hours. He was old enough to look after himself. He'd probably gone home to his wife. That was probably the real reason Dorothy was so pissed off.

I tapped the link to Brett Daniel's author website. It was just one static page that looked like it had been created in the nineties. The background was mustard yellow, and the 12-point Arial font was in blue. It was migraine-inducing. The author photo was of him looking out to sea, standing at the edge of a cliff.

I clicked onto his bio section.

Brett Sean Daniels grew up in a small coastal town in East Yorkshire. His first novel Oath of Titania *was published in 1999. If you have a question for Brett, please fill in the contact form below.*

There were no details about his family. The whole site was sparse, an afterthought. It was a pointless search. I put my mobile in the bedside drawer, got under the covers and pulled them up to my chin.

Brett had to be somewhere. He'd probably got annoyed with Dorothy bossing him around all the time, although he could certainly give back what he received, sometimes twice as bad.

But what if he *had* been hurt? He could be lying somewhere injured and no one was searching because no one outside this house knew he was missing. I had woken with blood on my hands and clothes, but how had it got there? It couldn't have been me who had harmed Brett, could it? I couldn't remember us arguing – I was sure he helped me to bed and that was that. Perhaps I'd used the bathroom in the middle of the night without turning the light on. That was the most obvious of scenarios.

I remembered everything about the night I killed Matthew. The questioning, the feeling as though it should've been me that night. It so easily could have. Would Matthew have been able to talk his way out of it? I could barely talk afterwards.

'I think I've killed my husband,' I told the woman on the end of the phone.

One of the paramedics had got up onto our bed.

'I think we're losing him,' he called out.

I should've felt concern. My husband was dying. But I didn't. What if he was going to live? What if he remembered what I did? I had no doubt that he wouldn't simply forgive me. If I didn't go to prison, he'd find me and kill me. He wouldn't stop until he did.

There were two police officers, a man, and a woman. They just appeared in front of me.

'Can you tell me what happened?' the woman said.

She knelt on the bedroom carpet next to me. She wouldn't look as sympathetic if she'd seen what I'd done. I opened my mouth to tell her, but I couldn't speak. My throat, my neck, was burning with pain.

'I stabbed him,' I whispered. 'I thought he was going to kill me.'

'Do you think you can stand?' she said.

I shook my head.

'How's he looking?' she said to the man tending to my husband.

I glanced at the paramedic and he pursed his lips, shaking his head slightly.

No. Matthew wasn't all right.

The two police officers didn't speak to me in the car on the way to the station; they didn't even talk amongst themselves. Voices sounded from their radios. I couldn't make out what they said.

I leant forward; the pain in my neck, shoulders and back almost made me vomit. Tears came to my eyes. 'Is he alive?' I whispered. I should've asked them earlier; they probably thought I didn't care. The one sitting next to me looked at me. 'Is my husband alive?'

He shrugged.

How did they see me? A crazy woman who could've been possessed by jealousy. Or perhaps they suspected I wasn't married to him – that I was a stalker who'd broken into his house. They didn't know me. They didn't know him. Would they believe anything I said, if I could do this to someone? I hadn't run away, though. I called them. I told them what I'd done. Should I have confessed so early? Didn't criminals usually say *no comment*. But they'd said, 'You do not have to say anything. But, it may harm your defence if you do not mention when questioned something you later rely on in court.' If I said nothing, would it imply I had something to hide?

Inside the station, the custody officer read me my rights again.

'Do you understand?' said the man behind the screen.

I hesitated a little too long. 'Yes.'

'You've been arrested for attempted murder,' she said. 'Do you deny the offence?'

'I . . . I don't know what I'm meant to answer,' I said. 'I didn't mean to try to kill him. He was on top of me. His hands were around my neck.'

The man typed on the keyboard.

'How are you feeling right now?' he said, not unpleasantly. 'Are you feeling suicidal?'

'No, I'm OK,' I said.

Was OK the wrong word? Were they going to scrutinise every word I said or was he merely gauging if I was about to harm myself? I don't think anyone truly suicidal would admit to being so.

'Would you like to put anything else on record at this time?' he said.

'I thought he was going to kill me. Can I say that?'

The man nodded. 'Empty your pockets, please.'

I looked down at my green dress. 'I haven't any pockets. I've nothing on me. I'm not usually allowed outside the house. I haven't had a phone or my keys for weeks.'

He raised his eyebrows and gave a slight tilt of the head to the policewoman standing next to me.

The policewoman took me by the elbow and guided me through a set of doors and into a white room.

'I'm going to take off your clothes and then I will take photographs of your injuries. OK? And then when the doctor arrives, she can examine you.'

'OK.' I stood still as she unzipped my dress, trying to stop myself shaking so much; I held my arms up one by one as she slid off the sleeves. 'Why do you need it right now?'

'It'll be sent to Forensics.'

'But I admitted what I did.'

She handed me a change of clothes and said, 'You might change your story later.'

'So, we're just going to have a chat now,' said a detective, after I'd been photographed and taken to another room, 'about what happened tonight.'

'A chat?' I said. 'But I don't have anyone with me. I can have a solicitor, can't I?'

She took in a deep breath. She thought I'd let them just talk to me. A woman who'd just killed her husband and arrested with my hands already up. She probably thought I was stupid.

'OK,' she said. 'But you'll have to go into a cell until we can get one here.'

She shouted to the custody officer to bring the keys.

'Number eleven,' he said, looking down at my feet. Checking for shoelaces, perhaps, but I was only wearing the pumps they made me shove on my feet. 'You can keep those on.'

Inside the room was every bit as awful as I thought a cell would be. I hadn't been offered a phone call. I didn't know who I'd ring anyway. No one knew what Matthew was really like. I had been too ashamed to tell anyone.

311

The tears came fast when I thought about my family. What would Jenny and Phil think of me? They'd hate me. They'd regret ever laying eyes on me. All those years they'd given a home to me when they could've given my bed to someone who really deserved it. They should've let me stay in care. They were too good for me.

After what felt like hours, my cell door opened, and a woman clutching a sheet of paper was ushered in. She was wearing a navy trouser suit with a white blouse underneath. Her messy brown hair was pulled into a ponytail at the base of her neck.

She held her hand out to me.

'Heather Elliot,' she said, not looking me in the eye. 'I'm the duty solicitor. Do you want me to find us a room to chat in?'

'Here is fine.'

She sat on the bed next to me, opening her black leather satchel. She took out an A4 notepad and a pen.

'Can you give me your version of events this evening, please?'

'Straight to the point, then,' I said.

She rested her arms on the notepad on her knees. She rolled her eyes slightly, smiling.

'Sorry. It's been one of those days ... nights. I've barely had time to think.'

'Oh.'

She pulled out a pair of glasses from her jacket pocket and put them on. She scanned the piece of paper she'd walked in with and placed it next to her.

312

'So, you've been arrested for attempted murder. Can you tell me what happened?'

'He's not dead?'

She frowned. 'I'm not sure,' she said. 'That's what's written on your sheet.'

'Oh. Where do you want me to start?'

'Did you have an argument with your husband?'

'Can I say no comment?'

'Not to me, no.' She pursed her lips as though wanting to laugh. 'There'd be little point of that seeing as I'm the one who needs to know everything about your version of events.'

'Sorry.' I glanced at the camera fixed to the ceiling in the corner. 'I'm confused. I didn't know if they were watching.'

'Would it matter if they were?'

'I suppose not.'

'Shall we start from this morning? How were you and your husband then?'

So I told her. From the moment he woke me until the time the police arrived.

And she seemed to believe me.

'What happens next?' I asked.

'The case will be heard at Magistrates' Court in the morning, then you'll be detained on remand before a plea is entered at Crown. You'll likely be detained until the trial.'

'What will I plead?'

'It depends on what charge they put forward. If it's murder, then I will advise you to plead not guilty, with self-defence as a defence, so to speak. If it's man-slaughter, then the same defence would come into play. It really does depend on the case the police build for the CPS.'

'Will I go to prison for a long time?'

'You'll have to see what your defence team says. I've given you the basics, considering what occurred previously with your husband.'

Some people back at home, even now, thought I was a liar. But why would I have made all those things up about Matthew? I was planning to leave him – I was a strong person. Though that was possibly the reason why they *didn't* believe me. *Someone like her wouldn't have put up with shit from a bloke. Matthew would do anything for anyone. As if he kept her in the house without anyone realising.*

But life was far more complicated than that. If they'd been present at my trial, they would have realised.

Now, Brett was missing. If anything had happened to him, people might think I'd harmed him. They'd say I shouldn't get away with murder a second time.

Outside, the windchime jingled in Dorothy's garden.

I knelt on the bed and opened the curtains. The lamp post on the street behind cast light into the back garden. A figure stood close to the tree with their hands in pockets. A long coat flapped in the wind. I couldn't tell if it was a man or a woman – or if he or she faced me.

I flicked off the lamp to help me see more clearly, but when I went back to the window, the figure had gone.

Chapter 46

Gordon reached over to his Fitbit and tapped it for the time. Half past five in the morning. He'd only had three hours' sleep – again – but this time he couldn't blame the residents of number sixty-three. For the second time in as many days, it had been perfectly quiet. There had been no loud noises, no parties, no shrieking or shouting. He had definitely made the right decision in contacting the police. Dorothy had completely surprised him. She must have respect for authority after all.

But what if his hypothesis had been misdirected? It wasn't in the realms of improbability for Bethany to have *silenced* Dorothy. That she'd become so tortured by the incessant noise that she . . . No, no. His night-time mind was taking over now. Such a ridiculous notion. The kind-hearted Bethany wouldn't take a pensioner's life merely because she partied too much. He'd read the posts on Facebook and Websleuths. Many theorised that Bethany was a victim of her husband's sociopathic tendencies. During her trial, several followed the live updates, the evidence pointing to a man who tracked his wife, keeping her a virtual prisoner. There were only a few who hollered from their keyboards that it was a miscarriage of justice and that Bethany had contrived the story of her husband's abuse.

Unless there was something he wasn't seeing. Why would Bethany have come here? She must have felt the need to hide from something or someone for her to change her name and start a new life. Or, more realistically, perhaps life had become too hard for her in the town where it had happened. Her husband's friends and family were vocal enough about it all.

'For heaven's sake.'

Gordon got out of bed and put on his robe that was draped across the clothes chair. He might as well do something useful with his time other than mulling things over lying down. He'd check the rest of the camera footage from the other night – the night before everything went quiet. He'd checked the rear cameras yesterday, but the past few days had been full of interruptions and he hadn't been able to check the rest. It would be good to get a couple of hours' peace before Mother woke.

First, though: coffee.

It was deathly quiet on the landing. He poked his head around his mother's door and, satisfied that it was *her* breathing and not only the cat's, he went downstairs.

He stopped at the bottom of the stairs. There was a strange sort of whimpering from next door, like whoever it was, was trying not to be heard. He couldn't tell which of the three women it was. Louise, more often than not, went home at around seven each evening, so chances were it wasn't her.

He put an ear to the wall. It was surprising how much could be heard when there was no ambient noise from either side. He pictured the woman crying being Bethany, draped along a chaise longue and dressed in a cream silk nightdress that skimmed her knees.

'Hey,' the woman whispered after several minutes. 'It's me.'

She must have been on the phone because there was no obvious reply.

'You have to,' she said, her voice high-pitched. 'It's only for a few more days.' She sniffed as she listened to the person on the other end of the telephone. 'It's the only way I'll get over him being gone.' She wasn't whispering any more. 'I know. I'll make it up to you.'

He leant closer to the wall; his cheek squashed.

'I ...'

Her voice was close. She must have moved; he couldn't hear footsteps. Could she sense him listening at the wall? Maybe they were kindred spirits with a psychic connection.

'I miss him so much,' she said. 'I know I've no right to ... ' She sighed. 'You can't say anything to anyone. Not yet.'

He wished she would put the speakerphone on.

Bethany must've been talking to a confidante. Keeping a secret — and such a big secret of murder — when it happened two years ago must've been difficult for

317

her. And after spending such a long time in prison on remand ...

He heard his heartbeat through his ears when there was silence from the other side.

Music began playing.

'Dream a Little Dream of Me'. The song that had played nearly every night since he moved in.

It wasn't Bethany at all. It was Dorothy.

Chapter 47

It had been three days since the party and three days since anyone had heard from Brett. Yesterday, I sat at my desk for most of the day before Dorothy came in at three in the afternoon. I asked her if she'd heard from him – the same question I asked every time I saw her, but the answer was always no. 'His wife hasn't heard from him either,' she said.

The blood still covered the bathroom. Every time I walked past it, it felt like the second hand of a clock tick-ticking, counting the hours until someone came to take me away. Should I take charge and just call the police – get it over and done with?

I half expected Brett to be in the kitchen when I walked in this morning, dressed again in Dorothy's dressing gown, having a sneaky cigarette at the back door. But he wasn't.

I opened the back door, and my eyes were drawn to light footprints on the damp grass down to the shed at the bottom of the garden. Curtains – shabby, faded blue, hanging from a loose cord – were closed across the small window to the right of the door. They might have always been closed, but I couldn't recall.

I walked to the edge of the grass and placed a foot on top of one of the prints. The same size as mine – size six.

'Nice morning again.'

I knew before I looked over the wall that it was Gordon, the ever-present observer.

I withdrew my foot from the damp grass.

'Did you see who walked across here this morning?'

His nostrils flared slightly. 'No. Was it someone who wasn't meant to be there?'

'I don't know.' The morning sun flashed in my eyes. 'Have you seen Brett recently? We haven't seen him since the other night and he's not been in contact with Dorothy.'

'I haven't, Rachel.' I suppressed a shiver. I didn't like the way he said my name as though we'd had more than brief polite conversations. 'I can check my CCTV for you. What times are we looking at?'

I hesitated. 'From about midnight on Friday ... anything you can find, really.' What if his cameras picked up something that *I* had done? Was Gordon the type to be discreet? 'I can't remember him leaving ... no one can.'

'Hmm,' he said. 'Brett's old enough to take care of himself, though, isn't he?' He narrowed his eyes. 'Has anything untoward happened in the house?'

Blood. Blood all over the bathroom.

'Not that I can see.' Technically it wasn't a lie. I couldn't see it right now.

'And if I find something ... shall I bring it round?'

'Yes please. Can you show it to me first? Just in case there's something too upsetting for Dorothy.'

'For God's sake, Gordon!'

Dorothy stood near the back door in fluffy heeled slippers and the same silk dressing gown. 'What on earth are you doing standing over the wall like that?' she said. 'Is this a Neighbourhood Watch meeting I've not been invited to?'

'We were just talking about the other night – Gordon thought he heard something strange through the walls ... just before Brett disappeared,' I said, feeling fleetingly guilty for pushing Gordon under the bus.

'Just the latest in a long line of conspiracy theories, eh, Gordon?'

'No!' He stepped down from whatever was propping him up. 'I was only trying to make conversation.'

Dorothy almost dragged me back into the house.

'Fucking hell, Rachel,' she said when the door was closed. 'Do I have to keep watch over you all the fucking time? You probably know by now that the man next door doesn't have any good intentions. He has no life and makes other people's business *his* business. Remember he called the police on us? Or had you forgotten about that?'

'You don't think someone's hurt Brett, do you? I kept it light in front of Gordon, but perhaps he hurt himself.'

Dorothy let go of my arm.

'No, no,' she said. 'He wasn't suicidal. He would've left a note. You know how much he loved talking and letting everyone know his opinions.'

She paced the short space between the sink and the kitchen door. She'd used the past tense: *loved*. She'd done that before, but I'd dismissed it as a mistake.

'You were the only one left with him at the end of the night. Perhaps if you were hypnotised, you'd be able to remember.' She leant against the sink. 'Do *you* have any theories about what happened to him? Is this all an act you're putting on, so I don't think you're to blame?'

'Hypnotised?' I said, my voice too high. 'I'm to blame? This is getting ridiculous, now. I'm going to call the police.'

Dorothy turned her head and looked at every part of my face. She narrowed her eyes slightly before raising her eyebrows. What was going on in her head?

'Not yet,' she said. 'I was just thinking aloud. I'm sorry.' She turned round and clutched the sink. 'This is all one huge nightmare and soon I'm going to wake up.'

I rested a hand on her back, and she flinched slightly. Was she afraid of me?

'I'm sorry,' I said. 'I didn't mean to talk to him next door.'

'I don't know what happened to him,' said Dorothy. She turned to face me. 'I think we *should* contact the police.' She stood straight and smoothed down her hair. 'Don't you think? If I don't hear from him by the end of play today, I'll call them myself.'

Did she really suspect me of hurting her friend? If she suspected that, wouldn't she have contacted the police as soon as she saw the bathroom?

I would have to tell the police my real name.

Everyone would know who I really was. And the nightmare would begin again.

Normal. I was going to try to act normally. Brett was probably hiding somewhere. Yes, Dorothy had said something to him, and he was teaching her a lesson. There must have been more to their relationship than just banter.

The list of tasks Dorothy had left me was verging on ridiculous and looked as though she must have been drunk while writing it. I couldn't concentrate and my gaze was drawn out of the window. Two ambulances were parked outside the care home; someone, covered in a blanket, was being carried out on a stretcher. After only a few weeks of staying here, this was the third person. At least this one had a mask over their face – at least they were still alive. The other two weren't so lucky.

I was surrounded by death. This house seemed to have brought to the fore all the memories I had buried about Matthew: the moment we met, the wedding and honeymoon, the night I killed him.

I opened the laptop and clicked on a tab I'd saved in the background.

GETTING AWAY WITH MURDER:
IS EMOTIONAL ABUSE OFFICIALLY CLASSED
AS DANGEROUS AS DOMESTIC VIOLENCE?

Matthew's face stared out from the page. I was in this picture, too, but this website pixelated my face.

God knows why they did that. My name was linked to hundreds of articles from the minute I was charged. But then came the lull, when I was in prison on remand and there was no new information for people to feed on.

After I appeared at the Magistrates' Court, I was guided back into the van, placed on a seat in the back, and locked in a tiny compartment. I couldn't think where the nearest women's prison was. Manchester, Warrington?

After forty minutes, the van stopped. I was ushered out and taken through two sets of doors, each one locked. I was stopped at a desk in front of a woman behind a plastic screen. People were either grabbing me or keeping their distance from me as though I were a leper.

'Bethany Arnold, date of birth 13 November 1985?'

'Yes.'

'Any personal possessions on you?'

'No.'

She tapped on the keyboard before leading me through another set of doors. I knew what was coming: they were going to search me. I felt like curling up in a ball and sobbing in the corner. In one of the booths, the prison officer patted me down. She lifted my arms, checked underneath, and put them down again; she slid her hands up and down my legs.

She stood aside and I chanced a glance at her. She wore no make-up, and her hair was scraped back. Her face was friendly; her cheeks flushed, which gave her a healthy glow like she should've been out hiking on the moors instead of intimately searching women.

'I know this isn't pleasant, love. It's not great for either of us. I need to search you, but we'll do it in stages. Take the top and trousers off first.'

I did as I was told, undressing in front of a stranger, trying to protect my mind by taking it elsewhere, but it wasn't working.

She lifted up my arms, looked in my ears. God knows what people could hide in there. She reached across and handed me a jumper.

'Now the crap part, pardon the pun.' She pointed to my underwear. 'Don't worry, it's not invasive.'

Her version of invasive and mine were two different things.

'That's it,' she said, handing me a pair of tracksuit bottoms that didn't match the jumper. 'All done. I'd say the hard part's over, but you probably realise it's not.'

'Is it awful in here?' I asked.

'It's what you make it, love. You just have to change your mindset.' She folded the clothes I'd arrived in. 'Don't pine too much for the outside. You're waiting for trial, though, right?'

I nodded.

'I'm sure you'll be fine.' She said that to everyone, no doubt. 'Quick exam with the doctor and then we can move you on.'

I was ushered, yet again, into another room.

The doctor silently took my blood pressure and pulse while I sat in front of her. She stood to examine my neck, lifting my hair as she moved round. She scribbled something on her sheet of paper, before taking photos of my bruises.

The nurse next to her smiled at me. It was such a warm, genuine smile, I almost burst into tears.

'How are you feeling?' the nurse said. 'In yourself?'

'I don't know,' I said. 'I'm a little bit in shock. I don't know how I ended up in here.'

'It's a strange time,' she said. 'You're doing really well.'

'Thank you,' said the doctor, not looking up from her notes.

The nurse walked me to the door and that was my cue to leave.

'Bye, Bethany.'

'Bye.'

I was about to turn and ask her name, but the door closed. I wished she could come with me to wherever I was going.

More doors, yet another corridor. The floor reminded me of school — worn salmon-pink and scuffed. The prison officer opened the door to a room with six chairs bolted to the floor, off-yellow walls, and an insipid painting of a cottage in the countryside.

'Wait here until your name is called.'

She left, and the door slammed shut on its own.

There were three women already sitting down. One in a tracksuit, like me; the other two in their own clothes. One of them, a girl who looked to be barely eighteen, nodded at me. Another, slightly older, looked me up and down.

It was like a waiting room at a doctor's surgery.

'What you in for?' said the eighteen-year-old.

'My husband died.'

The two other women looked up.

'Did you kill him?'

She was leaning forward now, arms still folded.

'Not on purpose,' I said. 'What about you?'

She straightened up and crossed her legs.

'Assault,' she said. 'I was pissed at the time ... can't remember the details ... so I'm pleading not guilty ... but ...' She shrugged. 'That twat had it coming to him anyway.'

'Was he your husband? Boyfriend?'

'No. My brother.'

'Oh.'

'Well, stepbrother. My dad married his mum fifteen years ago ... known him fifteen years too long, the miserable, smarmy bastard.' She smiled. 'Robbie, not my dad. I'm Rosie, by the way. What do you do? ... For a living.'

'I presume nothing, now.'

She rolled her eyes.

'OK, clever clogs, what did you used to do? You look a bit too prim to be in here.'

'I worked in an office ... well, used to. I haven't had a job for over a year. He doesn't ... didn't like me going out much.' I was saying too much. 'What about you?'

She tilted her head to the side. 'Social worker.'

My mouth dropped open a little. 'Really?'

She bent over, laughing.

'No, not really. Bloody hell! You should've seen your face.' She rested an elbow on the back of her chair. 'But you should *assume nothing* in here.'

After half an hour or so we were led to our cell. The prison officer unlocked the door and instructed us to enter with an over-exaggerated tilt of the head.

Inside was exactly how I imagined it would be. A bunk against the left wall, shelving unit on the right. Further along was a sink separated by a low partition, and on the back wall was a toilet. I hadn't thought about the logistics of sharing a space with no barriers.

Rosie got onto the top bunk. 'Comfy as ever, Miss,' she shouted to the cheerless prison officer.

The door was closed then locked.

'You'll get to hate the sound of that soon,' said Rosie. 'The jangling keys of doom.' She lay on the bed and stared at the ceiling. 'If only all the bitches were as quiet as that one.'

There was tapping on the window above as two birds scrapped, flapping their wings on the glass. Rosie swivelled her head to look at them, resting her chin on the back of her hand.

'A welcome party,' she said. 'They're special, you know. A reminder.'

'Of what?'

'That there's life outside.'

She turned her gaze back to the ceiling and I sat on the edge of the bottom bunk. The mattress was almost as thin as the one at the police station. I shuffled my bottom backwards and brought my legs up onto the bed, laying my head down. I turned to face the wall. It was filthy, with God knows what smeared on it.

'Don't know about you, Beth,' said Rosie, the gentlest I'd heard her speak, 'but I'm fucking knackered. Let's have some quiet time, eh?'

I closed my eyes and realised I'd not thought about home for a good twenty minutes. The tears gathered behind my eyelids. I wished I could carry on blanking everything out, but I knew I'd have to relive it again at the trial.

I was on remand for almost a year. In court, my life was examined, prodded, talked about, and that didn't stop when it was all over.

Wonder what the statistics are for kids in care – going from one system to the prison system because they can't handle real life? said a pseudo-intellectual on one of the Facebook groups. *I'd almost forgotten about this case,* someone had written on a sleuthing forum. *Ooh, I've been waiting for this one. Nice to see some of you back here again for the trial. At last, we will find out what really happened. Shall we do a poll when the jury's deliberating?*

I looked at the picture of Matthew and me. I was sitting on his knee in this picture – on a rare night out together – and his arm was draped around my neck, almost covering my face.

Now, I held his gaze.

'Louise has called in sick,' said Dorothy, barging into the room. She looked at her watch. 'Is there any chance you could pop out to the bakery for me?' She passed me a five-pound note, warm from being in her clenched hand. 'A cheese and tomato on white bread. I'm feeling unhealthy.'

'Of course.'

She walked towards the door and stopped as she grasped the handle.

'Did she go to prison?' she said, not turning around. She had seen the article I was reading on the screen. 'The woman who killed her husband in that story.'

'On remand,' I said. 'But the jury found her not guilty of murder ... because of what she had to put up with.'

'Maybe it won't end that way in my story,' she said and closed the door.

I'd seen that look before. The way she regarded me with a suspicion, the slight narrowing of the eyes.

She knew about me, didn't she?

Chapter 48

Gordon recalled Dorothy's words he'd heard through the wall early this morning. A one-sided conversation only gave some insight to the issue and he'd made that mistake before. Gillian at the library had been talking loudly when she was sitting right opposite Gordon. 'Oh, I think he knows how I feel,' and 'I think I might have to suggest a meeting,' all the time giving Gordon pointed glances. He was smiling at her for a good hour afterwards until he realised she was talking to the Neighbourhood Watch co-ordinator John Crenshaw about fly-tipping. She probably did it on purpose to get Gordon's attention. Adam kept saying that she *has a thing* for Gordon, whatever that thing might be.

He didn't mind Gillian, though. She talked a bit too much, but at least there were no awkward silences with her around. Actually, there was no silence, full stop, with her around. Not Gordon's type at all. He always imagined too much with potential suitors – way past the enjoyable parts of getting to know each other, and straight to the living together part to see how that would work out. He decided that Gillian would take up too much of his time and he'd have to constantly explain his movements to her. And that ridiculous gossip column full of tittle-tattle.

Gordon poised his pen as he watched the camera feed from two nights ago. State-of-the-art gear, he had. No blurry images here. The faces walking towards Dorothy's house were as recognisable as they'd have been with his own eyes.

He made his notes on each of them as they walked across the front of his house.

Blonde woman (7:02 p.m.) Aged between 29–32.
Dressed in a flowing (organza?) blue dress, beige
stilettos. Smiling.
Brett (7:05 p.m.) Walked from the house to the end
of the path. Walks back again. Dressed in a dinner
suit (hired probably), clean-shaven (for a change).
Blank expression.
Unknown male (looks like Adam from a distance,
but unsure) (7:10 p.m.) Blue jeans, black leather
jacket, white T-shirt, aviator sunglasses.
Gillian (7:15 p.m.) Black trouser suit with huge
shoulder pads, white frilly shirt, bright red lipstick,
cigarette holder (no cigarette). NB must be fancy dress.

What a strange mixture of people. Why had Dorothy picked Gordon's friends from the library and not included him? It was almost cruel to exclude him. He wouldn't have minded dressing up for the occasion, too. He didn't know if it was malicious or thoughtless and he couldn't decide if he would rather be a victim of spite or not thought about at all. He recalled a quote he'd read once: *The opposite of love is not hate, it's indifference*, and the thought of not being considered by anyone made his heart hurt for a moment. What was the point of doing anything if no one ever noticed? Since his dad died, Gordon had moments where he asked himself, 'Would I be content if I were to die at this very moment?' and right now the answer was no.

He blinked the thought away, along with any tears that threatened to form.

There had been no activity from number sixty-three for hours as he tabbed the camera through ten-minute intervals. Two ambulances for the home opposite, though.

At just after one in the morning on the night in question, he spotted the man he'd originally thought was Adam arm in arm with Gillian, almost as though he was trying to keep her in a straight line. Without the sunglasses he was wearing earlier, it was obvious it wasn't his friend. It took him and Gillian about four minutes to walk the short distance the camera spanned.

At 01:42, Louise strode swiftly to the end of the path and waited while the young woman in the organza gown danced around on the grass barefoot as though she were performing a pagan ritual in a forest. The footage wasn't as good in the darkness, but he caught that Louise shouted something and the other woman bounded over and embraced her rather enthusiastically.

Louise bundled her into the passenger seat of the car before she drove them both away. At least she was the one sensible person in that house. He'd always liked Louise, from what he could tell from their sporadic and brief interactions.

Gordon checked the footage five minutes at a time until one o'clock the following afternoon. There was no sign of Brett Daniels leaving number sixty-three.

Brett was somewhere in that house. Gordon was sure of it.

Chapter 49

It was 3 a.m. and I couldn't sleep again. I hadn't slept properly for so long. It had been a week since the party and still no one had heard from Brett. I checked at least twenty times a day for news online that Brett's body had been discovered but found nothing.

I swung my legs off the bed and tiptoed towards the bookcase. It was a selection you'd expect to see in a guesthouse or an Airbnb – a mixture of old classics and new thrillers. I had read *The Thorn Birds* as a child; hardly appropriate reading for my eleven-year-old brain. I grabbed *Gone Girl* and flopped back down on the bed. After reading the blurb, which everyone knew by now, I knew I'd not be able to read it. The hostile relationship was too close to my own story.

I placed it on the bedside cabinet and flicked off the lamp. The tiny flowers of the wallpaper became faces that glared at me. Contorted faces on top of one another – their eyes black and their gaze unwavering. It was how I imagined hell to be: misery upon misery.

'Enough!'

I sat up and grabbed my handbag, sure that there were still some tablets in there. I had relied on them the nights before Matthew died, to be able to think clearly during the day. I took one from the blister packet and swallowed it with water.

A small blue light shone from the space in the gap where *Gone Girl* had been. What the hell was that? I slid from the bed and crawled towards it. It was a small black device that I recognised; there had been one in every room in our marital home: a camera.

I stood outside Dorothy's study. The feed from the camera probably went to her computer. If I could access it, I could see what really happened the night Brett went missing. Had Dorothy not even thought to check? I took her study key out of its box and put it into the lock. A sound coming from the kitchen stopped me turning it. I slid the key into my pocket.

A woman was singing.

Lavender's blue, dilly dilly. Lavender's green. When I am king, dilly dilly. You shall be queen.

I'd heard that before, though it wasn't Jenny who used to sing it.

I tiptoed towards the kitchen, taking shallow breaths, my heart pounding so hard I felt the pulse in my neck.

Louise was standing by the back door, drying a glass with a tea towel, wearing pyjama bottoms and a fleece jumper. Her eyes were fixed outside. She stopped singing and placed the glass on the counter. She turned to me and pointed to the garden.

'There's someone out there.'

'What?'

What was she doing here at this time? And why the hell was she singing lullabies if there was an intruder outside? I went to the door, and leant forward on the balls of my feet.

'It's the reflection of the downlights under the cupboards behind us,' I said. 'They're making shadows. There won't be anyone out there.'

Now would be the time to mention that I thought I saw Brett standing in the garden the other night.

Louise went to the switch and flicked off the lights.

'Do you see,' she said, 'over by the tree?'

'I can't see anything.'

'Shall I go outside and have a look?'

She grabbed hold of the tea towel again and held it to her chest.

'But we're safe in here,' I said.

Whenever I'd watched a film and a character went out to *investigate*, I was always slightly disappointed with them.

Louise took a knife from the wooden block. The blade was longer than her hand.

'We can take this,' she said. 'We've had some trouble in the past. They might've been tipped off that my son Jamie was here. He's been mixing with people he shouldn't.'

'Really?' I said, standing back. 'Shouldn't we call the police if you're worried? If you use that, *you'll* be the one who ends up being arrested, not whoever's trespassing.'

She shook her head quickly.

'I wasn't going to actually use it,' she hissed. 'But if you saw two crazy women holding knives running towards you in the darkness, wouldn't you scarper?'

Louise slid her feet into slippers and opened the back door. She grabbed a jacket hanging on the back of the door.

She stopped halfway down the garden, flashing the torch from her mobile across the darkness.

I dashed towards her. If there was someone else here, I wanted to be with the person holding the weapon.

'Well?' I said. 'See anything?'

'Shh.' She stopped. 'What was that?'

Rustling came from the hedge near the back fence.

'It's probably a bird or a cat or something,' I said.

She shone the light straight in my face. 'You're probably right. I've been a bit jumpy these past few days.' She lowered the light. 'Things have been a bit strange, haven't they? I didn't expect Jamie to come walking through the door the other night.'

It seemed as though she was trying to confide in me, but something was holding her back.

'Do you know what happened to Brett?' I said. 'Did you see it?'

'I don't know what you're trying to say,' she said. 'If I saw something, I would've said.'

'I think we'd better get inside,' I said, gently tugging her arm.

She took hold of my hand.

338

'I must've been mistaken,' she whispered. 'I don't think there's anyone here. We're OK.'

Her gaze was fixed on the kitchen window.

'Are you sure about that?' I said, looking up at next door.

A silhouette of a man stood at the bedroom window. The man who was always watching.

I closed my bedroom door and picked up the packet of pills, surprised that the one I'd taken half an hour ago wasn't having any effect. I took another from the foil. It would allow me six hours of blissful sleep.

I lay on the bed and waited for the darkness.

I reached into my pocket.

I still had the key to Dorothy's study.

Chapter 50

Gordon was standing at the counter of the library. He and Adam had shared some great conversations in the past because they were both intellectuals. Adam wasn't a person who would go blabbing, whatever Gordon shared with him.

'No,' said Adam. 'I haven't seen Brett Daniels.' He was busying himself with some paperwork. Always busy was Adam. 'He's only been in here a couple of times.'

'What did you make of him?' asked Gordon.

'He's OK,' he said. 'Not had anything published since the nineties from what I gathered.'

'That's what his website says,' said Gordon. He picked a speck of dust from the counter. 'He's not been seen since the party Dorothy hosted the other night. Rachel seems quite worried about him.'

Adam stopped writing.

'Really?' he said. 'Does she know him well?'

'Do I detect a hint of envy?'

'No, Gordon,' he said, smiling. 'Well, maybe a little.'

'I see.' Gordon drummed his fingers. 'A parcel came to mine by mistake the other day. I looked up the name online.'

'Oh, right,' said Adam.

He picked up the books accrued on the returns trolley, and Gordon followed him to the Science Fiction section.

'I saw you talking to Rachel the other day,' said Gordon. 'She's a bit of a closed book, so to speak. Do you know where she came from – what area, I mean?'

'You know I don't repeat other people's conversations, Gordon,' said Adam, putting two books on the shelf.

He couldn't tell if Adam was mocking him. He might have said those exact words to Adam in the past because he was once a firm believer in personal privacy.

'I know, I know,' he said, 'But I'm not asking to be nosy. The article I read seemed to suggest there was more to her story than she's letting on.'

'What story's that?'

'Oh, I don't know. I haven't put everything together just yet. I suppose what with Brett going missing ...'

'You don't seriously think Rachel's in danger, do you? Doesn't she work for a writer ... just typing and stuff?'

'No, no. It's more the other way round.'

'What do you mean?'

'Perhaps it's Dorothy who's in danger.' Adam pulled the trolley into the Romance section. 'You're more Rachel's age.' He followed the trolley again. 'Why don't you go round there and see if everything's all right. It wouldn't be too odd, would it?'

Adam folded his arms.

'You really have to take up a hobby, Gordon. Do you just sit at the window all day?'

'My CCTV sends notifications to my mobile if there's activity outside.'

He pulled out his phone and showed Adam his home screen.

'See. There are five already and it's only one o'clock. And this is just a small area covered by the camera.'

'Do you have CCTV of the night Brett went missing?'

'Actually, that's why I'm here,' he said. 'My printer's run out of ink and I need to print out the findings for Rachel.'

'For Rachel?' Adam frowned.

'Yes. I know it sounds odd, but I can't talk to Dorothy. She seems to dislike me.' He put his phone in his chest pocket. 'Has she lived here long? Dorothy, I mean. I expect she's lived here for years. Mother only started mentioning her when I moved in. She's not usually so discreet.'

'She arrived just a few weeks before you moved into your mum's, I think,' said Adam.

'And that is ...'

'About four and a half months.'

'Oh.'

'I know.' Adam folded his arms after he put *Outlander* back in its rightful place. 'And the strange thing is, I was sure that the author Dorothy Winters had died. Early

342

two thousand, I think. But I must've been mistaken.'

He watched Adam push his trolley away.

Gordon felt the butterflies in his stomach. He stood a little taller and fetched the memory stick from his pocket. He certainly hadn't expected this turn of events when he woke up this morning. He had a lot more investigating to do.

Gordon had printed off his findings and notes, detailing the comings and goings of number sixty-three, along with a complete list of Dorothy Winters' works. As he was about to pass through the gateposts to next door, the woman in question came out of the door.

He stopped on the footpath.

'What do you want now, Gordon?' she said. 'We are in the middle of something at the moment and I haven't got time for any more complaints.'

Gordon stepped aside as Dorothy headed straight towards him. If he hadn't moved, she would've most likely pushed him out of the way.

'I've got a few pages for Rachel,' he said.

She stopped and turned round.

'For God's sake, Gordon,' she said. 'It's embarrassing the way you're fawning after her. She's at least twenty years younger than you. Just leave her alone.'

'It's not like that ...' But she'd already begun to walk away. 'We seem to have got off on the wrong foot, Dorothy,' he shouted. 'But I can't think what I've done.'

She stopped, and it took her a few moments to turn round.

She walked slowly towards him. He had never seen her smile at him before. He grasped the pages in his hands a little tighter.

'Do you know,' she said, 'you're absolutely right. It would make things a whole lot easier if we could just get along. Or rather, just be like normal neighbours – brief hellos on the street, that sort of thing. Don't you think?'

'That would be nice,' he said.

'Well, I must be—'

'I've read all of your books,' he said.

He cursed himself. He didn't want to appear to be ingratiating. He could have worded it a little more carefully, but he hadn't had much time to think about it.

'That's very kind of you to say,' she said.

She smiled, but it wasn't a kind smile. Her eyes were lifeless; there was no shine to match her expression.

'My favourite,' he said, 'was *Judged for Revenge*. What inspired you to write such darkness? Especially when the wife killed her husband's parents. Don't you find yourself quite melancholy when you're writing?'

She frowned for a fleeting moment.

'*Judged for Revenge*?' She glanced at the pavement. 'Well, yes. I did have to go to the depths of my imagination for that one. You have to get into your character's mindset, you see.' She tilted her head to the side. 'Your mother told me you were trying your hand at writing.'

'That's right.'

'Well, any time you want me to look over your pages, just let me know.'

344

'Really?'

'Yes, of course.' Still with that plastered-on smile. 'I've got to be going now, Gordon. Bye for now.'

He walked up the path of number sixty-three, glancing at Dorothy as she walked to the end of the road, head tall, shoulders straight. The woman didn't seem worried at all about her friend Brett.

Judged for Revenge. It was a title Gordon had made up on the spot. None of Winters' books featured a woman who killed her husband's family.

Whoever that woman was, it wasn't Dorothy Winters.

Chapter 51

The flat Kathryn had been renting for the past couple of months was only a few streets away from her daughter's house. It was the same as all the other flats she'd rented in the past. Smelled slightly of damp; had crap furniture that hundreds of people had probably used. She tried to stay away from home as much as possible.

Maybe in the next few months she would contact Andrew again. She saw on Facebook that he'd come into some money now that his grandad had died, and his business was still doing well. The girlfriend with the huge brood seemed to be absent from his more recent photos, too. He was still in love with Kathryn and it was obvious he was waiting for her to feel the same. And she did – as much as she could.

She was sitting at a table in the pub next to one of her new friends. Kathryn was getting older now. She could put up with Andrew in exchange for the comfort he could offer her when she was supposed to be near retiring.

'I like this song, Kath,' said the woman next to her.

Her name was Sophia, and it didn't suit her at all. Kathryn had only met one Sophia before, and she had been shy and apologetic. This Sophia wasn't like that at all. She made Kathryn's name sound like a brand of beer, and she was the type to get proper fisty if someone argued with her. It was one of *those* pubs. And 'Kath' seemed to fit right in here. She fitted in well anywhere, really. If she didn't get too drunk and let rip what she really thought.

Lou walked in, ordered a drink, and sat at the table. She rolled her eyes at Kathryn while Sophia wasn't looking.

Kathryn shrugged and mouthed, 'Sorry.'

Bad timing.

'What you sorry for?' Sophia hollered, slightly swaying.

'She wasn't saying sorry,' said Lou. 'She was saying it's loud in here. Anyway,' she pushed her gin and tonic towards the one least in need of another drink, 'I bought a G&T for you.'

Sophia put a hand on her chest. 'For me?' she said, her eyes wide. 'No one ever buys me a drink.'

What a surprise.

'I'll just get mine,' said Lou, standing back up.

'Ooh,' says Sophia. 'There's that guy over there.' She tried to stand but almost tripped on a leg of a chair. She collapsed back on the chair. 'Think I need some Dutch courage.'

'That'll be it, love,' said Kathryn, giving her a wink. 'You'll be fine after another gin.'

347

God, she wished she didn't have to placate idiots.

Lou came back from the bar.

'We should've found somewhere else on our day off,' she said. 'We know too many people here. I could do with not seeing them.' She studied the rest of the pub. 'Come on, Kath,' she said, standing. 'Let's go into the restaurant. I can't hear myself think in here.'

'What about her?' said Kathryn. Sophia was resting her cheek on the table, dribble sliding out the corner of her mouth. 'We can't just leave her there.'

'Oh, can't we?'

Lou smiled and grabbed Sophia by the crook of her arm.

'Come on, Sophia, love,' she said. 'We're just going to move tables.'

'But I have to go over there,' said Sophia, looking down at the carpet.

'She'll go back to sleep when we've sat her down again,' Lou said over her shoulder.

'Eh, Kath,' shouted Steve the landlord. 'She's better off home.'

'She isn't. She's going to sleep it off with us. I don't trust her perv of a housemate when she's in this state.'

Kathryn lay Sophia down across one of the booths and she fell asleep.

'Thank God for that,' said Lou. 'One more drink and I reckon she'd have started a fight with an empty chair.'

Kathryn laughed. 'I feel sorry for her,' she said. 'She's not had it easy.'

'Nor has anyone,' said Lou. 'But sometimes people

have a choice. They can choose to wallow in misery and disappointment, or they can do something to change it.' Her head jerked towards the door as it slammed open, the colour draining from her face.

'Oh no.'

A man, tall, with a shaved head, stood next to another with greasy hair. They lingered near the doors as they surveyed the pub.

'Who are they?' said Kathryn.

She turned to Lou, who was pressing her back into the booth, desperately shielding her head behind Kathryn's shoulder.

'They came to our house a few nights ago,' she said, 'looking for Jamie. He owes them money, but he won't tell me why.'

Kathryn could feel Lou's legs shaking next to hers.

'I think they could seriously harm him.' She sniffed. 'Or even kill him.'

'How much does he owe them?'

'About five thousand pounds,' said Lou, her hands trembling as she put the drink to her lips.

'Shit, Lou.' Kathryn leant forward as the two men approached the dining area, turning her back on her friend. She was ready with a few choice words, were they to approach the table, but they barely glanced their way. 'They're going,' she hissed, watching them strut their way back through the pub. The taller one punched the door open.

She turned to face Lou. 'You can't live like this, Lou. You'll have to get Jamie to deal with it.'

'You know what he's like, Kath,' she said. 'Charms everyone to their faces but runs away when there's any real trouble. And it's not as though I have anything to sell.' Lou reached into her bag for her mobile phone and began texting. 'He'll have to stay with my mum for a while. His dad won't deal with him any more.'

Kathryn leant back in her seat.

Jesus. Her life wasn't going to get any better, was it?

Kathryn was sitting on a bench in front of the church near her daughter's house, but she hadn't arrived home from work yet. She'd been coming here every day since deciding now was the time they had a proper talk.

Kathryn looked out for the car; she was due home in ten minutes. She made up her mind that if she arrived alone, then she'd wait a few minutes before getting up, walking across the road and knocking on the door.

She spotted the car turning into the road.

She was alone. She got out of the car, walked through the gate and down the path.

Part of her wished that she hadn't been alone, that she could delay it for just one more day. But she couldn't procrastinate any longer.

Her legs shook as she stood, as she walked across the road.

She could walk away now – leave her to get on with her life.

But Kathryn rang the doorbell quickly before she changed her mind.

She opened the door after only a few seconds.

She narrowed her eyes at her.

'You've been watching me,' she said. 'Do you think I didn't notice? What the fuck is wrong with you? You're lucky I didn't call the police.'

She stood closer.

'I know you, don't I?' she said.

Kathryn thought she saw tears spring to her eyes.

'Yes,' said Kathryn. 'It's me.'

She took off her sunglasses; she'd forgotten she was wearing them.

Her daughter slammed the door in her face.

Chapter 52

Kathryn stood at the graveside. Her son's funeral was the one ceremony she'd been allowed to attend because he had no say whether she attended or not.

I paused typing and looked at Dorothy's handwritten page. It wasn't just one typo – the rest was the same. Kathryn had a son now. Was it intentional that she hadn't mentioned him before?

She would never be able to explain to him why she left him with her sister – how she thought he would have a better life with Christina than he ever would with Kathryn. She had rehearsed what she was going to say to him. Written it down as some of her best work. Now, he would never hear it.

Dorothy walked into my office clutching a new notebook. 'Hello, Rachel,' she said. 'I'm popping out for the afternoon. How are you going with the latest batch?'

'I've made a start, typing it word for word,' I said. 'Louise and Sophia will be pleased they get a mention.' I smiled at Dorothy, but her expression remained the same: mouth in a straight line, brows in a slight frown.

She was probably still suspicious of me after I found her lost study key. I turned to the screen and moved the cursor to the beginning of the new chapter. 'But you wrote that Kathryn has a son who's just died. He's never been mentioned before. Does she have two children?'

She placed the notebook on my desk.

'There's no new character, Rachel,' she said. 'Everything has slotted into place since I changed it. I can feel it now. It was always meant to be her son. There never was a daughter.'

'Shall I go back through the whole thing and change *she* to *he*?'

'That's right,' she said, looking out of the window. 'It shouldn't take much time, as she ... he isn't mentioned many times. Oh God, there's Gordon. Why is he always sneaking around? He really has nothing better to do, has he?'

'He's OK really,' I said. 'Perhaps if you were nicer to him, he'd leave you alone.'

'Hmm,' she said. 'Maybe. Ta-ta for now.'

I picked up the new notebook. The fleeting notion I'd had that Dorothy had been writing about my biological mother was ridiculous. The photograph in my file in her cabinet must be there by mistake – my details shoved in there with it.

In Dorothy's manuscript, *Chrissie*, Kathryn's sister, had become *Christina*. Writers probably changed things as they went along all the time.

Christina ... Tina.

No, no. I rested my forehead on the edge of the desk. This house was getting to me.

I sat straight and stretched my neck. It was going to take me hours to go through the whole thing again. I flicked on the radio. Perhaps a bit of background music and chatter wouldn't be a bad thing today. I made a note of the page number I was on and began to type the new pages:

Kathryn pushed open the doors to the police station, introduced herself to the woman behind the plastic screen and took a seat on one of the plastic chairs.

Just half an hour before she'd been standing at the foot of his grave; the grass was just beginning to grow on top – like wisps of baby hair – on what was a pile of earth. It would be another few months before the ground settled enough to install his headstone. She'd already ordered it – even though Christina had said she wanted a say in what it said.

'You always do this, Kathy,' she said. She wasn't angry when she said it – her sister hardly ever showed her anger. 'But I suppose it doesn't matter. It's just granite.'

'I haven't told them to just put my name on it, have I?' said Kathryn. 'I just wanted to pay for it. You can have what you want carved into the stone.'

But Kathryn didn't mean that, and her sister knew it.

'Beloved son of Kathryn and Jack.'

Because, in the end, those were the three names that mattered. Together forever in stone. Even if they weren't together now.

Gordon was walking quickly up the path, holding sheets of paper. He was almost smiling. He must've gone through his CCTV footage; Brett might have been caught leaving the house.

I jumped from my seat and answered the door as he lifted a hand to knock.

'Did the camera capture Brett leaving?' I asked.

Gordon handed me his printed sheets.

'I'm afraid not,' he said. 'I can't find any footage of him leaving the house since the night of the party.'

'Oh.' I flicked through and scanned his notes. They didn't tell me anything new, though my cheeks flushed when it described me sitting in the back garden with Brett. I'd had vague recollections of that, though I couldn't remember what we were talking about. The grass must've been freezing and damp. 'Do you want to come in? I think Dorothy's going to be out for the rest of the afternoon.'

'That'd be very nice. It's pretty chilly out here.' He stepped inside. 'Thank you.'

Chapter 53

Gordon had never been inside number sixty-three. It was very different to Mother's house – dark wood everywhere. Bethany was dressed in the same maroon-coloured jeans she was wearing the first day he saw her.

'How have they managed to squeeze in so many rooms?' he said, looking at the three doors leading off the hallway.

'Do you want to have a look around?' said Bethany, opening the door nearest the front. 'This is the office I work in. Go in if you like.'

Bethany's laptop was in the centre of her desk; a Word document was open. There were about a hundred more words on the screen than he'd ever written. In fiction, at least.

'That's Dorothy's new book,' she said.

'Oh, is it?' Gordon read the first few sentences. 'How's it coming along?'

She bit her bottom lip. He wanted her to tell him that it was the worst thing she'd ever read, but that might be a little vindictive.

'It's not bad,' she said. 'I'm not really taking to the main character. It's all a bit ...'

'A bit what?' Gordon sounded too keen; he needed to bring it down a notch.

'A bit pointless,' she said. 'I've been waiting for her – Kathryn – to kill someone, yet nothing like that has happened. She wanders from one place to the next and she doesn't feel anything for anyone else. Not enough to kill them.'

'What made you think she'd kill someone?' Gordon glanced again at the Word document.

'Dorothy asked me to research undetectable poisons.'

'Ah, I see. Perhaps she was asking for herself.' Gordon picked up the notebook and flicked through the pages; Bethany didn't try to stop him. Perhaps she wasn't as faithful as Dorothy expected. 'And is it like her previous works? Can you tell it's written by the same author?'

'I guess all books are edited quite a bit, aren't they? I've had a lot of time to look into it all because I had the same questions you have. It doesn't seem anything like the rest of her books.'

Gordon replaced the notebook and stepped towards the fireplace. What a ghastly painting. Fancy having to work with that grim bunch all day.

'Can't you put a cover over that?' he said. 'I wouldn't want that lot watching me.'

Bethany laughed lightly.

'I've gotten used to them,' she said. 'I've given them names. And backstories. People don't seem as

357

frightening when you know a little more about them.'

'That's very true,' he said. 'And how much do you know about Dorothy?'

Her head jolted to the side. 'What do you mean?'

'Just a passing thought.' That would have to wait. He needed to dig a little deeper before he revealed his theory. 'I'd love to see the rest of the house.'

Brett was in here somewhere; he could feel it.

Gordon knelt on the window seat in the dining room, craning his neck to see how much of his house could be seen from this vantage point. Even though the two houses joined, this was part of a huge extension. Obviously flaunting her wealth. That was if it actually belonged to Dorothy. She had lived here only a short time before he moved in. He would have to ask Mother, who lived here before.

Bethany placed a hand on the wall. 'Between here and the library is Dorothy's study.'

'Is it really?' Gordon had suspected a secret room; the panelled area in the library had been the only one without a bookcase. It had obviously been one room – like Mother's generous living room – divided into three tiny rooms. 'Are you allowed in there?'

'With permission,' she said. 'I'm afraid that's a room I can't show you.'

'Have you checked all the others in the house?'

'Checked them?'

'For Brett?'

She stood away from the wall. Her gaze went to the

floor, her eyes shifting from side to side. The body language course he'd taken online had pointed out this was a sign of lying, a way of looking for an escape route perhaps, in case their lies were uncovered.

'Three places I haven't looked,' she said. 'The shed at the bottom of the garden, the cellar and the attic. And Dorothy has cameras everywhere ...'

Bethany frowned and rubbed her forehead. She looked extremely uncomfortable – her eyes danced as though she were having an internal argument with herself.

'Well,' said Gordon, zipping up his coat. 'Let's start with the shed then, shall we?'

He followed her through the long, narrow kitchen. All the mod cons in here, but they lacked personality. White, surgical, stark. He much preferred Mother's homely wooden kitchen. All the magnets she collected on the fridge. Occasionally, clutter was a comforting factor; it showed there was life inside the house.

Bethany slipped on her flat pumps that were under the radiator.

'They'll get soaked through,' said Gordon. 'It rained last night, and the grass'll be sodden. Haven't you got anything more sensible for this time of year?'

'No,' she said, pressing her lips together in a self-deprecating smile.

'And what about a ...'

He was going to say coat. He was beginning to sound like her father.

He was right about the grass. Even in his practical

shoes he could feel the cold beneath his feet. The bottom of his trousers had gained a water line by the time they reached the shed. Dorothy really should've given it a final mow before the weather set in.

Bethany wiped the grubby window with her sleeve.

'You're going to get filthy,' he said.

'It can be washed,' she said, trying the door.

She pulled it hard until it stuttered open. Out came a cloud of dust, sparkling in the sunshine. She wafted the air around her.

'Jesus,' she said. 'It looks as though no one has been in here for months at least.'

She stepped inside; Gordon looked over her shoulder, which wasn't difficult. He was over a foot taller.

On the right were two lawnmowers: one, a small petrol; the other a Flymo hover mower. Ineffective for a garden this size. A rusty metal shelving unit was against the back window with a huge toolbox on the bottom and pots with various plants in stages of decomposition.

'It certainly looks that way,' said Gordon. 'Fancy planting them and leaving the poor things to die. What a waste.'

'Definitely no sign of Brett in here,' said Bethany, stepping back outside.

If he'd been alone, Gordon would have happily spent a few more minutes having a good look around, but Bethany was already making her way across the garden.

'I'll just close everything back up then, shall I?' he said, but she wasn't in hearing distance.

He wiped his feet on the mat behind the kitchen door.

'The cellar door was locked the last time I tried,' she said. 'I don't know where Dorothy keeps her big set of keys.' She walked out of the kitchen and Gordon followed. She stopped in the hallway and tried the cellar door. 'You don't really think Brett could still be in this house, do you?'

'I didn't see him come out.'

'He might have sneaked out,' she said. 'There must be some blind spots.'

'There might be,' said Gordon, trying the handle after Bethany had given up. 'Yes, it's definitely locked.' He bent over and peered into the keyhole. 'I did a course on lock-picking a few months ago.'

'Really? Like a lesson for wannabe burglars?'

Gordon laughed. 'Not exactly. It was a YouTube video.'

'Oh,' she said. 'Do you need specialist tools for it?' She rested a hand on his arm. 'What if Dorothy comes back? I don't know how she'd react to us sneaking around. We could get into trouble.'

'Paper clips,' said Gordon. 'Have you got any? Ideally a few in case they snap or get warped.'

Bethany winced slightly. Was she actually worried about getting caught? Her reaction caught him off-guard.

'Don't worry,' said Gordon. 'It won't damage the lock or anything. We could just say a sheet of paper wafted under the door or something. I can feel a draught on my ankles so that would sound authentic.'

'OK,' she said. She came back with a clear plastic box

of paperclips. 'Here you go. I'm dying to see this. You never know when this sort of thing will come in handy.'

'Indeed,' said Gordon, taking out two of the largest paperclips.

He straightened half of one, keeping the other half folded as a handle. He inserted it into the lock and bent it slightly to get a 45-degree bend. He'd only practiced this manoeuvre twice but he fiddled with the paperclips, trying to look as professional as possible, until the lock cylinder moved freely. He turned the handle and the door opened.

'I can't believe you managed to do that,' said Bethany.

Gordon couldn't either.

She pulled the short cord next to the bare bulb at the top of the stairs.

'Would you prefer me to go first?' said Gordon.

'I don't mind,' she said, squeezing past him. She held the rail tightly. 'I've been down here before.'

'I thought you said ... oh, never mind.' Gordon stepped into the semi-darkness. 'But Brett might be down here, you know. I wouldn't want you to see anything macabre.'

She stopped a few steps from the bottom.

'Actually, yes, please.'

'Stand aside then ... Rachel.'

He pressed himself against the wall, so he didn't touch her accidently as he shifted to the front. He sniffed the air. It was damp, but there was no sign of decay. He switched on the light for the main room, illuminating the collection of stored items. Chairs, rugs (which would be ruined down here), cabinets and general nick-nacks in flimsy boxes. Against the far wall were two teak cupboards. He opened one of them to find pages and pages of A4 paper.

'What's in here?' he said, knowing it couldn't have been Dorothy Winters' shelved novels.

'I didn't look through much of that lot,' said Bethany. 'There were a bunch of letters that were really weird. Nothing to do with Brett, though.'

Gordon grabbed a pile of bundled letters held together with a buff elastic band.

'These, you mean?' He held them up. 'What was strange about them?'

She shrugged. 'The same letter was written again and again.'

'Do you think she'd notice if I borrowed them?' Gordon loved reading other people's correspondence, but he had to keep the excitement from his voice. 'There might be some clues in here.'

'I doubt it,' she said, climbing on a box to peek out of the tiny window at the front. 'But she probably wouldn't notice if they weren't there for a few days. There's so much junk down here.'

Gordon placed the letters in his coat pocket; he knew extra-large ones would come in handy one day. He pulled out his mobile phone to shed light into the dark corners.

'There are no signs of blood,' he said, 'but to highlight cleaned areas, we'd need luminol. I don't suppose you've—'

'No, Gordon,' she said. 'I don't have any luminol.'

'It was worth a try.'

'But ...' She hesitated. 'I don't think you'd need luminol if you went upstairs and looked in the bathroom.'

Gordon's ears tingled. This was his very first investigation and it was getting interesting. Picked a lock – tick. And now blood in the bathroom. Wait until he told his mother.

'Can you describe the scene?' he said.

'The bathroom is literally covered in blood.'

Gordon's arm jerked up and his torch flashed into Bethany's face.

'Sorry, sorry.' He stepped towards her. 'Why didn't you tell me this about before? We should have looked there first.'

'I ... I don't know.'

'Rightio,' said Gordon, striding to the bottom of the stairs. 'Let's go and take a look.'

'OK.' Bethany lingered. 'I'll join you in a second. I just want to check ...'

Her voice faded as he reached the top and stepped into the hallway.

The shape of a person lingered at the front door.

'Rachel,' he shouted down the stairs, 'I think there's someone at the—'

'Gordon!'

He stepped out of the vestibule.

Dorothy Winters stood at the threshold. Her heels tapped on the floor as she came towards him. She grabbed hold of the cellar door handle and slammed it shut.

'Wait,' said Gordon. 'Rachel's—'

'What are you doing sneaking about in my house? I thought you were just posting some pages through the letterbox.'

'Rachel invited me in. She said she needed help with a technical issue.'

'I think it's time you left,' she said, her mouth in a snarl.

Her make-up was caked on – the powder had set in the lines around her mouth and on the tiny hairs on her face. The mascara was layered on in spiders' legs spouting from her eyes.

'I'm going,' he said, stepping aside and walking towards the door.

'If I catch you in here again, I'll call the police.'

He stopped at the open door.

'I'm not afraid of you,' he paused for two beats, '*Dorothy.*'

He slammed the front door, taking a deep gulp of the bracing air outside. He felt the oxygen flood inside him, his heart racing as though he'd run a hundred metres.

It was turning out to be the best day he'd had in months.

Chapter 54

I raced up the stairs and tried the door.

Locked.

I knocked lightly. Dorothy must surely still be there.

'Dorothy!' I said. 'I'm locked in. Could you let me out, please?'

There was an intake of breath from the other side.

She knew I was here. What the hell was she doing – punishing me for letting Gordon into the house?

'I'm sorry about Gordon,' I said. 'He came round with the CCTV footage from his house to see if Brett had left.'

Still no response. I pressed an ear against the door. The sound of shoes being taken off. A shadow at the gap in the door. She had placed her shoes in front of it.

'Dorothy, please.' Louder this time. 'I know you can hear me. Please let me out.'

I heard her pick the shoes up. She padded towards the bottom of the stairs.

I made a fist and pounded the door.

'Dorothy! Please let me out!'

She started up the staircase. 'I can't hear anything,' she said. 'Can you?'

'No, Dorothy. I can't hear a thing.'

She was talking to herself. She'd finally lost it. I didn't have my phone with me, but who would I call anyway?

I slid to the floor and leant against the door. She might return in a few minutes. Pretend she hadn't heard me. Perhaps her hearing was fading. I pulled my legs up and put my arms around my knees. It was so cold in here and I was only wearing jeans and a light cotton shirt.

At least there was ligh—

Both of the lights went out. How had she done that? Had she flicked a fuse?

'Dorothy! Please let me out. I can't be in here.'

I shouted as loudly as I could, but I knew it was pointless. My arms were shivering. I brought my knees closer to my chest and buried my face.

It was pitch black with only a sliver of daylight from the bottom of the door. It was like being back in my prison cell after lights out. A blanket of darkness, left with my thoughts and the constant sounds from outside.

Why was Dorothy doing this to me?

My mind raced with images I didn't want to see, the thoughts I'd managed to keep buried for nearly a year. Matthew the week before he died, Matthew the day before he died. Matthew on the night it all went wrong.

I'd finally found my passport hidden in a box disguised as a book on the shelf in the living room and had packed only the basics I'd need for a few days. I had warned Jenny that I might be coming, but I didn't know exactly when.

Matthew had discovered my suitcase under the stairs. He unzipped it in the hallway, taking everything out. He held up each item of my clothing, examining it. Making me watch from the floor. The front door was locked, and he had made me strip to my underwear to stop me screaming for help at the window.

'I was planning a surprise trip for us,' I said.

'Where's my stuff?' He tipped the rest of my things onto the floor and flung the case into the living room. 'Do you think I'm stupid, Bethany? I know you've been pilfering this stuff away for weeks.'

'I ...'

'You what?'

'I'm sorry.'

He shook his head. 'No wonder everyone gave up on you. You're so ungrateful. After all I've done for you.' He stood and kicked my clothes aside. 'I really tried with you.' He walked towards me. I clasped my arms around my knees. 'And look how skinny you've got. It's not attractive, you know. All your bones sticking out everywhere.' He reached out a hand. 'Come on, I'll carry you to bed. We've both had a shock and the rest will do you good.'

He bent down and scooped me from the floor. 'You're so light now, Bethany. We'll have to feed you up. I'll get you some of those protein shakes you like from the chemist.'

He must've put something in the hot milk he brought me because I slept for what felt like days afterwards. Occasionally I'd hear a knock on the door and him shouting to someone on the doorstep. On what was the third or fourth night, he brought a knife into the bedroom.

'If you try to leave me again,' he said, 'I won't be afraid to use this.'

He put it under his pillow.

'No one has contacted you, you know,' he said, after a week. 'I had thought to tell them you had glandular fever, but no one has bothered to ask.' He laughed and stroked my cheek. 'Those shakes seem to be working. You're getting some colour back.' He lifted the covers. 'And you're getting a bit more meat on you. That's good to see.' He kissed my cheek. 'I do love you, Bee. I'm glad to see you're sorry. You are sorry, aren't you?'

I nodded.

'Good, good. Because I've got a treat for you. There's a meal after work on Friday night. All other partners are going. They've been on and on at me to bring you to one of these things for months now and I've run out of excuses. I'll go shopping and get you something nice.'

It was a green dress covered with sequins.

The fabric scratched my skin, and the neckline skimmed my throat.

'Well, don't you look beautiful,' he said as I stood in front of the full-length mirror.

I wanted to say that it was far too hot outside for a dress like this but instead I said, 'Thank you.'

He grabbed me around the waist and rested his head on my shoulders. For a moment, my body tensed, and I looked into my own eyes reflected back at me. I looked at him and felt the nausea rise from my stomach to the back of my throat.

'The taxi will be here in five,' he said. 'I'll just pop to the loo. Go and wait in the living room.'

Wordlessly, I walked out of the room, down the stairs and stood next to the fireplace, staring at our wedding photo. Him and me, Jenny and Phil, Tina and Shane. I held up my left hand and removed the wedding ring, placing it on the mantelpiece. This was how it would look if I were free.

I swiped back the ring when his footsteps started down the stairs.

'Right,' he said, rubbing his hands. 'Let's go.'

We left the dinner early, as was typical. Matthew had drunk too much, yet he was always aware when he had. He didn't want to make an idiot of himself in front of his work colleagues.

'I saw how you were looking at Mark,' he said, hissing in my ear. 'It was embarrassing. Everyone saw it.'

I stared at the road ahead, knowing that whatever I said wouldn't be good enough.

The taxi driver glanced at me in the mirror. I tried to tell him what I was thinking through my eyes, but the words were stuck in the back of my throat.

Help me, please.

Too quickly, the taxi pulled up outside the house.

My cage. Allowed out for a few precious hours.

'Cheers, mate,' Matthew said, handing the driver a twenty-pound note. 'Keep the change.'

Always so generous to people he didn't know.

I waited next to him as he unlocked the door, and followed him inside.

Chapter 55

Camera_1>Hallway>22.14

'You go upstairs,' he said. 'I'm just going to get a whiskey.'

Camera_3>Bedroom>22.15

She lies on top of the quilt still in her dress.
After several minutes she seems to have fallen asleep.

Camera_3>Bedroom>22:21

He enters the bedroom.
'Bethany,' he says.
He removes his tie and crawls towards her, starting from the bottom of the bed.
He places his knees either side and lies on top of her.
'Why did you fall asleep without me?' he says.
He pulls out a knife from the pillow on the left side of the bed.
She opens her eyes.
He holds the knife against her throat.
She rolls out from underneath him, and lands heavily on the floor.

She runs out of the room.

Camera_1>Hallway>22:28

She tries to open the front door, but finding it locked, bangs on the front door.

She shouts, 'Help me, please,' through the letterbox.

He comes down the stairs.

'Oh, my little Bee,' he shouts. 'You frightened little Bee.'

Camera_2>LivingRoom>22:30

She attempts to open a window, but it appears to be locked.

She stands behind the living-room curtains.

He swipes the curtain open.

'You silly Bee,' he says. 'I could see your feet at the bottom.'

She runs past him and out of the room.

Camera_3>Bedroom>22:33

She sits behind the bedroom door.

Camera_3>Bedroom>22:35

He enters the bedroom.

He puts the knife under the pillow on the left-hand side.

'It was only a joke,' he says. 'You know that.'

He sits on the bed and removes his shoes. He places the shoes side by side on the carpet near the end of the bed.

'I know you're there,' he says. 'I'm not in the mood for playing any more.'

He leans back and reaches over the bedside cabinet on the right-hand side. He picks up her mobile phone.

'Are you all right?' he says. 'I'm worried about you, it says.' He laughs. 'So you have got friends.'

He throws her phone against the radiator under the window.

He lies on the bed.

Camera_3>Bedroom>22:58
He begins snoring lightly.
She remains seated behind the door.

Camera_3>Bedroom>23:09
She gets up. She walks towards the mobile phone, lying on the carpet.

He opens his eyes and sits up.

He gets off the bed, picks her up and throws her onto the bed.

She lands face down.

He takes hold of her wrist, flips her over and puts his left hand around her throat.

She grabs the lamp from the bedside table and smashes it against his shoulder.

It stuns him, briefly.

He kneels on her chest and brings his other hand towards her throat.

He appears to squeeze tightly.

Her arms hit the bed as she struggles.

Her right hand reaches under the pillow on the left-hand side.

374

She stabs him once in the chest with the knife (EXHIBIT #1).

He collapses on top of her.

She shuffles out from underneath him.

She sits on the carpet next to the radiator.

Camera_3>Bedroom>23:47
Paramedics Andy Carlisle and Riya Srini enter the scene.

Camera_3>Bedroom>23:49
PC Hannah Glover 7984 and PC Peter Wignall 5423 enter the scene.

*** End of report ***
Transcription by PC Kirsty Davies 8026
7 August 2019

Chapter 56

Mother was waiting at the living-room door when Gordon let himself in.

'What was all that about?' she said. 'I saw you nattering away to Dorothy Winters outside half an hour ago. I've been waiting by the window for you to come back and tell me all about it.'

Gordon sat on the bottom of the stairs and untied his shoelaces.

'It was only for a couple of minutes. I'll tell you about it in a moment,' he said. 'I'll have to have a cup of something sweet. I've had quite the afternoon.'

'Have you, Gordon?' She shuffled towards the kitchen. 'I'll stick the kettle on and plate us up some biccies. I noticed you bought some of those digestive thins. They'll be just the ticket.'

He placed his shoes in the cupboard under the stairs and went into the kitchen as Mother was fetching the step from under the sink.

'You go and sit yourself down, Mum,' he said. 'I'll sort out the tea.'

He hummed to himself as he dropped the teabags into the pot and waited for the kettle to boil. He actually felt like singing this afternoon. He turned the radio on. 'You Make Me Feel Like Dancing', Leo Sayer. Perfect.

The water almost splattered down the side of the pot; he was enjoying himself rather too much. *Rein it in, Gordon.* A little decorum.

Still, his hands shook as he carried the tray.

'Which room are you in, Mother?' he shouted.

'Living room, love. Thought we could keep an eye out in front in case of any further developments.'

'Perfect,' he said, as he placed the tray onto Mother's table. 'Do you know, you'd make the perfect assistant.'

'Assistant to what?'

'All in good time, Mother.' He tugged his chair closer to her. 'All in good time.'

She rubbed her hands. 'I do like it when you're in a good mood, love.'

'Me too.' He passed her a cup on a saucer. 'I'll leave the biscuits on the plate. Don't want the chocolate melting.' He hooked the handle of his cup with a finger. 'I'll tell you what happened next door after you've told me what you already know.' He took a sip of lovely hot sweet tea. 'How long has Dorothy Winters lived next door?'

'Ah, now that's a tricky one,' she said. 'It was during the time your dad was poorly in hospital. Do you remember?'

Gordon nodded.

'I came home after your dad had passed and there

377

was a couple – Dorothy and Brett, though they didn't introduce themselves for weeks after – unloading suitcases from the back of a car.'

'Didn't they have a removal van?'

'No, love,' she said. 'It's still Estelle Williams' house – do you remember me telling you about her? She's always off travelling – next door is only one of her houses. She rented it out to Dorothy and before Dorothy it was a young couple, but they were never in.'

'And Dorothy moved in a couple of weeks before I moved in?'

'Yes, that's right. Estelle leaves all the furniture in – stores a few things in the cellar, from what she told me last time.'

'Why didn't you tell me about this before? I thought Dorothy had bought the house.'

She placed her cup and saucer on the tray.

'You've not had a good time of it, love,' she said. 'First losing your dad, then that bitch of a wife left you.'

'Mother!'

'Well, she was. I've never met anyone as cold as her before. Fancy, just a few weeks after your dad died. It was heartless. Cruel.'

'Thanks, Mum.'

'You've no need to thank me. I'm your mum. I'll always be here for you, Gordon.' She tapped his knee. 'So, are you going to tell me why you're all excited?'

He leant forward. 'The new assistant next door isn't who she says she is.'

'Who does she say she is?'

378

Gordon rolled his eyes. 'You're losing your touch, Mother. I thought you kept abreast of everything on this street. She said she's called Rachel, but she's actually called Bethany.' He placed his cup on the table and clasped his hands. 'And she murdered her husband just over two years ago.'

His mother's hand went straight to her mouth.

'She never did!'

'She did.' Gordon glanced at the window. He stood when he saw a figure walking past the house. He went closer to see Dorothy striding away from number sixty-three with hands clenched in fists. At least he didn't have to worry about Bethany being on her own with the woman. He turned around to savour the look on his mother's face. 'And I believe, from the digging I've been doing, that the woman claiming to be Dorothy Winters isn't Dorothy Winters at all.'

'No,' she said, leaning forward and resting a hand on her lap. 'Who would lie about being a writer? Wouldn't everyone know who the real Dorothy Winters is?'

'Obviously not.'

'Who is she, then?'

Gordon stroked his upper lip. Perhaps he'd grow a moustache.

'Now that, Mother, is my next puzzle.' He frowned. 'And to be honest, I have no idea where to begin with that one. Anyway,' he said. 'I'll be able to tell you more once I clarify a few things. Is it OK if I switch the telly on for you while I continue my investigations?'

'Course it is. I'm looking forward to your next

instalment, Gordon.' She wiggled her shoulders to get comfy in her chair. 'Fetch us my blanket, will you? And can you turn it onto ITV?'

'No problem.'

'I've really enjoyed our chat, Gordon,' she said.

'Me too, Mum.'

He almost reached the bottom of the stairs.

'Before you head up,' she shouted, 'get me the rest of those biscuits, will you? They really hit the spot.'

'Right you are, Mother.'

Gordon pulled up the Twitter account for Dorothy Winters' publishers and composed a message to Fox Glove Publishing.

To Whom It May Concern,
I am in the process of writing the biography of Ms Dorothy Winters after being a fan of her written works for many years. Please, if it's not too much trouble, could you let me know the details in regard to her date of birth, etc. I have searched online to no avail. If, indeed, you have a short biography of Ms Winters, I would be most grateful.
Mr G. Anderson.

Now, if Gordon were the recipient of such a message, he would be extremely wary about any aspiring writer attempting a comprehensive biography about Dorothy Winters when they didn't even know her date of birth. But he lived in the hope that they'd see past that.

He had thought about writing the same message to Brett Daniels' publisher, but according to Companies House, they went under in 2004.

The man next door probably wasn't Brett Daniels at all. What possible reason could there be for that pair to pretend to be authors? He really couldn't fathom it. Did they have a connection to Bethany? Perhaps he would never find out because he had no way of learning about them unless he asked them outright. He seriously doubted they'd accommodate him in answering.

The Twitter message had been marked as read.

He minimised the screen when he didn't see the replying dots after five minutes. He got up and paced the room. Would they have that kind of record on file? A database of authors' details they could bring up with a click of a button? Gordon would love to have information like that at his fingertips.

A ting of a notification brought Gordon back to his chair.

He could hardly bear to open the message once he'd maximised the window.

OK. He was going in.

Dear Mr Anderson,

Thank you so much for your message. We are so pleased to hear that you have enjoyed Dorothy Winters' novels. Her family will be delighted to learn that you will be writing about her – this will be her first biography. I do hope you get some interest from publishers (unfortunately we are purely a fiction team here). Here

are a few details, which are available in public records,
should you choose to pursue your project.
  DOB: 12 March 1932, Liverpool
  Date of death: 19 December 2008, Cornwall
  I wish you the best of luck!
  Sarah Tomlinson.

It confirmed what he suspected. His instincts had
been spot on, although a little late coming. What other
clues did he have to discover the woman's identity?

He shot up from his chair and dashed downstairs
to fetch the letters from his coat pocket. How had he
forgotten about the letters? They might have a wealth
of information – if they didn't belong to the Estelle
Williams' whose house it was.

Once he was back in his office, he took them from
their envelopes, read each one, and laid them on his
desk. The writer of the letters to Jack sounded completely unhinged. Sending it once was bad enough, but
nine times? Gordon didn't recognise the name Ms K.
Holden. He couldn't trace the woman without a first
name, but there was a full address for Jack Lawrence.

Gordon typed the man's information into the search
engine. One of the results was a link to an electoral
roll entry, giving details of additional residents at that
address. The latest entry was 2011 and the fellow occu-
pant was Eleni Maria Lawrence.

Gordon loaded Facebook and typed in Eleni's full
name. There was a high probability that she was Jack's
wife. If it was another relation, she was obviously close

enough to have a Mr Jack Lawrence on her friends list.

There was only one entry for Eleni Maria in Bolton and Gordon clicked on the profile. The main photo was of a man and a woman, who looked to be in their late sixties. They were sitting on a terrace, a clear blue sky in the background. Eleni's hair was coiffed in an intricate beehive style and she was wearing a bright yellow dress that showed off her olive skin. Jack's nose and upper cheeks were flame red. Perhaps through sun, perhaps from alcohol. His hair was thinning and was a mixture of grey and auburn. He was probably handsome three decades years ago. Gordon clicked to reveal the comments.

Retirement suits you, Lenny, said one of them – to which Eleni replied, *I deserve it after these hellish past few years!* Another person wrote, *Get back to work, you lazy bastard, Jack*.

He had found the right profile. Jack Lawrence had replied to the comment. Gordon clicked on the man's profile. His photo was of him alone: smart suit, hands in pockets, sunglasses. He was leaning on the bonnet of a silver Aston Martin DB9.

Gordon clicked on to Jack's friends list. There was no one by the name of Estelle Williams, the owner of next door; no one with the surname Holden. Facebook certainly wasn't the best investigative tool, but it was a start.

He clicked back to Jack Lawrence's timeline. The only posts visible had the world symbol next to them: public posts. Gordon scrolled down: 2020, 2019. He paused when he reached an article shared from a Lancashire news website.

WOMAN FOUND NOT GUILTY OF HUSBAND'S MURDER – Jury acquits Bolton-born woman.

Gordon's face went cold. Was it by chance Jack had shared this article? There were no comments under his post. Gordon swivelled his chair to face the wall. The letters were found in the cellar of number sixty-three. Had the woman who was posing as Dorothy Winters left them there?

Gordon picked up one of the letters. Whoever wrote them was deranged – the suggestion that Jack's wife had come to harm was extremely intimidating and upsetting. Was the woman disturbed enough to set up home and pass herself off as someone else? But to what end? Gordon couldn't think of a connection between Jack, the woman pretending to be Dorothy, and Bethany Arnold.

He needed to talk to Bethany again; he prayed she wasn't in immediate danger.

Chapter 57

I'd been banging on the cellar door for around fifteen minutes when I heard the front door open and close. There were no footsteps inside; Dorothy must've left.

I stood against the cold brick wall and assessed the door. It was solid wood, but the lock was old, just a simple mechanism. The frame might have been weak. I took a deep breath. One, two, three, and I propelled myself against the door, putting all my strength into my right shoulder.

The door barely moved. My neck and shoulder burned with pain.

There must be something here or downstairs that I could use to bash the door with. I was still in darkness, so I sank down to the floor, searching with my fingers for something heavy. There was a doorstop that was too light, a vacuum cleaner too flimsy.

What had I seen last week when I looked down here? The dining chairs would only make a dent in the door. Perhaps there was a loose brick I could smash the lock with.

I grabbed hold of the metal rail and carefully stepped down the stairs. My fear of lying undiscovered in a heap at the bottom was fast becoming a reality. I tried the switch on the wall. This one didn't work either. Dorothy had definitely cut the power to the cellar.

I followed the wall round to the window, which offered a little daylight. I kicked as I went, searching for any loose stone. I stood on the flimsy cardboard box and hoisted myself up, banging on the window, my fist covered with my sleeve in case the glass smashed.

'Hello,' I shouted. 'Can anyone hear me?'

Footsteps. I could hear footsteps.

They were inside the house.

It couldn't have been Dorothy unless she'd come in through the back door.

I retraced my steps back to the stairs and crawled up them. When I reached the top, I pounded the door with both fists.

'Help me! I'm locked in the cellar. I'm under the stairs.' Footsteps were right above my head. It could've been Louise. 'It's me – Rachel. Can anyone hear me? I need you to let me out.'

I leant my head against the door. Light steps on the wooden hallway floor – someone wearing only socks.

'Please let me out.'

A key went into the lock; I stood back as the door opened.

Standing in front of me was Brett Daniels.

*

386

His shirt was creased, his trousers crumpled. He looked as though he hadn't slept since the day he went missing.

'Where have you been?' I said. 'Everyone's been worried about you. Are you hurt?'

'I haven't been anywhere. I've been staying in the attic room.'

Stubble had shaded his face and the glow his skin once had had faded.

'What? Why? Does Dorothy know? She's been so stressed about you going missing. She's been crying every night – I've heard her.'

'Come with me,' he said, walking towards the dining room. He sat in his usual chair, next to Dorothy's, and gestured for me to sit opposite. 'There are a few things you should know.'

'She locked me in the cellar,' I said, sitting down. 'I've been there for almost an hour. I don't know if she realised.'

'She knew you were there. That's why I had to come down – to let you out.'

'I don't understand. Why have you been hiding upstairs? Why would she lock me in the cellar?'

'She wanted to scare you.' He looked up to the ceiling. 'And I didn't know she was going to coat the bathroom in blood.' He rolled up his sleeves, then dabbed his forehead with the back of his hand. 'I'm sorry that all of this got so out of hand.'

'What are you talking about? Coating the bathroom with blood?'

'She wanted you to think something had happened to me. It wasn't real blood ... well, not human.'

'But why?' Dots of light began appearing in my vision. 'Was it research for her book? Watching what happened when a person thought they'd hurt someone?'

He brought both hands to his face, rubbed his eyes.

'She's not writing a book, Rachel.'

'What? Then what was the point of me typing her pages?'

He patted his shirt, but gave up when he realised he must've left his cigarettes upstairs. In the attic. Where he'd been staying while I thought I was going mad.

'She's not who she appears to be,' he said. 'None of us are.'

I pinged the elastic band around my wrist. This wasn't a dream. Brett was really sitting in front of me.

'My name's not Brett,' he said. 'It's Andrew.'

Dizziness clouded my vision; the floor seemed to move.

'She knows who you really are,' he said.

Why did he keep saying these things? Sentence after sentence firing at me.

'She's always known. From the minute she interviewed you. From the minute she left the newspaper with the job advertisement outside your hotel room.'

Events of the past weeks rewound in my head. The paper outside my door. The advert in the centre of the page. Me, thinking I had been given the job through cunning. Her escalating odd behaviour.

'Why would a writer be curious about my life?

388

There are plenty of interesting people out there to write about.'

He raised his eyebrows, his lips straightened.

'She isn't a writer at all, is she?' I said. 'Her name isn't Dorothy Winters.'

He shook his head. 'And there weren't any previous assistants. There has only ever been you.'

'But why?'

'Have you read her story?'

'I've almost finished.' I rubbed the tops of my legs. 'Is Dorothy actually Kathryn?'

He nodded, slowly. 'And what did you gather from her writing towards the end?'

'Have you read it?' I said, but he didn't reply. 'I'm only just getting to the end. She gave away a child. The child, her grown-up son is now ...'

The words stuck in my throat. *Dead.*

It couldn't be him. That would be impossible.

'I haven't read the last chapters,' I said, flatly.

He stood and left the room, returning with the notes from my desk.

'Then I suggest you read it,' he said. 'It's her version of things, though, remember. That's all.' He pushed the papers towards me. 'She had painted you so differently, you know. She said that you'd killed him out of spite – that you were manipulative, vicious, cold. But you don't seem like that person at all. When she talked about keeping you down in the cellar, I had to put a stop to it.'

The tears were gathering in my eyes, my heart was

racing. I needed to get out of this house. Where the hell had I left my phone? Would he stop me? If I read these pages, would he let me go?

I picked up the notes with shaking hands and began to read from where I had left off.

Chapter 58

If Kathryn were to die now, there'd be no one left with her genes; she would have no grandchildren. That sort of life had never come her way. She supposed she wouldn't have changed most things if she had the chance to start again. She'd have stopped him dying, though. She could've done that if she'd been around from the beginning.

She had left everything too late. She was nearing retirement age now and her life seemed to have passed in the blink of an eye. What had she done with it?

But she wasn't dead yet.

There was plenty more she could do.

'Mrs Arnold,' the officer said. 'I've got your son's things here.'

She signed for them and went back to her car. She prised the cardboard envelope open. It was Matthew's shirt. The one he'd died in. Had they given it to her by mistake? His blood covered almost all of it.

She put it to her face. It was the only part of him she had left.

She placed it on the passenger seat and reached into the envelope. His mobile phone. Kathryn would have to get someone to unlock it for her.

She'd get to know him that way.

Kathryn saw her this afternoon, strolling down the supermarket aisles like she didn't have a single care in the world. She wasn't even wearing her wedding ring.

Bethany had planned it all along, hadn't she? Made Matthew look bad on the camera footage for everyone in the courtroom to see. The jury fell for her victim act, but Kathryn wasn't fooled.

Fancy her, having the gall to go round the supermarket, not giving a shit who saw her. Though no one else seemed to have noticed her. People's memories were so fleeting. Kathryn's wasn't. With every passing day since the not guilty verdict, the rage inside her was like a growing ball of fire.

'Aren't you going to eat that?'

Kathryn blinked. Andrew must've been rabbiting on again and she hadn't heard a word.

'I know you're thinking about her,' he said. 'You need to get past this.'

She picked up her fork, stabbed it in the middle of the spaghetti, and twisted it slowly. The thought of getting over this was impossible. Kathryn saw her everywhere: on the street, every time she closed her eyes.

'What if I were to speak to her?' she said. 'What if she could explain to me why she did it?'

Andrew placed his fork and spoon either side of his plate.

'You heard what happened,' he said. 'We went to court every day.'

'But that was all—'

He rubbed his face. 'I know,' he said wearily. He'd heard it a hundred times before. 'It was all lies.' He shuffled his chair back and stood. 'She'll never meet with you, Kathryn. Not after those letters you sent.' He took the plate from her. 'We need to get ready.' He carried the dishes into the kitchen.

'She doesn't know who I am,' she said, even though Andrew was out of earshot. 'I'll find a way.'

'I don't know why you've brought me here,' said Kathryn. 'This isn't my type of thing at all.'

'It's only for an hour or so,' said Andrew. 'We have to support him. It's taken him years to get published.'

Even though she didn't want to be here, she wanted to look the part. She'd gone for the Beatnik look: black polo-neck jumper, black capri pants and large hoop earrings. She looked a hundred times better than the scruffy idiots who surrounded her, clutching their huge canvas shopping bags. No style whatsoever.

Kathryn looked around the bookshop. She could've written a book. Her life had been far more interesting than some of the crap that was written these days.

After the mind-numbing reading of naval-gazing bullshit, Andrew dragged her with him to the signing queue. The two women behind her were talking far too loudly.

'Is it her?' one of them said.

'I don't know,' said the other. 'I thought she was dead.'

'She was a hermit, you know. So, she might still be alive.'

Kathryn felt a tug on her sleeve.

'Are you Dorothy Winters?' asked the short woman with hideous, blue-rimmed glasses.

'I've no idea what you're talking about,' said Kathryn.

'The famous author in the nineties,' she said. 'You're the spitting image of her.'

Kathryn turned on her heels.

'Am I really?' she said. 'In what way?'

The pair glanced at each other.

'You're very glamorous, blonde. You dress well.'

'That's very kind of you to say,' said Kathryn, examining her hand, admiring her latest manicure. 'What kind of books does she write?'

'Thrillers, mainly.' She looked at her friend. 'Remember that one she wrote about the man whose daughter was murdered? He employed the guy who got away with killing her – it was a live-in job, remember? He tortured him for weeks, messing with his mind ... said he shouldn't have got away with it. Do you remember, Connie?'

'I remember the story,' said Connie. 'But that was written by someone else.'

Her friend's face dropped. 'Oh.'

'What was the book called?'

'*Silence the Fury.*'

Kathryn turned round to see Andrew already at the signing table. When she reached him, she put her hands around his waist.

'Thank you for bringing me here, my darling,' she said. 'Life is such a funny thing. Sometimes you're right where you're supposed to be.'

It had been nearly a month, and nothing had worked. My Little Bee, the nickname Matthew had given her, which Kathryn had found in his mobile phone, was spelled out on the Ouija board; it had barely caused a reaction. Kathryn had etched his name thirty-four times in the wardrobe – for each year he was alive – and she just seemed to forget about it. The shirt he was wearing on the night she killed him, she'd burned. The blood in the bathroom, well, she seemed to have compartmentalised that in her mind. She should get Bethany to clean it up. That might push her closer to the edge.

'You should stop spying on her.'

Andrew was standing next to Kathryn. How did she not notice him coming in?

'You shouldn't be down here,' she said. 'Someone might see you. You're meant to be—'

'What am I meant to be?'

'You know what ... She was meant to think she'd stabbed you. She was meant to feel guilty ... hide away, maybe hand herself in.'

Andrew stood behind her and rested his hands on Kathryn's shoulders.

'I've been hiding up there for nearly a week,' he said. 'Enough's enough. It wasn't meant to be like this. You said you'd arranged all of this to get to know her, to try to find out what really happened.'

Kathryn shook herself free of Andrew's hands. 'She can't even speak his name. It's like he never existed.'

He crouched in front of her, placing his hand on hers.

'Do you think that, maybe, you arranged all of this because you feel ...' He took his hands away. 'Never mind.'

Kathryn clenched her jaw. 'You think I feel guilty?' She stood and shot past him, almost knocking him over.

'Not because he died,' he said, standing up. 'That wasn't your fault.'

'Of course that wasn't my fault.' She grabbed the packet of cigarettes from the mantelpiece. 'I shouldn't feel guilty for letting my sister bring him up. It was what was best for him – a stable home that I couldn't offer.'

'I know, I know. I'm sorry for bringing it up.' He walked towards her. 'Perhaps it's time to tell Bethany everything. Then you can let her go. We can travel to somewhere far away. A villa by the beach.'

She took out a cigarette, lit it and took a deep drag. 'Just a couple more days.'

'What will that achieve, Kathy?'

He watched as she returned to the desk in front of the laptop.

'I'll think of something,' she said. 'Don't worry, I won't hurt her.'

She clicked back onto the feed from bedroom one. Asleep without a care.

What would Andrew do to stop Kathryn anyway? He'd gone along with everything else. He never could say no to her.

Chapter 59

The street was empty, save for an elderly gentleman having a cigarette under the shelter outside *Whispering Oaks* over the road. Gordon raised his hand in a wave as he hopped over the wall to next door. The man didn't respond; Gordon didn't want the man to think he was up to anything untoward and telephone the police.

Gordon headed towards the window just above ground. He knelt on the damp grass and peered inside. The cellar was in darkness, even shining his phone torch was no use – it just reflected the light back at him. He tapped on it gently.

'Are you still in there, Rachel?' he hissed.

He placed an ear to one of the tiny cracks in the window but heard nothing. He relaxed a little. For a brief moment he had imagined her trapped in there.

Should he knock on the front door? What if Dorothy had come back while he was in his office. He should've checked his camera feeds, but it would've wasted precious time if Bethany was in danger. And there was a chance of that. There was a connection between the woman masquerading as Dorothy, Jack, and Bethany, but he didn't know what it was. All he knew was that Ms Holden was capable of sending threatening letters to a man who appeared to be a powerful businessman.

The clicking of heels sounded on the pavement in the distance.

Gordon looked to his left.

Dorothy was coming back.

Chapter 60

I placed the pages down after reading what she'd done to me: using the tracker on Matthew's phone to find me, sending abusive letters and packages when I was staying at Jenny and Phil's, watching my every move in this house, steering the planchette on the Ouija board after reading the text messages he sent me, calling me his little bee. How she scratched the name Matthew in the wardrobe, and covered the bathroom in fake blood.

'What was she going to do to me?' I said.

Andrew looked up, eyebrows raised.

'What do you mean?'

'What was she going to do to me next?'

I slid the pages across to him and he flicked to the last.

'I don't know,' he said. He folded the pages in half. 'When she messaged to say she'd locked you in the cellar, I knew I had to step in.'

'Would she have left me down there?'

'I really don't know any more. She's been a totally different person these past couple of weeks. Perhaps that's how she's always been, but I didn't see it. She's very good at telling me what I want to hear.'

'But why did you, Louise, everyone ...' I began. 'Why did you go along with it all?'

He looked down at his shaking hands and clasped them together tightly.

'She said we could get on with our lives if I helped her get over Matthew's death.' He looked into my eyes. 'And as for Louise, I don't think she knew what was really going on. Her son Jamie was in a lot of debt and Kathryn offered to pay it off if she did her this little favour. They're not as close as Kathryn's been making out. They went to the same pub a few years ago. They're not best friends at all.'

'What about Sophia and Gillian?'

'They had no idea. And Jamie's so bloody self-centred that he didn't even ask where his mum got the money. It helped that it was a murder mystery party – everyone was playing a role that night. And Sophia, well, she's had a lot of problems. I don't think any of them know who you really are.' He reached across for my hands, but I slid them from the table and tucked them under my legs. 'I'm really sorry, Bethany. Really, I am. It all got so out of hand.'

'Why did she pretend to be a writer, though? It all seems so elaborate.'

'She didn't want to be some old lady who needed a carer.' A hint of a smile was on his lips, but it wasn't funny. 'She wanted to get you under the same roof ... find a way to dig a little deeper. Kathryn's very good at

401

pretending to be another person. I had to drink far too much alcohol to be able to deal with it all, which you probably noticed. The night of the murder mystery, I almost blurted everything out to you.'

The front door opened.

Oh God. She was back. The sound of her heels slowly came towards us.

She slammed the dining-room door against the wall. 'You let her out of the cellar?'

'Of course I've let her out,' said Andrew. 'You can't keep her locked up forever.' He shifted in his seat. 'I've told her, Kathryn. That you know who she is, and that you're Matthew's biological mother.'

'He never mentioned you,' I said quietly. 'He talked about being abandoned but I didn't think it was any-thing like this. He always asked about my childhood, but he never brought up his own.'

'Oh, stop with your misery act,' she said. 'I've had enough of your pretence. What I wrote was just a part of it. I anguished over him. He was the only part of me that was left. Just because your mother fucked off and left you, doesn't mean I did that to Matthew. I left him with my sister. I knew she would give him a better life. She was able to give him normality.' She walked up and down, her heels click-clacking on the wooden floor. 'You barely reacted to his name when I spelled it out for you.'

'I did react,' I shouted, gripping the edge of the table. 'I left the room that night. I thought Matthew was haunting me.'

I glanced at Andrew; he didn't take his eyes off Kathryn.

Kathryn. She was Kathryn.

'It was all about you, was it?' She slammed a hand on the table. 'What about me?'

'I didn't know ...' My heart was pounding, and my legs were shaking. 'I didn't know who you were. If I had known, I'd never have pretended ...'

She stood straight and folded her arms. Her gaze felt as though it was burning holes in my skin.

'We both pretended,' she said, 'didn't we?'

Her words winded me.

She was right. I had.

She had.

'But what did you gain by putting me through it all again? Sending me the bloodied shirt, the mess in the bathroom, Brett disappearing.'

She slumped down onto a chair. 'I wanted to know if you'd planned it. I wanted to know if you were sorry.'

I couldn't hold back the tears any longer. They were hot on my cold skin and streamed down my face. 'I *am* sorry,' I said. 'I didn't want to hurt him. Even after everything he did to me.' I clasped my hands together tightly under the table, digging nails into flesh. 'He was going to kill me, I know he was. It was why he kept the knife under his pillow, drugged me every night for months.'

I looked up. She was staring at the floor, but her face was streaked with black from make-up.

'It all started after we got married. He'd tell me that

I'd done things, to make me think I was going crazy. He'd tell me the wrong time, so I was always late. He convinced me that I'd been sleepwalking – drugged me, carried me downstairs and cut a chunk out of my hair.' She looked up at me, her mouth slightly open. 'I am so very sorry, Kathryn. Please believe me. My life won't be the same again. I loved him. I loved the person Matthew was. Please don't think I've forgotten him. I think about him all the time.'

I pulled the sleeves of my cardigan over my hands and wiped my face.

This wasn't happening, it wasn't happening.

But it was. Tina was Chrissie.

The baby was Matthew.

He always talked about being abandoned and I'd assumed it was the aftermath of a previous failed relationship. Why hadn't he talked about it with me? Even when he was drunk, he would get angry at stupid little things rather than talk about himself. He always spoke about how average he was – how normal his family life had been. If he'd talked about it, would it have made a difference to how everything turned out? His upbringing was more like mine than he ever let on. Was that why he felt an affinity with me so early on?

Kathryn didn't speak. She was sitting still, her gaze fixed on the folded written pages on the table.

It was only when the clock struck the hour, seven minutes later, that she moved.

She stood, smoothed down her skirt and walked towards the door.

She opened it and paused.

'You can leave now, Bethany.'

Chapter 61

Dorothy had been inside number sixty-three for nearly fifteen minutes and Gordon was still lingering at the side of the house, crouching under the open kitchen window. There had been occasional raised voices – no words he could decipher – but there was no suggestion of any violence occurring. Still, he had his mobile in his hand in case he needed to call the police.

He turned to face the wall, grabbed hold of the windowsill, and pulled himself slowly up.

The kitchen was empty, but Gordon could still hear raised voices coming from the dining room. After a few minutes, there was silence. Gordon stood at full height. What the heck was going on in there? In front of his face was a ceramic York minster saltshaker, the printed illustration had faded over time. There was a pile of dishes in the sink. Had Louise left?

Inside, a clock struck the hour. He heard a woman's voice and the kitchen door opened. Gordon ducked back down, wobbling on his feet. He placed a hand on the brick wall for balance.

'You did the right thing, letting her go. Nothing good ever comes from revenge.' It was a man's voice. 'I have to go,' he said. 'I've been cooped up in that attic for far too long.'

It was Brett. And seemingly unharmed. Had he been hiding in the house since last week?

'You can't leave me now,' said Dorothy. 'I thought we were going to go away together when this was all over.'

'I need time to think,' he said. 'Bethany wasn't how you said she'd be. And when you brought Jamie here ... as if Louise hasn't been through enough. You should have let her go when she said she wasn't comfortable with all of this.'

'Well, it's done now. I can't change the past.'

A door slammed shut.

Gordon couldn't let them find him eavesdropping below them. He side stepped away from the window and walked quickly to the front of the house. At the front door, his heart pounded as he took hold of the brass knocker. He banged it heavily against the door three times.

He stepped off the step and looked up to the house. There was no sign of movement inside, no one peeking through a window. He knocked on the door again. Light footsteps on the wooden floor came closer towards him. The door opened.

It was Dorothy.

The clip in her hair had dropped close to her face and her shoulders sagged. She seemed to have aged ten years in just a few hours.

Adrenaline pumped through Gordon as he placed a foot on the step.

'Can I speak to Bethany, please,' he said. There was no need for pretence – he'd heard them discussing her. He braced himself for her onslaught, the vitriol towards him.

'Hello, Gordon,' she said quietly. She let go of the door and walked down the hall away from him. 'Bethany will be down in a sec,' she called behind her.

What the heck had happened to make her look so defeated? She not only looked like a different woman but behaved like one.

Should Gordon go inside?

His question was answered when Bethany came down the stairs carrying the suitcase she'd arrived with.

'Gordon!' she said, stepping outside. She closed the front door. Her eyes were red and puffy. 'Are you all right?'

'That's a question I should be asking you,' he said. 'I read those letters from the cellar. It seems there's a connection between them and your husband.' Bethany's expression remained unchanged. 'You know that now, don't you?'

'Yeah.' She rubbed her face. 'Dorothy is actually called Kathryn. She's my husband's biological mother.' She started down the path. 'I need to go now, Gordon. I need to get home.'

Dorothy – Kathryn – was Matthew Arnold's biological mother? Good grief. Gordon hadn't even contemplated that scenario. The 'author' next door had known all along she had a murderer in the house. The killer of her very own son. Gordon had so many questions, but now obviously wasn't the time to ask them.

'Wait, Bethany.' Gordon broke into a light run to catch up to her. 'Where are you going to go?'

'Back to Bolton,' she said. Tears were running down her cheeks, the wind dispersing them across her face. 'Back to my family.'

He placed a hand on her arm.

'I can drive you there if you like,' he said. 'My dad's car is in the garage.'

She stopped and turned slowly towards him.

'That's so kind of you,' she said, sniffing and dabbing her face with the sleeve of her jacket. 'Thank you.'

She leant her head towards his chest and began sobbing loudly.

He raised a hand hesitantly behind her back before encircling her in a hug.

'There, there, love,' he said. 'We'll get you home.'

Chapter 62

I walked through the iron gates and down the path to where he was. I'd never been here before. I'd expected the clouds to be heavy with thunder, for lightning to strike me as I made my way towards his grave, but it didn't. The sun was shining and there was a light breeze across my face.

I turned and walked along a narrow gravel pathway until I found it.

MATTHEW ARNOLD
14 April 1985 – 26 July 2019
Beloved son of Kathryn and Jack

I took the necklace out of my pocket and placed it on the ledge of his gravestone.

The sterling silver bee. It wasn't mine. I wasn't any-one's *little bee*.

I looked aside to see Gemma walking towards me. She put her arm around my shoulders.

'Is it strange,' I said, 'that I miss him ... miss the way he was? The man I thought I married.'

'Maybe,' she said. 'Sad about the life you could've had.' She took hold of my hand. 'You're still young, Beth. And you've been through more shit than people would go through in a lifetime. You could do whatever you wanted to, now.'

My phone buzzed with a message; I took it out of my pocket.

It was a picture message from Gordon; his new business card.

G. Anderson

Private Investigator

'Who's that from?' said Gemma, craning her neck over my shoulder.

'A new friend,' I said. 'I think you'll like him.'

'I can't believe you managed to make friends while you were living in the house of horrors. But Adam seems like more than a friend?'

She nudged me and I tugged her hand. We headed towards the exit, the gravel crunching beneath my feet was satisfying in my new winter boots.

'I'll sit in the back again, shall I?' she said.

'Gemma!' I hissed, opening the passenger door of Adam's car.

'Was everything OK?' he said.

'It was the same inscription on the gravestone that Kathryn had written about.'

He switched on the ignition and pulled out of the car park.

'Bloody hell,' he said. 'I still can't believe all that went on in that house. The woman's insane.' He flicked on the radio, but changed the station when Radiohead came on. 'Have you heard from her at all?'

'God, no,' I said. 'And I hope I never do.'

'I wonder where she is now,' he said as he turned into Jenny and Phil's road.

'I don't,' I said. 'I never want to think about her again.'

'Do you think she'll ever think about you?'

Jenny opened the front door and stood on the step. Since I came home, she'd started greeting me at the door as though I'd been away for years.

'Let's hope not,' I said.

It was time for another fresh start.

Chapter 63

Two weeks later

The air was so baking hot here that Kathryn thought she might faint. The coach, filled with pale-skinned tourists clutching guidebooks, was equally as bad. The only fresh air came from the three windows that actually opened.

So far, they had stopped at three shitty-looking hotels. Kathryn had dreaded her name being called out at each one of them.

After a couple of perilous turns on the mountain roads, they halted at the Hotel Cassiopeia and it was the first decent one they'd stopped at. It must've been a sign. She'd watched a film with him that had mentioned that constellation. He probably didn't remember that. It was the curse of a good memory she wished she didn't have.

She glared at the rep at the front of the coach and willed him to read out her name. They might find her dead from heatstroke if she had to stay on this bus any longer.

How much had Andrew spent on her little getaway? Probably enough that she wouldn't complain about it, and enough to keep her away from him for a month or longer. She didn't mind that he wanted some distance from her – especially after he'd paid for the rental at number sixty-three, too. And it was only fair; she'd supported *him* financially for nearly ten years.

'. . . and Kathryn Holden.'

Thank God.

Her room overlooked the small coastal town in the distance. She had already unpacked and opened the welcome wine and she sat at the round plastic table on the balcony. She opened the Instagram app on her phone, waiting as it loaded the images.

Kathryn looked to the horizon where the sun was setting. Andrew was right. He was always right. He was probably the best friend she'd ever had. He knew her better than anyone else, especially when he'd pointed out that Matthew's troubles had started long before he'd met Bethany. That Bethany had the same shaky start, probably even worse, than her own son.

If only Matthew had known that Kathryn thought about him every day. That was what made her forgive Bethany. She said she thought of Matthew every day. Kathryn had never said that aloud about her own son. She'd pretended to everyone that he didn't exist. Was she any better? In some ways they were the same, her and Bethany. Pretending to be someone else to get over something horrific.

414

She tapped on Jack's profile. He'd tagged himself in a bar overlooking the beach. It was one of the many she'd passed on the way up here. Did he think that because she was nearly seventy that she wouldn't be bothered with social media – not be bothered to make the trip here?

Not once had he messaged her after their son's death. He hadn't even attended the funeral. Such a cold-hearted bastard. At least, after nearly seventy years of being on this earth, she could say she had feelings. That this is what it felt like. It was what she'd read about.

Yes. Matthew's problems started at the very beginning of his life. The same time Kathryn's problems had begun. With Jack.

Kathryn would make sure he understood that. With what she had planned, he would never be able to forget them again.

Acknowledgements

What a strange time this past year has been for us all. I finished the first draft of *The Vacancy* during the first lockdown, and to say it was a challenge would be an understatement. My editor, Francesca Pathak, has been fantastic – so patient and understanding. Fran's insightful suggestions helped shape *The Vacancy* to what it is now – thank you so much. I have never worked so hard on a manuscript as I have this one! Huge thanks to my agent Caroline Hardman and thank you to everyone at Hardman & Swainson – the best literary agency in the world! Thank you, too, to Lucy Frederick and Clare Wallis. Thank you to my family and friends for their unwavering support.

Thank you to you, my lovely reader. It is so wonderful getting messages to say you've enjoyed my stories. I really hope you enjoy this one!

Credits

Elisabeth Carpenter and Orion Fiction would like to thank everyone at Orion who worked on the publication of *The Vacancy* in the UK.

Editorial
Francesca Pathak
Lucy Frederick

Copy editor
Clare Wallis

Proof reader
Kati Nicholl

Audio
Paul Stark
Amber Bates

Contracts
Anne Goddard
Jake Alderson

Design
Debbie Holmes
Joanna Ridley
Nick May

Production
Hannah Cox

Editorial Management
Charlie Panayiotou
Jane Hughes

Finance
Jasdip Nandra
Afeera Ahmed
Elizabeth Beaumont
Sue Baker

419

Marketing
Tanjiah Islam

Publicity
Ellen Turner

Rights
Susan Howe
Krystyna Kujawinska
Jessica Purdue
Louise Henderson

Sales
Jen Wilson
Esther Waters
Victoria Laws
Frances Doyle
Georgina Cutler

Operations
Jo Jacobs
Sharon Willis
Lisa Pryde
Lucy Brem

If you loved *The Vacancy*, don't miss
Only A Mother ...

ONLY A MOTHER ...

Erica Wright hasn't needed to scrub 'MURDERER'
off her house in over a year.
Then her son, Craig, is released from prison.

COULD BELIEVE HIM

Erica has always believed Craig was innocent,
but when he arrives home, she doesn't recognise
her son anymore.

COULD LIE FOR HIM

So, when another girl goes missing, she questions
everything. But how can a mother turn her back on
her son? And how far will she go to protect him?

COULD BURY THE TRUTH

And you'll be gripped by
The Woman Downstairs ...

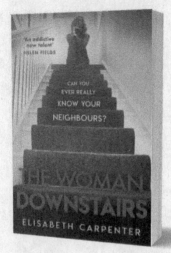

Can you ever really know your neighbours?

When human remains are found in a ground floor flat,
the residents of Nelson Heights are shocked to learn
that there was a dead body in their building for over
three years.

Sarah lives at the flat above and after the remains are
found, she feels threatened by a stranger hanging around
the building.

Laura has lived in the building for as long as she can
remember, caring for her elderly father, though there is
more to her story than she is letting on.

As the investigation starts to heat up, and the two
women become more involved, it's clear that someone
isn't telling the truth about what went on all those
years ago . . .